lullabies for little criminals

'Vivid and poignant... O'Neill's novel builds to a riveting climax... deeply moving'   *Independent*

'Told with shafts of wit and a lightness of touch which few novels on such themes achieve. Baby, like Holden Caulfield in *Catcher in the Rye*, is totally believable. Although few people suffer a childhood like hers, everyone can identify with her feelings, on the threshold of adolescence longing for stability and recognition'   *Times Literary Supplement*

'O'Neill bombards the reader with piercing observations and magical imagery... Her story is bleak, yet not bitter; full of pathos, spirit and, overwhelmingly, innocence'
Independent on Sunday

'An enchanting tale of imagination and survival... This is lovely stuff... A fine debut – a great curler-upper with of a winter book'   *Dublin Evening Herald*

D0227143

lullabies for little criminals
heather o'neill

Quercus

First published in Great Britain in 2008 by Quercus
This paperback edition published in 2008 by

Quercus
21 Bloomsbury Square
London
WC1A 2NS

Published by agreement with HarperCollins
Publishers, New York, USA

A CIP catalogue reference for this book is available
from the British Library

978 1 84724 393 5

10 9 8 7 6 5 4 3 2

Printed and bound in Great Britain

lullabies for little criminals

life with jules

1

Right before my twelfth birthday, my dad, Jules, and I moved into a two-room apartment in a building that we called the Ostrich Hotel. It was the first time I could remember taking a taxicab anywhere. It let us off in the alley behind the building, where all the walls had pretty graffiti painted on them. There was a cartoon cow with a sad look on its face and a girl with an oxygen mask holding a tiny baby in her arms.

Jules was wearing a fur hat and a long leather jacket. He was all in a hurry to get our stuff out of the taxi because it was so cold. 'Stupid, lousy prick of a bastard, it's cold!' Jules screamed. That's the only type of thing anyone could say while outside in that weather. I think he was also in shock that the cabdriver had charged him ten bucks.

Jules took a suitcase filled with his clothes in one hand and a record player that closed into a white suitcase in the other. I was sure that he was going to drop it because he was wearing a pair of leather boots with flat soles that he had fallen madly in love with at the Army surplus store. They didn't have any treads on the bottom, so they gave his feet the funny illusion of moving in all directions at once. He slipped just outside the door of the hotel and had to land on his knees to break his fall.

I had my own little vinyl suitcase with green flowers and my name, Baby, written on it with black permanent marker, bulging with my clothes and my homework. I also had a plastic bag filled with dolls that I was dragging on the ground behind me.

There was a glass window over the front door on which were painted gold cursive letters that spelled out L'Hotel Autriche. This of course meant the Austrian Hotel, but Jules wasn't a particularly good reader. There were old-fashioned radiators all along the hallways with designs of roses on them. Jules loved the radiators. He said they were the only things that could keep an apartment warm. You had to stand on a floral carpet and wipe your boots before going up the stairs. Jules had already picked up the keys, so we just ignored the woman sleeping at the desk.

The apartment was small, with a living room and a tiny bedroom for me in the back. Like all the apartments in the hotels on that street, it came furnished. The wallpaper wasn't bad, although it had peeled off in spots near the ceiling. It was blue with tiny black stars on it here and there. The carpet had been worn down so much that you couldn't see what pattern it used to have and the light switch was practically black from so many hands turning it on and off.

It had the same smell of wet clothes and pot that our last apartment had. It smelled as if a florist shop had caught on fire and all the flowers were burning. I didn't mind any apartment so long as there weren't any tiny amber-colored cockroaches that disappeared into holes. Our last apartment was bigger but wouldn't stay warm. The heat from the electric baseboards just made Jules sweat and then get colder.

We had decided to leave abruptly in the end. Jules was

nervous about a friend of his named Kent murdering him in his sleep. Kent had gone to Oshawa to work in a ski pole factory for the winter season and had left his two electric guitars, an amp, and a bag of clothes at our apartment in exchange for two cartons of cigarettes. They were reservation cigarettes and they had three feathers on each box. Jules smoked the cigarettes one after the other, as if he had an infinite supply. Even though he said they were like smoking shredded-up tires and chicken bones and they were going to kill him before he turned forty, he chain-smoked them nonetheless.

Jules had a little kid's sense of time and after a month, when all the cigarettes were gone, he didn't seem to believe that Kent was ever going to come back. He sold the equipment for fifty dollars. Two days later, Kent called and left a message saying that he would be coming back into town to pick up his stuff. Jules didn't have any problem-solving skills and he panicked.

'I can't get his shit back! I threw his clothes in the trash.'

'What's he going to do?' I yelled, jumping up on the couch, as if I'd seen a mouse.

'Fuck, he'll run me over with his car. All I need is a couple of broken legs. I can barely walk down the street as it is. You know what they call someone who can't walk? An invalid!'

'Can't you buy back his guitars?' I screamed, hopping from foot to foot on the couch cushions.

'They're worth like a thousand dollars. I only got fifty dollars for them. I'll never be able to get them back. What did he expect me to do? Keep his instruments here for the rest of my life? I've already probably got arthritis from stubbing my toes against his shit.'

That night I had a dream that a pair of running shoes were following me down the street and I woke up in a cold sweat. I had never met Kent, but Jules got me so worked up about him that I couldn't eat my lunch at school the next day. And that evening, when the doorbell finally did ring, my belly button felt as if it had come unthreaded and had fallen down through the floorboards.

Jules and I sat nervously next to each other on the couch, until we heard the footsteps walk away. Then he jumped up and peered out the peephole for five minutes before deciding the coast was clear and opening the door. He stepped out into the hallway and came back holding out a note for me to see. It read: 'Where the hell are you??? I came by for my stuff.'

'This doesn't mean anything,' Jules said, holding up the note. 'You have to send it registered mail.'

He and my mother had both been fifteen when I was born. She had died a year later, so he'd been left to raise me all by himself. It didn't make him any more mature than any other twenty-six-year-old, though. He practically fell on the floor and died when a song that he liked came on the radio. He was always telling people that he was color-blind because he thought it made him sound original. He also didn't look too much like a parent. He was boyish and had blue eyes with dirty blond hair that stuck up all over the place. It sometimes had the shape of a hat he'd been wearing earlier. I thought of him as my best friend, as if we were almost the same age.

If I'd had parents who were adults, I probably would never have been called Baby. The little stores on St Catherine Street I made Jules walk me past always had gold necklaces with pendants that said 'Baby'. My heart skipped a beat whenever I heard it in a song. I loved how people got confused when Jules and I had to explain how it wasn't just a nickname. It was an ironic name. It didn't mean you were innocent at all. It meant you were cool and gorgeous. I was only a kid, but I was looking forward to being a lady with that name. I had stringy blonde hair and was skinny as hell, but Jules's friend Lester said I'd be a heartbreaker someday soon.

But having a young parent meant you had to pack up your stuff in an hour and run away from a twenty-two-year-old from Oshawa who was going to be mad at you for having sold his guitars.

The bathroom in our new apartment was tiny, but it managed to have a little blue bathtub. This was a good thing because Jules claimed that it was necessary for his self-preservation to sit in a hot bath for at least an hour a day. A glass soap dish shaped like a shell had been left behind and a set of fake nails were lying in it, like petals that had fallen off a flower. It was strange that someone had lived here just hours before, and now it was all ours.

There was a restaurant right under us, and you could reach out the window and unscrew one of the lightbulbs from its sign, if you wanted to. Jules ran downstairs to pick us up some hot dogs and fries from there.

'We're localized here!' Jules yelled, kicking open the door with his foot. 'We should have moved here a long time ago.'

I could tell that Jules was finding it a real treat that the hotel was right on busy St Laurent and St Catherine. He didn't like having to walk even a block to the convenience store. St Laurent Street wasn't an ideal place to raise a kid. It ran right through Montreal, dividing its east and west sections. It was also the red-light district and, to me, the most beautiful section of town. The theaters where famous people used to perform in the twenties and thirties had been converted into cheap hotels and strip joints. There were always prostitutes around. They made me feel bad when I was little because they always had beautiful high-heeled boots, while I had to wear ugly galoshes. I closed my eyes when I passed them. In general, everyone dressed like they hadn't gone home from a wedding the night before. You could go to the Salvation Army, buy a pin-striped jacket and stick a plastic flower in the lapel, and call yourself an aristocrat—everyone was living a sort of fictional existence.

The French newspapers of the district had strippers on the front pages with their wrists in handcuffs and their breasts falling all over the place. These were people who didn't care about international news. If you never thought about Paris, you'd never think about how you were so far away from there. There were a lot of Hell's Angels around, buzzing down the street like bees. It was a joy to see them all drive by, like a parade, on their way to blow up a restaurant.

That first night in the new place, Jules dismantled the fire alarm so that he could smoke in peace. I loved when he smoked a cigarette with the lights off. The smoke in the dark looked like the dove that whispered the future to saints in paintings. He had on a T-shirt he always wore that had a little hand at the bottom, holding about twenty balloons. When he wore it, the song '99 Red Balloons' would play in my head. Across the street from us was an old theater with a million lightbulbs on the marquee. Only seven or eight of them worked, as if they were the first stars at night that you were supposed to wish on. Jules stretched out to sleep on the foldout couch and I climbed into our small bed with a brass headboard. He opened his little white record player and put on a record. He fell asleep before it was over and I listened to the needle going around and around. There is always the sound of children roller skating at the end of every record.

Since I had to take a new route to school, Jules decided to walk me there the next morning. It was more for a sense of ceremony, though, because I knew my way around the area so well that I never got lost. I wished that I could get lost, just to know what it felt like. I wanted to be able to wake up in the morning and not know where I was, but no such luck. We'd just moved too many times for that to happen. That neighborhood looked the worst in the morning. The street was empty and there was vomit on the sidewalk. All the colorful lights had been turned off and the sky was the color of television static.

Outside my school, we gave each other seven kisses for good luck. Then Jules announced that he had to go to the bathroom and took off running home. The kids started laughing at me when I walked into class because they had seen Jules pecking at me like a hen from the window and my face was all red from the stubble of his beard. The teacher shushed everyone up as she handed back our book reports on *The Cricket in Times Square*. Jules had helped me with it the week before. He had told me that nothing was what it appeared to be in a book. He'd said that a cricket in a subway represented the Jewish People. According to him, the cricket was the same thing as the Fiddler on the Roof. I don't know why I had taken his advice, seeing as how he hadn't actually read the book. The teacher handed back my paper with a zero and said I had to redo it.

As I was walking home, I spotted Jules on the street corner. He was craning his neck all over the place, looking around for someone. He started gesticulating in a way that made it seem as if he was having an imaginary argument in his head. He kept putting his hand, palm up, in front of him, as if he was asking the universe, 'What? What? What?' His hat was down over his eyes, and when I called out his name he had to tilt his head way up to get a look at me. I knew it wasn't me that he had been looking for, but when he saw me, he shouted out happily anyhow.

His girlfriend had told me that the only thing Jules had going for him was a smile. At the time, I thought this was such a wonderful comment. It made me happy because I thought everyone saw that he had a nice smile. I didn't like how people always gave him the right-of-way when he was walking down the sidewalk. He tripped on nothing as he walked toward me.

'Hey, it's my sweet little apple pie,' he cried out.

'Hey, Jules,' I said.

'Did you get your book report back?'

'I got an A,' I lied.

'Far out!' he yelled. 'I told you I was a genius. An undervalued genius.'

2

A week after we'd moved to the Ostrich Hotel was my twelfth birthday. Jules made me a cake and brought out a piñata that he'd made by gluing layer upon layer of newspaper on a balloon and painting it white with Liquid Paper. It looked like something you'd find at a construction site, or something you'd transport drugs across the border in. I hit at it with a wooden spoon, but eventually the handle broke. So then I smashed it with a chair leg and still nothing happened. I swung the leg again and hit Jules in the shin. While he was hopping around, I tried to rip it open at the top with my fingers without him noticing.

'What are you doing? That's not how you bust a piñata! I worked all night on it.'

His best friend, a twenty-five-year-old blond guy named Lester who drove a green Trans Am, showed up. They washed dishes at the same restaurant and were almost always together. Lester had a temporary job once, handing out pamphlets for an electoral candidate, and still had stickers of the guy's face on his leather jacket. He hugged me and I looked into what was left of the candidate's smiling face. Lester always wore a chain with a golden Bambi pendant hanging off it, which was how I had learned the meaning of irony.

Taking in our piñata situation, Lester said that he wished he'd brought his gun. He took a big bowie knife out of his packsack and started stabbing at it instead. I put my hands over my ears as Lester hacked into it. Afterward, we all sat on the couch and picked candies out of the thin slit Lester had made in the piñata. There weren't that many sweets inside, so we ate slowly. Each candy was like taking a chick out of its egg too early.

Jules also gave me a little white fur hat and I immediately put it on. I looked at my reflection in the mirror and thought that I was good-looking enough to be in a circus with men throwing knives at me. I was especially good-looking after I'd eaten spaghetti sauce and my lips were all stained orange. Whenever things were going well, I started to feel vain.

I could tell that the hat was secondhand because the care instructions had worn right off the inside tag. Jules had a gift for finding wonderful garbage at the thrift store. Once he had found five dollars in a pair of pants that he had paid a dollar fifty for. Next he handed me a cardboard shoe box, and when I pulled off the cover there was an old-fashioned marionette wearing a blue dress with tiny red flowers inside it. She had a long nose and peach cheeks and was really human-looking. I named her Roxanne and I loved her instantly and passionately. I made her dance on the coffee table, recounting her life story, until Jules and Lester were ready to commit suicide from boredom.

Afterward, we were all hanging out in front of the television watching *Benny Hill*. Jules and Lester were lounging on the couch, laughing their heads off. I was lying on my belly on the floor, and I'd start laughing whenever they did because their laughs were so contagious. We were having a good time.

'Let's go get some chocolate milk,' Lester said all of a sudden.

'Oh, yeah!' Jules jerked upright. 'It's been on my mind too. I'd like just a little taste to strengthen me up.'

'I know this guy who's selling it dark brown.'

'Jesus! Let's find him. I've only got ten bucks, though.'

'That's okay. I've got about twelve. It'll do.'

On the television screen, a policeman opened his car door and three girls in their underwear scrambled out of it and ran down the street. Neither Jules nor Lester laughed; they had both totally lost interest in the show. They sprung up off the couch to go get their chocolate milk. Lester almost stepped on me while reaching for his coat, which was lying on the coffee table.

'Watch out!' I screamed.

'Sorry, Baby,' Jules said, even though he was on the other side of the room and hadn't done anything. 'We're just going to the store. We'll be back in fifteen minutes. Don't move an inch. Watch the show and tell me everything I missed when I get back.'

Jules and his friends had been calling heroin chocolate milk for years. They did it so they could at least pretend I didn't know what was going on. I don't know exactly how I knew, but I just did. Jules had a backgammon set with electrical tape around it that I wasn't allowed to touch that he kept his drugs and works in. He had red marks like mosquito bites on his arms even in the winter. A boy had made hickeys on his arm in class and had shown me and it had reminded me of Jules's arms.

For a kid, I knew a lot of things about what it felt like to use heroin, just from looking and listening. Supposedly, it was like shaking hands with God. It was cool like a Black Panther. It was like putting your face on the fur collar of a great leather jacket. If you passed by a poster of a band of singers coming to town, you could hear them singing.

I looked at the television screen and the credits were rolling. Jules went out the door hopping on one foot, trying to tie his shoes without slowing down. I heard him and Lester go down the stairs, jumping the last few steps. I usually waited in the apartment for them, but their excitement was too overwhelming. I wanted to be a part of it. I put on my new white hat and my ski jacket with yellow stripes like lightning bolts on the side. I grabbed Roxanne and ran down to the corner after them.

They kept walking ahead of me down the street, as if not to include me. I had to run to stay close behind them.

They both had such long legs that they were hard to keep up with at the best of times. They could smoke and drink coffee and eat and reenact a bar fight while walking down the street without even slowing down.

They got to a skinny building that had tiny different-colored ceramic tiles all over the front and black tiles with gold stars on them on the lobby's floor. It was a more modern building than the rest on the block, so it must have been built in a spot where an older one had burned down. A drug dealer named Paul lived there. I'd been to his apartment once about a year before. He'd just gotten a dog from the SPCA named Dostoyevsky. He couldn't pronounce it, so he changed it to Donut. I was looking forward to playing with it.

'Baby!' Jules turned and yelled at me. 'Quit following us. Go play with your doll! Get lost, okay?'

'I want to come with you,' I said. 'I like Paul!'

'*I like Paul*,' he repeated sarcastically. 'Go find some friends your own age, okay? Trust me, you don't like Paul.'

'I'll wait here then.'

When the buzzer sounded, Jules and Lester pulled open the door and stepped in. It was one of those metal doors that slams shut after you let go. Once it banged closed, there was no way I could get in. I pounded on the door. Jules leaned over and opened the mail slot that was made to put circulars through.

'Look, go run and play and you can eat dinner with chopsticks tomorrow, okay! I'll give you some money to see a movie!'

As he shouted out all my favorite things, they seemed so cheap to me. They paled in comparison to my desire to be with him.

'Screw the chopsticks,' I whispered to myself as he and Lester ran up the stairs.

I spotted a big rock on the ground. I picked it up and pretended it was an injured bird and held it in my hand and stroked it. I encouraged it to stay alive and whispered to it that it would fly again soon. Then I put it in my pocket with the other rocks I'd rescued. I sat down on a bench outside the building and waited a few minutes, but they didn't come back down.

I was still clingy like a little kid with Jules and I hated when he dumped me like that. I was so lonely all of a sudden. When I felt lonely, I really felt lonely. I couldn't believe that anyone else in the world could manage to feel as lonely as I did. When I was a baby, Jules had made up a story in which I was the main character. In the tale, I was on a ship sailing to Europe that sank in a storm. I survived by climbing onto a floating armchair that had been in the captain's cabin. I floated all the way to Paris in that chair and there was a big parade for me in the streets when I arrived. I used to beg Jules to tell me this story over and over again. I had loved the part where I realized that everyone else on the ship had drowned and I was all alone on the giant ocean. It had given me such a chill. Now I regretted that he had ever told me that story because there were times, like now, when I found myself on that armchair. I could even sort of feel the sidewalk rocking under my feet, as if I were on some waves.

The moon was out already and looked like a melting bit of ice in a glass of water. A few big snowflakes started falling here and there, all slowly, like spiders on their invisible webs coming down.

I held Roxanne up in front of me and discovered that

she didn't impress me much anymore. I was annoyed with her because I was stuck with her instead of Jules. I got up and dragged her down the street. I decided to go to the indoor ice-skating rink a few blocks away. It was by the housing projects, so all the kids who lived there hung out at the rink all day.

Strings of Christmas lights lit the place up all year. People there would steal everything you had, so you had to skate with your shoes in a plastic bag at your side. But I wasn't even able to skate. Jules had gotten me a pair of skates, but I had unscrewed the blades and banged them off with a hammer. I wanted to have a pair of fancy white boots like the kids in the illustrations in a book I had read called *The Railway Children*. The skates were impossible to walk in, though, because the soles didn't bend, so I had to throw them away, weeping.

I saw some kids I knew in the bleachers. They were eating a little jar of maraschino cherries that they had all probably pitched in to buy. Someone had come up with the idea that maraschino cherries were soaked in whiskey, and everywhere I went kids were eating them by the jarful. I'd asked Jules about it and he had said it was bullshit. I'd told some kids that, but they thought Jules didn't know anything because he was so much younger than all the other parents. They'd informed me it was quite likely that Jules was a numbskull.

A boy named Todd spotted me first. He was wearing a tight blue T-shirt with motorcycles on it and burgundy corduroys. His mother wrote his name on the outside of his clothes with a magic marker so that nobody could steal them. That was a considerable waste of time because nobody would be caught dead in his clothes. He had to be extra aggressive to overcome the stigma of having his name written boldly on every single thing he owned.

'What have you got there, a doll?' he said increduously. 'Oh, man! I can't believe it. What the hell are you doing with a doll?'

'She's been following me around,' I said. 'I can't get rid of her.'

'What?' they all demanded, now that I was messing with their sense of reality.

'She's a pain in the butt, I swear to God,' I continued. I held the puppet up to my face. 'How come you have those holes in your elbows, Roxanne? Is that like a bad polio vaccination?'

All the kids laughed when I insulted her. The boys made lewd comments. 'Come on, Roxy, please, Roxy. How about giving me a little piece of ass.'

Roxanne just laughed. She was a survivor, Roxanne. I guessed that I'd give her that.

Someone called my name loudly from the other side of the skating rink. I saw it was Marika, my old neighbor. I used to be madly in love with her because she was missing a finger and she would never give a straight answer about where it had gone to. It was disgusting and beautiful at the same time. She also had greasy black bangs that she wore down to her nose, and I found them really debonair or something. She was four years older than me, but she didn't ever seem to notice our age gap.

I walked over reluctantly, though, because, despite her great beauty, she was always making me do creepy things with her. Once she looked up a strip joint in the phone book and we called up to ask if they were hiring. When they said they were, we almost lost our minds, because before we had somehow assumed that strippers were fictional creatures, like mermaids. The last time I'd been over at her house, she had taken the lace curtain down from the kitchen window and bobby-pinned it to my hair. Then she had convinced me to marry her brother. She wouldn't let me go home until I had kissed him, and now we were married.

She was wearing a black patent-leather jacket that was a size too big and made her seem like she was somehow dressed in a wet umbrella.

'Did you see Quincy?' she asked, nodding toward the rink, where her brother was skating.

He was skating with a cast on his arm. He had drawn a naked lady on it last week, but the principal had made him cover it in Liquid Paper. I cringed at the sight of him.

'Is it your birthday?' she asked.

'Yeah, I'm twelve.'

'You have to lose your virginity when you turn twelve,' she told me.

She had a tiny jam jar filled with beer and she offered it to me. Jules sometimes drank beer that had a beautiful unicorn on the label. I used to beg for a sip just because I found the label so lovely. It tasted bitter and always made me feel as if I'd been crying. I shook my head at the jar.

'Suit yourself,' she said, taking the tiniest sip possible.

'I thought you were going to get me and Quincy divorced.'

'Do you know how long a divorce can take?'

'Did you even start?'

'I'm not going to dignify that question. My brother isn't interested in you anymore. He says you are too flat-chested.'

I shrugged, pretending not to be offended. She was

troubling me already. A couple teenagers on the ice started yelling obscenities at each other and the echo of their voices made it sound as if we were all at the bottom of a well.

'You could make a lot of money in that little white hat of yours. You could have anything you want,' Marika said suddenly.

'Yeah, I know,' I said, not having any idea what she was talking about.

'Do you want to see something crazy?' she asked me.

'All right.'

She reached into her pocket and pulled out a handful of bills. I'd never seen one of my friends with that much money in her hands. We were broke in a way that only kids can be broke. Our toes were black with dye from wearing boots that weren't waterproof. We had infected earlobes and green rings around our fingers from cheap jewelry. No one ever even had a chocolate bar. We'd steal containers of cottage cheese and eat them together in the park. It was a miracle to see so much money in the hands of someone so young. It seemed to be a magic trick and I stared at it, waiting for it to turn back into something else.

'I had sex with a man for fifty bucks,' she said. 'Me and my cousin have been doing it on Ontario Street. It's easy. She made two hundred dollars one night.'

I wasn't sure whether or not she was joking, so I laughed loudly and briefly. My laugh sounded different than usual, as if I was laughing in a room with no furniture. I was still uncomfortable with the idea of sex. When I first heard of French kissing, I thought it was something that only mental patients and the kids who failed grade four would do when they grew up.

'Do you want to know the details?' she asked, leaning her face so close that it was almost touching mine.

When she spoke, her breath smelled like cigarettes and dead things. There was something inhuman about her, suddenly, as if when she opened her mouth and tipped it backward you would see mechanical inner workings, like a little dumb weight instead of a tonsil. If she coughed and you looked in her Kleenex, you would see nails and screws. That's probably why she was missing a finger. She had probably just fallen and it had broken off. I felt so lonely all of a sudden, as if I were the only human left in the world.

I whispered that I had to go back home and I turned around and walked away from her.

People gave you a hard time about being a kid at twelve. They didn't want to give you Halloween candy anymore. They said things like, 'If this were the Middle Ages, you'd be married and you'd own a farm with about a million chickens on it.' They were trying to kick you out of childhood. Once you were gone, there was no going back, so you had to hold on as long as you could. Marika was beckoning from the other side.

I stepped outside into the cold, and since I hadn't taken off my jacket while inside the skating rink, it was twice as cold as before. It was dark outside now. My breath in the cold air was bleach that accidentally spilled on a black T-shirt.

I started walking in the wrong direction, heading toward our old apartment building, and then I remembered that we had moved. I turned in the right direction, and this time I started running. Jules had always told me that if I met someone dangerous to run back home.

Home was something that you could fit into a suitcase and move in a taxi for ten dollars. Home was wherever Jules and I were together.

I hurried up the carpeted stairs of the Ostrich Hotel. The metal banisters curled up at the ends like the waves in Chinese ink drawings. I opened the front door of our apartment and felt the heat come out at me. Jules had already cranked it way up and had put masking tape all along the sides of the windows, so that nothing, not even the air, could get in.

I walked into the living room and saw a man I didn't know sitting on the couch between Jules and Lester. They were sitting there like Wynken, Blynken, and Nod: three little boys who were tucked in together, about to sail off into the starry universe. They all had a similar expression when I walked in, with their eyebrows raised and their eyes closed, as if they were bored aristocrats. There were glasses and jars filled with water all over the coffee table in front of them. It looked like a dismantled chandelier.

Jules was holding a teacup daintily in his hand to tip his cigarette ashes in. He opened his mouth and I waited several seconds for him to get the words off the tip of his tongue.

'This is Kent,' Jules said, pointing in the opposite direction of the stranger on the couch, but obviously meaning him.

Kent half opened his eyes and smiled. He closed his eyes again, but his face kept its jolly expression. Once you smiled on heroin, your smile could last a whole hour. Kent had a Fat Albert key chain attached to the zipper of his ski jacket. He had black hair with gel on it that had frozen outside and turned white. He had purple running shoes with fat green shoelaces. Looking at Kent, I felt incredibly safe all of a sudden. If this was our worst enemy, Jules and I had nothing to worry about.

Jules came into my room later that night after Lester and Kent had left. He had his hands in front of him feeling around, although it wasn't particularly dark. He did that even when the light was on when he was stoned. He squeezed in next to me. He was in the mood to talk, I could tell. We lay on the bed as if we were crammed in a confessional booth together. When he was stoned, he was honest. I loved when he told me his secrets.

'So Kent showed up freaking out and saying stuff he didn't mean. It was out of control here. But Lester offered to give him that guitar he found backstage when he was working at the Medley.'

'You mean the guitar he stole from the Medley.'

'If Lester didn't take it, someone else would have, so it isn't exactly stealing.'

'What about his clothes?'

'His clothes were ugly. He can't dress. I gave him that top hat I got at the Salvation Army.'

'You loved that hat!'

'And my green suit jacket with the sparkly thread.'

'No!' I cried. All his friends were after that jacket and so I was proud of it.

'None of that stuff matters, Baby,' he said sweetly. Although he might feel differently about his losses in the morning when he wasn't high, I decided to enjoy our carefree reprieve.

'I'm sorry I told you to get lost earlier,' he continued. 'I didn't mean it. Did you have a nice birthday?'

'Yes.'

'My dad's birthday is also coming up in a couple days. That horrible, horrible bastard,' he said. As he spoke, he stared amorously into the eyes of my stuffed lion.

'How come you don't like your dad?' I asked. I'd been given hundreds of explanations over the course of my life, but I wanted to start up a conversation.

'Jesus! He ripped a handful of hair off the back of my head. He dragged me down the hall and threw me out of the house. He broke my collarbone once.'

'Why was he so mean to you?'

'Everyone was mean in Val des Loups. It's in the water. We had a dog that always drank from the river and he became clairvoyant. He could tell the future.'

'How did you know he could tell that?'

'Because his eyes were all bugging out of his head and he was always barking for no reason.'

Jules had grown up on the outskirts of a town called Val des Loups, about an hour outside of Montreal. To Jules it was the antithesis of all that was good and civilized in the world. According to Jules, in Val des Loups the dogs were all missing legs and the women were hideously ugly. I had a teacher from elementary school who told me that she was from Val des Loups. I almost lost my mind when she described it as a nice little town. I kind of figured out then that the Val des Loups Jules described wasn't really a real place.

Once he'd told me that everyone boxed in Val des Loups. It was part of life. His dad made him go into a makeshift boxing ring once. When it was Jules's turn to fight, he started coughing his brains out in the middle of the ring, finding it chilly standing there with just shorts on; he passed out cold the first time he got punched. He said his dad had tried to strengthen him up by making him do a hundred push-ups. He was outside for hours working on the hundred push-ups. That's why he had lousy lungs now and always had to see doctors about them.

I knew a lot of the little details about Jules's past just from things he'd told me here and there. He claimed he didn't take a bath for the first five years of his life. He said they used to eat hard-boiled eggs out on the lawn for breakfast, lunch, and supper. When Jules was eleven years old, he broke his arm riding a bicycle and then a car hit him six months later. Then, to top it all off, he set his bed on fire with a cigarette when he was fifteen. He had fallen asleep smoking and had started to dream about giant white gardenias floating above him and it hurt his eyes to look at them. He woke up realizing there were flames all around him. After that his father kicked him out of the house.

I also knew that when he was little, he had a red raincoat with yellow flowers on it that was for girls. He couldn't read very well, but he liked to draw. Once he had drawn a dog and the teacher accused him of tracing it from a book. He'd been told when he was a little kid that he had severe learning disabilities. He was taken out of school when he was in third grade and went to a tutor instead, and that hadn't helped.

This was so tragic. It made me feel almost as sad and creepy as the story about being stranded at sea. I loved to hear these terrible stories, as they were like Grimms' fairy tales to me. The stories about Val des Loups helped me to feel better than other kids. Unlike them, I had come from a country of great mystery and pain.

Jules was still under the impression that he was a big shot for having moved to Montreal. It was his biggest accomplishment. Once he'd picked up a broken pair of glasses from the grocery cart at the Salvation Army and put them on. 'These are so Val des Loups,' he'd claimed. 'How so?' I had asked. 'They're just ugly and have no style.'

We had left Val des Loups right after my mother died. He would tell me everything about the place except anything that had to do with my mother. I'd given up asking about her, but I started pleading for more details about his own life in Val des Loups. He lit a cigarette, closed his eyes, and got a big smile on his face. Jules was able to smoke in slow motion when he was stoned. The smoke came out of his mouth like ribbons being pulled off a present. Then he started getting ridiculous.

'We had fried snowballs for dessert. I had one toy. It was a chair. My mother put a wig on it and told me to pretend it was a horse. I'd take my chair outside and ride it. I found a key chain with a rabbit's foot on it and I kept it as a teddy bear. I named it Louis and it was my best friend. I brought it everywhere and talked to it. I had to keep him with me all the time. If my mother had found him, she would have used him to scrub the pots.'

I was waiting for him to continue but then realized that his head had slumped over to the side and he had passed out. I took the cigarette out of his hand and put it in a glass next to my bed. He was hot as hell, but I liked him there right next to me, stoned and not going anywhere. I felt protected and perfect. I could forget what Marika had said. Everything in the world was designed for a child and was safe. Even the little cockroaches in the wall were clockwork. They were made with the most beautiful tiny bolts from a factory in Malaysia, with little buttons underneath to switch them on and off.

the last time we were children

1

Despite the central heating of our new apartment, Jules started feeling lousy. He coughed all the time. He got the shakes at Burger King even though we were sitting as far away as possible from the door to avoid getting a draft. His fork, loaded with eggs, started trembling on its way to his mouth. He held it out for me to see and said, 'Watch it go. Jesus, I am one pitiful bastard.'

He always said that he had terrible lungs that picked up any cold. Now he'd leave the oven blasting with the door open and sit on the couch in a ski jacket and long johns. He wore his overcoat outside even though nobody else was wearing theirs and it was spring and the air smelled like mud and wet dogs. It was embarrassing because I thought that only bag ladies did that.

When I got up one morning, Jules was sitting sunken down into the couch taking little baby sips from a bottle of cough syrup. He said he'd had a terrible bout of coughing, and now he had to sit still to recover. Later he shuffled off to the hospital up the hill from where we lived, one of those giant hospitals with soot-faced gargoyles out front. They said he had tuberculosis and couldn't go home.

I just wanted to live in the hospital while he was

staying there. Then I wanted to stay with Jules's girl-friend, a rocker named Marie, but he said that she was too unstable. The smallest that a family can be is two members, and that was Jules and me.

When I was a kid I had a tuxedoed clown that I used to hide around the house so that Jules would find him and get surprised. It was our big inside joke. He'd open his drawer to get some boxers and there he was. This was great fun until one day Jules came home in a bad mood and yanked the clown out of the mailbox so hard that his leg came off in his hand. Jules felt so bad that he stayed up that night and stitched the clown's leg back on, but he sewed it on backward. After that, Jules and I called him Mr Limp. With his foot pointing the wrong way, he became more precious to me. All of a sudden that doll had personality. Because I felt so sorry for him, I started taking him everywhere I went. One night I accidentally left him on the steps of our building, and when I came down the next morning there he still was, sitting against the wall in the exact same position I had left him in the night before, his back perfectly straight. I thought it was a miracle. 'The maniacs of the night have spared Mr Limp,' I'd told Jules.

I sat in the social worker's car with my back as per-fectly straight as Mr Limp's. I had just met her that morning at the hospital. She was taking me to a foster home in Val des Loups that I'd stayed in when I was a baby. I couldn't remember the place at all. Jules said he'd had to leave me at the foster home sometimes when he needed to sleep for a couple days and couldn't afford a babysitter.

I was always the kind of kid who was up for a road trip,

but I didn't like the feeling of traveling without my dad. He thought it would be good for me to be in Val des Loups since he grew up there. I found this hard to believe given the way he had always trashed the place.

As we drove, the social worker didn't even bother trying to make conversation with me. I didn't know if I could open up the windows all the way. I didn't insist that we stop and look at the bulrushes. When I was with Jules, I used to pretend that they were lions' tails and I would pet them as we drove slowly along, enjoying the feeling of their raspy softness. Instead of my little case, I had Jules's suitcase that was covered with Chiquita banana stickers and Easter Seal stamps. Jules thought the stickers would make me look like a world traveler. All my stupid ugly things were in there: a couple T-shirts and jeans, a *National Geographic* magazine with an article about killer whales, my dolls, and a toothbrush.

The foster home was in a little town just outside of Val des Loups. Everyone there either worked in a factory or had just come out of prison. People meandered around looking out of place, like dogs without owners. There were a lot of trailers, and you could tell they hadn't been moved in a long time because the grass had grown up around them. There were no tall buildings and the houses reminded me of milk cartons.

I wasn't ready to go into the house all at once. The woman who ran the foster home told me her name was Isabelle, and she brought out an aluminum chair and let me sit in the front yard. Her husband brought me a cup of tea to drink. It was the beginning of spring, one of those days when you feel as if you should be wearing rubber boots even though it isn't raining, and the sound of a seagull carries for miles and miles. The sky had the feeling of cold, wet underwear on a clothesline. The trees around there looked like garbage. They looked like a pile of old fences and car parts leaned up one against the other.

When I was starting to think they'd forgotten me outside, Isabelle came to the door and held it open until I stood up and walked inside.

2

There were five boys living in the foster home. As far as kids went, they were all losers. When I first came in, holding my suitcase, they were sitting watching an exercise show without doing the exercises. One boy was always pretending to have an epileptic fit. It was his gift, his big talent. Another boy would weigh himself before and after he went to the bathroom and record the results. He carried around a microscope that had been donated to the foster home.

'You don't want to know what I am looking at,' he would say. No one else would touch the microscope.

I saw one boy pick up a discarded asthma inhaler on the ground and squirt it in his mouth.

'Not bad, not bad,' he said. 'Kind of pepperminty.'

For the first week I was there, the other kids would get shy around me and look at the ceiling or down at the ground, as if they'd dropped something. Then, one morning, I told them about a game where you take a chair out to the middle of the road and just sit on it. When the cars honk at you, you have to act natural and pretend not to hear them. We sneaked a kitchen chair out and we all tried to sit on the chair at once. We were piled on the chair for fifteen minutes, screaming and pinching each other, and still no car came. Nonetheless, we decided that we'd had a lot of fun. We started taking the chair out in the middle of the road every day right after breakfast. When cars did come, they just got used to driving up on the grass and around us.

After that, I was part of all their sad little rituals. We threw all our tennis balls onto the top of the grocery store, and then there were no more tennis balls to play with.

Behind the house was a row of ten-speed bicycles that we were allowed to use. None of them seemed to be the right size for anybody and we were always having accidents on them. My bicycle was too tall for me and the only way to get off of it was to just let myself fall off. I ended up with a big cut on my shoulder blade and forehead.

'Why do you all fall off your bicycles so much?' Isabelle asked. 'I swear to God, I've never seen anything like it. It's not your fault, of course. It's just the world has given you some bad luck. It's good to remember if you try anything new. That you're unlucky.'

Every new kid who showed up at the foster home had a few personal things that they were clinging on to. One boy used to have a little piece of felt that he would rub against his cheek. New kids always wanted to watch the TV shows they had watched at home. The only show Isabelle ever wanted to watch was *Barney Miller*. The change in TV shows made a lot of kids cry. When you are a kid, if you watch *The Jeffersons* with your family at seven o'clock, it seems like a natural phenomenon, like the sun setting. The universe is a strange, strange place when all of a sudden you can't use your glass with the Bionic Woman on it anymore.

It was humiliating to have the same schedule as a bunch of strangers.

Also, nobody cared about you as an individual anymore. In class at my new school I wrote a story about a magician who accidentally pulled a tiger out of his hat instead of a rabbit. When he reached down into his top hat, the tiger bit off his arm. My dad would have said that all the other kids were writing fluff and that I was a genius, a real poet of the streets. He said that one time when I'd written a report called 'Why the Dodo Is Extinct.' Walking home with my story that had a C+ on it, I missed Jules terribly all of a sudden.

Jules told me on the telephone that he also got very depressed and lonely in the hospital. He only got channel six on the television there. He said it was a terrible thing to have insomnia in a hospital. The only other people who were awake were the people who were brought in from accidents in the middle of the night. If they had just been sleeping, none of their tragedies would have happened. Jules said that he had met one man who had stepped out onto the fire escape for a smoke and then realized that it wasn't the window that led to the fire escape at all.

I'd figured when I first showed up at Isabelle's that after a short while everything was going to be better and Jules and I would be right back together. Then one night Jules called me and his voice was funny on the phone. He sounded like a little girl, or like he was imitating a cartoon character, and at first I wanted to laugh because I thought he was trying to make a joke. Then I realized that he was talking like that because he couldn't help it. Jules told me that he was taking a turn for the worse and that he was going to be in the hospital longer than we'd thought, maybe even three months.

After I got that news, I started wearing a star sticker that I took off my math test and stuck on my forehead. I stole Isabelle's eye shadow and mascara even though she'd told me not to. She said young girls looked prettier without makeup anyway. I started cursing more and throwing bottles against the train tracks. I did these things for no good reason. I didn't know anyone whose father lived in a hospital.

3

After I'd been living in Val des Loups for a month and a half, we were told that a new boy named Linus Lucas was being moved to our foster home from another home that had burned down.

Linus Lucas was fourteen years old, a number that made the spoons fall right out of our hands. Isabelle said that he could look out for us. She said it would be like we had a big brother. He could walk us to the pond and save us from drowning.

When Linus Lucas arrived, he wasn't in shock the way kids who had just been separated from their families were. I'd shown up wincing like the spring breeze was giving me a black eye. In fact, Linus was in a good mood when he got out of the social worker's car. He had his Walkman on and he was carrying a gold gym bag. I found out later that he'd been in foster homes since he was seven years old and that's why he was so blasé when he showed up.

Linus wore a fedora and a skinny leather jacket with a fur collar. He was mulatto. He explained how his mother was white and his father was black. This was new to us. 'His mother is white and his father is black,' we would say over and over when he wasn't around. He had a long face and big freckles, only about five or six of them on either cheek. His lips were fat and in the shape of a heart. He was fourteen, but he was as tall as a man and he almost had a mustache.

His father had left the family to go live in Montreal. He rode the subway asking good-looking women what time it was. He'd given Linus a guitar pick with a silhouette of a naked woman on it a couple years ago, when he had seen him last. His mother had to go to Montreal on her own to find some work and then she was supposed to come back and get him, except that she never did.

He had spent his whole life in Val des Loups, and Montreal was like the Emerald City to him. The only person who really kept in touch with him was an uncle who was awaiting a court date in the city. His uncle would drive all the way out from Montreal to the foster home to come and chat with Linus. He'd always bring him cool things, like a pair of sunglasses with mirrors for lenses and music tapes.

Lucas would go into the bathroom to smoke. We could smell it all the way in our rooms. He also liked to pretend that he was a drug addict. He'd smoked pot a couple times in his life and he went on and on about how he needed to go into rehab now. He used to say that his orange juice was methadone. He walked around the house with a blanket wrapped around him.

'I'm going through withdrawal,' he said.

He wore his big mirror sunglasses to the breakfast table, drinking a big cup of coffee, his shiny lenses staring at nothing.

He said we always had to turn our cups upside down and shake them before we used them so that if there were any cockroaches in them, they would fall out. We didn't ever see a cockroach there, but we started doing it just for fun. He made everything exciting, like this was the place to be, which is a strange feeling to have inside a foster home.

'If you want to buy heroin,' he said, 'you call it brown or horse. You got some horse, my man? You have to learn the codes.' I'd personally never heard these terms used. 'You have to hide your drugs in very original places. You can keep them in your houseplant or you could keep them in dolls.'

He was always taking the heads off my dolls to see if he could fit little baggies into their bodies.

He said that we should try and make Isabelle's dog, Bone, deadly like a drug dealer's dog. He thought it would be cool to have a ferocious dog that we could walk down the street on a leather strap, pulling like crazy and barking and yanking our arms out of their sockets.

He liked to talk about New York City all the time. New York City this and New York City that. In New York City nobody did anything stupid or they would get themselves shot.

'If this was the States, we'd all be shot by now.'

Everyone nodded their heads, solemnly acknowledging this fact.

When Linus Lucas found out that I was from Montreal – the big city – he named me his personal assistant. I told him a story about how a friend of my dad's named Thumper had been pulled over by some police officers when he had LSD in the car and he'd swallowed all of it. Now sometimes Thumper would do strange things, like he would pick up our telephone and start talking even though it hadn't rung. Thumper would refer to people as numbers for no reason. 'Hello, XC-27-18,' he'd say. Linus thought it was the greatest story he'd ever heard. He gave me a backstage pass to his room that he made with a little piece of cardboard and a gold marker.

Linus always listened to the same tape that his uncle had picked up for him in Montreal. He wouldn't even play it in the boom box downstairs because he didn't want anyone else listening. He would only play it on the Walkman that his uncle had given him. He said that we would not comprehend this type of music. I could only watch him as he grooved to the invisible beat and try to imagine what it could possibly sound like.

I walked into his room one night and flashed my little backstage pass. I saw the Walkman lying on his bed, so I asked him if I could listen to it. I expected him as usual to tell me to get lost.

'All right,' he said to my surprise and handed it to me. 'Get ready to have your mind blown, though. You might not enjoy the awakening. You'll think all the kids are fools. Are you ready?'

'I think they're all fools anyway.'

'Good answer. That's 'cause your dad's cool. I'm cool because my uncle's cool. It's something you just have to be born with.'

I sat on the bed and spread out my arms, waiting for the music to begin. When it started, it wasn't what I had expected. I guess I'd expected a whole chorus of skinny girls screeching and moaning. Instead there was a man singing along to a piano. I think it was Stevie Wonder, although it could have been someone else. I closed my eyes and the roof was gone. I could see the stars while the piano tinkled. I could see Jupiter and it was blue, and Neptune was silver like a tennis ball sprayed silver. I could reach out and touch it, like cold water.

After that, when another kid in the foster home would ask me if I thought Linus was full of it, I would say, 'No way! He's the real thing!' I wouldn't tell them what the music had sounded like, though, because that was a nice secret that I shared with Linus.

'Is my uncle coming to visit me today?' Linus always asked Isabelle.

'How should I know?'

'Maybe he called and said he was coming by.'

'He calls and says he's coming and then never shows up. And then he doesn't call for a couple of days and shows up out of the blue. I've told you kids a million times, just because your family or nobody doesn't come and visit you, it doesn't mean that you're not lovely people just the same.'

Linus Lucas's uncle was a black man with long legs that stretched across the room. He wore sunglasses all the time and his Afro was pulled up like a lit matchstick. He always talked like he was an important blues singer who had been touring for months and was now being interviewed during a much-needed reprieve from the road. The two of them were sitting together on the couch discussing things one afternoon. I was curled up in an armchair, minding my own business.

'Baby, I know your dad. Is he still selling weed?' he called out to me, loudly, so that everyone heard.

'No, he's in the hospital.'

'So anyway,' he said. 'I was down in the East End.

I went to see Sarah, who works at a strip club there. It hasn't wrecked her yet. I asked for a date when I saw her dancing. Those legs are one in a million. When you've looked at legs as many times as I have, you begin to distinguish between them quite easily, my man. These were fine legs. So anyway, I got this bag of terrible strong weed, not like the usual stuff I have, and we smoked the whole thing. People are always like, why the fuck do you sell such lousy goddamn weed, and I say if I was carrying some great stuff I would just smoke it all myself. It would be too irresistible. This stuff I'm holding is really truly unquestionable, just a smash-up success story on its own. But smoking it with her was like heaven. Now that is one fine mixture: women and pot. Better than ice cream and pie. When she said sweet things in my ear, they would slide right down into my heart.'

His uncle could just go on and on. He was like an encyclopedia of sleazy things and Linus Lucas drooled over every word.

Linus was coming to the conclusion that just because I was from Montreal and my dad was cool didn't necessarily mean I was cool. Once he caught me with my face up against the neighbor's chicken coop, saying, 'Hey, girl, aren't you a pretty thing, come here! I like your soft feathers. Sexy!' He told me that I had to get out of the country fast. Another time I was collecting a paper bag full of white stones from someone's driveway, which I thought would impress him for some reason. The bottom of the bag ripped open and they all fell out all over the kitchen floor and Linus just shook his head.

Isabelle gave me a box full of dolls and Linus came in the room and held up each one in the air, trying to decide whether or not he would sleep with her if she were a real person. He said that if you put Spanish fly in a lady's drink, she'd do anything for you. He said that he would like me if I was older, but if he so much as looked at me for a minute straight, he'd end up in jail.

I thought I'd be the perfect girlfriend for Linus, if he'd wait for me a couple years. I was only just twelve. I stood up on a telephone book on my tiptoes and pulled my belt really tight to see what I'd feel like when I was old enough to date Linus. But then Linus went and started dating a girl named Brandy who was the most ridiculous girl in town. She never said anything; instead she'd just stare at people. She wasn't attractive at all, but she had big boobs. She wore a sweater with a picture of a woman walking a poodle on it and there were real bows attached to the sweater on the poodle's ears. She had the tiniest shorts that I had ever seen. They were like a little heart-shaped purse for dolls. You couldn't wear shorts like that in the city, or you would cause a car accident. She and Linus would sit in the living room and make out like crazy with their mouths wide, wide open.

One time, he put her up on his shoulders and pretended that they were at a rock concert.

'Did you ever see Twisted Sister in concert?' he asked me.

'No.'

'Did you ever see Judas Priest in concert?'

'No.'

'You don't know what's going on.'

Isabelle drove us into Joliette one day so she could visit her sister. She made a big deal about us going to visit our 'auntie'. We knew that her sister couldn't stand the sight

36

of us. She was always telling Isabelle that we were going to murder her in her sleep one night. After we said our awkward hellos, Isabelle left us all in this really big park that we liked while she and her sister went to do their hair. There were lottery tickets all over the ground in that park. That was because the drug dealers used to wrap up heroin in bits of old lottery cards folded into flaps. Before Jules had gone to the hospital, there had been a lot of lottery tickets under his bed. The seagulls in that park were so used to being fed that they attacked you if you took out a sandwich or even if you stuck your hand in your pocket. They came down out of the sky to check us out. They reminded me of a scene from a movie I'd seen, where a flurry of hands wearing white gloves were applauding at the opera.

We lay on the grass outside the zoo, criticizing a mime who was wearing a tuxedo and standing perfectly still in front of us. We were insulting him under our breath and laughing really, really hard. He couldn't walk away because he was pretending to be a statue, so it was really a good time.

Right about then, I noticed a whole group of kids walking straight toward us. They had this angry look about them, as if they had been falling off swings all day. A pack of masochists, that's what Jules would have called them. They looked right at Linus Lucas, who was sitting by himself, hitting the ground with two sticks as if he was playing the drums, while listening to his Walkman. One of the kids tripped right on top of him on purpose.

It was obvious from his attitude that the boy was the leader of this gang. He stood back up, and instead of apologizing he just got a mean look in his eyes. Linus stood up and dusted himself off. The boy blew into an empty Chiclets box casual-like while staring at Linus. Chiclets had freckles all over every bit of his body and had bushy dark eyebrows. He wasn't even dressed cool. He had a pink T-shirt and striped shorts and he was wearing old men's sandals. The boy next to him was wearing girl sunglasses and one of his arms was shriveled up.

'Why were you sitting in my way?' Chiclets demanded.

'I didn't see you coming,' Linus answered.

'Well, I'm still going to have to sue you, my man!'

'And why are you wearing that stupid bandanna so tight?' asked the boy with the shriveled-up arm. 'It's going to cut off all the circulation to your brain.'

Linus just stared at them, not knowing what to say. His face was taking on that expression you get right before you cry: all wavy and sad. I knew that the trick to save yourself from this type of situation was to act totally crazy; to act fearless, like you would try to poke one of their eyes out with a library card if they came any closer. He should have called them all motherfuckers by now. All the kids in the gang moved in closer around Linus, encircling him. They started flailing their arms outward and accusing him of having assaulted their dear friend.

'Give us your Walkman, man, and we'll forget about the whole thing,' said Chiclets.

'Yeah! Or give us a hundred dollars! Motherfucker! Motherfucker! Motherfucker!' the shrivel-armed boy chanted.

'My uncle gave me this Walkman,' Linus said, making the sorry mistake of being polite.

One of the boys started kicking his legs up karate style and the rest of them joined in, making those whiny martial arts noises. Then Chiclets punched Linus right in the face. The other boys started punching him too, and we all put our hands over our faces, not looking and hoping it would end soon. I peeked and I couldn't see Linus. All the other boys had surrounded him and were throwing punches down at him. They looked like old women going through a bag of clothes at a community center.

When Chiclets finally got Linus's Walkman, the whole gang ran away right out of the park. We all sat down next to Linus, who was lying facedown on the ground and crying. We were very quiet because we didn't know what to do. He couldn't even look at us. His face was covered in blood and he couldn't open one of his eyes. All the kids from the foster home stepped back because his nose was bleeding. The blood that was coming from his nose was mixed up with snot. I was afraid to get down on my knees and hug him.

'Oh, my God, that's so nasty,' they all whispered.

The next day there was a huge purple pouch under Linus's eye. It made my own eyes water to look at him. The stitches on his lips were big and swollen. They reminded me of train tracks, but I didn't tell him. He was allowed to stay home from school so that no one had to look at his face. When I came home from school, he was sitting on the sofa watching soap operas.

That night things got even worse for Linus. His uncle showed up at the foster home with his hair all over the place and his clothes looking like he'd just pulled them out of the laundry hamper. I guessed right off the bat that he was the kind of guy who yelled at you when you hurt yourself.

'I got that Walkman for you and you just let some kids take it away from you!' he screamed at Linus, not saying hello or anything. 'Shit, you remind me of your father. He doesn't have any shame whatsoever. When I see him on the street, he always wants to borrow five dollars. You're going to start acting like that too now? You have to act like a man! Didn't I ever tell you what to do if you get in a fight? Haven't you ever watched a movie?'

'I think you're scaring the children, sir,' Isabelle said.

'Scaring the children! Look at the goddamn reality of this situation. His face is what's goddamn scaring them. You're going to be ugly for the rest of your life. And it's not like you were a pretty boy before. At least the kid who hit you went and earned himself that Walkman. You can't appreciate it because it was handed to you on a silver platter. A spoiled motherfucker, that's what you are. I want you to make some money and pay me for that Walkman. I bought that downtown.'

'I could do that after I move in with you,' Linus said in a small voice.

His uncle looked terrified for the briefest second before going back to being enraged.

'You know how we were talking about you coming to live with me in the city after I tied this legal business up? Well, I don't think that you can handle it. You're just too spoiled to come and live with me.'

That night I hung on to the door frame of Linus's room and leaned in. He was lying there reading *Stranger in a Strange Land*. He looked a lot younger without his music, just sitting there and minding his own business.

'Are you all right?' I asked.

He sat up on the side of his bed with his legs dangling and looked at me sadly.

'Yeah, but I hate my uncle and I always will.'

I went into the room and sat next to Linus on the bed.

I put my hand on his shoulder. I was always surprised at how soft other people were. I thought that I felt his heartbeat, although it could have just been my own.

The other kids were disillusioned with Linus after they'd seen him sobbing in the park. Now he seemed ordinary and just a loser like anybody else. One of the boys ripped up his backstage pass to Linus's room. The kids started saying that Linus was unlucky, and they'd make the sign of the cross after he passed and wasn't looking.

'I like men with black eyes,' I said. 'They look like raccoons.'

'Kind of like Alice Cooper?'

'Yes, like that.'

4

During the first warm days of May, Zachary showed up at the foster home. He was from Montreal and was twelve, like me. He was the saddest kid I had ever met, pale and really small for his age, with a big round beauty mark on his cheek. His curly blond hair was long for a boy. I thought he looked a little like Marilyn Monroe might have when she was twelve. He had a pack of Starburst that he divided up between us. He didn't even keep one for himself because he was so confident that his mother was going to come and get him.

Zachary's mother went to a sewing school downtown and she'd made him a school bag out of different squares of material. He was carrying it with him on the subway when he fell asleep on one of the scratchy cushions on the seats. He woke up and his mother was gone. He stayed on the subway all the way until the last stop, until someone figured out that he was lost and called the police. Zachary was convinced that his mother was still out there looking for him.

He always packed everything he owned in the morning, as if a horn would honk and he would only have a second to get his stuff together, because the meter would be running in the cab and his mom would be waiting for him in it. After he had been staying with us a week, Isabelle asked, 'So what movie do you guys want to see on Saturday?' Zachary said that he wasn't going to be here, so it wasn't right for him to vote.

Zachary cried at the end of any TV show, even *Happy Days*. He threw up after being on the merry-go-round. He always came out of the bathtub with shampoo still in his hair. He couldn't tell the time, and if you teased him about it, he got all upset.

We were fascinated by Zachary in the same way that we'd been taken with Linus and his hipster ways when he first showed up. Linus had permanently retired to his room, where he practiced cursive and read *Stranger in a Strange Land*, never seeming to get past page twenty. Zachary would ask if Linus wanted to play and we'd all shake our heads to indicate he was to be left alone. Linus Lucas told us that he was suffering from depression, an emotion that we were too immature to understand.

I had my own room in the group home since I was the only girl and all the boys were perverted. One boy claimed to have had sex with seventy-eight women. Another boy would call out, 'What's behind door number three?' and pull down his zipper. Isabelle knew Zachary would never do anything like that, so he was given the empty bed next to mine.

Zachary and I actually tried talking about Montreal, but we didn't seem to know any of the same places. Every time I asked him where he had lived, he said a different street name. All he knew was that there was a butcher next to where he lived and his mother didn't like the smell so she made him hold his nose when they passed.

'My mother and I are vegetarians,' he said.

'So you don't eat hamburgers?'

'No, we eat hamburgers.'

'So how are you vegetarians?'

'We just are.'

He would fall asleep as soon as he touched anything soft. His hair was like baby chicks and it always reminded me of dandelions when it was sticking out of the top of his blanket.

One night it was cold outside because there was a thunderstorm coming. Even though it was May, it felt as if I was lying on top of a pile of snow. I tried to hold myself rolled up into a little ball under the bedcover to keep warm, but it didn't do any good. Finally, I got out of my bed and climbed under the covers with Zachary. That night I fell into the deepest sleep I had ever had. Sleeping next to Zachary was like sleeping in the middle of a cherry pie that had just come out of the oven. No wonder he was so mellow every night! I figured that he was warm like that because he still had his mother's love in him.

The next day it was raining outside so we all stayed in. We usually didn't mind the rain and liked to sink our sneakers into the mud, but that day the raindrops were the size of nickels and dimes. We were all wearing matching sweaters that had come in a box. Zachary and I were in our room. He was only wearing his sweater and underwear; he liked to wander around half dressed. He pointed out his birthmark that covered half of his leg and told me that his mother said it was beautiful and reminded her of chocolate and made her want to bite it.

From what I had gathered about the world, you couldn't trust what mothers said. A mother would tell her kid that crossed eyes were beautiful and made you look like a scientist. If you saw someone walking around in their rubber boots even though it was sunny outside, you knew their mother thought those rubber boots were just about the cutest thing she'd ever seen.

Linus was walking down the hall and took a look into our room. He was wearing the same sweater as us. Since the sleeves were too short on him, he wore them pushed up to his elbows.

'What are you two doing?' he asked.

We'd actually been trying to play an adventure board game. We were inventing the rules as we went along because we were too lazy to actually read the instructions. Since our version of the game made no sense, we were about to give up on it.

'Can you teach us how to play this board game?' Zachary asked.

'Board games were invented to keep people from thinking so they won't plan a revolution.'

'Oh,' said Zachary, and he quickly kicked the game under the bed.

Noticing the effect he was having, Linus strutted into the room and sat on a chair.

'You want me to show you how to draw a panther?' Linus asked Zachary.

'Sure!' Zachary said, rushing around the room in his underwear, looking for a pencil and paper.

Linus drew a picture of what looked to me like a regular black cat, except with slanted eyes and crooked teeth. Zachary exclaimed that it was a thing of beauty. That morning, Zachary was in awe of Linus Lucas. The next day he let Linus draw a dragon on the back of his jacket. It was the ugliest dragon I'd ever seen. It looked more like a praying mantis. Linus had a can of gold spray paint that he had shoplifted from a hardware store a while ago and he'd spray-painted his running shoes. Zachary begged him to do the same to his ratty old sneakers. So off they went to the backyard to do the deed. They laid the sneakers down on the ground. Zachary stood back as if they might explode and screamed excitedly when Linus started spraying them. In an effort to do a complete job, Linus spray-painted all the grass around the sneakers too. I went out to check out the damage and Zachary was tiptoeing around in his new golden sneakers trying to do break dancing moves. The ground was silvery, as if some stars had fallen there. It was the first time I had seen Linus smile in a long time.

A bakery used to bring day-old sweets to the foster home. Sometimes they brought us fancy cakes that hadn't been picked up. One day we got a cake that had 'Happy Birthday Zachary' written across it in turquoise icing. There were tiny plastic birds and big blue roses all over it and it looked very expensive to us.

'Look, Zachary, it's a cake especially for you,' Isabelle said.

Zachary was so delighted about that cake that he started acting as though he were some crazy duke, throwing a dinner party. He laughed and laughed as he ran around the table, helping Isabelle set up the glasses for milk. She let him cut the cake, naturally, and he was very fair about dividing it up evenly.

'Blue is my favorite color! Isn't this cake good! It's ice cream flavor, I think!'

Zachary washed off the plastic birds from the cake and kept them under his mattress. That night, all Zachary could talk about was things that his mother had done for his birthday. One time she had made him a cake that was shaped like a cat with licorice whiskers. He wanted to kiss everyone good night. We all stayed up late passing kisses back and forth until Isabelle said enough was enough.

As I lay in the dark, I knew everyone was thinking about their mothers. I wanted to think about my mother, too, but I couldn't come up with much. Jules never liked talking about her. All I knew was that sometimes she went to the library when she wanted to cry. Also, she didn't snore. If you put your ear right up to her mouth, you wouldn't hear a single thing. I thought of her sleeping face and how it must have looked as peaceful as the moon. When Jules gets better and takes me home, I thought, I'm going to ask him to watch me sleep and see if I look like her.

napoleon street

1

'Well, Baby is completely out of her mind,' I overheard Isabelle saying to the social worker.

They were both sitting in the living room drinking coffee. I stood in the hallway quietly, listening.

'God bless her, but the child is wild. It's not her fault. But she'll never be normal. At least let her enjoy her childhood. You read the report, didn't you? There was rotten food in the fridge, clothes all over the floor. She came here wearing one of her father's T-shirts and his baseball cap. You just wanted to throw out all the things that she had in her suitcase and give her a chance to start all over again. And the child's fingernails were long. Who ever heard of long fingernails on a twelve-year-old? And she smelled!'

'Is she worse than Rodney?'

'Rodney? No, God no. She doesn't need psychiatric help. I'm just saying that she needs a couple extra things like a sweater or some new toys of her own.'

Later that afternoon, Isabelle came into my room with a box filled with girls' toys. I pulled out a blue pony with long yellow hair and pink seashells on its butt.

'Who was Rodney?' I asked her.

'A little boy who lived here and used to wear swimming

goggles all the time. Who's been talking to you about Rodney?'

'You mentioned him to the social worker.'

'Lord! Don't worry what I say to the social worker. I have to make you sound like a real sorrowful case to be able to get you more things. See, I got you a pretty pony, didn't I?'

I guess it was worth having your self-esteem destroyed if there was a free toy involved. Isabelle told me that she was trying to get us a subscription to *Ranger Rick* magazine. I didn't want to hear what she was going to say about me to get it. I sat next to her on the bed and leaned on her as I played with the pony's hair. I loved the way that Isabelle could make you feel so lazy.

And then, when it seemed like an impossibility, Isabelle informed me that I was going to live with Jules again. His decision to come and get me took me by surprise. I'd become used to living at the foster home and had given up on looking forward to his return. The morning of his arrival, I packed my little suitcase and went down to the kitchen to wait for him. Isabelle hugged me about a million times, which made me feel weird, as if she expected something bad to happen. She also called me every pet name in her repertoire: 'lollipop, little fool, kitty cat, bumblebee…'

I sat around the kitchen table with the other kids. We sat there and sighed and said, 'Yep, yep, yep.' We had sat around the table muttering like this two times before when kids were transferred to other foster homes. We thought it was the thing to do. Isabelle gave me my going away present early. I opened up the envelope she handed me and took out the card. Each of the boys in the home

48

had signed it. Someone had signed Hulk Hogan. 'Yeah, right!' I said, and everyone laughed. Inside the card was a five-dollar bill with the words 'I love you' written on it with a blue pen. I wondered how I could spend a bill that had the words 'I love you' written on it. Somehow I knew that I would, on movies or comic books. Love is a big and wonderful idea, but life is made up of small things. As a kid, you have nothing to do with the way the world is run; you just have to hurry to catch up with it.

When Jules drove up in his friend Lester's car, I was really excited but embarrassed at the same time. I didn't want my two homes colliding. For some reason, I didn't want Jules to see how I felt about this place. I wanted him to think I was above the kids here and had sat alone in my room reading for the four months he had been gone. I was worried that he was going to stand around drinking coffee and getting the scoop from Isabelle about everything that had gone on. What if he saw the name tags that Isabelle had put on the backs of all our chairs because of all the fistfights we had at supper time over who would get to sit next to her? Jules would think I was so lame.

When he finally drove up into the driveway, he didn't even cut the engine. He waited for me to run outside and meet him. Isabelle walked me out, her arm squeezing me to her side. For a second, I wasn't sure whether I wanted her to let me go. Isabelle was very good about making me not worry about things. For instance, she would write the phone number of the foster home on the inside of my coat in case I got lost. The nights at Isabelle's house were very quiet. I could really fall into a deep sleep because I knew I would be able to sleep until the morning. Jules used to get me out of bed in the middle of the night to help throw towels all over the kitchen floor because the sink had flooded. Once he woke me up to look at a bill because he thought that he had been overcharged.

Jules shook hands with her without saying anything and then jumped back in the car. One of my rag dolls fell from my arms and onto the driveway. I had to step back out to get it.

'Come on, you little bitch,' I whispered.

I closed the car door and Jules pulled back onto the road. As we drove away, I started to wish I'd done something dramatic, like thrown my arms around the other kids and Isabelle and wept. I should have done something I could remember my whole life. Something that would signal the end of an era. I was driving off to a real home. I tried not to think about those I'd left behind.

I shoved my suitcase over the seats into the back. I couldn't put my feet down because there was a box of records under the front seat. The records all seemed to be of bands I had never heard of.

'Where did you get these?' I asked.

'Someone gave them to me. They're rare, I think. There might be a couple that are worth a lot of money.'

I rested my feet up on the dashboard. I had on a pair of bright green sneakers with yellow stripes down the sides and they caught Jules's attention right away.

'Where did you get those?'

'My other pair got too small so the social worker brought me these.'

'The social worker! How dare she have the audacity! They look like Jamaican shoes. They're pot dealer shoes.'

'They are not!'

'They are one hundred percent Saint Henry shoes.'

I started to try and sit Indian style to hide my feet.

'Hey, I'm just kidding,' Jules said. 'You look great! You look like you've been eating really well. And, man, did your hair ever get long.'

'Thanks,' I answered.

He wrapped his finger around one of my ponytails and pulled it gently. He leaned over and opened the glove compartment.

'Look what I got from the hospital,' he said as he pulled out a stethoscope. 'I lurked around a good half hour waiting for the right moment to strike. It's impossible to acquire. If they sold them at the pharmacy, anyone could be a doctor.'

He handed it over and I held it out in front of me, admiring it.

'All the kids will wish they had something like that. I mean it's cool, right?'

I nodded and put the stethoscope on my chest to listen to my heart. I had always wanted to be on the other end of a stethoscope. I envied the doctors who were able to hear what hearts really sounded like. But mine only sounded like a flat tire thumping down the highway. I pulled it out of my ears and let it hang around my neck.

'Do you still sing a lot?' Jules asked.

'No! I never sang a lot.'

'Yes, you did. When you were seven years old, you used to sing this song called '*Dialogue des Amoureux*' that played on the radio sometimes.'

'I've never even heard of that song.'

'It goes, *Quand je te détesterai pour que tu le crois bien, quand je te détesterai, je mettrai ma casquette.* When I don't love you anymore, so as to let you know, I'll be wearing my hat.'

'I don't know that song.'

51

'Well, I learned it from you. *Quand tu ne m'aimeras plus, je me ferai des tresses.* When you don't love me anymore, I'll be wearing my hair in braids!'

I started laughing. The idea that I used to sing that song seemed kind of wonderful to me. Jules was the only person who could remember nice things about me that I couldn't remember myself. It felt really comfortable to be with him again.

'Who are we going to be staying with?' I asked.

'With ourselves.'

'You got an apartment already?'

'I've been living there a couple months.'

This was news to me. The whole time I'd been in the foster home, I thought Jules was still in the hospital. I thought the day they'd release him, he'd hitchhike right over to the foster home and get me. I must have looked really hurt because he immediately pulled the car over to the side of the road. He stopped the car next to a bush covered in flowers with tiny round white petals. His voice always got screechy when he was being defensive. I remembered that much.

'I had to get all my shit together if they were going to let me get you. I had to get a place to stay. I have a job lined up in a couple months when my disability pay runs out.'

I nodded, trying not to cry, to make him feel better. I'd been looking forward to this reunion for a long time and I didn't want to ruin it by making us both sad. I reached out the window to pull off one of the flowers. As soon as I touched the branch, all the petals fell to the ground, as if someone had emptied a hole puncher.

'I swear to God, Baby,' Jules said. 'There wasn't a second that I wasn't thinking about you since we got separated.'

He leaned over and just squeezed me really hard. I was still small enough to enjoy a hug in a car, actually anywhere.

'I'm feeling really good,' Jules said. 'You don't have to worry about me going anyplace any time soon. I missed you so much that I'm really going to take care of myself so I don't end up in the hospital again. No more smoking or doing drugs or stuff like that. I gotta be aware of what I'm missing out on. How does that sound to you?'

'Good!'

I settled back into my seat as we drove back into Montreal. It had been a lot easier to mellow out in Val des Loups than in the city. Zachary and I would take three-leaf clovers and crazy glue extra leafs on them to try and pass them off as lucky. In the city there didn't seem to be time for that kind of hobby. Things were always hectic.

There was a way that you could sleep properly when a house had been straightened up, when all the *Ranger Rick*s were put up on the shelf and the toys were put in the plastic box and tomorrow's clothes were laid out neatly on a chair. But then again, when everything was left out all over the floor and the dishes were still in the sink, there was a way that you could dream.

2

He took me to a small apartment on Napoleon Street. In this apartment, there was yellow wallpaper covered with pink roses and water stains. The cracked window in my new bedroom looked out directly onto the wall of the building across the alley. A twin-sized bed took up the whole room. It had been there when Jules moved in and it reminded me of a photograph I'd seen in a National Geographic magazine of a hospital in Romania. We were both afraid to even sit on it, but after a few days we forgot that it wasn't always ours.

Jules and I taped some record covers on the wall. There was a singer wearing enormous sunglasses on the cover of one and a man in a blue suit holding a rose on another. These gave our apartment a real touch of class.

There's something that moving around all the time is supposed to do to you morally, but I didn't feel it. It felt good to be back in Montreal. There was a TV show that took place at the Apollo Theater and I assumed it must be somewhere downtown. You could walk to the river from where we lived. There was a concrete wall between the grass and the river that people sat on and fished from. It was so polluted that putting your feet in the water could kill you on the spot, apparently. I went down the street in my bathing suit and rubber boots and found a cardboard box to sunbathe on by the water.

I just tried to do the things that I used to love to do before I went away. There was a record store with glass tiles out in front of it that made this great noise when you danced on them with dress shoes. I bought mango juice from the store that everybody said was a front for selling cocaine. There was a tourist shop, and if you went in and begged enough they would let you inhale a little helium. Jules slapped me once for inhaling it at a birthday party years ago, as he believed that I could get addicted to the stuff.

If you walked up the hill from the bus station, ours was the first street you saw. It was the street of illusions for newcomers, filled with run-down cafés, bars, heroin dealers, and street vendors. You could live la vie en rose there. Our building was next to a hotel called Istanbul Tourist Rooms that had cardboard boxes on some of its windows for curtains.

I hoped that we would stay there forever and that we would never be separated again. For this to happen, I thought Jules would have to start acting more adultlike and responsible. You get very religious about the idea of parents in a foster home. They seem as fragile as a glass horse on a shelf. While Jules was in the hospital, I had learned that our relationship was a vulnerable thing, but it turned out that he hadn't. Because I had come back from the foster home looking healthier and with good color, Jules got the unfortunate idea that I could handle myself without him. He acted as if no matter what he did, everything would still turn out all right.

He bought a gun from a friend of his for ten dollars, although he had no idea where on earth to get bullets for it. He put it in the elastic waistband of his jogging pants and the gun slipped out and landed on his toe. He hopped around the living room screaming. He took off his sneaker and his sock later and made me have a look. His little toe was completely blue and black. It really shocked me. If this could happen to him, anything could happen. It didn't seem like the kind of thing that happened to other people's parents.

He did other worrisome things. Like he stole a pair of boots with steel toes from the Salvation Army and left his running shoes in their place. He lit a cigarette on the back of the bus and kept his hand dangling out the window, sticking his face out the window when he wanted to take a drag. He assured me that since the cigarette was outside, it was perfectly legal and he had nothing to worry about.

55

Because I'd been in foster care, the social worker came by to check up on us and make sure that he had a job. Jules lied and claimed he'd gone to a lot of interviews. Really he was looking into a career of selling stolen items out of garbage bags on the street corner, which was what his best friend Lester was into at the time.

He was still using heroin; he had even used it while he was at the hospital. I know because he told Lester and his friends about one time when he was desperate to get high. He had wheeled his IV to the front door of the hospital and had told the guard that he wanted to get a hot dog from a vendor on the corner. He had sworn up and down that he would be back in exactly two minutes. As soon as he was around the corner, he had started to run. He'd shown up in St Louis Square, a lowlife park off St Denis Street, to meet his dealer hooked up to an IV and dressed only in a hospital gown that kept blowing open and showing his underwear. This story almost killed Lester and anyone else he told it to. It always guaranteed Jules a laugh, so he told it a lot. When he had gotten back to the hospital, the nurse confiscated his shoes so he couldn't escape again. I wished that I could hide Jules's new steel-toed boots, too, in order to keep him out of trouble.

As a gift to himself on his twenty-seventh birthday, Jules decided to give himself a tattoo. I walked along beside him as he headed to a tattoo parlor called Iris on Ontario Street. I had to hurry to keep up with him. I didn't like the idea of a tattoo, as I associated them with creepy guys who wore headbands in the park. Tattoos weren't as pretty as they are now. They were like the pen drawings that rocker kids drew in high school, doodles on pieces of loose-leaf paper. I was trying to talk Jules out of it the whole way there.

'God, what if it comes out ugly?' I whined. 'You can't erase it, you know. I hope you know that! You can't just Liquid Paper it out. You'll be too embarrassed to go to the swimming pool ever if it's ugly. Don't expect me to come to the swimming pool with you, either. No way I'm hanging out with a dad who has a goofy tattoo. No sir!'

'They know what they're doing at this place,' Jules said calmly.

'Elaine's cousin told me that getting tattoos is addictive. He said that you can't just get one. You might end up being one of those freaks who has tattoos everywhere. Even on their face! That's so ugly. Have you really thought this out?'

'I've spent twenty-seven years without a tattoo. That's a long time. Now I'd like to spend some years with a tattoo. It sounds pretty rational to me.'

'Would you like me to knock out one of your teeth to go with your tattoo? So that you can have the full bum look?'

'Don't be a wiseass, Baby. Why don't you use that smart ass of yours to try a little harder in school so that you can get some good grades?'

'But I do get good grades at school!'

'But you don't act like someone who does.'

'Tyler's older brother went to get a tattoo,' I continued. 'But he couldn't stand the pain, so now he only has half a tattoo.'

'I'm just going to be getting something small.'

'I don't think it's a very good idea at all. How do you know that they clean their needles? You could get AIDS!'

'Why are you even coming with me if you're going to be such a drag?' Jules yelled, quickening his pace.

'Well, if you're going to do it anyway, then I want to watch.'

When we got there, it turned out that kids under sixteen weren't allowed in. I tried to physically prevent Jules from going in without me. God knew what crazy tattoo he'd pick on his own. I wrapped my arms around him. He always seemed so skinny that you might assume that he was the weakest person on the planet. I was weaker, though, because I couldn't hold him, and he yanked my arms from around him. I pulled on his T-shirt and managed to stretch the neck all the way down past his nipple.

'Get lost, Baby. I hate when you completely lose your goddamn mind! Don't I have enough problems in life without you being a wacko!'

Finally I let go. I leaned against the wall of the tattoo parlor, waiting for him. I was singing a song under my breath, trying to pretend that I wasn't the one who was actually singing the song. I was trying to believe that there was someone next to me and that they were singing to me.

Time went by unbearably slowly. Jules walked out of the tattoo parlor forty minutes later. He looked very pleased with himself. He pulled down the piece of gauze that was taped to his chest and whistled at the same time because he had a swallow tattooed there. It was all 3-D and bright like tattoos are before they heal. For a moment, I was impressed. Who could not be taken in by a newborn tattoo, glowing as bright as a stigmata?

That little swallow did turn out to be bad luck, though. Jules went outside a few days later with his jacket on and no shirt underneath so that people could get a look at his tattoo. The cops stopped him for looking ludicrous.

Making people uncomfortable is a crime, I guess. They found a point of heroin in the pocket of his jeans. He didn't warn one of the cops that he had a syringe in his pocket and it stuck the cop in the hand. That enraged the cops and they shoved my dad in the squad car.

I came downstairs and a friend of mine pointed out to me what was going on. I ran across the street to get to Jules and to try and save him. I didn't even look; I flew across.

I will let you in on a little secret about being hit by a car. Sometimes it doesn't hurt at all. It makes the same noise as when you jump on a suitcase to close it. Everywhere that should have hurt just ended up feeling heavier. I was so distracted by Jules being arrested that I didn't feel anything. There wasn't much that pain on the outside could do to me at that point.

A group of people immediately surrounded me and looked down. It was as if they had opened a sewer cover and there I was, lying down there. They were all angels trying to decide if they should bring me up to heaven or what. I ignored their emphatic advice to keep lying on the ground until an ambulance came. I got back up and hurried a few steps toward Jules. Another cop car came around the corner and a woman officer ran over to me. She asked me my name about a hundred times and wanted to know where my mother was. I didn't even try to answer her; I just stared across the street in shock. Finally, she told me just to sit tight, that someone was on their way for me.

As the cop car pulled away, I waved to Jules in the backseat. He had been too distracted to even notice me being hit by a car. He gave me a desperate little thumbs-up as he drove away, I guess to reassure me. I wished that they had put handcuffs on me too and taken me off with my dad. I walked around the corner and sat down on the curb. I was feeling terrifically weak and couldn't stand anymore. I pulled up my pant legs and saw that my knees were cut open and bleeding. I blew on them, but that made them feel worse. If I hadn't looked, I wouldn't have known I'd been hurt at all. I slowly pulled my pant legs back down and just waited for whatever it was that was going to happen next.

3

Since Jules had started using heroin again, it was inevitable that he would be arrested. He still had a disability pension because of his lungs, but that only covered the basics. It certainly didn't cover the forty dollars a day he needed to get stoned. He was selling joints every afternoon in the park. He stole television sets even and he was always stealing bicycles. He stole dictionaries and sold them to students outside the university. He tested every car lock as he walked down the street. Once, at the supermarket, he picked a purse out of a grocery cart and stuck it down his pants. I tried to focus on the stuff that he had gotten away with in order to cheer myself up.

He wasn't going to have to do any jail time, naturally. You never did in Montreal. The court wanted him to spend a month at Doorway, a rehabilitation center out near Saint Jerome. It was in a really mountainous area with tons of trees and country cabins, a place that was supposed to be the opposite of a heroin addict's natural environment. Much to my astonishment, Jules agreed.

I was going to stay with a neighbor named Mary who

used to babysit me sometimes. Mary was a nurse and owned a little bungalow at the end of the street. She was about forty years old. She had pretty, light blue eyes and she liked to wink. Strands of her long blonde hair floated up over her head, as if she had just rubbed a balloon against it. She seemed like the kind of person who would be a free spirit if she had the energy. She was overweight, but only about twenty pounds or so.

Mary talked to everybody in the neighborhood and she'd do anybody a favor. She gave the impression, even to me, a twelve-year-old, that she would go for just about anyone. I'd seen her being flirtatious with men that nobody spoke to. I thought she was maybe interested in Jules, although I knew nothing would ever happen between the two of them since Jules wasn't interested in girls while he was on junk.

Jules gave her some money. It couldn't have been very much. I think she was also getting money from the government to look after me, who knows. Jules claimed that he had known Mary for years and that she was like a sister to him. I didn't buy that, though. He was always calling people his brother; I'd heard him say that about people he'd only known for two weeks. There was a landlord who'd lowered our rent fifty bucks and Jules said he was like a father to him.

He assured me that we'd be back together again in a month. I knew that Jules would be gone for more than a month; he was always gone longer than he said he would be. Even when he went out to the store for bread and said he would be back in five minutes, he would be gone for an hour. Linus had warned me at the foster home that when a parent splits on you once, they are guaranteed to do it again.

The social worker walked me across the street to Mary's house. I hadn't been able to bring very much. I had a plastic suitcase that looked like there might be a record player inside. But, believe me, there wasn't.

I was missing Jules bad. I started thinking about mean things I'd done to Jules and regretting them. He had bought me a raccoon hat that he'd been so excited about, but I had never worn it. I had lost it on purpose in the park. Once I had to do a project on a great artist for school. He'd begged me to do Michelangelo because he'd seen a documentary on him and could help me out. I'd already taken out a book on Chagall, though, so I'd told him I didn't need his help. I was getting sick with guilt and nostalgia. It was going to kill me before I even got to Mary's house.

If you want to get a child to love you, then you should just go and hide in the closet for three or four hours. They get down on their knees and pray for you to return. That child will turn you into God. Lonely children probably wrote the Bible.

Mary showed me where I was going to sleep, in a room that wasn't much bigger than a walk-in closet at the end of the hall. She'd taken everything out of it and stuck a little cot in there for me. There wasn't a window. It was like being buried alive when you shut the door. You couldn't really offer much proof of your existence while shut up inside that closet.

I turned on the lamp and sat by myself, then opened up my suitcase and took out a big conch Jules and I had bought at a gift shop by the ocean. It was the one time we had ever taken a trip anywhere. Everyone said it was impossible for me to remember that trip since I had been only five at the time. But I remembered everything about it, perfectly.

I put the conch up to my ear, as I often did. Sometimes I didn't hear the sound of the beach at all. Sometimes I was sure that I could hear the sound of my mother laughing.

4

Mary had two sons. The older son, Johnny, was eighteen, so he didn't have much to do with me. Felix was my age. The year before Felix and I had gone to the same school, same class. He had blond hair and green eyes and lips that were always pursed, which is usually a nice combination. He would have been cute except that he had these massive eyebrows that almost met in the middle, and his forehead seemed oddly big.

The teacher had hated Felix, and she'd made it clear to everyone that he gave her the creeps. He whacked his head and pulled his hair when he was trying to come up with the right answer during our spelling tests. He'd always have a cupcake in his desk that he'd try to eat in class without the teacher noticing. Because the teacher despised him, all the children felt a vague unease and disgust around him. There were ridiculous rumors about him. It was said that he had been caught masturbating in the science room by Mr Malony.

Felix hung out with a blind kid at school. Felix would sing songs from the radio and the blind kid would have to guess the titles. Felix liked holding the blind kid's hand and guiding him down the hall. Felix always had a bit of a desperate look about him when he was doing this.

It was as if he was worried that someone else was going to take the job from him.

We were sort of friends. Once he'd come shuffling up to me as I was walking home from school. He was wearing a one-piece purple jogging suit. I noticed that he had a stitches scar above his top lip that would disappear when he smiled.

'I really liked your story,' he said.

We had all written a story for homework the night before. I wrote a story about a little boy who had climbed down a hole in the ground and had found himself in China and liked it very much. Since it was an adventure tale, I put exclamation points at the end of each one of my sentences. The teacher read my story out to the class, reading each sentence in an exclamatory fashion. The kids almost lost their minds laughing. She was making a point about how exclamation points were rare and were supposed to be used only in case of emergency.

'Shut up,' I said to Felix.

'No, I really mean it. It was very exciting. My heart was really beating fast.'

'Yeah?'

I felt comforted when I saw him at Mary's, standing in the hallway with a sweatshirt down to his knees. He was the most unthreatening child, and any sort of fright at the moment might have killed me. Felix was happy to have a friend with him all the time; he wanted to spend every one of his waking minutes with me. I started to do the things that he liked to do.

Felix had a little box of flavored toothpicks. We sat and sucked on each one until it ran out of flavor and then threw it onto the street and started on the next one. After that we walked pigeon-toed down the street.

There were all these little things that Felix did. He wore a sling around his arm some days for no reason. There was a bicycle out front, locked to the gate; he had forgotten the combination, and he would try guessing it every morning. He liked to throw Kleenexes up in the air, spin around and then catch them. He showed me how to pour bubble bath in the tub and then mix it up with a manual blender.

The home is the most ritualized place in a society; each house is like a religious order with its own ceremonies. There was something decadent about playing with Felix. It made his family seem like the center of the universe instead of my own.

Every night Felix insisted that Mary check his hair for lice. This is something she had been doing for him since grade one and he was crazy about it. 'Keep checking!' he'd cry whenever Mary showed signs of letting up. Afterward, Mary would check my hair for lice too. It did feel amazing. She gently told me the endings of TV shows that I'd had to miss the night before because it had been my bedtime.

Felix liked to take the eggs out of the fridge and draw faces on them. He wanted to put one of the eggs in an empty Kleenex box, directly under a lightbulb, so that a chick would hatch. I knew this was an impossibility, but I didn't tell Felix. I drew a face on mine and stared at it for a while when I was done. It did seem to have some sort of personality. I kissed the egg, and I decided to try and save mine too. When my chick was born, I would name him Joel. I thought that I had heard of an angel named Joel in the Bible. Also I had never met anyone named Joel. 'Good night, Joel,' I whispered in the darkness of my room to the egg tucked away in the Kleenex box next to my pillow. Who knew what the physical laws and limitations of this universe were? Perhaps in the morning there would be a wee chick in there.

5

When I went back to school, nobody made fun of the fact that I was staying with Felix. Instead, they were blown away that I got to live with his older brother, Johnny. He'd graduated the year before but still managed to be the most popular boy in school. The girls in my class were always asking me what he looked like naked.

Johnny wore his dark hair hanging in his face. He had big blue eyes and puffy, puffy lips like a girl. He lifted weights while lying on a white carpet next to his bed every morning for half an hour so he had a nice body. He possessed style, too. He wore a yellow T-shirt with a decal of a Rastafarian smoking a joint. He drove a black car that he made everyone call the Black Stallion. He would go around insinuating that he had a dead body in the trunk.

I didn't consider myself so lucky to be living with him, though. There was a picture that Johnny had drawn on the kitchen fridge, held up by butterfly magnets. It was of a wolverine ripping apart a girl, limb from limb. Mary and Felix were both so generous at heart that my being there didn't seem out of the ordinary for them. Johnny, however, looked shocked every time he saw me in his house.

Johnny was usually out, but a couple nights after my arrival, he came to the table to eat dinner with us. He sat on the opposite side of the kitchen table from me, staring and patiently waiting for our eyes to meet. I could feel him looking right at me, and I tried to concentrate and not look up at him. Inevitably, though, our eyes did meet, and he leaned over the table and shoved his fist in my face. 'Get your eyes off me!' he screamed at me. 'I told you, I'm not in love with you! You can't have me. Can't you understand that?'

Mary reached over and patted Johnny on the head, as if he were a ridiculous pet dog showing too much affection.

When we bumped into each other in the hall later that night, Johnny yelled at me to stop stalking him. He would tackle me on the couch, screaming, 'Let go of me! Get your hands off me. Mom! She's gone crazy. She's raping me!'

Johnny started referring to Felix and me as nerd and nerdette. He would give us penalties for being morons. We had made these kites out of sticks and newspaper and were running around with them in the yard, jumping up and down, trying to make them fly. The kites just couldn't get off the ground. We looked stupid, but we didn't care. Johnny grabbed Felix and tried stuffing him in the laundry hamper upstairs, which he referred to as a penalty box.

Once Johnny stormed into the living room, where I was reading a book, turned the radio on and snatched me off the couch. He made me dance around with him by thrashing me all over the room. I was worried to death that my neck was going to snap and that I'd have to spend the rest of my life in a wheelchair. He yanked me toward him and his chin smacked into my face. I felt something in me come undone and put my hand up to my mouth and spit out a tooth. Johnny stopped dancing and we both stared at the tooth.

It was my last baby tooth and already had a chip in it. Jules had said it didn't matter if my baby tooth was chipped since I was going to lose it anyway. Jules used to get down on his hands and knees and beg me for my teeth to put under his own pillow, telling me that he needed the money more than me. Mary had a little bottle filled with Johnny's and Felix's baby teeth and she put mine in with them. We both found this funny. I would think about that tooth in the little jar long after I left that house. It would be forgotten in there. In a few years, nobody would know it had been mine at all.

Being attacked by Johnny wasn't any worse than having to eat their favorite cereal or join Felix's karate class. They were just the natural consequences of living in someone else's house. Jules hadn't packed me any fall clothes other than my white fur hat. When it got colder, I had to wear a pair of Felix's silver rain boots that he himself refused to touch. Mary gave me an old sweater of Johnny's that he constantly demanded back. In a way, it was kind of horrific living in someone else's house. I preferred being in the foster home. There, we had all been lost and we all had to wear castoffs. I was the only one who was lost and dispossessed in this house. The contrast was unforgiving.

One day after I'd been there a couple weeks, Felix gave me his tape recorder and told me to go and listen to a song that he had recorded of himself singing. He wanted me to tell him whether he had any talent. He suggested that I go listen to the tape in the privacy of my own room.

I went in my closet and closed the door and turned on the tape. Felix was singing both parts of the duet 'Say,

Say, Say' by Michael Jackson and Paul McCartney. His singing was awkward and out of tune and there was no music at all behind it. It sounded like someone singing after the apocalypse. For some reason Felix's rendition made me feel sad and very alone. Now I felt as if I were the last person alive on the planet.

Felix knocked on the door. 'Go away,' I yelled. My voice was all choked up so that anyone in the world could tell that I had been crying. I don't know how long I was in there. There's hardly such a thing as time in a dark space like that. As I mentioned before, once I started crying, it was difficult for me to stop. Finally, Mary opened up the door. I squinted at the light from the hallway. I probably looked like a wreck. The light gave me that same shocked sensation you get after having been slapped in the face.

'Oh, my dear Lord,' Mary cried when she caught sight of me. 'You poor, poor little thing. What did those beasts do to you? Those awful, awful beasts. Monsters! My sons are monsters!'

She pulled me out of the closet and patted me on the head. She was probably contemplating looking through my hair for lice just to cheer me up. That wasn't at all what I wanted, though. For some reason I was surprised myself when I said, 'I miss my dad a lot.'

6

Mary drove Felix and me out to the rehabilitation center to visit Jules. The two of them were going to go for a walk through the forest that surrounded the center while I went inside. Mary insisted that Felix needed exercise and some fresh air. Felix had wrapped a sleeping bag around himself; although, it wasn't even cold out. He was just trying to prove a point. A worker took me by the hand and led me alone down a long corridor, into a wilderness of posters and bulletin boards.

I felt nervous in the big communal room. Jules and I were sitting in folding chairs on opposite sides of a plastic table. We hadn't had too many occasions when we had to look directly at each other like this. Jules was always moving around. Even when he was eating, he was always wandering over to the window with his plate in his hand. It seemed like we should be saying important things to each other. Since I was feeling a serious bout of low self-esteem, I felt incapable of coming up with anything important. So we sat there quietly for a bit. I looked at Jules without looking into his eyes.

Jules had managed to lose more weight and he looked skinny like a girl. His legs were crossed politely as if we were meeting on a blind date. He was wearing a T-shirt over his pajamas. He had a Ziploc bag filled with cigarettes laid out in front of him. I noticed that he was chain-smoking them. He was wearing a pair of socks, and his big toe stuck out of one of them.

'They don't let certain patients here have shoes,' Jules said when he saw me staring at his toe. 'It's a matter of principle. It makes the possibility of escape less possible.'

Then he remembered that he had gifts for me. He went and got them from the other room. He had decorated a pot by gluing felt circles on it and had planted a tropical plant inside it. It seemed as if they must have put a gun up to his head for him to make something like this. He had never had the concentration for crafts at home. He had also apparently learned the art of origami, as he had a plastic bag filled with a dozen paper cranes. He said that he'd made them in some sort of workshop, and he held them out for me to see.

'You can take them home with you if you like.'

I nodded. I had also brought him a gift. I reached into the pocket of my coat that was slung over the back of my chair to get it. I handed him a copy of our Charles Aznavour cassette. He nodded a thanks back but said that he couldn't take it.

'It'll remind me too much of the old times.'

I was silent and confused as I put the tape back in my pocket. One thing I thought I really knew about Jules was that he liked Charles Aznavour. It was my favorite too. I had tried to get some friends of mine into that tape. They looked at me with a pity and disgust that was way above their age and maturity. I guess you had to be a child with some tragedy to understand that music. You had to have your mother die to enjoy Aznavour, who had a voice like someone reading handwritten Valentine cards. I imagined Aznavour sleeping in a tuxedo and owning a cat named Moustache.

I was wearing my T-shirt with a baby duck on it. Jules loved when I wore that T-shirt; he found it so cute. That's why I'd put it on today, even though it was getting a little tight on me. But Jules hadn't said anything about the T-shirt. In fact, he avoided even looking at it. I realized that part of his therapy was probably to give up his personality bit by bit. I hoped that part of his therapy wasn't to give up his interest in me.

'What do you do here all day?' I asked, to change my own train of thought.

'We have discussions. Now I know what it's like to be a rock-and-roll star and to always be on talk shows. Tell us about yourself. What do you think you'll be doing next year? What motivates you? It's not really conversation.'

'Do you have to exercise?'

He looked startled a little by this question. It was as if I knew something that he didn't think I knew. I'd only asked this because Mary had told me that at her hospital they made patients do lots of exercise and eat plenty of healthy food as a means to recovering. This information had really upset me because I knew that Jules despised both exercising and eating. The thought of him being forced to do sit-ups had upset me greatly.

'When I first got here, they tried to get me to go jog a lap around the yard,' he answered finally. 'I'm a goddamn infirm, I told them. They had a doctor come by and check out my lungs, and he said, What in God's name are you doing? This man doesn't need to jog. He needs a coffin with some feathered pillows. If he makes it for three more nights in this joint, he'll be lucky. Touching his toes is probably enough to kill him.'

'Is it difficult to stay off drugs?'

'It's really hard. There's a drug dealer named Norman who comes by the gate and sells dope.'

'Do you buy any?'

'I haven't got a cent.'

We were about to start being silent again when a young guy sauntered into the room. He sat down next to Jules and handed him a coffee. Once he sat down, Jules began to look more comfortable all of a sudden. The guy introduced himself as Oliver. Unlike my dad, Oliver was fully dressed and not in pajamas. He was barefoot, though, so I figured he must be in the same category as Jules was: the ones who were too risky to be given shoes. His hair was dyed different colors in different places, kind of like a dusting brush. He looked about sixteen years old. I noticed that his fingers were all chewed up. I had never seen anybody's fingers bitten down so much. He had a huge scab on his hand that he must have spent a lot of time picking at. Oliver smiled as if he were having his picture taken in elementary school. That was his trademark smile, I guess. I hated people who had trademark anything.

I was able to stare at Oliver and take note of all this because he wasn't paying attention to me. He was staring at Jules mostly. He was sitting there as if he were Jules's interpreter. I don't know why he got to be on Jules's side of the table. They were both smiling as if they had something to smile about.

'I was just telling Baby what it's like here,' Jules told Oliver.

'When I first got here,' Oliver said to Jules and not to me, 'I kept thinking that my clothes were shrinking. I was afraid they were putting them in the dryer.'

Jules laughed at that. Oliver started brushing his hair up from the back with both hands. This was something that Jules did all the time. It was disconcerting to see Oliver do it in exactly the same way. That's what happened in rehab: people were always trying to rip off someone else's personality. People used to say that Jules and I had the same laugh. They also said that we had a similar walk. If Oliver was stealing Jules's personality, then he was also stealing my personality. I wished that Jules would be more careful and see through this guy.

'I kept thinking that everything that had happened had been a dream,' Oliver continued. 'Like the nurse came up to me and said, I told you yesterday that you had an appointment with me at two o'clock. Oh, I said, I thought that conversation was a dream.'

They started to laugh at this. I tried to smile, but I couldn't.

'Have you started to see angels yet?' Oliver asked Jules excitedly. 'Martin, you know Martin, right? He says that after you're here for about three weeks, because of all the Haldol and whatnot in your system, you start to see angels.'

'I'm going to start going to church once I get out, though, that's for sure,' Jules said.

'I don't believe in God,' Oliver said. 'You believe in Jesus, man? I didn't know that about you.'

I wanted to interrupt at this moment. I wanted to say that the reason we didn't like Jesus was because there used to be a guy on our block named Greg who talked about Jesus all the time. We couldn't stand Greg and now we couldn't help associating Jesus with him. But I couldn't find a way to interject my thoughts. This conversation didn't really include me.

'Trust me,' Jules said. 'I'd like to believe in Jesus as much as the next guy, but I don't. Who says that you have to believe in God to go to church? I need to join a choir. It'll make my lungs open up. I like singing.'

'You have a really great voice. Super deep and good. You should really record it, man. You're like a genius at that. I can't do it. I'm all nerves. There's like all this compressed energy in me.'

'Come on,' Jules said, smiling. 'I could never be a real singer.'

'This is what Suzanne was talking to us about in the meeting this morning. You have to reinvent yourself. As if you have a blank page and you're writing your own story on it. I think that we should start our own band.'

I sighed loudly, which managed to get Jules's attention.

I hated people who wanted to be famous. There was nothing so depressing as people with ridiculous plans. Most of Jules's friends who came out of rehab wanted to be famous. Now that they weren't heroin addicts, they wanted to be something marvelous. They wanted careers as rock stars or bestselling novelists.

'What's new with you, Baby?' he asked me.

'I had a fever a week ago. I went and woke up Mary in the middle of the night and told her that there was a big dog in my room. She almost had a heart attack. I was just sleepwalking, though. I didn't remember any of it the next day.'

Neither of them seemed to react to this story. I felt stupid for having told them. What was I, two years old? I should be telling him fun stories that impress. I wondered if I should tell him about the autograph book that Felix and I had made. We had signed a bunch of celebrities' names in it. We showed it to other kids and most of them were fooled. I decided against bringing it up since Jules didn't know any actors anyway. The only actor he seemed to have ever heard of was Jack Nicholson, and *One Flew Over the Cuckoo's Nest* seemed to be the only movie he'd ever seen.

I didn't like that Oliver had a million things to say to Jules. He was acting as if he knew my dad better than I did. I wasn't used to this; Jules and I had always been best friends. When he was broke, I was broke. When you considered his situation, you also had to consider mine. I had somehow stepped out of his world.

When he was walking me to the door, Jules gave me some news that really upset me. He told me that he was going to volunteer to stay at the rehabilitation center an extra month. He said that his supervisor strongly recommended it. I stood there, unable to move, just staring helplessly at Jules. He seemed uncomfortable meeting my gaze. He spun around, making as if he suddenly needed to read a pamphlet that was stapled on the bulletin board right behind his head. Then he spun around again, probably hoping that I had stopped looking so sad.

As I walked to the car where Mary and Felix waited, I turned and looked back. Jules was looking out the window and waving to me. The building was made out of brown bricks and reminded me of an elementary school. All the window frames had been painted yellow to make the building look more homelike. Jules obviously didn't want to have much to do with the outside regular world. Of his own accord, he was going to stay locked up there making his cranes. That's what he and Oliver were smiling at. They both knew that it was better on the inside than on the outside. As I walked out into the evening, I wished that I was on drugs too. Oliver was a junkie and so he had more in common with my dad than I did. They would be eating dinner together in their stockinged feet. Just like they had known each other from the day they were born.

After much insistence, Mary let Felix sit on her lap and steer the wheel. I hoped that he would crash the car. I sat in the back of the car not saying anything. I couldn't beg for a turn at the steering wheel too. I couldn't plead for any rights because I didn't have any.

It was dark by now. I hated riding in cars in the country at night. In the temporary illumination of the headlights, the insects were scribbling out messages from God that we couldn't get. You couldn't see what was up ahead. How did you know that the universe still existed a few feet in front of the car? How could you know that God was continuing to imagine it all? How could you be sure that he hadn't forgotten about the road and that you wouldn't soon be driving into nothingness?

7

I was very firm on the idea that I would become a drug addict too now. I didn't care what drug I was going to be addicted to. A fool like Oliver could hang out with my dad just because he was a stoner.

When Jules did junk, all the other heroin addicts came around and they weren't so bad. They made me laugh so much. I thought they were the coolest group of humans that ever lived. I really did. They were the only ones who had the habit of making a fuss over me. They touched my hair and said that I could be a fashion model. When I sang along with a song on the radio, there was always someone screaming that I had to get an agent and get a recording contract. When I danced to a TV commercial, they said I had natural rhythm and had to take ballet lessons to bring out my talent. Naturally my friends at school didn't speak to me like that. They didn't think there was anything special about me at all.

Jules had a friend named Frederic who used to bum for change. Jules would keep him company while he was out panhandling. Frederic used to carry around a suitcase and pretend he was a stranded traveler who needed money to get home. It was a gimmick that only really worked at the bus terminal, but he and my dad had been banned from the terminal a couple years before. Frederic had been on our street corner every day for the past year with his suitcase. Everyone knew his face and nobody believed he was a lost tourist. Jules made him a cardboard sign that said he was a Vietnam vet. We all laughed so hard when Frederic came over and Jules gave him that sign. I fell right off the kitchen chair.

He had another friend named Jimmy who came from California and wore a blue leather jacket.

'What was it like in California?' I asked Jimmy one night.

'Oh, I'm not really from California. That's just a cover.'

'So where are you from?'

'Well, actually, I'm not from this planet. I moved here to Earth when I was seventeen.'

I asked him what the planet he was from looked like; he said the same as the one on *Blade Runner*. I'd seen that movie and it took place on planet Earth, but I didn't mention that. He said that there were so many people on his planet that it took about half an hour to walk down a block. He said that he never drank milk because there was no such thing as cows.

'What did you do for a living on your planet?' I asked.

'It's a job that you wouldn't understand. It would have no application whatsoever in this world.'

On his planet voices could travel long distances through the air. You could hear someone whispering to you in bed from all the way across town. That was one of my favorite things about his planet.

I had been polluted with the ridiculous dreams of junkies. I had gotten the ridiculous ego that comes with a heroin high by proxy.

Usually you get drugs from the crowd that you hang around with. But I was twelve and none of the people I hung around were into drugs. There were simply no cool kids my age. Maybe coolness was intending to entirely skip a generation. It seemed possible. Felix was in his room singing into a tape recorder then playing it back and exclaiming, 'My God. Do I actually sound like this? All this time I thought that I was a great singer, but I don't have any talent whatsoever!'

I made it a point to really observe the kids in my grade the next day. I wanted to see if any of them also had the potential to be drug addicts. There was going to be a 3-D movie on television so the supermarket at the corner had been giving out 3-D glasses for free. Everybody showed up at school wearing a pair. They wore them like sunglasses, like they were really cool. One boy was making himself sneeze by looking up at the sun, and a group of children had gathered around to watch him. A boy named Eddie tied his head in a plastic bag and made everyone count how long he could stay like that without breathing. The girl who sat next to me in English class put the mimeographed handout up to her nose, exclaiming how good it smelled. I knocked that off in grade three. A boy named Sherwin showed me how he was writing the lyrics of songs from the radio out in his notebook. 'It's the first step to being a rock star,' he said.

Drug dealers wouldn't want to have anything to do with these pathetic specimens. You had to be relaxed and professional to associate with drug dealers.

I was hanging around in Felix's bathroom a few days later, washing my hands with a soap that smelled like cocoa butter. I thought that if I washed my hands a few times in a row with it, my hands would smell like cocoa butter all day. That seemed like an interesting idea to me at the time. I opened the cabinet and took a stick of Mary's lipstick off the shelf and painted my lips. I stood there staring in the mirror with my brand-new red lips pursed for a long time, I guess.

Suddenly, I heard the front door open and Johnny's voice booming. He walked into the bathroom without knocking and leaned over the sink next to me to stare in the mirror. He stuck the tip of his finger under the faucet. He'd cut it open and the cold water turned red for a moment, just like the tail of a fancy goldfish.

I usually split any time Johnny was around. That day I just sat down on the toilet seat and observed him. I remained very still. I was surprised he hadn't attacked me yet. He opened the cabinet door to an angle that allowed him to see my reflection.

'What in the world are you doing here?' he asked.

'I don't know,' I answered, since I didn't really know myself.

'You see this,' he said, turning and holding up his finger. 'I cut my finger with a knife. I was using it as a screwdriver. I was too lazy to go and get an actual screwdriver. What do you think about that?'

'You should disinfect it with some iodine.'

'Someone told me that iodine was just a myth.'

I shrugged. He kept staring at me. I couldn't begin to guess what insult was going to come out of his mouth. Instead, I was surprised by what he said next.

'I'm sorry I've given you a hard time. That's how I treat everyone, though. I just want you to feel at home. You know that, right?'

'Right,' I lied.

'So if you need me to get you anything, just let me know.'

I was always moved when mean people were suddenly nice to me. It was a weakness that would lead me into some bad relationships later in life. At that moment I believed Johnny might be the only person in the world who could understand me. So I popped the question.

'Can you get me some magic mushrooms?'

'What!'

I felt myself get all red. I stood up to leave, but Johnny pushed me back down onto the toilet lid.

'What did I just hear you say?!' he sputtered in mock outrage. 'What is the world coming to! Are you not just out of diapers? Are you not just out of elementary school! My Lord. The shock of it all!'

Again I tried to leave, but he easily held me down.

'You're not old enough to be asking that question. You have to start dressing differently if you're going to use 'shrooms.'

He squatted down and looked into my face as I sat on the toilet.

'You know, you're not going to be bad-looking. Of course, you might try behaving more like a girl. You can comb your hair, for instance.'

He made his fingers like two little legs and walked them all the way up my leg. They pushed up my skirt as they walked along. When they touched the elastic of my underwear, it was as if I had peed a tiny butterfly. He leaned over and kissed me and his tongue opened up my mouth. And then he grabbed me and started tickling.

'Oh, my God, the girl's in love with me!!!'

'No, I'm not!' I whispered.

'She wants to marry me. No, I'm not going to mess around with my brother's girlfriend. I'm a stand-up guy. You'll get over it, though. Just don't go and kill yourself over me now. I don't need another one of those.'

He took the rest of his clothes off and got into the shower. 'Turn on the radio on your way out, Baby,' he called to me. I slinked out, still without any connections and deeply humiliated. I had been turned away at the door of the adult world.

I couldn't think straight as I walked down the hall. I had run into my friend Sherwin earlier in the day wearing a motorcycle helmet that he'd found in the trash. I was just as childish as he was.

I don't know why I was upset about not being an adult. It was right around the corner. Becoming a child again is what is impossible. That's what you have legitimate reason to be upset over. Childhood is the most valuable thing that's taken away from you in life, if you think about it.

After I'd been living at Mary's for about a month, she started dating a guy named Jean-Michel, a tall black guy who smelled like Noxzema. She met him one night when she went to get some milk at the corner store.

I knew Jean-Michel before he hooked up with Mary. He was one of those guys who liked to stand in front of a particular store that had a neon pot of gold in the window and a big sign advertising that they sold bus tickets. The store put a sign up that said NO LOITERING OR WE'LL CALL THE POLICE, just because of him, I think. He walked with a cane even though he wasn't lame or sophisticated; he just pointed it at people when they passed through the store. He had a friend who pushed a shopping cart around, scavenging, and Jean-Michel would riffle through the contents of his friend's cart and say, 'Nothing. This ain't nothing but garbage.'

I had seen him a million times all over the place before I had seen him at Mary's place making a quick-mix box of cookies. He was famous in that kind of way. He liked this bench that was right next to a pay phone. They were so close together, you could sit on the bench and talk on the phone at the same time. He was always talking to someone he had borrowed twenty dollars from. This guy kept on charging interest on the twenty dollars and now Jean-Michel supposedly owed him six hundred dollars.

Jean-Michel's face was flat and almost sort of one-dimensional and had gray pricks all over his forehead. I have to admit he did have a nice smile, even though he talked as if he had just shoved a spoonful of burning hot macaroni in his mouth. He was clumsy and he always stepped on Felix and me while we were lying on the floor watching TV. He was always trying to guess what people were going to say on TV shows, but he wasn't even good at it. He'd predict the girl on the TV show was about to say, 'How about breakfast?' and she would say something like, 'I'm leaving you.' But Mary said he brought some light into her life.

I had always liked watching him from afar, just because he was so odd. It's not that there was anything wrong with Jean-Michel; it's just that I'd always identified him as a bum. I mean, if he wasn't, then who the hell was? But Mary treated him as if there was nothing unusual about walking around in flip-flops at the end of September with sores all over your feet. I decided Mary was right about him, because if she was wrong about him, then she might be wrong about me. Her compliments made me feel so good about myself. For instance, she always said that I naturally smelled good. She said that I naturally smelled like soap and that she should rub me in her hair before going out on a date. I sat on my bed and decided to change my opinion about Jean-Michel. I just took the words 'bum', 'hobo', and 'street person' out of my vocabulary. You could never really get to know anyone when you associated them with those words. Afterward, I thought of him as being very gentle and very optimistic.

'The white dress! The white dress! The tight one! I like that! Hallelujah. You look great.' Jean-Michel applauded and banged the walls whenever she put on anything other than a sweat suit. On the first night that he came over, he gave her earrings that made her earlobes turn green and get infected. But she was desperate to wear them. She froze her earlobes with ice cubes so that she could stick them in. She yelped every time he tried to nibble on one and threatened to murder him with the ashtray.

Felix had no idea what to make of Jean-Michel. He was all that Felix wanted to talk about. His presence in the house day after day made Felix nervous.

'I don't understand why he spends all his time here,' Felix whined. 'He's always here. Why? I don't understand why! Can you tell me why!'

'He just doesn't have anyplace else to go,' I said and shrugged. 'Trust me, I wouldn't worry about Jean-Michel. He's harmless.'

'How would you know?' Felix demanded.

One night, Jean-Michel made us all a huge pot of spaghetti. He dumped everything in the fridge into the sauce, and it actually wasn't that bad. When we were all in the middle of dinner, he told Mary that he had to hide out in her apartment on account of the whole loan problem.

'I told him yesterday, I'll give you twenty dollars... loan-sharking is illegal, don't you know, Mr Shark? It's immoral and it's bad. What are you going to do? Break my fingers. What do I care? What do I need fingers for? All I need are my eyes so that I can look at Mary. You are just sensational, Mary. Did you know that? Did he actually come and kill me already when I wasn't looking? I think I'm in heaven because there's a beautiful angel right here in the room with me. But seriously, the man is out to get me. I think he has my place staked out. I think it would be better if I stayed here with you. What do you think of that, Mary? You ever been on a honeymoon?'

He moved in the next day with only a plastic bag that had a few things in it, like a brown sweater and a sticky-looking yellow telephone. These things made me think that he didn't have a house at all.

'Where do you live?' I asked as he was washing his T-shirt out in the sink with some dish detergent.

'I live in a palace. Thank you very much for asking.'

'No. Really.'

'I live in that big white building downtown.'

'Isn't that a Holiday Inn?'

'Well, the building right next to it.'

'Can we go there and pick up some things for you?'

'My mother lives there. If she sees a stranger in the house, she'll think she's being mugged. She'll have a heart attack.'

'What's it like inside?'

'Yeah. It's a nice place. We use a pinball table for like a real table.'

That shut me up for a bit. It was hard to figure out if it was a lie or not, or even if he was bragging. Although that little detail threw me off, I felt safe coming to the conclusion that he was a liar. I was glad of it, because I liked liars. I especially liked what were referred to as senseless liars. Jules used to tell senseless lies to people on long bus rides. One of Jules's favorite lies was that he was a professor who lectured at universities all over the continent on the benefits of street wisdom. I felt somehow relaxed talking to Jean-Michel, knowing that everything that came out of his mouth probably had nothing to do with the mundane world around me.

After that, I found that I was always trying to initiate discussions with him. He was the closest thing to Jules in the house. He was part of the world that I'd grown up with. It was as though we spoke the same language.

'Were you ever in rehab?' I asked Jean-Michel another time.

'I've been all over the place in all kinds of living situations. Due to the fact that my mind is my own worst enemy. In a way I am perpetually and permanently in a state of rehabilitation. In an attempt to rehabilitate from the shock of being born. Some people are too sensitive to withstand that.'

People often nod their heads at this kind of assertion. It's no different to them than having someone shake a foam cup in their face and ask for change. It is the speech of a homeless person. It is a sermon to no one in particular. I was feeling homeless and I in turn felt the need for that kind of spirituality. I wanted to be a mixed-up and pitiful soul too. His voice had this chalklike quality, like it was writing out words on the blackboard. That was the mark of a voice that had been stylized by smoking weed and other illegal substances. I knew that Jean-Michel could get me some.

*

I was walking home from school by myself when I spotted Jean-Michel leaning up against the wall of the liquor store and talking to a panhandler. I went up to him.

'Hey, Baby,' Jean-Michel said, nice and casual, which I liked. 'What's up with you?'

His friend walked off right away. Most homeless people were afraid of people that weren't. They didn't like to be addressed directly by them. They didn't mind children, but I was getting older now. I was glad that he'd left right away so that I could ask my favor of Jean-Michel.

'Can you get me some magic mushrooms?'

'You got some money?' he said, completely unfazed. 'I'm broke.'

'I have five bucks. I just want a couple. You can keep the rest for yourself.'

'All right, sure. Joey has some, and he's in the park now. You got the money on you?'

I handed Jean-Michel five dollars, which was all the money I had in the world. He gestured for me to wait for him and headed across the street, waving to someone in the park. There was a white guy on a bicycle. Jean-Michel walked past him and dropped the money. The guy picked it up and placed a baggie delicately on the ground. It was all very efficient and professional.

Being judged by society makes you disregard it altogether after a while. Jean-Michel didn't know that he shouldn't get a twelve-year-old drugs. He didn't even really know what a twelve-year-old was.

He took some mushrooms out of the bag and put them in his pocket. He gave me the bag and indicated by jerking his head back that maybe I should get lost now, just in case any cop got suspicious about us standing together. I skipped down the road, feeling like I'd accomplished something. I put the baggie under my bed and waited for the right moment.

8

At dusk, Mary went out with Jean-Michel and left Felix and me alone in the house. We carried the space heater from Johnny's room into Felix's even though it wasn't that cold outside. Johnny had bought the heater a week before but had never let anyone touch it, so we were curious about it. We had turned it way up and now we were boiling hot and uncomfortable. We also had Mary's tape recorder, so we turned it on, hoping it would put us to sleep, but the singer's voice on the tape gave me the creeps. It felt like the kind of song that people who weren't in love would make love to.

'My mother named me after Peter Pan,' Felix told me.

'But then shouldn't your name be Peter?'

'I don't know. She said she named me after him. That's all I know.'

Then we were quiet. There's no use talking to someone who's being nostalgic.

'I wish my real dad was here,' Felix said as he lay sweating beside me.

'Where is he?'

'I don't know. He used to be a good dancer. He used to play in a band, I think.'

'What instrument did he play?'

'I don't know. Look, I don't know the names of all the instruments. I got to make a telephone call,' he said, rolling out of bed.

'Who are you going to call?' I asked.

He picked up the receiver and pointed to a sticker with a phone number on the side of the phone. There was a white flower on the sticker and it had the words 'Teenage Help Hotline' written on it. Someone on the other end picked up right away, I guess because if someone had swallowed enough pills, they might already be dead by the third ring. I could only hear Felix's side of the conversation.

'I'm feeling down,' he said. 'My brother, he's going to move out soon. And my mother didn't come home from the bar. I feel terrible. I'm always worried now that she's going to go away with her boyfriend. I'm twelve years old. Well, she didn't leave me alone in the house because my friend's here. She's twelve... Baby, did you have your birthday, yeah, you did. She's twelve, same as me. Ever since she met this guy, she likes to go out and have good times. He says she deserves it. I worry not that something bad will happen, they just wander around, and neither of them have a car. I'm worried that they'll have a really, really good time and never come back.'

Man, I thought, what an open book.

He sat in his pajama bottoms with his legs crossed, listening to whatever it was the stranger on the other end of the line was saying. He grabbed a notebook and started jotting things down. I peeked over at the notebook. He'd written, 'You are a special person and no one can take your place.'

'How come you feel so comfortable talking to that woman?' I asked him after he got off the phone.

'A friend of my mom's at the hospital set it up. My mom calls there all the time. She makes Johnny and me call there if we're getting out of line. She thinks all kinds of things are signs that people are going to commit suicide. The first time I was sitting on the balcony railing, the neighbor saw me and told my mom. She thought I was attempting suicide so she made me call. Johnny drank all the beer one night and she said it was a cry for help and made him call. It's like free therapy.'

'Is it the same woman every time?'

'No, but after you talk to her for like ten minutes, it feels as if you've known her all your life.'

'So she's kind of like your sort of girlfriend?'

We both giggled at this. Then we rolled on the floor, laughing at the top of our lungs. Then, of course, Felix started to worry again.

'He probably takes her to that Boom Boom club with the drawings of palm trees on the windows.'

The Boom Boom was a poolroom down the street that people liked to go and drink at. It was like a bar except the lights were always on and there were plastic plants hanging from the ceiling. Kids never went in there because it made them feel sad.

'Every time I pass by there, they're playing that song about scooping the girl up. Do you know that song?' I asked, trying to change the subject.

'He's going to make her forget about me. He'll tell her she needs a vacation.'

'Where's he going to take her?'

'He'll tell her there's a place where there are real palm trees. He'll tell her she deserves it.'

'You can't drive to palm trees. You have to take a plane and go over water to get to palm trees,' I said.

'No, you don't. You can drive to Florida. I think I hate that Jean-Michel.'

'I got something that will take our troubles away,' I said.

I went into my room and came back with the mushrooms. Since this was a night for opening up and talking
about our feelings, it was a time for drugs. I took out the
bag and showed it to Felix.

'What the hell is that?' he asked.

'Magic mushrooms.'

'I've always wanted to try those,' he exclaimed. 'They
sound so cute.'

'Yeah.'

'Where'd you get it?'

'A friend of mine. I don't know how to use it, though.
Do you eat them raw?'

'Let's cook them up!' Felix suggested.

He grabbed the bag and headed to the kitchen.

I was already feeling light-headed and delirious from the
space heater being cranked up. I'd rolled the pajama legs
right up to my butt. Felix took his pajamas all the way off
and was in just his underwear. We got to work making
ourselves some spaghetti. We were singing that Swedish
cook's song from *The Muppet Show*. Felix whipped a
wooden spoon in the air and almost took out one of my
eyes. We mixed up the mushrooms with a jar of spaghetti
sauce and served it on the spaghetti. We ate it, happily,
and laughed as we awaited our hallucinations, waiting to
be anointed cool and troubled people.

After twenty minutes, nothing seemed to be happening. Felix got bored and went to lie down in his room. I
sat sadly by myself. Then I stood up and started to walk
down the hallway to join Felix in the bedroom. As I
walked down the hall, I noticed that it was snowing.
I was pleasantly surprised to see that it could snow
indoors. As far as I could remember, I hadn't ever seen it

happen. As I stood there marveling at the lovely flakes, I realized that it wasn't possible for snow to fall from a ceiling. I looked closer at the snowflakes and realized they were thousands of tiny origami cranes that had taken flight. They were so small that they must have been made out of rolling papers and grocery receipts. I walked through Felix's doorway and they were swirling around the room. The room was filled with them. Felix was lying on his back and didn't seem to notice anything unusual.

'I think I've smelled my scratch-and-sniff stickers one too many times,' Felix said. 'They've given me a sore stomach.'

I realized that I wasn't feeling good either. I felt rubbery and nauseous. I was afraid to move. It was as if the world had turned to ash and if I moved even the slightest inch it would all turn to powder and vanish. Here we were, wanting to be death-defying pirates, and we had seasickness just a few minutes off the shore.

Felix and I just lay together in bed for what could have been five minutes or two hours until the dizziness had gone away. Slowly, the origami birds came down from the air and settled under the bed and on the floor. I figured there would probably be several inches down there. I had that feeling you get when you step outside after it snows. Everything in the world was dead and quiet and calm.

You wouldn't be stunned by anything in this state. A magician could cut you in two or pull doves out of your pocket, but you wouldn't be surprised. There would be nothing horrific in life, but then again, there wouldn't be anything wonderful either. It made me nervous that I wouldn't give a damn about brushing my teeth in the morning, or remembering to put my math homework in my bag, or getting to school on time on the day of a field trip. Some people wanted to feel this way, but I didn't. This separation from feeling was Jules's remedy to life. But I was going to have to find other things to make me feel good and confident in life. I was just going to have to start being my own person.

going to war

1

When my dad got out of rehab, I had only seen him once in three months. Felix walked me over to the new apartment that Jules had rented, helping me carry my stuff in plastic bags. Mary had given me all sorts of pots and dishes to help us set up house. Felix put on his coat over his pajamas. He thought that since we were going from his house to mine, there wasn't any reason to put on clothes. According to his logic, we weren't actually going into the outside world.

Felix was confused when Jules got out of rehab and it was time for me to leave. He had somehow been thinking that I would be living at his house forever. Maybe Mary had insinuated that it was a possibility to him. She had mentioned a few times during the past couple days that there wasn't any reason for me to go anywhere, but I wanted to get home while it was still possible. One wrong move might mess up everything and I would never get to be in my own skin again. I wanted to be able to sing in the shower and fart while watching television. I wanted things to be the same between Jules and me as they had been on Napoleon Street.

I liked the preparations for my leaving. They seemed

all helter-skelter. It was getting Felix all worked up. He flung his shoes out the window for no good reason.

'What are you doing!' Mary shouted.

'My feet need to breathe!' he yelled back frantically.

I was having trouble finding all my stuff. Mary had an obsession with buying Felix and me cheap trinkets. Someone told me that if it weren't for the people who bought all this stupid stuff, the world economy would collapse. I got down on my hands and knees and pulled out a plastic lion, a Smurf, and three hockey cards from under the couch.

Felix and I divided up our marbles. We had made a model of the solar system with Styrofoam balls and wires and acrylic paint for the science fair at school. For some reason it had taken us two months to complete and we'd been shocked to find out that we didn't even get an honorable mention. We both wanted to keep the model, so we decided to divide up the planets. It was sort of stupid to have only Neptune, Venus, Pluto, and a handful of moons, but we were both very devoted to that particular universe. As I packed away the orange ball that was supposed to be Saturn, I found that, although I deeply wanted to live with Jules again, it hurt me to leave here.

Mary came running outside after me. There was no reason to run since I was just standing there. I was glad, though, because she always bounced up and down and seemed so soft when she ran. She was wearing her housecoat. Plastic barrettes in the shape of seashells held her hair up, and, for a second, I couldn't even look at her because I found her so beautiful. I couldn't blame Jean-Michel for being in love with her. The desire to touch her was overwhelming. I wanted to put my hand in her pockets and mash my face up against her belly and all sorts of other weird stuff. Johnny had warned me about touching his mother. He said I was obscene, and I realized that he was sort of right.

The clouds got thick and gray over us and it seemed as if it was going to rain any minute. The calm before the storm made me feel excited. It gave me the feeling that things were about to change. I sighed happily when I saw Jules walking down the street. I couldn't be expected to stay in that house all my life, I told myself. Felix's tapes wouldn't take him anywhere and Johnny was bound to lose his looks. I was meant for bigger things. Jules had implicitly taught me to turn my back on anyone but him, the way he had done to his family. At that point in my life it probably saved me from an awful lot of heartbreak.

Up close, Jules looked tired and nervous. He was wearing a green ski jacket that wasn't even his style. He leaned forward with his hands and neck stretched out awkwardly, not sure whether he was supposed to kiss me or hug me. I couldn't remember either because I'd only ever done it automatically. All of a sudden we were actors who were trying to play ourselves, not exactly sure what our subtext or motivation was. I settled on hugging him. There was a way that he felt lighter, though. As if something was missing.

Once I got my things unpacked in the apartment, I felt as if I was in an entirely different reality. I had a window that looked out onto the street and would need a curtain. I thumbtacked a pillowcase up. I was going to miss a woman's touch. No matter what apartment my dad and I moved into, there would never be a mother there. If there was, we'd have a glass to put lilacs in on the kitchen table. The towels might even have a pretty pattern of a seashell on them. The social worker had two beds and the ugliest couch in the world delivered to us. I didn't mind, though. I was just happy to be living with Jules again, even though we got off to a rocky start.

To tell you the truth, Jules looked five years older. He'd given up wearing dentures for his missing front tooth. His hair was matted and impossible to comb, as if he had been lying in bed for six years. His eyes had gotten bluer. They were that shade of intense blue that only crazy people seem to have.

He had lost a lot of weight and seemed sickly all over again. Once he coughed all day, and he acted as if each cough was a kick in the stomach. It got worse and worse over the next couple days. He coughed for ten minutes at a time. It sounded like an umbrella being torn apart by the wind. The way I remember it, dishes bounced up and down in the sink when he coughed and the lightbulbs started to flicker. He was always squeezing a pillow against his chest. I came home to find him lying on the bed with no shirt on and the pillow on his chest. He reminded me of a doll whose stuffing was coming out.

The doctors said that he had a modern form of TB. They gave him medication and insisted he take it. He always complained that the pills made him crazy. He fell off the kitchen table during the night. I came out to see what was going on, and he said he could have sworn that the table was his bed. The next morning, he thought that a bird was in the house someplace. He'd seen it flying from one corner to another. He accused me of leaving the windows open at night, saying that was how the bird got in. I didn't know what to say. I just agreed to keep the windows closed.

Actually, he started blaming all kinds of things on me.

He thought I was getting up in the middle of the night and breaking things around the house. A couple days later he was watching TV at two o'clock in the morning and the sink overflowed. He said I had sneaked out of my room and turned the tap on.

'I don't understand why you do all this hateful shit, man,' he said to me, standing in a puddle on the kitchen floor. He had dragged me out of bed to check out the mess. 'You used to be a sweet kid. I don't know where you got that mean streak. You must have picked it up from Mary or maybe those black kids at the foster home.'

Then one evening he accused me of being on drugs. I'd never ever tried drugs again since the mushrooms. I had to sit there listening to his speech. I burst out crying from frustration.

'Don't lie to me. You're sitting there stoned. Your eyes are popping out of your fucking head. I won't have a drug addict in my house. I've battled that demon. I hate it. I just fucking can't stand it. You've got those fucking junkie ways.' His face got all red as he leaned over me and screamed. I sort of wished that he'd just go back on heroin, chill out and leave me alone.

He sent me out to buy some milk and then followed me down the street. I knew he was behind me, ducking behind trucks and into the alleys. He wanted to catch me in the act of buying drugs from drug dealers.

He went around acting as if we were enemies and were at war.

It seemed unfair because I hadn't changed the way I felt about Jules. I sat by myself in my room in the evening; my arms and legs felt longer and gangly. It was the first time I felt like that. When you're little, you don't really feel ugly because your parents are always looking at you and rewarding you for your cuteness. I think he was disgusted that I was going to be turning thirteen soon. Then one night when I went to the bathroom, I realized that I had my period. I didn't even want to tell Jules at first. I thought that it would separate us even more. Someone had yelled at me from a car that I had the longest legs in the world. So maybe there were some advantages of getting older that Jules didn't care for.

Jules had never really talked to me about my period. Our moral ed. teacher had explained it to our whole class, though. She'd handed out photocopies with a drawing of a naked man and woman standing side by side on it. I had a pair of paper dolls when I was younger who came with top hats and party dresses and leisure wear. These figures, however, weren't given any adjoining pages with clothes on them to cut out and put on, and they were just stuck being naked forever. There were arrows pointing to their bodies that you were supposed to write the scientific names for their private parts on. These words sounded like the names of devils and wicked angels. I didn't want to think about my body as being that of an adult. I wanted Jules to like me the way he had when I was a baby, and now that seemed impossible.

But I knew it wasn't just me because he was on bad terms with the rest of the world too. He was constantly arguing with the Vietnamese neighbors who lived downstairs from us because he couldn't stand the smell of their cooking. He made me stand there and bang the floor with a broom handle for fifteen minutes whenever I smelled it wafting up. When my arms got tired and I started slowing down, he called out for me to continue.

'It's like I'm living in a Communist country!' he

screamed down the hallway. 'It's fucking with my karma!'

He sent me down to the landlord's apartment with the rent check. I couldn't help but read what he had written on the back, in his messy handwriting: 'There are fucking leeches in my lungs.'

Nobody's all bad, though. I still loved him so much. He was my only dad and all that. One nice thing I remember him doing for me around that time was buying me a pair of cleats. I had asked for a pair once when I was in grade five, but I had no use for them now since I didn't play soccer anymore. I guess he'd seen them on sale in some window. They were black with white stripes and had little metallic cleats at the bottom. I didn't want them, but I didn't want to hurt his feelings. I wore them outside every weekend. I clicked down the street, looking around and hoping no other kid would see me. I kept to back alleys. No matter how scuzzy and crazy their parents are, kids still try to make them feel good about themselves.

2

We had moved onto Christophe Colomb, which was about seven or eight blocks east of St Laurent and was a much more residential street. We moved into the only apartment building on the block. The rest of the houses had colorful turrets and wooden eaves on them. It was the first street that I had lived on that had a lot of trees. It was fall and the leaves were all over the ground, the color of old men's checkered clothes. The kids there all seemed to know one another. The street was filled with pages of misspelled words that had fallen out of binders along with the autumn leaves.

I didn't have too many friends on our new block. Part of the reason was Jules. He used to scream at kids if they got within five feet of the yellow five-speed bicycle he kept chained outside our building; once Jules went outside wielding a tennis racket like a baseball bat and threatened to smack a kid who was leaning on the bicycle.

The kids started calling my dad John McEnroe, and they laughed at me when I walked by. Jules was so anxious about his bike being stolen that he decided to keep it in his bedroom at night. He had an asthma attack and then a near stroke carrying his bike up the four flights of stairs. I had to go carry it from the third floor to the fourth, scratching all the walls as I went. He couldn't go through that ordeal again, so from then on he rode my bicycle around, a pink girl's bike with a yellow basket on the front. He kept a pair of pliers in the basket and went around cutting the cords off appliances that people had thrown out. He thought there was money in it. There's no need to explain to you how the kids on the street reacted to all of that.

Still, I remained confident that I could make friends at my new high school. I resolved I would keep Jules away from my school and new friends. At my last school, Jules used to steal clothes from the lost-and-found box. A boy in my class had asked me once why my dad was wearing his hat.

Anyhow, Jules would be happy to stay away from my friends. He was always criticizing them by predicting what they were going to be when they grew up. He said my friend Earl was the kind of boy who would grow up to have sideburns. Ian was going to be the type who stole from the meat section. Adam would paint flames on the backs of leather jackets for a living and Ricky would end up riding a bicycle all day and going through garbage cans looking for washing machine parts.

On the morning of my first day of school, I sat in the kitchen drinking a banana and egg milk shake. Jules said it was healthy and it saved time on washing dishes.

'These milk shakes don't have any pizzazz,' I said.

'You go for crappy shit. This is what milk shakes are supposed to taste like. They were invented to be healthy.'

I was having sad and insecure thoughts that morning and I knew making conversation would distract me and calm me down.

'So how did my mom die?' I asked.

Jules looked at me like I was crazy.

He had told me a million times about what happened to my mother, who died when she was only sixteen years old. I would ask about her when I was nervous. It was a terrible habit, but I couldn't help it. Every time he gave me a different answer. That morning, he told me they had been on a cruise ship and she dove off and had never come back.

'I was just standing there, drinking my piña colada, and then she was gone. They say it was the sun that drove her to it.'

'You think she was eaten by sharks?' I asked.

'No, I think she's living on a tropical island with a bunch of Mau Maus. Of course she was eaten by sharks!'

One time he told me she had entered the pie-eating contest at a country fair and had eaten too many pies and died.

He didn't have that many good baby stories about me. I think he was drinking too much after my mother died to be able to remember any funny details. His stories always seemed to be about me almost getting hit by a car or falling down a sewer. 'You had this crazy thing about always wanting to cross the street by yourself. And when you cried, you sounded like a goddamn alley cat.'

I much preferred stories about my mother. There was this story about how as a little girl she had been jumping up and down on her bed and had fallen off and cracked her skull open on the radiator. Nobody even knew that her skull was cracked open until she started writing things backward.

'She was always getting into incidents,' Jules said.

I picked up my bag and left for school, feeling terribly nervous. I used to be able to meditate on these stories for hours and they would take my mind off anything. That morning, they just seemed ridiculous.

My last school had been in a small converted factory building. I had thought it the ugliest school in the world. It had always been on the verge of closing because of lack of enrollment. My new school was within walking distance of many more houses, so it didn't have to worry about having enough students. It took up most of the block and was made out of large gray stones, like a museum. I didn't mind changing to this school at all and was very optimistic about it. I hoped that I could be in a school play. There was a stone gargoyle of a woman's face on the side of the front door. I put my hand up against her cheek and it felt unexpectedly warm.

In class I was seated next to a girl named Lauren. She had a big blonde ponytail and curly bangs, blue eyes, and freckles and I thought she was beautiful. She also had great style. She wore a little gray jogging suit with a rainbow belt that wasn't attached to any belt loops and she had about forty plastic beads on her shoelaces. She had a gold locket of a mushroom or a clover, I wasn't sure which.

She was very friendly with me. I sat with her and some other girls at lunch for the first week. Lauren and I ended up walking home together because she lived in the same direction as me. On Friday, we were walking past my building when Jules happened to step out the front doors. He seemed to be in a good mood when he came up and introduced himself. He asked Lauren if she wanted to come over for dinner. Lauren said yes and came upstairs with me and called her mother for permission.

I showed Lauren my room. It was really bare. Jules had thrown out all my toys because he thought the dust they collected was going to kill him. I'd only been allowed to keep one special rag doll. It was a doll that my mother had bought for me when she was pregnant. The doll had black hair and buttons for eyes. It always made me a little sad. I thought that if my mother met me now, all grown up, she would be disappointed. The doll also made me feel sweet inside, too, because it made me feel that at some point, even before I existed, I had been loved. I showed the doll to Lauren. I could tell from her expression that she found it really ugly, so I stuck it back under my pillow.

Jules called out to us from the kitchen that it was time for dinner. We opened the kitchen door and he had his arms spread out, as if to say, Surprise! I was happy to see that he was wearing a shirt and pants. He usually opted for one or the other at supper time. He'd heated up a couple cans of Chef Boyardee, but he had gone on to light a dozen candles and stick them in bottles around the kitchen, in order to make the whole affair seem fancy. Lauren smiled.

'I love candlelit dinners,' she said.

For about five minutes I was happy. Jules opened a bottle of wine, and since Lauren and I were both only twelve, he had to drink the whole bottle himself. Then he started talking. Lauren and I weren't able to say one word to each other over dinner because he didn't stop for a second. He just rattled on, and everything that came out of his mouth seemed inappropriate. At one point, he leaned over in Lauren's face and told her that if she ever started using birth control pills, she'd end up with cancer. He told her that she should just tell the filthy boys to keep their hands off her.

Then Jules started talking about how beautiful my mother had been. How she used to wear a fluffy brown coat and how even the other girls would turn around and look at her. Then he started crying, which was a horrible sight. His face got all messed up, like it was made out of pink Play- Doh and had just hit the floor.

'Nothing means anything now that I'm not with her anymore. Not a thing. All garbage.'

He stood up and took his wallet out of his pocket, and to illustrate his point he pulled out a five-dollar bill and tossed the wallet behind him onto the floor. He waved the bill over the table like a magician, and then he leaned over toward a candle and stuck the tip of it into the flame. I bolted upright, knocking over my chair, and screamed. We had been so broke lately, five dollars was a big deal. I'd begged him for some money to pay for school supplies and he hadn't given me any.

I grabbed his arm, trying to get the money away from the flame. He tried to shake me off, and we started knocking the plates all over the place while wrestling for the money. Finally I got it away from him. I stuck it in my jean pocket and then sat down at the table. I turned to smile at Lauren. I was hoping that if I acted as if nothing had happened, nothing would have happened. I shoved a spoonful of ravioli in my mouth.

Jules sat down too. He was way past eating, though. He was hunched over a little and he was staring at me. I tried to imagine that he wasn't staring at me. I hoped that Lauren didn't notice the hateful look he was shooting. Although it was near impossible since the man wore his emotions on his sleeve. 'Why don't you wash these dishes!' he screamed at me.

Lauren jumped and almost knocked over her bowl.

'But we haven't even finished eating,' I explained.

'You're a lazy bitch. You try and talk to me like that to impress your friends. You want to look down on me! That's not how I was fucking raised. I respected my parents. You disgust me. You get it from your mother's side. Get out of my face now. Get into your pajamas!'

'But my friend's here. I can't go to bed!'

'And could you remember to brush your hair and comb your teeth! Go brush your hair and comb your teeth! Always the same thing! You never do anything. One single thing without being told. It's making me old before my time.'

I stared at the kitchen window. I swear that I contemplated jumping right out of it. I think my dad noticed my sadness, because all of a sudden he seemed distraught too.

'Fuck it all,' he said quietly. 'I'm going to get the classifieds and find myself a tidy little one-bedroom apartment. I'll save some money without you.'

Jules weaved out of the kitchen and down the hall to

his room. He ran his hand along the wall and knocked one of the pictures off of it. I heard him undressing with the door still open. He turned on the television full blast.

I figured that since he was watching TV, he'd leave Lauren and me alone now. I took the cake that was for dessert out of the fridge. I cut two slices from it and put them on plates. Lauren got up, though, and went into my bedroom to get her stuff. She didn't even say good-bye. She just ran out the door and down the stairs. I carried the two plates down the stairs in my stockinged feet. I stood there, shivering in my T-shirt. I realized it was stupid to run after her. I tried to imagine I was the last person on earth for a while, but then I was too cold, so I walked back upstairs as slowly as I could, taking a step only every thirty seconds or so.

The next day everybody in school had heard about how I'd been in a fistfight with my dad over a five-dollar bill. All during the day kids kept coming up to me and asking, 'What does that mean: Go comb your teeth?'

Lauren had gossiped to everyone about me. I'd expected her to do as much. She stuck her finger in her mouth as if to show that she was going to gag as I walked by. She tossed a pea from her lunch at my head in the cafeteria.

After that, the kids started saying that I was learning disabled. There was no good reason for it, seeing as the grades on my tests were fine. They said I was a drug addict too, and that my dad was unemployed, because he and not my mother walked me to school.

When I sat down on the toilet, a bunch of girls peeked at me over the top of the stall door. The music teacher had a tattoo of a flower on his hand and I had tried to make eye contact with him to see if he liked me; the girls started saying that I was having sex with him. I tried to read the page in the reader out loud really quickly to show what a good reader I was and how I didn't stumble on any of the words. Afterward I heard a girl say, 'She's so stupid, she doesn't even know what a period is.'

Kids would ask me questions that weren't really meant to be questions, but were meant to be insults.

'How come your pants are falling off your hips?'

'How come one of your shoelaces is brown and the other one is blue?'

'What exactly is that in your sandwich?'

'How come you have a jacket that's like an adult's jacket?'

'Why do you have a Stop Forest Fires bag instead of a regular schoolbag?'

'How come your dad wears that big fur coat and it's not even winter yet? It scares my dog.'

'How come your mother named you such an unfashionable name?'

A boy called me to find out what pages we had to do for homework. My dad thought he sounded twenty-eight years old. Jules told him he was going to call the police and have him arrested for statutory rape.

'My mom says your dad is schizophrenic,' the boy told me the next day in class.

'Well, your mother's a prostitute.'

'No, she isn't. She works at the drugstore.'

The kid behind me tapped me with his pencil. I leaned back very carefully to hear what he had to say without the teacher looking.

'You smell,' he said.

I didn't feel like being friends with anyone at school. It

was just too hard. I went to eat by myself and read my Agatha Christie book that was translated into French. I got a hundred percent on my quiz about the book, which made me feel good. Not great, of course, but it made me feel calmer.

3

Jules used to like to go to a leather goods store on St Catherine Street where they sold belts and cowboy boots and stuff like that. He would try on six or seven pairs of cowboy boots every time but never buy any. I'd go with him and wait outside, seated on the curb.

There was a community center upstairs from the store. I was standing outside the store waiting for Jules and collecting red leaves when I noticed a bunch of kids my age coming down from there. I imagined them putting on plays and singing songs upstairs. I'd asked Jules if I could go before, but he had scoffed at the idea. He said that program was only for welfare kids and fucked-up half-retarded juvenile delinquents. He said that the kids were sleazy.

He did have a point. They all dressed like crack addicts. A boy wore a white leather belt as a tie. A lot of the kids had bandannas on, holes in their jeans, and words written in Magic Marker all over their dirty jackets. One girl wore her bangs in a ponytail at the front of her head. She had cut holes in the toes of her gym socks and was wearing them as wrist bands. Another girl wore a pair of scuffed-up high heels over a bulgy pair of wool socks. She tripped every few minutes. She had drawn big black cat eyes around her eyes with eyeliner.

Any time anyone with a cigarette would pass by, they'd all scream, 'Can you spare a cigarette?' at the same time. They were sitting around saying 'Boombaclot' over and over. It was a Jamaican swear word and they were trying to say it with the right accent.

Then a man came down with buckets of paint and brushes. He had long blond hair and was tall and athletic-looking. 'James!' they cried out at the man in unison. He smiled and joyfully called them all over.

The gang was painting a mural on the wall by the leather store's parking lot. I really wanted to do something like that; it seemed so exciting. So the next day, I begged and begged Jules for permission to go. Finally he said okay. I ran as fast as I could to the community center. I was running so that I didn't have to notice how fast my heart was beating.

It was pounding noisily as I went up the narrow staircase, though. The community center itself was just a big open space with gray floors and a lot of small windows. There were some rooms off to the side that the social workers used as their offices. The organizer noticed me, but he didn't look as if there was anything out of the ordinary about me showing up out of the blue. He introduced himself as James and told me to go sit in the circle, while the kids put on some improvised skits.

I sat down next to a boy who was wearing a white glove with silver circle stickers on it. He had funny, wandering eyes. He was holding an extra-large cup of coffee, even though he couldn't have been more than eleven.

The boy in the center of the circle was drinking out of an empty bottle, pretending that he was getting drunker and drunker. He stumbled around until he lay on the ground, having some sort of seizure. Then a girl stormed in from one of the offices and walked into the circle. She was holding a doll in her arms, pretending that it was a baby. She was wearing an old blonde wig. She started screaming at the boy as if he were her husband.

'I'm not taking this anymore. You get out of my house, mister. You hear me, mister? You backstabbing drunk. I'm going to raise this baby up by myself.'

Everyone gave them a standing ovation when they were done. I was really impressed. I'd never seen a play like that before!

James called out to me as I was leaving.

'Wow!' he said. 'Slow down. I like that jacket you have on. It looks like an authentic dirt bike jacket.'

I looked behind me, like an idiot, just to make absolute certain he wasn't talking to someone else. It was kind of shocking that he liked my ugly ski jacket.

'You want to sign up with the group?' he asked.

I nodded, not daring to say a word that could change his mind.

I started going there all the time. James made all the kids feel welcome and safe. They would gather around close to him, always almost touching him. He made us believe that we were cool by virtue of hanging around with him. Most of the kids went to schools that I'd never heard of. One school was in a storefront that used to be a chicken restaurant. They all seemed to have failed a couple grades, floating somewhere indefinable between eighth and ninth.

A lot of them were in foster homes and had parents who were homeless. One boy's father played harmonica on the subway. They were the most nonjudgmental kids I'd ever met. They seemed to accept everyone, even me.

*

One day James announced that we'd been invited to join in a Caribbean-themed Halloween parade. I jumped for joy. The parade was being organized by the Jamaican Social Club. There was an artist who came in and showed us how to cut wings and crowns and other fantastic items out of sheets of cardboard and paint them with acrylic paint. The costumes were fantastic. This one kid looked like a giant robot and another one was just a giant skull. I had a costume of a dragonfly. I came up with the idea myself. I had a long tail made out of balls of nylon stocking. I had a black cap with antennae. My wings were made out of these long wires with shimmering cloth on them. It was beautiful. I was a little worried because my running shoes were so ugly, but I put that out of my mind.

There was this professional hockey player that I liked. I imagined him watching at the parade and falling in love with me. It didn't occur to me that he probably wasn't interested in twelve-year-olds.

Jules didn't really object to me going to the center since he had started working as a dishwasher and liked me out of the house when he wasn't there. He still insisted that I was being used and was too stupid to know it. He said the parade was just a front for selling pot. He told me a story about a Rastafarian who had been arrested for speeding or something like that. When they brought him down to the police station and took off his huge tam, they found that he had a Chihuahua living in there. He kept it under his hat because he liked the feeling of the dog scratching at his dreadlocks all day. Jules was being so dark and negative these days that I had gotten used to ignoring these types of fabrications.

One day as we were all working prodigiously on our

costumes, a boy named Theo came by the drop-in center. He was a scrawny kid with a skinny face, enormous eyes, and red hair with a natural streak of black in it. He had on an oversized and unbuttoned pea coat, under which he had a shirt with yellow and purple stripes and these ridiculously wide collars. He walked like he was riding a unicycle.

I had met him at the indoor swimming pool about a year before. He had sat next to me on the side of the pool, wearing the top half to a girl's bathing suit that he'd found in the lost and found. He scrunched up his lips and asked me, 'Don't you find me sooo loveliee?' We'd played together in the pool that whole day. He had walked me home because it had started raining and he had an umbrella, even though it was way out of his way. I didn't know if he remembered me, but I remembered him.

All the kids seemed to know him already. They gathered together and made a sort of wall against him, insisting that he leave immediately.

'You can't be here. James said you can't come anymore.'

'You're not allowed. You lost your privileges to be here.'

'We'll call the police. This is private property.'

I'd never seen them act this way. Finally James came out of his office and told Theo that he had to leave the building. I wondered what could be so wrong with this kid that he was making these losers react the way they were.

Theo just stood there expressionlessly while everyone yelled at him. I thought that maybe he was going to cry, but instead he turned around and wiggled his butt at them. He ran down the stairs shouting obscenities.

When the drop-in hours were over, we ambled

downstairs. Theo was sitting on a cardboard box out front, screeching hysterically. He'd caught a pigeon in the box. He stood up and danced around it. Every time the box moved, the kids screamed their heads off, as if it were a scene in a horror movie. They were worried that when they let the pigeon out, it might be so mad that it would pluck out someone's eyes.

We all gathered some bricks and put them on top of the box. After about half an hour of sitting around cross-legged and biting our nails, we decided what we were doing was cruel. We all stood back while a girl with bleached hair named Zoë kicked the box off. The pigeon lay there dead. We all started moaning and cursing and poking at the pigeon with the toes of our sneakers. James came out to see what the commotion was.

'What the hell is this? You went and hurt a defenseless creature.' James picked up the pigeon with a piece of newspaper and put it in the garbage in the alley. 'I'm closing the drop-in center next Saturday. I'm really disgusted with all of you.'

He gave each of us a long look and then went back upstairs, shaking his head angrily. All the kids started giving Theo hell.

'Get out of here, you death bringer!' a kid cried at Theo. 'Shit disturber!'

Another kid picked up a tiny pebble from the ground and flung it at Theo. Theo stuck his chest out and started butting it into the kid who had thrown the pebble at him.

'You wanna piece of me? I'll kick your goddamn ass. I'm going to burn your fucking dick, stinky mother-fucker!'

Theo pushed the kid to the ground and kicked him, then turned and bounded off, laughing and hollering.

'Aaaaah! Haaah! Aaaah! Haaaah!' he yelped his way down the street.

'He's so mean,' Zoë told me afterward.

'How come he's banned from the center?' I asked.

'Because he hit this really sweet kid, Ray, right in the face with a hockey stick. He knocked out Ray's two front teeth. Ray's never going to get a woman now.'

Theo hadn't shown up at the center for a while because he'd been in a soccer league that practiced on the weekends, but he'd been kicked off the team. I heard it was for beating up a player on his team who didn't pass him the ball. Another kid told me that it had been for kicking the soccer balls into the traffic on purpose. Zoë told me he stole one of the balls and made a hole in the side so that he could stick his dick in it.

Zoë also told me that she and Theo had gone to the same school for a while, one of these alternative schools with a ridiculous name like Open Minds. Zoë said one of the teachers used to always bring Theo a sandwich because he never had any lunch of his own. That much was probably true. I mean, who wants to make up something sad like that.

Theo came the next day too. He was told to stay out again, so he hung around downstairs. I quickly figured out how mean he was. He found a dirty knit hat in the garbage and started screaming that it had lice, then he pinned down a boy and forced the hat onto his head. He yanked the boy's shoe off and dropped it down the sewer. Everybody knew that boy got hit by his dad. The poor kid went home crying, knowing that he was going to get beaten for having lost a shoe.

It got so every day Theo hung out downstairs, waiting

for us to come down. He'd grab kids' arms and bend them back, really hard, until they had to beg him to stop. Man, he was giving everybody nervous twitches. He could kill you, too. One day we came out of the community center and he started throwing glass bottles at us.

Once he was walking down the street with his pants down around his ankles. He had on a pair of boxer shorts with polka dots on them. I guess he wanted attention. One day I saw him get hit by a car outside the community center. I could tell he wasn't hurt bad. He just lay on the ground. The driver of the car came out of his car all traumatized. Theo lay there writhing in mock pain.

'You hit me in the ass, man! How am I ever going to sit down on a toilet now? You hit my ass, you pervert! You touched my no-no zone.'

I started laughing my head off. Everyone looked at me, irritated that I was encouraging him. Who knows why I found that funny, but I did.

Maybe it was because I was raised to think that idiotic things were funny. My dad had a pile of Chinese firecrackers, and he would light one and toss it out the window whenever a middle-aged woman walked by. He would lie on the carpet afterward, convulsing in laughter. He used to make a loud duck noise while we were walking down the aisle of the supermarket. Once a woman was so startled by the sound that she knocked over a wall of cereal boxes. My dad laughed about that for days.

The other kids stared in shock at Theo no matter what he did. They did retarded things themselves, but whatever Theo did still seemed appalling to them.

One day Theo drew a mustache on his face, and every time I looked at him I just had to laugh. I had to sit down; I was laughing so hard. After that little incident, he came up to me as I was walking home.

'Didn't we used to be friends when we were little?' he asked.

'Yes,' I answered.

'I thought so,' he said.

He started singing a Motown medley from a commercial that was on the television at the time. He couldn't sing it properly, but I thought that he hit some of the high notes very nicely. That night I started singing the commercial in my room. My dad stuck his head in angrily.

'Stick to one goddamn song!' he yelled.

After school one day, I was looking for a place to mellow out and read my comic books. I saw a stiff bed of chrysanthemums in front of a building. I sat in the middle of them. It always seemed warmer, sitting among the flowers. It was going to be one of the last days that you could hang around outside.

I saw Theo walking down the street toward me, his coat wide open as usual, and underneath it the same chocolate milk T-shirt he had been wearing all week. He was swinging his hips from side to side, snapping his fingers. He looked like a Diana Ross backup dancer. I got anxious as he approached. I thought that now, since we were alone, he was going to knock my teeth out. But he didn't. He sat down on the grass next to me and looked at the comic I was reading.

'I live here,' he said, pointing to the building behind us.

'Oh,' I said.

'I like that comic,' he said.

We sat next to each other quietly reading it. The only

time he put his hand on me was to stop me from turning one of the pages just yet.

A woman's voice called his name from one of the building's windows. When I looked up, I could only make out some dyed red curls. She called down to ask Theo if *Star Search* was about to start. She spoke in that cartoon mouse voice that I noticed people who had had nervous breakdowns speak in.

'No, not yet, Ma! I'll come up and tell you when it's on, okay?'

'Okay, sugar cube. But don't forget, okay?'

'I won't. Go back inside now. You'll catch a cold.'

When Theo talked to her, he also used a babyish, syrupy voice that I'd never heard him use before.

'Is that your mother?' I asked.

'Yeah. *Star Search* is her favorite show. She likes to watch it while having a nice glass of chamomile tea with a spoonful of honey in it.'

'Theo?' she whined. 'Are you sure *Star Search* isn't on yet?'

Theo didn't answer, but she pulled her head back in. Theo suddenly looked as if he'd done something wrong and kept staring at the door of his building. He jumped up as soon as he saw his mother push open the door. He ran over to her, took her arm and guided her back into the building. He turned and waved good-bye to me abruptly and then disappeared.

The next day at the center, we were making some drums out of plastic laundry buckets we were to beat as we walked down the street. We practiced a beat on them and we sounded great. We all applauded ourselves.

I kept peeping out the window that looked out onto

the street to see if Theo was still sitting outside. Since he had nowhere to go, he'd just wait for us to get out, looking sad. He had stolen about fifty little milk containers from the café at the gas station and sat on the curb drinking them.

When we came outside, he had slicked his hair to the side and was walking pigeon-toed. He walked around introducing himself as Simon. I knew that he was trying to be funny, but that day it just made me sad.

4

One afternoon, Theo jumped out from behind a car and stuck a cap gun to the back of my head.

'Where you going, Baby?' he asked me.

'To the center.'

'Oh, no! That's so stupid. Come to the pool with me instead.'

'No.'

'Please, Baby!' He got down on his knees. 'Please, come with me. Don't leave me alone, come on!'

He toppled over onto his side. He grabbed on to my foot, wailing loudly. I knew that he was just playing around, but at the same time I knew that he meant it. I don't know why I always felt so much for him, why I felt so bad when he was unhappy.

'Okay, already. I'll go to the pool with you,' I relented.

We weren't going to be working on our costumes anyway that day. I think the activity of the day was charades, which I hated. No matter how you looked at it, it wasn't real theater.

He waited for me outside my building while I ran up

to get my bathing suit. He had boxing shorts that could pass. When we got to the pool, Theo refused to take his T-shirt off and just jumped in the water with it on. He did bombs off the side of the pool, trying to land on other people. He ripped this little kid's goggles off his head and ran to the other side of the pool, laughing. He put them on while the kid cried and begged for them back. The little kid went and reported him to the lifeguard, who finally got down off his ladder and walked over to us. He told Theo he couldn't go in the water with his T-shirt on, but Theo wouldn't take it off, and instead opted for sitting all wet in the bleachers next to the pool.

Theo leaned over and called obscenities out at the kid who had told on him. He had the filthiest mouth on the planet. I could never even repeat some of the things he said. They were gratuitous nonsense descriptions of genitalia. They went something along the lines of: 'You pussy wet you stupid fat white ass. I'm going to come with my microwaveable oven and fry your dick off.'

The lifeguard told Theo enough was enough and he was banned from the swimming pool. Two other lifeguards came out of the office to help drag Theo out of there. I picked up my towel and went to dry my hair before leaving the pool to meet him. He was out on the sidewalk trying to dry his own hair with a wet towel. He was happy to see me. He started jumping up and down and throwing punches that kept narrowly missing the side of my head.

'Knock it off!' I yelled. 'Or I'm going back to the pool.'

'All right. You're so goddamn sensitive. Women! I swear to God!'

As we were walking to the park, Theo threw cans at a

guy who was driving a bike with a grocery cart.

'All those guys are assholes. They take up too much of the sidewalk.'

'It's not his fault he has to drive that grocery cart.'

'You're going to remember my face, mister,' Theo called after the guy. 'Trust me! You're not going to forget me. I'm going to go down in your history books.'

He grabbed my hand and insisted that we stop in front of the entrance of a karate studio for a while. He'd wait until a kid came out after his class and then start karate chopping him.

'Come on! Show me what you learned in there, dipshit!'

When we finally got to the park, I went to mess around on the monkey bars. Theo took over the water fountain and wouldn't let the kids take a drink.

'You are too ugly to drink this water. I don't want your herpes. Go ask your mama to buy you some Coca-Cola! Go on! You never drank Coca-Cola in your life. What you want with this water? You ain't gonna die of thirst. This ain't the Siberian desert. It's October. *October!* Get lost and come back in ten minutes and I'll let you have some then.'

Afterward, Theo and I decided to crawl inside the cement tunnel, and we got comfortable in there. When any kid came to look in, Theo would yell at them to fuck off, his voice echoey, like it was coming out of the hole in your sink. We were feeling very cozy and warm in there, and now that we had forced all the other kids out of it we felt that we had to stay there all day just out of spite. We lay there as it started to get darker outside. We were leaning against the curved wall next to each other. We started kicking each other's sneakers for a little bit.

'Yesterday was my birthday,' Theo said.

'How old are you?'

'Thirteen. You?'

'I'm twelve.'

'Oh, you sucker! I hated being twelve. I really feel sorry for you. It explains why you're so stupid, though.'

I shrugged, angrily.

'No, I'm just kidding. Don't be so sensitive.'

'What'd you get for your birthday?'

'I got a hundred dollars from my grandmother. And I hired myself four prostitutes and had sex with them all at the same time. At one point they started fighting over me and I just had to stop the whole thing and tell everybody to just cool out.'

I liked when boys told me these kinds of lies. I could listen to them for hours. They were better than Nancy Drew mysteries. They were like looking at books of Ripley's Believe It or Not! They were appalling but at the same time full of wonder.

'I thought you were a virgin,' I said, encouraging him.

'Me? No way. I've had sex with a bunch of girls.'

'Who was the first one?'

'This sixteen-year-old. She used to live in our building. She invited me over one time. We went into her bedroom and she took off all her clothes. Then she covered herself in vegetable oil. I kept trying to get on top of her but kept sliding right off. I slid off her at one point and hit the radiator and knocked myself out cold.'

We were sitting close together as he told his story. Our pinkies were really close. I was imagining what it would feel like if my pinky touched his. I wondered if such a thing was actually possible.

All of a sudden, I heard a woman's voice calling Theo's name. There was something about the sound of her voice that filled me with a sickening feeling. Theo and I both scrambled out of the tunnel. She was wandering through the playground wearing a big winter coat; her hair stuck up all over. She had a plate of spaghetti in her hands.

'I'm over here, Ma!' Theo called.

She turned toward him. Her face was wild.

'Where the fuck have you been?' she screamed in her high-pitched voice, making dogs cringe all over the neighborhood. 'I've been looking everywhere. I made supper and it's on the table. What's wrong with you? You stupid fuck. I hate you. I made supper for nothing.'

She took the spaghetti and threw it at the monkey bars. She grabbed a hunk of his hair and started shaking it around. She was so strong and terrible. When she started punching him, he didn't even fight back; he just let her. She hit hard, too. None of the kids in the park made fun of him. It just made us all feel terribly sad; even the sparrows looked the other way.

Theo started hurrying home as she followed, screaming at the top of her lungs.

'You lousy bastard. Wait till I get your ass home!' she was screaming over and over. 'I am going to turn you into a motherfucking blueberry.'

I told my dad about the whole thing and he told me that whatever I did, I shouldn't bring up the thing and embarrass Theo.

'I feel sorry as shit for these poor little creeps who are stuck with depressive cases for mothers. I hope you thank your lucky stars every day that you have me. I'm your ace in the hole. Remember that.' I shrugged, since I didn't even know what that meant.

I didn't take Jules's advice much anymore. Since he

quit dope, he had had to rediscover the meaning of things. It was as if he had to rewrite the dictionary from scratch. His definition of a beetle would probably be a small hole that changes places. When you clean up your act, naturally there are certain aspects of your life that you have to change. For instance, you should probably stop stealing and staying out all night. But Jules had somehow knocked off loving me in a certain way that he had when he was a junkie. I wished that they had told him at rehab that hanging out with me and dancing and eating sundaes and drinking Coke out of green-and-yellow teacups were all okay. I wish that they had told him that all that was not part of the junk addiction.

I ran into Theo outside the community center a couple days later. I couldn't understand why he had one of his mother's big purple lipstick kisses on his forehead. I didn't feel like hanging out with him. The sight of him made me feel as if the world was a terrible and creepy place. He didn't look like he wanted to spend time with me either, so I went upstairs without even saying hello. Upstairs we were practicing our moves for the parade. That got my mind off Theo.

5

Poor Jules was under a lot of stress. He wouldn't have enough dishwashing work until the next summer season, and we were living off the little money he had stashed away in a bank account. He was constantly terrified of spending it all. He was hoping his friend Lester could hook him up with a job selling these quilts door-to-door.

Selling quilts had apparently turned Lester's life around and was helping him stay off junk. I tried to stay optimistic, hoping he'd get the job, but I couldn't picture Jules as a salesman. I couldn't imagine who would look through the peephole at Jules standing there and still open the door. Never mind his missing tooth and messy hair, his state of mind had affected his ability to wear decent clothes. He always tucked his pants into his socks. He wore a red leather jacket and a pair of boots that the neighbors had thrown out. He smelled pretty bad, and on top of all that he swore too much to be a door-to-door salesman. What would his sales pitch be: 'So you want to buy this fucking blanket, man! It's a fuckin' good deal. It'll bust up your fucking washing machine if you try sticking it in there, but what the fuck? That's what those shithole Laundromats are for anyway, right?'

He rarely said a noun without attaching a swear word to it as an adjective. He swore for absolutely no reason. 'What fucking time is that show about that fucking immigrant who fucking talks funny? I hate that shitty show but there's nothing the fuck else on.' I brought up the swearing with him, but he didn't seem to know what I was talking about. I didn't know how he was supposed to fit into the regular world while talking like that. In the meantime we both had to keep our fingers crossed while we waited and waited for Lester to get my dad this job.

We had been waiting for three weeks and the pressure was really getting to Jules. He started getting all crazy with me, accusing me of tinkering with his clocks. He yelled at me when he caught me looking up at the kitchen clock during dinner. Seeing it as proof of some sort of conspiracy, my dad got out a roll of masking tape and covered the glass surface.

'That'll stay there until you learn,' he said. He then proceeded to put masking tape on the other clocks in the house. I think there was one uncovered alarm clock that he kept hidden under his bed.

One morning he yelled at me for at least an hour about having broken all his umbrellas. He said he knew for a fact that I snuck them out of the house and used them as walking sticks, thereby destroying them. He stared at his plastic jar filled with coins in the evenings and accused me every day of taking more and more. He said I gave them to my boyfriends. He swore that I was trying to break his television set. He took the knob off it so I couldn't use it unsupervised. He lost the knob a couple days later and was forced to turn the television on and off with a pair of pliers. This was a procedure that could take him up to five minutes. I never heard the end of that.

Another evening Jules sent me to a grocery store that had a special on concentrated orange juice. It was about an hour's walk away. I had to cross the overpass and then walk along the interstate for forty minutes. He had given me a long, complicated grocery list. I wouldn't have been able to carry all the bags home, so I had to take a grocery cart that Jules had stolen once and kept in the alley behind the apartment building.

On the way home a gang of kids from the other side of the highway made fun of me for pushing a grocery cart. They started whipping garbage at me. I hurried back up onto the overpass. I knew that I should just ignore them and go on my way. You will get very far in life with such a policy, but when I saw some pebbles and bottle caps lying on the ground on the overpass, I couldn't resist the urge to avenge myself. I picked up a handful of debris and rained it down on the kids below. I don't think I actually hit any of them, but they jumped up and started up after me. I ran off as fast as I could, rattling the cart in front of me with all my juice cans bouncing.

I ran and hid in an alleyway underneath a fire escape with my grocery cart. I sat under there for maybe twenty minutes until I was absolutely sure they were gone. I could probably have handled them on my own, but I had the groceries. Naturally, they'd take them and smash them against the ground. God could only imagine how my dad would react to something like that.

Jules was still hysterical when I got home because I had been gone so long. He was positive that I had been sitting on a bench somewhere contemplating taking off with his grocery money. He demanded the change and bill immediately, saying he was going to make sure I hadn't spent any of the money on drugs. After he had recounted it on the kitchen table for the sixth time, I snuck off to my room.

As I walked in, I saw a horrible sight on my floor. While I'd been out, Jules had knocked over all my things. He had torn up the homework I had left lying on the bed. I would never be able to finish my project on time now. But then I saw something even worse. There, lying on the floor, was my rag doll, its arms and legs ripped off. I dropped to my knees and picked her pieces up. I'd never get another one. Jules never thought to buy me pretty things like that. That doll had been like a miracle to me. It had reminded me that I'd been loved by a mother. Now I was a nothing, a real nobody.

'It's like you're good for one day,' Jules said. He was standing behind me in the doorway, but I didn't turn to look at him. He was trying to keep his voice level, as if he had a very intelligent observation to make. 'Then the next day you're bad. Every second day you act up. I have to yell at you and you learn your lesson. You're good for one day and then you go right back to acting up. I don't know why you're like that, but you are. You're taking years off my life.'

'Why'd you have to do this to my doll!' I screamed.

Our eyes met, and I saw that he felt terrible for having hurt me like that.

'I'll sew it back together,' he promised quietly. 'I'll use some good thread. It'll make it stronger than it was before.'

I went back outside. It didn't matter what he did with the doll to fix it now. How was I ever going to love that doll after I'd seen it lying mangled and dismembered on the floor? The teenagers who were sitting on the stoop across the street started twisting and contorting with laughter when I passed by. They'd heard Jules screaming at me from the open windows. My dad had just made their day.

'Why'd you spend the grocery money on drugs, kid?' a teenage girl said as I walked by.

I wandered down the street. As I passed Theo's building, I noticed his mother standing in the doorway of the building in her big winter coat again. It was the first time I'd seen her since that evening in the park. I didn't think she'd even know who I was since she seemed so out of it, but there she was, waving me over. I stopped and faced her from the opposite side of the street.

She waved to me again. 'Hi!' she kept saying. She motioned for me to come over to where she was. I was allowed to ignore adults, but it seemed like somehow I wasn't allowed to ignore people's parents. I went across the street to talk to her. I was feeling very low and self-destructive and wanted to see if she would try and hurt me the way she had hurt Theo. I'd take her punches just like Theo had.

She took a huge drag of her cigarette and blew the smoke out of both nostrils as she smiled.

'Hello, sweetie! You're a friend of Theo's, aren't you? I saw you two playing in the alley the other day. I was watching you out the window. You two play so sweet together. I could just watch you for hours.'

I knew what time she was talking about. Theo and I had been breaking these old glass picture frames and then scattering them all over the street, hoping to puncture some tires.

'I hope you all get married. I do! I was in love for the first time when I was three years old. With my cousin. His name was Joey Delorio. I just loved the sound of his name.'

She was one of the worst breeds of parents going, the ones who are really mean but then don't even give you the satisfaction of being able to hate them. They just break your heart. They were able to do whatever they pleased and then still have you love them.

'Theo has a bit of emphysema,' she said, making her voice sound as sweet as she could. 'He's always breathed funny since he was a little baby. I don't want to smoke in the house because it's bad for Theo, but my legs get so sore when I come down the stairs. I feel like just going to the doctor and having them chopped off. Chopped right off! You could come and help Theo push me around in the wheelchair. I've wanted to be in a wheelchair. It looks like fun! Oh my! I'm crazy. That's for blessed sure.'

Then she got all quiet, fantasizing about being pushed around in a wheelchair. I took her silence as my cue to leave, but as I started to walk away, she called me back.

'Come here, Baby,' she said. She threw her cigarette into the grass and spread her arms to me. 'I want to give you a hug. You don't get enough hugs. I can see that. I'll give you one of my special teddy bear hugs.'

I stepped closer to her to receive my hug and get it over with. She squeezed my cheeks and smelled my hair. She put my head between her two palms. Then she pulled my whole body to her and hugged me. I waited for her to let go of me, but she didn't. At first I thought I was going to die of claustrophobia, but then I noticed that she smelled like cocoa butter. I liked her smell. It reminded me of postcards and pictures of brown palm trees. It made me think of Mary's housecoat and how Felix and I would sometimes sit on her lap even though we were almost as tall as she was.

Then I decided just to enjoy it. She had fat arms, the type of arms that held sailors and soldiers and thieves. The kind of arms that held someone who was going away to jail for ten years. They were the arms of a woman who had eaten a hundred delicious cakes and pastries to get them this comfortable. I wrapped my arms around her and squeezed her tighter. I wanted to feel every part of my body touched by her. We stood like that, just hugging, for a long while.

Afterward, at home, I felt guilty about having let her hug me. I felt violated and dirty, as if I'd raped myself. Falling in love with a mother like that was about as low as you could go in this world.

I took a bath to clean her smell off me and scrubbed myself. Usually I filled the bathtub and jumped in, washed my hair maybe, and jumped right out. That day I made sure to scrub myself harshly with a rag and even get in between my legs. The bathwater didn't make me feel clean at all. It was as if I were taking a bath in a bathtub filled with tears.

6

At the center, James told us he was going to drive in a car behind us during the parade with his sound system cranked up. He told us to try and decide on what music he should play on his car radio. We got all hysterical trying to decide what was the coolest music on the planet, screaming and yelling about our favorite bands until James had to kick us all out.

The next day after school, we all showed up with our different tapes. I had a Prince cassette. I wasn't even particularly passionate about Prince, but I'd brought it because it was the only English tape that we had in the house. Lester had forgotten it once. When James said he thought my tape was a good choice, a girl pushed me on the ground. She rounded up five kids and they all started chanting at the top of their lungs and in unison: 'Def Leppard, Def Leppard, Def Leppard.' They pumped their hands up in the air as they chanted. It was all very exciting!

At that moment, the community center was definitely the center of the universe. I'm sure people could hear us screaming out in the street. Theo couldn't help but want to come upstairs. Indeed, he snuck up, and I saw him sticking his head into the glass of the door, watching us. He also took out a red marker and drew a dog with a huge penis on the door. He made it say; 'My name is James and I like girls with big tits! Come inside and suck my dick.' Upon inspection, we noticed that Theo had also scribbled, 'The Jazz Man Was Here, Suckers!'

James came over when he heard the commotion. Everyone was saying what a loser Theo was for referring to himself as the Jazz Man. James, naturally, was upset about the other stuff that Theo had written, but he kept his cool.

James told Theo that he wasn't allowed to hang out on the sidewalk around the community center anymore. He said he'd be forced to call the police on him the next time. Theo walked off, looking for once as if he might have gone too far. All the kids that he knew, even though they hated him, hung out at the community center.

I turned to watch him. He looked sad and small walking in the middle of the street, deliberately slowing down the traffic. Sometimes I forgot how skinny he was. It was like a little kid had drawn him with a crayon. He looked like he was going to disappear into the horizon. I had this crazy idea that I would never see Theo again and I concluded that, really, it was for the best.

But he caught up to me as I was walking home. I didn't know where he'd popped out of. He must have been lying under a car or something.

'I didn't do it!' Theo said. 'You believe that I didn't do it, right?'

'I don't care if you did it or not,' I said truthfully.

'So you think I did it?'

'I don't know. What does it matter?'

'Because I want to know whose side you're on.'

'I'm not on anybody's side.'

'James did it himself and set me up. He came down and wrote down all that stuff himself. He just wants to have sex with you. You're too stupid to know it.'

'I hate when you talk like that.'

'You're a fucking snob, you know that?'

I made to cross the street and get away. He grabbed my hand and squeezed it as hard as he could. I don't know why boys are so much stronger than girls, but it's an unfortunate fact of life.

'Let me go,' I begged.

'Why should I? You're just going to run away. You're just going to go right back to being a bitch.'

He twisted my arm around as if he were hiding my hand from me. He continued twisting my arm until I lay on the ground. My face squished right into the cold wet grass and I prayed into it that he would let me go soon. It was then that I felt my shoulder pop. It was a terrible sound that I heard right inside me. My arm was in a new freakish position, as if I was reaching for something just behind me. How unattractive, I thought for a second. Then for a moment, just a moment, I felt pain. Theo helped me get to my feet and, immediately, I leaned over and threw up.

The ground sank as I felt myself go into shock. I was see-through, I was static on a television screen. There were these small black moths fluttering around me. I decided that later I would have to figure out where they came from, but for now I would focus on getting home. I managed to stand up, but it was hard for me to get one foot in front of the other. I realized I couldn't hear very well. That was good, because it made me feel as if I was hiding and that I was protected. My arm was at a horrible angle, but I wanted to hide from that too. I tried to be as quiet as possible as I walked away on tiptoe. 'Shhhh...,' I said under my breath. I crept along, terrified that the pain would finally find me. Theo walked along next to me, not knowing what to do. He kept sticking his face right up close to mine and making goofy expressions to get my attention and to make me laugh. This situation, and the position of my arm, was very distressing to him, obviously. He was upset that I wasn't consoling him.

'You bitch! Why you got to treat me like that? White bitch,' he screamed finally, and stormed off.

I turned for a second and watched him go. I could hardly make him out, though, through the huge flock of moths between us. I marveled at them, as there must have been about a million, covering everything. Then I fainted in front of the steps of my apartment building.

I spent two nights in the hospital and came out with a sling around my arm. The doctor had given me a plastic container of painkillers to take whenever I needed one.

I rode home on the bus next to Jules and he kept shaking his head in disbelief. He'd spent the whole two days pacing up and down the halls of the hospital. He didn't even know how to react to what had happened, as I'd never been in the hospital before. A social worker had taken him into a little room to ask him questions about how my arm had been dislocated. He had settled on being indignant about that: indignation is a much easier emotion to sustain than sorrow.

'You're going to have us both thrown in jail before you're satisfied.'

The kids at the center were all very excited by my little container. One girl asked if they were making me hallucinate yet.

'You're so lucky. I've never hallucinated, but when I do, I know exactly what I'm going to hallucinate. Some little cute pink bunnies. I totally know it.'

They kept asking me if I was addicted to the pain-killers yet. When I took one in front of them, they were all impressed. They were very excited to be friends with a junkie.

'Soon you're going to prostitute yourself for more pills,' said Zoë, all starstruck.

Over the next week, I was feeling melancholic. I started to like the feeling of melancholy: sitting around and feeling sorry for myself. The way that it felt good when you put a thumb on a bruise and pressed down. It made me feel like getting hurt more often, since after-ward you were able to experience this soft, reflective state.

When I got home after school one day, there was a folded piece of loose-leaf in the mailbox. I opened it and read: 'I am going to rape you and cut your fucking head off. I am going to feed your feet to a dog.' Naturally, I knew it was from Theo. It didn't even hurt my feelings, to tell you the truth. Instead I was sad that Theo was feeling this way. I knew that he was pretending to hate me because he figured our friendship was over and he didn't want to lose face. I kind of missed him for some strange reason, but I wanted him to know that he couldn't hurt me.

I folded his note back up and put it in my pocket. I carried it around for the next few days and even felt sentimental about it, as if it was a postcard that some-one had sent me from Paris, one that smelled of perfume and was written in cursive. It might have been the painkillers that were making me feel that way. Actually, they were probably behind my enjoyment of melan-choly, too. I was glad when I went to the doctor and he said I could knock off the pills and take my arm out of the sling. He said it was necessary to feel pain now, so that I knew if I was being hurt.

7

Early Sunday morning, we had a dress rehearsal at the community center, as the parade was the next weekend. James had a bunch of long johns for us to wear under our costumes and we were hopping around looking like the Lost Boys in *Peter Pan*. I carefully fit my bad arm into the wire loops that were attached to the wings. Everyone said my costume was the nicest, right after Paul's, but that was understandable since he was dressed up as a skeleton.

When I got home before noon, my hair was still slicked back with gel and sparkling. Jules looked me up and down a minute and said I was too young to use hair gel. Then he announced that I wasn't allowed to hang out at the community center anymore. He reminded me that he hadn't liked me being there to begin with. Now the delinquents over there were breaking my bones. Next they'd turn me into a drug addict or at least murder me. I didn't bother explaining that they had tried smoking banana leaves and were very unsuccessful at being drug addicts. Nor did I explain that they were all still upset about the pigeon we'd killed, which indicated that they weren't serial killers by nature.

Instead, I only asked that I be allowed to participate in the parade. Actually, I fell down on my knees and begged. Jules simply opened his can of pop that seemed to be called Thirty Five Cents and shook his head. I knelt on the ground, my head spinning in disbelief. It was too unfair and cruel. What were the other kids supposed to do without me? I was the first one in the line. No one else had memorized any of the footwork. They just followed behind me and imitated my moves.

I yelled that I was going to the parade no matter what he said. To this, Jules answered that if he saw me in the parade, he would stop the parade and slap me in front of everybody. I knew that he would do it, too. I just lay on the floor, sobbing hopelessly.

It was impossible to reason with Jules. His brain had been a mess lately. A couple days before, he'd asked me if I had seen a pattern in the carpet moving.

'I could have sworn it just flew through here,' he'd said. It wasn't his fault that he was unfair. Rehabilitation had driven him batty.

Jules shuffled into the living room, but I stayed on the floor by the door and engaged in some of that mad, frustrated crying: the kind where you talk with your teeth clenched together. Everything in the apartment, even the print of a geisha nailed on the wall, was making me angry. Finally, I put on my ski jacket and picked up my shoes and got up and left the apartment.

I stumbled out into the street, hoping that I looked like a drunken sailor. Everything was all topsy-turvy because my eyes were filled with tears. I clutched my shoes to my chest as I went. I cried loudly, not even bothering to wipe the tears and snot off my face. I just let it all pour down, allowing everybody walking by to see what this world had done to me. If a kid my age walks down the street in her socks, crying her eyes out, then it makes it a bad neighborhood. I was glad I was making their world a shitty place to live.

I sat on an empty bench at the bus stop on the corner.

A few people walked up to wait for the bus, but they didn't sit on the bench with me. They were afraid of me, of my sadness. I put the shoes down next to my feet. It was like there was an invisible man sitting next to me, naked, except for his shoes.

Out of the corner of my eye, I noticed someone come and sit next to me. They were leaning over, obviously trying to get me to look at them. I turned a little and saw it was Theo. As soon as our eyes met, he put both his arms around me and hugged me.

'There, there,' he said gently. It was the way that his mother talked when she was being nice. 'Don't cry like that. Poor little sweetie. Too sweet to sit here and cry.'

I squealed, pretending to be disgusted, but I didn't even try to push him away. I liked being squeezed tight like that. I even liked that it hurt my shoulder a little.

'Get off of me, you weirdo,' I said.

Theo shook his head and just squeezed me tighter. He let go and patted me on the head. He gave me a Kleenex to blow my nose on. I'd never been treated like that by another child. It was creating very pleasant sensations in me. He lowered his head, so that our faces were right in front of each other's.

'You know you're my best friend, right?' he said.

I shrugged. I guessed it was true. Now that I wasn't going to be at the parade, they would all hate me. Everything had been carefully choreographed, and me not being there would throw them all off. I realized that kids like Theo and me weren't even supposed to have real friends. We were supposed to be alone and confused. By being each other's friend, we were defying our laws of gravity.

'Are you upset because of the letter?' he asked.

It took me a couple seconds to figure out what he was

referring to. Then I remembered the nasty letter I was carrying around like a poem in my pocket.

'No.'

'I'm sorry. And I'm sorry I dislocated your arm.'

'It's okay. It's practically cured now.'

'I never told you this, but I saw you hugging my mother.'

'Yeah. She's nice.'

'You like my mother?'

'She smells good.'

'That's true. She wears cocoa butter! She screams a lot. But it's not her fault. She gets really nervous.'

'Yeah. My dad's like that too.'

'Does he whack you sometimes?'

'He throws things at me,' I said.

I leaned my head over so that he could see the big cut on my head from where Jules's slipper had caught me a couple days before.

'That's pretty bad, but really it isn't shit. You want to see something worse?' he asked.

'Yeah.'

He lifted his pea jacket and T-shirt at the same time over his head. Then he turned around so that I could get a good look at his back. There were little thin scars running all the way down to his waist. They reminded me of tall blades of grass. Looking at his scars gave me the feeling that I was seeing something intimate and dirty. It was more secret and I felt myself get excited. I ran my finger along one of the scars, then shivered.

'I got those when I was a little baby. My mom whipped me with a telephone cord and then poured salt in my cuts. She did that right before she had to go to the hospital. I had to go live in a group home for a while.'

'They're not that bad,' I said.

'Yes, they are.'

We were very quiet. When he took off his shirt, it had changed the way we felt about each other. There wouldn't be any reason for us to keep secrets from each other now. It occurred to me that Theo was the first person in the world that I trusted. We sat there next to each other and he put his arm around me. Strangely, it wasn't a big deal at all. It just felt comfortable. Neither of us wanted to move even the slightest bit. I had this distant feeling after I had cried, like I was far away, someplace on holiday. It was easy to keep still next to Theo.

I snapped out of my reverie when I looked down the street and saw Lauren walking in our direction. She was with her cousin, a really mean girl in her own right. The two of them were trailing behind their parents. They had on beautiful black tailored coats. From the way the whole family was dressed, I guessed they were on their way to the church around the corner. Lauren and her cousin had their heads leaning together, the way that girls did when they were about to do something rotten. I hurried to put on my running shoes. I didn't want them to say I was barefoot and pregnant, or something like that. I was yanking desperately at the shoelace, trying to get a knot untied. Theo looked at me confusedly, obviously not understanding why I was being all crazy about my shoes.

Lauren and her cousin slowed way down as they passed the bench.

'Hey, Baby?' Lauren's cousin said. 'How do you comb your teeth?'

'Yeah,' said Lauren. 'You better get home. It's twelve o'clock. You'd better get your pajamas on and go to bed.'

Theo stared at Lauren with his face squinched up,

trying to figure out the meaning of what she'd just said. He was completely lost. If he had known what was going on, he'd have jumped up and slapped both of them in the face. I had no doubt about that. Lauren and her cousin walked off quickly, bending over with laughter.

'Was she being serious?' Theo asked. 'Or was she trying to insult you?'

'I can't stand her,' I said, finally managing to tie my shoelace. 'She's always bothering me at school.'

Theo's face went all red. He jumped up and climbed on the bench and looked down the street to see if he could catch a glimpse of them, but they were gone.

'Oh, man! That bitch said that shit to you while I was sitting right next to you! No fucking way! Let's wait for that bitch to come out of church and stab her to fucking death! Come on, we got to!'

He was getting all worked up and excited. He had been presented with a legitimate enemy for once. He was also very happy that we were both on the same side and were, therefore, no longer enemies. He made me swear not to move an inch and ran into his apartment. He came running back out a couple minutes later with a huge kitchen knife waving in his hand.

'Do you think this is a machete?' he asked.

'I don't know.'

'Don't worry. I'll never let her get away with saying that shit to you. Nobody talks like that to you ever. You hear me? You have to respect yourself.'

Theo tried to figure out how he could keep the knife on him and out of sight. He pulled his gym sock all the way up to his knee and stuck the knife into it. He walked a couple steps to try out his new system and screamed out in pain. The tip of the knife had cut the side of his leg.

He pulled it out and, hopping on one foot, tried to stick it in the pocket of the pea coat he was wearing. The pocket was much too shallow for the knife; it toppled out and landed on the ground. I suggested he tuck it into the waistband of his pants. He informed me that if he slipped, the knife might cut off his canary patch. Finally, he just held the knife in his hand, for the whole world to see.

Theo and I went to sit on the church steps. Neither of us had any idea how long church was going to be. I picked up some leaves that were on the church's lawn and started making them into a necklace to pass the time. Theo, however, was getting impatient, and started pacing back and forth. He ran the blade along the grass, trying to decapitate the heads of the few remaining flowers, but it was no use. We realized, after sitting there for ten minutes, that we weren't going to be able to wait it out.

'I know where she lives, man!' Theo screamed. 'I used to have a paper route there. Let's go trash her place while her whole family's in there praying.'

So we set off down the street toward Lauren's house, Theo swirling the knife around his head as if it were a light saber. He couldn't resist chasing a couple five-year-olds down an alley with it.

'Don't look at me like that,' he said to a boy who was sitting in a hockey net in his driveway. 'I'll come over there and stab you right through the heart.'

I really hoped no one was going to be at Lauren's. I had seen so many people murdered on television it seemed as if I was going to have to murder someone at some point, but the thought of Theo and me murdering a whole family was making me nervous. I had to run into a gas station and use the bathroom.

When I came out, Theo was standing on the corner singing 'Señor Don Gato' at the top of his lungs. He sang it in a really deep, deep voice for fun. I had learned that song in elementary school and it had been my favorite for years. I started singing too. We sang it together as we walked down the street.

'Oh Señor Don Gato was a cat. On a high red roof Don Gato sat. He was there to read a letter, meow, meow, meow, where the reading light was better, meow, meow, meow. 'Twas a love note for Don Gato!'

All of a sudden, I was in a good mood and didn't seem to have a problem in the world. All the stuff my dad had said to me was completely put away for the moment. That was one of the beautiful things about being a kid, how you could just feel such complete joy in the middle of everything.

I picked up a stick. Theo and I started sword fighting as we sang.

'Oh Don Gato jumped so happily. He fell off the roof and broke his knee. Broke his ribs and all his whiskers, meow, meow, meow, and his little solar plexus, meow, meow, meow. 'Twas the ending of Don Gato!'

The sun was shining that day and the fall colors were everywhere, as if an army of children had passed through here, smashing crayons under their heels as they went. I walked like a peg-legged pirate with one foot on the sidewalk and one on the street. I kicked an empty bottle of bleach for a couple blocks. It made the sound of a whale. The air was filled with tiny white fluffy bits, flying everywhere. They stuck all over Theo's jacket. It was as if a check had been left in his pocket during the wash.

He tried to cut a clothesline in half just for fun, but his knife couldn't get through the line at all.

*

The back alley behind Lauren's house looked the way the world would look if a child had built it. Some underwear and a couple T-shirts that had fallen from clotheslines lay on the pavement. A single sneaker was stuck up on a fence post. There was a toy bucket with rocks in it and a sled that had been left behind from a day when there had been snow on the ground. A wooden door leaned against a wall, leading nowhere. There was a lamp and a bathroom sink in the same garbage heap. You'd think that these houses were being blown apart by the wind, the way that pieces of them were lying about. Not one of them would be a match for the Big Bad Wolf.

'Is this her window?' Theo whispered.

I looked up and he was right. Lauren's bicycle was leaning next to the back door. The window wasn't even closed. Theo jabbed open the screen with his knife and we climbed through. We didn't even look up and down the alley to see if anyone was witnessing our crime. Now that I was becoming a criminal, I thought there should be a big audience applauding me.

We both tiptoed around the apartment, staying really close to each other until we were sure no one was there. I think we were both somehow fantasizing about living there together. I didn't know that these houses were so different inside. I assumed, somehow, that the interiors looked just like those of poor apartments. If it was unfair that we had broken into her apartment, it seemed much more unfair that she got to live here. It was big and lovely. The ceilings were high and there were paintings on the walls. A vase filled with fresh flowers sat on the kitchen table.

Theo said we should put the things we wanted by the

144

back door, so that we could be sure we took them when we left. He came into the kitchen dragging the comforter from Lauren's parents' bed. He seemed to think that it was really expensive. Apparently his mother had gone on about a goose-down comforter she had when she was little. We thought about taking the television just because we knew that it was something that people took when they broke into houses, but we couldn't even carry the color TV set over to the door. That was very strange. I didn't understand how it was that thieves stole people's television sets. They must bring cars and put stuff in the trunks. We both already had television sets anyway, so we dropped the idea.

I went through a change jar in the kitchen and took out some quarters and stuck them in my pocket.

Lauren's room smelled like perfumed erasers. There was a little barrette with a giraffe in a bureau drawer that I took and put in my pocket. That would go a long way toward making me beautiful. I looked over the shelves for something else that might catch my fancy. There was an adorable wooden turtle that I decided to take.

'There's a box of jewelry here,' Theo called from the other room.

'I don't like jewelry,' I said.

'Are you sure? There's some nice stuff here.'

In our old apartment, my dad and I had this creepy neighbor who wore tank tops and leopard-skin balloon pants. He always wore lots of jewelry, five gold chains around his neck and these big chunky rings on his fingers. Now jewelry always reminded me of him, and even the thought of a simple band depressed me. I didn't know anything about pawnshops then, so I yelled for Theo to leave all the jewelry where it was.

Theo came out of Lauren's sister's bedroom with a pair of her underwear on his head. He was carrying a stuffed tiger in one hand and his knife in the other. He jabbed at the tiger's neck until the head came off. Theo had a ferocious expression on his face, as if he was engaged in a difficult fight. Then he put the head on top of the fridge, where it would be sure to be seen. At some point Lauren had once told me about that tiger. His name was Marshmallow, I think.

We looked at each other and a peculiar feeling of excitement came over us. We just started wrecking everything we could think of. There was a statue of a ballerina that I threw against the wall. All its limbs broke off at once, poor fragile thing. We knocked everything on the floor. Theo ripped the shower curtain off the hook. He took a marker and scribbled on the wall, 'You are a bitch and you are going to hell. I am going to kill you all.' He took his machete and started stabbing the couch cushions. Theo handed it to me and I cut through some paintings on the wall. We knocked their stereo system over. We did a whole bunch of other things that I can't really remember.

I dumped a potted plant in the sink. I rescued a little flower from one of its stems and stuck it behind my ear. At this point we'd lost all sense of reality. It was like being in a dream. What made everything feel so strange was how easy it had been to break into someone's house and wreck their things.

Violence never gives you a specific feeling that it's time to knock it off. That's because it is impossible to satisfy. All your actions are like shoveling mud into a hole with no bottom. After we had wrecked a good portion of the apartment, Theo and I sat down in the kitchen and each had a big piece of chocolate cake that was in a box in the fridge. He poured us two glasses of milk, which we drank all out of breath.

When we were done, we threw the dishes on the floor and threw the rest of the cake down the hall. We couldn't get the back door open, so we climbed back out the window. Theo got stuck for a couple seconds because he was hauling the ridiculous comforter out with him. Amazingly, it was the only thing he'd found to be of any value in the house.

I noticed Lauren's bicycle near the back door again. I pushed it out of the backyard. When we got into the alley, I got up on the bike and cycled through all the garbage. The cats scurried out of the way. Jules had been borrowing my bike for his so-called work, so I hadn't had a chance to ride one in a while. I had forgotten how good it felt to get up on one, sailing along. It made me feel at peace. A crowd of boys called out to me that my bike was ugly and I waved happily to them. As I rode faster, I imagined that I was a stunt man and that I was about to jump over a chasm with thousands of people watching.

Theo ran after me, quilt in his arms, as if he'd just rescued a dog from a burning building. He called, begging for a turn on the bicycle.

Theo tied the quilt around his neck as he rode. It was pretty to see. I thought he looked just like a superhero. Mind you, I was thinking of a superhero from one of the low-budget television shows on Saturday morning, who carried around a spray-painted pack of cigarettes that he used as a teleporter. Still, we were both very happy and impressed with each other.

He double rode me down a steep hill down one of the streets that led to the river. There were always strange stores on this street because it was out of the way and the rent was cheaper. They were stores that you could pass a million times and never go into. One sold framed pictures of Jupiter and the moon. Another had busts of different composers and broken violins hanging from wires in the window. One was an extermination company with a stuffed rat on display. The world was sweet!

We rode past the end of the street to where the ground got all gravelly and led to a cliff over the river. We stood at the edge looking over. There were rusty wire fences at the bottom of cliffs back then. A huge filthy puddle the color of dead fish lay under us, full of seaweed that looked like hair clogging a drain.

I found a piece of concrete. I picked it up and brought it over to the edge, counted to three, and flung it down. It made a big splash and a clanging noise. I was staring over the cliff at my masterpiece when Theo came up from behind me and grabbed me around the waist.

He squeezed me really tight and leaned forward with me, making like he was going to fling me into the mucky water. I begged him not to throw me. He was squeezing me so tightly that I had to make sure not to exhale too much so it hurt my rib cage and my side.

'You're my prisoner, you know. I'm going to hold you hostage. Okay?'

'Okay,' I said and relaxed.

And I closed my eyes. It felt like we were flying. It was necessary for him to hold me this tightly so that I wouldn't fall. Together we were going to be very strong. The world was going to pay for what it had done to us. If I wasn't going to get to be a dragonfly, other people would also feel the pain along with me.

I heard Lauren talking about the break-in at school. She didn't suspect it was me. She couldn't even fathom that it had been me. Only Theo knew that I was capable of such things. I didn't mind not going to the community center, because Theo and I met up every day after school for the next week. Jules had nothing to complain about: he had won his argument about me not hanging out at the center. He left me alone for a while.

Shortly after our adventure, Theo's mother had another breakdown and he was put into the foster care system. No one who goes into the system even writes a good-bye letter. The first thing they teach you is that you aren't worth good-byes.

It was sad because I had been picturing us as boyfriend and girlfriend. I ran into a girl from the community center and told her that I liked Theo. She promptly told me that I, by far, had the worst taste on the planet. She thought of me differently once I'd confessed my affection toward Theo. Maybe there was something wrong with me. I wondered if I was one of those people who were doomed to always love the losers and the ridiculous.

Other girls in my school knew what pop stars and television heroes to care about. Unlike them, I was completely lost when it came to knowing who to find attractive. Or at least my tastes differed vastly from theirs. I had no innate sense of who I was supposed to like. Nonetheless, I wanted to love someone as much as anyone else. As I walked home from school one day, I stopped in front of a life-size poster of Arthur H that had been plastered to the wall of a building. He was a tall skinny Parisian singer who sang ludicrous love songs. There were posters of him all over town because his new album had just been released. Everyone in my school hated French music with a terrible passion. Other girls would rather kill themselves than like Arthur H. Most of his posters near our school had been entirely defaced by mustaches or the word 'pervert' across his forehead, but this poster hadn't been marked at all.

It didn't matter what anyone else thought. I stood on my tippy toes and kissed Arthur H on the lips. I was going to make my own decisions about love from now on. I hurried up the stairs to our apartment.

the devil in a track suit

1

Jules was in a better mood when he was drifting. He'd get crazier and crazier in the apartment. When he was getting ready to go somewhere, he'd get his suit on and shave. Sometimes he just walked all day and I didn't know where he was. He was always falling asleep at his friends' apartments. They squeezed in together on the couch and watched late-night movies and fell asleep with their heads on each other's shoulders. He came home in the morning as if a piano had fallen on him, as if he had been run over by a herd of antelopes.

Then he started disappearing for longer stretches of time. He'd put twenty dollars for groceries under the bed and take off for a few days. He was always bringing things to the country to sell, going door-to-door selling the quilts he'd bought in Joliette. There was always a big pile of quilts in the corner of our living room. They were covered in autumn leaves and berries, which was a popular pattern back then. Mary's housecoat had that same pattern, and every time I lay on one of those quilts, I thought happily of her.

I was almost thirteen and he thought I was old enough to be left alone in the house. I didn't think that I was because I was still afraid of the dark. Plus, if someone decided to kick the door in, I wasn't going to be able to beat them up.

Sometimes he'd leave for reasons that weren't even business. One day he decided to go with a friend out to the country to meet Lester's cousin, who had been some sort of boxer and had been on television. Jules thought it was a great opportunity to be able to meet this guy. I thought it was stupid.

He put on a tweed suit, a giant scarf, and wallabies. He looked too young to be wearing a suit and look sophisticated in it. It was more the kind of suit you saw on the cover of a reggae album. He looked like a gypsy about to be married. But I didn't say anything.

Jules said that he might be gone overnight, so he had a plastic bag with his toothbrush and underwear. He also had a danish wrapped up in cellophane in case he got hungry. He sat on the couch waiting for his ride. He smelled like aftershave. When I passed the Ritz-Carlton once, I imagined that it smelled like Jules's aftershave inside.

The doorbell rang and Jules split. He ran down the stairs to meet his friend Lester, who was waiting downstairs in his car. I looked out the window at them leaving. Lester was driving a borrowed car. It was a beat-up black car that made me think of a crow. I just decided to go to bed early and get one day over with.

That whole weekend I missed waking up to Jules screaming at the radio.

'Play another song, motherfucker,' he would scream at the announcer. 'Come on! I can't stand all the commercials!'

Jules and I were living in a new apartment again. It was in a skinny old building tucked in between a barbershop and a tango studio. There was wallpaper on the walls in the stairwell, something that I'd never seen before. It was like living in a dollhouse. I'd go sit on the stairs and try to read a book when being alone in the apartment freaked me out. Mostly I just ended up staring at the golden stickmen on the wallpaper who were sailing on gondolas across a red ocean.

The landlady was Russian and looked like she was wearing a dozen sweaters and about three scarves on her head at the same time. It was hard to imagine what she actually looked like under all those layers, or what her face must have looked like when she was young. She was probably from another generation, a time when people were uglier. There were little black hairs on her nose and her glasses had tape holding them together in the middle. For some reason the lenses seemed murky, as if they'd been permanently steamed up. It was like I was looking at her under a microscope because there were so many faults.

She liked to hug me when I passed her in the stairwell and say, 'Poor little thing. Terrible, oh, so terrible. Your coat isn't thick enough.' She gave me plastic bags filled with oranges or boxes of tea cookies. I liked her, but older people made time stand still when you spoke to them. Standing under the yellow light of the bulb in the hallway, I felt like a bug trapped in amber. Sometimes she gave me *Cosmo* magazines and I'd leaf through them looking for the perfume samples. When she gave me a pile of old *TV Guides*, Jules yelled at me that they weren't any good. Didn't we have enough of our own garbage that we didn't have to go around taking in other people's? I couldn't say no to the landlady when she offered me something, though. I didn't want to hurt her feelings.

One time she gave me a cassette without a case. It had

the words 'Vladimir Vysotsky' written on it in scratchy old person's handwriting. I didn't know for sure if Vladimir Vysotsky was the singer's name. It could have been, say, the name of the landlord's cousin, who had maybe owned the tape at one time. I thought that I should probably throw it right out into the alley. I might listen to it and it might be horrible, like the bad rock and roll they played at the Jupiter café on the corner. It would depress me all day if I had to hear that.

I showed it to Jules and he stuck it in the cassette player. It was a shock when we turned it on. It was a man singing and shouting in Russian. He screamed at the top of his lungs when he sang. I had never heard a man sing like that. He sounded like an irate drunk screaming at his wife through the bathroom door to hurry the hell up. Instead of sounding like birds singing or pretty ladies, or wind chimes, it sounded more like garbage bags being dropped out windows, or like people throwing cups and dishes up against a wall because they were outraged. These were all sounds that you wouldn't think were music. It was exciting.

Jules liked the tape as much as I did. It became the tape that we listened to all the time. We simply couldn't get enough of it. I listened to it in the bath, or lying on the carpet doing my homework. Jules and I even listened to it while we watched TV.

We tried to figure out what he was singing about because, of course, we didn't know a word of Russian.

'Maybe he's singing about how he isn't speaking to his best friend?' I suggested.

'He probably came home drunk and ran over the family dog. Now he knows his wife is going to kick him out for good. He's feeling real sorrowful.'

I thought that Jules became a poet when he interpreted these songs. These days he only seemed to speak to me when I'd done something like leave the bathtub a mess. Then he cursed me and the day I was born so hard that even the neighbors heard. But now, sometimes, when the music was playing, he would say something just regular and thoughtful, as if we were still friends.

When Jules was away in the country for the weekend, I found myself waiting outside the landlady's apartment, hoping she would come out and invite me inside. I kicked over a telephone book that was lying on a step so that she'd know I was there. Sure enough, she opened the door and invited me in. It smelled like almond cookies inside. She had masking tape all over the floor where a tile was missing. There were newspapers lining the floors in the hall, and there was a photograph of Jesus in the kitchen, or, rather, an actor dressed up as Jesus.

I couldn't figure out how well she spoke English because instead of speaking she mostly pointed at things and made funny little noises. She kept forgetting that I was there. When she walked back into the kitchen, she almost had a heart attack because she was expecting the room to be empty.

She gave me these jelly candies to eat and I couldn't get the idea out of my head that I was eating sugar-coated slugs. I gagged right while I was sitting next to her, but luckily she didn't seem to notice. She just patted me on the head and took out a plastic bag filled with stamps that we looked at, one by one, trying to organize them.

Afterward, I helped her wash the stairs in the hallway. I couldn't really enjoy it because I knew that Jules might come home any minute and catch me working for no pay, and that type of thing would upset him.

It might have seemed ludicrous for a twelve-year-old to be hanging out with an old woman, but that was the way I was. I'd started looking for adults to hang around with. They had more quality time for me and said sweet encouraging things and gave me gifts.

2

I'd get excited when grown-ups paid attention to me. It always made me feel special. I didn't have a mother and my dad wasn't ever around anymore. I was even friends with the retarded people who stood rocking back and forth on the corner. I used to push this guy Emmet around in his wheelchair. He was a junkie and he had to get up a hill every day to his dealer's house. Nobody else liked to push him up the hill on St Laurent Street because he'd scream and insult whoever was helping him. He complained to me the whole way up.

'You keep knocking me into things, fuckin' shit. Not so fuckin' swervy. It's like I'm on a goddamn ship. I'm going to puke all over my fucking lap. Slow the fuck down, will you? I don't know why you're in such a rush. It's Saturday. You have to hurry off to smoke pot with your friends?'

Jules said he'd slap me right in public if he saw me pushing Emmet's wheelchair. Jules always let me push Emmet's wheelchair when I was younger, but now he said it wasn't appropriate for me to be associating with him anymore. But I'd still sneak around behind my dad's back and push him and that wheelchair up the hill. Emmet always told me the funny jokes he'd seen on *Saturday Night Live* since we didn't have cable.

I used to call out insults to a guy named Peaches, a man who Jules had also suggested I not bother with anymore. He told me Peaches didn't know what a kid was. Peaches was a skinny twenty-year-old kid who was always trying out new stupid styles in order to be original. Like he'd wear two different colored socks or two pairs of sunglasses at the same time. I used to insult his clothes every time I saw him and that would make him really happy.

I saw him walk by wearing a gray woolen sweater and a big tie with a blue bird on it one day.

'Peaches!' I shouted. 'What's with that tie? What is it with that ugilieee tie? I don't want to insult you, but I just need to know for scientific reasons, why would you wear such an ugly tie? Are you color-blind? Are you experimenting with food coloring?'

'Did your mother kick your butt out of the house 'cause she got sick of your face?' he answered. 'Hmm. I bet you got a spanking lately. At least I don't get spanked! I heard your mother yell at you the other day. She said, "Get in your room!" It's true! You're blushing. I heard it all the way down the block!'

I just laughed. No matter how many times I reminded him, he couldn't remember that I didn't have a mother, so I didn't bother anymore.

One day I was sitting in the lobby of my building doing a report on endangered animals. Mine was on the cheetah. I was tracing a picture of one out of the encyclopedia for the cover page when Peaches pushed open the front door to the lobby and sat next to me on the stairs. Instead of insulting me, he tried to make conversation.

'So did you draw that?' he asked. 'That's nice. I have a

cousin who's really, really good at drawing. She could have gone to school in Paris, but you have to know five languages to study there.'

'That's not true. Come on, Peaches! They speak French in France and that's it.'

'You don't have to call me Peaches. You can call me Benjamin.'

'I like Peaches, though.'

'Just go on and try Benjamin. You might see that you like saying it. Just say it once. I want to hear you say it.'

'Benjamin,' I said, but then right away I wished I hadn't.

Calling him Benjamin at this point gave me a similar sensation to letting him lift up my skirt and kiss my thigh. I knew that he was coming on to me, although I couldn't figure out why. There were plenty of good-looking teenage girls around. I was sitting there wearing a long-sleeve shirt with dragons on it and a pair of green Adidas shorts. On my feet were a pair of brown walla-bies. I dressed like people in Haiti who'd been sent cast-off clothes. I'd grown up with men around the house and there'd never been anyone to help me match my clothes or fix my hair. I had scabs on both my knees, for crying out loud.

Then again, everyone knew Peaches had terrible taste in women, because for a while he had dated a girl named Oana who wore huge glasses and worked at the Laundromat. She always told everyone they were stupid and didn't know how to use the machines properly. She slapped my hands once when I was fiddling with the knob on a dryer. It didn't mean that you were attractive if Peaches liked you. He had a cousin named Alphonse who was always surrounded by pretty women. If Alphonse liked you, it meant that you were one of the foxier girls in the neighborhood.

After I knew that Peaches sort of liked me, it made me wish that Alphonse would notice me one day and just wink my way. But then again, the one adult I was afraid of and got all quiet around was Alphonse. I couldn't even sit near him, so he was the one I most craved attention from.

Alphonse was a big guy, with dark red hair and big blue eyes. He had a tattoo of a rose right on the top of his spine that would peek out from the top of his shirt sometimes. He had a scraggly beard and his hair was in little dread-locks that stuck up. It reminded me of the way cartoon cats looked after they'd been blown up. It was beautiful.

Alphonse wore expensive outfits and a white angora baseball hat. He had a pair of gold pants and a shirt with goldfish that matched the pants exactly. Once I saw him out on the street corner on my way to school, wearing a burgundy overcoat over some green silk pajamas with blue leather slippers and drinking out of a plastic milk container. It was then that I realized that he could never look anything but spectacular.

Although Alphonse was terribly interested in women, he never seemed to notice me. But that's because I wasn't really a woman. He didn't have friends who were kids, and in fact he picked on us kids. Especially ones whose parents weren't ever around.

There was one kid on my block who knew how to sing really well. Alphonse would catch him and keep him in a headlock until he sang 'Blackbird' by the Beatles for him. Once I saw some kids playing with an empty refrigerator box, pretending it was a spaceship, and Alphonse started shaking the box like crazy. 'Engine trouble, men!' he kept yelling. When he finally stopped, a kid rolled out of the box crying.

My friend Zoë and I had this large piece of plastic that her father had been using to cover a window during the winter. He gave it to Zoë to drag out to the trash. Zoë and I laid the piece out on the sidewalk. We took off our shoes and started slip sliding in our socks, practicing crazy dance moves. Alphonse came by and chucked the remains of a bottle of water on us. I started to cry out of humiliation.

'Come on!' Alphonse had said, laughing. 'Don't be a crybaby. Get your shit together. Jesus Christ, what a fucking sap.'

I tried to forget that I had ever even liked him after that.

Alphonse lived in a big building that had 'Jesus Saves' spray-painted on its bricks out front. He often sat outside it with a giant boom box. Even though it was starting to get damn cold out, friends of his would gather around him to listen to his music. The music put Alphonse in a good mood, and when he was in a good mood, he would start to insult people who were passing by. Once I heard him making fun of Jules. Jules was walking down the street carrying a lamp in his hand that he'd obviously just pulled out of some garbage heap.

'Look at the garbage picker man!' Alphonse said. 'That motherfucker is sad. He tried to sell me a comforter once! I said get the hell away from me. He's out all night looking for rags and bones. What year we living in, man? Get a real job, motherfucker.'

Jules couldn't stand Alphonse either. He said Alphonse was a pimp. I didn't know what a pimp did exactly. I was almost certain that it meant he had prostitutes working for him, but I wasn't sure. I told a kid at school that I knew a pimp and he said, 'Bullshit. It's not fucking possible. You're making it up.' So I guessed I'd made a mistake. Or maybe the word 'pimp' had two different meanings.

I didn't do anything to make older guys want to treat me like I was one of them, but I had some friends who did. My friend Zoë wore these running shoes with high heels. She slicked her ponytail back and wore blue eye shadow in enormous rings around her eyes. She tied her T-shirt under her breasts and carried a fake leather purse with straps so long it dangled down to her ankles. Guys would whistle at her from cars and she'd give them the finger all heroically.

I couldn't dress like that or Jules would throw a fit. He didn't even let me braid my hair. He thought that bobby pins were invented solely for attracting black men, that elastic bands with big plastic balls on them were for prostitutes. He didn't let me put a Pink Panther temporary tattoo from a stick of gum on my arm because he said any woman with a tattoo was a tramp. He insisted on cutting my bangs really short, the way that five-year-olds did, and made me wear a ridiculous turtleneck with strawberries on it and a pair of bell-bottoms whose waist went right up to my nipples. He gave me a secondhand fur coat that was an ugly orangish color that was popular in the seventies. I looked like a kid from a rerun. Jules argued that the clothes were made of good material and if I didn't want to wear them it meant I was trying to be a whore.

Then Zoë started smoking pot. She got it from her older sister. She said it made you feel like a woman. She told me that every guy would go nuts for a girl who smoked pot. I didn't know about that, but I did like the idea of smoking up. Jules had a bottle of white wine in the fridge once for about three months. I liked to sneak a few sips while I was pretending to look for the jam. The wine would make my feet feel soft and buzzy like hummingbirds. I loved to take a little drink and then sit on the fire escape. It felt like there were toads in the wind that whispered, 'Kiss me, kiss me, kiss me.'

The first time Zoë handed me a joint, I remember thinking that it smelled like a skunk, just like Pepé Le Pew. I took a toke from the joint and held it in. My throat started burning and I coughed and retched really hard. Zoë acted as if this were perfectly natural. I stood looking around, disappointed but somehow relieved that nothing at all was happening. Then I noticed that I was feeling numb, as if pain was impossible. I wanted to go up to a dog and get him to bite down on my arm. I had funny impulses, too, like taking off all my clothes. The mere thought of getting naked on a park bench made me burst out laughing. My laughter was like warm water running through my body. It was funny to me and made me laugh some more.

'God, you are such a stoner,' Zoë said, smiling.

3

Zoë gave me two more joints to take home as a symbol of our friendship. I smoked them over the next week. It would only take one good drag to make me high. I'd smoke them a little at a time in alleys and other such dismal places.

One Friday Jules came into my bedroom to tell me that he was going to sell some comforters in a flea market in Trois-Rivières. He was getting a ride up there and he wasn't going to be back until Monday morning. I didn't look at him while he told me about his plan. Instead I picked up a stuffed animal, an orange dog that I'd named Butchie. I knew if I looked at my dad I would start to cry. I cradled Butchie in my arms and stroked his head. I picked up a tennis ball and waved it in front of his nose, trying to interest him in it. Then I tossed the tennis ball across the bed. Jules and I sat there silently, as if we were waiting for the dog to jump up and fetch. Then my dad left and went to his room to get ready. I pulled the blankets over me even though I still had my running shoes on, and I fell asleep with Butchie in my arms.

The next morning I woke up, still wearing my clothes from the day before. The house was empty except for me. It was so quiet it was as if the bomb had dropped the night before. I remembered that I had hidden a little joint that Zoë had given me in a wooden box under my bed. I leaned over and pulled it out.

I took my lighter out of the pocket of my jeans and smoked the last of my joint just like that, lying in bed, the way that bank robbers and rock-and-roll stars did it. It was the best joint I'd ever smoked.

I got out of bed and wandered around the apartment. I felt like I had died and was a ghost and was just hanging out and observing things with no worries whatsoever since I was no longer one of the living. I took a bath and tried to float on top of the water, as if I were in the ocean off a tropical beach. The T-shirts were right: it was better in the Bahamas.

I wrapped myself in a towel and went to get dressed.

I looked through the pile of clothes that Jules had brought back from the laundry the day before. My clothes were downright ugly and I was the first to admit it. I didn't want the delicate good mood spoiled by wearing a T-shirt with a rooster advertising a chicken restaurant downtown.

I went into Jules's room and looked in his closet. He was skinny, and I was almost as tall as him, so I could get away with wearing some of his stuff. Of course, he never let me, but he wasn't here. I found a black suit that was strictly for weddings or for joining the Mafia, so he never had an opportunity to wear it. I put on a white dress shirt with a huge collar and the jacket over it. The pants were way too long, so I rolled up the cuffs. His shoes didn't fit so I had to put on my running shoes, but I didn't mind. I looked in the mirror and, in my altered state of consciousness, thought I was ready to host the Johnny Carson show. I threw on my fur coat but kept it wide open.

I went to sit on the front steps. I brought down the whole pitcher of orange juice and drank straight out of it in the manner I believed to be that of a big shot. My friend Bobby came up and sat with me. He was fifteen years old and was very impressed with my new outfit. He said there were strippers who dressed up in suits like that, and that they took all their clothes off and had fancy underwear on underneath. He said that no man could resist that kind of a strip show because there was nothing so sexy in the world as a good-looking lady in men's clothes. I just smiled and took another swig of my orange juice. A couple other kids came over to find out why I was dressed up so crazy.

'Because I died last night,' I said. 'And they dressed

me up in my fanciest suit and laid me down in a coffin. It's such a nice day and you are all my good friends, so I decided to get my butt up out of the coffin, just like Jesus Christ, and come and chitchat with all my beautiful and soulful friends.'

That's the way I talked when I smoked pot. It was a gift. Every time I smoked up, these pretty phrases and ideas just popped into my head. Usually I went around with so many ugly insecure things flying around in my head that when a pretty thought came to me, it usually died a lonely death, afraid to come out. But when I was high, I simply had to utter it. One time I'd been out by the river getting high with Zoë and her sister. On the bus ride home, I'd turned to a guy sitting next to me and said, 'Somewhere there is a sparrow singing in B minor.' I swear to God, pot made me a genius.

Someone in an upstairs apartment turned on their radio too loud. The sound of some goofy song filled the air around me, and I stood right up and started dancing to it, rolling my hips around, spinning an invisible Hula-Hoop, just like a stripper. All the kids were laughing their heads off. Bobby stood up and started grooving with me. That's when I noticed Alphonse standing across the street, checking out the interior of a car with some friends of his. Alphonse wasn't interested in the car, however. He was looking right at me.

Later that afternoon, after my high had long since deflated, I was sitting on my steps with Zoë. The rest of my friends had split to go and eat lunch or visit their cousins, or whatever. Her family couldn't stand her, so she was always a good person to waste the afternoon with. We were quietly rereading all my Archie comic books and minding our own business. Because of the cold, I'd closed up my fur coat and didn't look like I was wearing anything fancy at all anymore. Peaches walked over to me in that long-legged stride of his. He handed me a little paper bag.

'These are from my cousin Alphonse. He just wants you to know that you are a hot tamale.'

Peaches had this way of stopping and looking around him, as if he was about to cross a busy street. Then he ran across the parking lot, trying not to get hit by any imaginary trucks. Zoë and I looked in the bag. Curled in the bottom was a pair of skinny little delicate white kneesocks. I shrugged and put them in my pocket while Zoë begged me to ask Alphonse for another pair for her. She said I was lucky as shit because maybe Alphonse wanted to be my sugar daddy and I'd never have to work a day in my life. I told her I had to go. I picked up all my comics and ran up the stairs to our apartment.

I took out the stockings and laid them out on my lap. I stroked them as if they were kittens. They were the first pretty things I'd ever owned. I put them on and stood tiptoe on the toilet seat, trying to see myself in the bathroom mirror. I wore them every day for the next few days, even though my thighs and butt were freezing. I rinsed them out at night and hung them from the shower curtain to dry. I couldn't believe that he'd called me a hot tamale.

On Friday night, I came home at nine o'clock. That was my curfew and I felt guilty about staying out past nine even when Jules was out of town. It just made me feel strange and adrift when I disobeyed. My dad had told me that if you stayed out after nine and you were a girl it meant that you wanted to have sex with whoever was passing by. He told me that if I got raped after nine o'clock the courts would probably say I had deserved it. I didn't believe it, but I liked having a curfew. Without a curfew the nights seemed shapeless, like floating through the Milky Way. The idea of an infinite universe unnerved me.

When I walked into the apartment, Jules was sitting in the kitchen. He was in a bad mood. He'd had an argument with a guy who was selling the comforters with him. The idiot had wanted a 50 per cent cut even though my dad had paid for the comforters with his own money. After he finished his story, he looked me up and down strangely and his face went red. I realized suddenly that I was wearing my knee-high socks.

'Where'd you get those socks?' he asked in a voice you would use to command a dog with.

Zoë had told me that if I wore these socks every day of my life I would be popular until the day that I died. She told me to tell Jules that her sister worked in an undergarment factory and that she got samples for free that she gave to Zoë and all her friends. This seemed like a complicated and foolproof lie. Another friend of ours used it to explain her fancy underwear to her mother. But Jules didn't even give me a chance to tell my lie. As I opened my mouth, he stretched out his arm and punched me in the eye. There was a bright light and a sort of popping sound.

I sat down on the floor and took my shoes off. I peeled off my socks and reached up and handed them to him. He yanked at them furiously until he had ripped them into pieces, and then he threw them in the garbage. He didn't give me a chance to tell my story but just started yelling at me.

'No fucking twelve-year-old gave you those socks. You're a goddamn liar and you're a whore. If you start with guys now, you'll be all used up and no guy will want you. You're going to be a pervert! No guy likes a pervert! You'll know all these moves and shit that he won't know. You'll only be fit for drug addicts. Why can't you be a normal girl? I think I should just throw your ass out and move into a one and a half. I don't need this. I gave you the best of everything and this is how you turn out! You don't get it from me! I'd be embarrassed to walk down the street with you, everybody knowing that my kid's a whore.'

It was that speech and not the punch that made me cry. I felt so bad. He stepped over me and went to his room. He slammed the door, and I heard him muttering curses under his breath. I crawled across the kitchen floor and pulled myself up by holding on to the handles of the drawers, sobbing as if I'd been beaten close to death. I opened the cutlery drawer and took out a bread knife and pushed it against my belly. The edge wouldn't go through my skin so at last I flung it across the kitchen floor. I didn't actually think it was going to work, but I just wanted it to be on the record with myself that I had tried. I felt so sorry for myself that I hugged myself like a baby.

'It's okay. It's okay, sweetie,' I whispered until I felt better.

4

The next morning, I just couldn't stop looking at my reflection in the bathroom mirror. It was my first black eye. I remembered how Linus Lucas had a black eye at the foster home and it had destroyed him. By contrast, mine intrigued me. It was perfectly round, just like the ones that people had in comic strips. In a way I was sorry that it was Saturday. The black eye would go over great at school, and I hoped it was still this dark on Monday.

I put on my fur coat over my bell-bottoms and an ugly T-shirt that was faded like a pillowcase. I thought Jules was still going to be mad at me when he woke up, so I decided to stay out of his way. I was too ashamed to look at him. I was determined to stay away from grown men from then on. I went outside with my schoolbag. It was nice out and I thought I'd go to the park and find a quiet bench and catch up on my homework.

As I walked down the street, I noticed that everybody turned to look at my black eye. I liked the feeling, although I couldn't quite understand what I liked about it at the time.

I got to the park and sat down on the edge of the swimming pool, which had been emptied for the winter. I started reading my French book for class. I took out my notebook and opened it on the sidewalk beside me and started jotting down vocabulary words. I had a bag of lollipops in my schoolbag. I'd stolen those from the grocery store a week before and had completely forgotten about them. I took one out and started sucking on it contentedly.

'Say, what's with you?' I heard a voice behind me say.

For a split second it felt as if a hole had opened up in the sidewalk and had swallowed me. My body recognized Alphonse's voice before I even did. He had on a long camel hair coat over a dark blue terry-cloth track suit and he looked good. His clothes always fit him beautifully.

I looked all embarrassed at the tattered hems of my bell-bottoms. He was holding a lone flower in his hand, smiling. I didn't know what kind of flower it was and I still don't. Its blossom was white and tilted over like pouring milk.

'What are you reading? You're a little thinker, huh? You look cute as a button when you sit there reading. I've seen you do it before. You'd look good with tiny glasses.'

'Thank you,' I said.

'You are the prettiest girl on this street. I'll tell you that much. I know because I was walking around over there and I got bored to death. Just a lot of people who are not my style. Where did you buy that crazy-looking lollipop?'

'I stole a whole bag of them from the supermarket.' I pulled out the bag and showed it to him.

'Oh, my holy shit! You're like a thief. That's cool. I love girls who are thieves. Sitting out here reading a book and eating stolen candy. Do you even realize how cool you are?'

We just stared at each other. For the life of me, I couldn't figure out anything to say. He squatted down so that we were face-to-face. He handed me the flower.

'Here, I got you a flower,' he said in a low and sweet voice. 'I'm not going to tell you that I bought it because I know you prefer a stolen flower. I bet that tastes better to you because it is stolen. Smell this flower, though. Isn't it good? I wish I could manufacture that smell.'

I leaned over and smelled it. It did have a lovely smell.

'Wear the flower in your hair!'

I did as I was told. Putting that flower behind my ear made me feel like a gypsy. I didn't feel bad about myself anymore. This was turning out to be an interesting day.

'You don't even look like you're from here. You look like you just came over in a rusty truck from Mexico. Hey, you want a job over at that dance club? They're hiring dancers. You dress up as a black cat or a pirate and dance on the stage. I know the owner. It's not a strip club or nothing stupid like that.'

'I'm not allowed in there. I'm not eighteen yet.'

'How old are you?'

'Twelve.'

'You are just like a wee little chick. That's so goddamn crazy. No wonder you're so cute. I think my grandmother married my grandfather when she was twelve. They were Spanish. You know what my grandfather used to do for a living? He made these wooden roosters and Cadillacs that people like to put on their gravestones.'

'That's neat,' I said, really meaning it.

I liked to hear new things. I'd never heard about knickknacks on people's gravestones. My mother was buried in a little cemetery in Val des Loups. Jules always said that we should go and put some flowers on her gravestone, but we never did. I'd never encouraged him to either because I hated the trip out to Val des Loups. Now I sort of felt like going to put a Hot Wheels car there or something. Jules usually came up with original ideas, but he'd never thought of that.

'You got any poetry written in that notebook of yours?' Alphonse asked. 'You should write poems about stealing shit. You'd be good at it.'

'Yes,' I lied, and then put the notebook up to my chest so that he couldn't see that I was working on lame homework. 'I like to write poems at night sometimes.'

'You know what I did last night? I went to see Tito Puente! I love that guy. I have never seen anybody so alive in my life. He was vibrant. An electric shock. I wish you could have come with me last night.'

He reached into his coat pocket and took out a handbill with a picture of Tito Puente on it. I thought Alphonse might be pulling my leg. Tito Puente was a grinning middle-aged man wearing a black wig that appeared to be made out of wax. When I realized that Alphonse was serious, I came to the conclusion that he was the most unique person I'd ever met. As we spoke, I found myself imitating the movements his hands made and tilting my head at the same angle as his.

'I notice you got a little something around your eye,' Alphonse said, taking me off guard.

I'd gone into shock when he'd said hello and I'd completely forgotten about my black eye. I'd been planning on telling the kids in school that I'd been in a high-speed car chase and that the car had turned over and that the stick shift had hit me in the eye. I knew that Alphonse would never believe a story like that. Adults were harder to lie to than kids. He had probably figured out exactly where it had come from already. I was overwhelmed by humiliation and I looked at the ground.

'That sort of makes me angry as shit, but I'm not going to bug you about it,' he said softly. He had this gentle way of talking. There was something about his voice that reminded me of smoke. 'Because you already know what's so fucked up about that whole thing. I think that you should trust me. I got a nice place and you've always got a place to come to if you need some time to just get away from things. I know you're friends with Peaches and he's my cousin, so you know I'm not a stranger.'

I looked into his eyes. I didn't know what to say. I

didn't know if I should thank him or what. The idea of going to his house seemed terrifying. If Jules knew some guy had made a proposition like that, he'd throw me out the window. I realized that I'd already done something wrong by just sitting here and letting him talk to me. I'd fucked up again and now felt the guilt coming on.

'Anyway,' Alphonse continued. 'I'll just put that out there. I left home at fifteen, I never looked back. Fuck all that prisoner shit. You know what you want. Don't let anyone fuck with your soul.'

A car started honking on the street at the edge of the park. My heart was skipping beats all over the place, as I was afraid Jules or one of his friends might be in it. I would be a dead man if he was. I squinted to see who was in it. They were all wearing fashionable brand-new coats, so I knew they had to be Alphonse's friends. Jules's bummy friends wore corduroy jackets and berets and ballpoint pens that didn't work behind their ears. Alphonse waved to them. I couldn't tell if they were all looking at me suspiciously or as if I was a complete idiot. I still couldn't read a lot of adults' facial expressions.

'I'm getting into that car now,' Alphonse said, standing up. 'But we're going to meet up again soon, right? I'll play you a Tito Puente album. We're going to do some dancing and all that.'

'All right. See you then,' I said, throwing up my hand to wave.

I just sat there, smiling, letting him look at me. The wind came up from behind me and my hair blew all over my face. I felt like a gypsy again.

'Precious!' he exclaimed, and then walked over to the car and climbed in.

I was a little bit obsessed after that. No one had ever made me feel that wild, unusual way before. I started watching out for Alphonse, trying to bump into him. I spotted him sitting on a bench next to a girl a few days later in the middle of the afternoon. I wasn't sure if they were together. I started walking really slowly so that he would notice me. He looked up and waved me over. I sat down on the bench and slid up next to him. He shifted a little toward me too. I didn't know if he knew that our legs were touching. I liked being close to him. I liked the way he smelled.

I could tell from his eyes that he was stoned on grass, and I was hoping that he had some for me too. He just stared at me, serene, like a body that had just been drowned. The first thing he said was how he was going to take me to the hairdresser for fun one day and have my hair done in little braids and swirls, all fancy.

The girl next to us stood up and left. A couple other girls came and squished onto the bench to say hello to Alphonse. One of them had a ponytail on top of her head and pink high heels. The other one was wearing a gray leather jacket over a pair of silk pajama bottoms that weren't staying on her very well, and a pair of untied running shoes.

He had intense gravitational force. He was like Saturn because Saturn has so many moons. If I kicked my shoes up in the air, they would go into orbit around him. Girls were always talking to him and he sat there and listened and listened. He never told them to get to the goddamn point. It would take them forever to get to the point because usually their stories were pretty lame anyhow.

I was always kind of smitten by women. Probably because I never had a mother. The women that I was most crazy about were the young drug addicts. They'd be sitting on the hoods of cars late at night wearing white leather jackets with wide flaps and jean shorts. When they were stoned, they'd always smile at me. They had smiles that were so sweet and tender, smiles that made them seem as if they might have been crying a couple minutes before. They were always laughing and talking hard and being funny. These were the type of girls that Alphonse had around him.

Alphonse pulled out a dragon-shaped pipe from his pocket and asked if I wanted to do a shotgun. I nodded and he lit up the pipe and sucked the smoke into his mouth. He leaned over and I puckered up my lips and he blew into them. There was something monstrous about his mouth, as if he could open it wide and I would fit all the way in. It was the first time our lips touched and I shivered all over.

I leaned back and waited for the dope to hit me. I knew it must be working because all of a sudden I could feel his heartbeat. It was like the sound of a drum. He started talking, but I couldn't make sense of what he was saying. There was a funny hum to his low voice that I was feeling for the first time. It was like the hum that old refrigerators and half-broken appliances had. I felt like he had been part of me since the day I was born.

'Hey, Al,' a voice a few feet away called.

Alphonse and I both turned to look. It was Leelee from rue Napoleon. It was impossible not to know Leelee if you lived in that neighborhood. She was skinny, with a big nose and tons of freckles. She was one of those blonde girls who looked as if they'd just been rained on. She always seemed to be in some sort of situation. Once I'd seen her with her arm stuck in a revolving door. Another time she had dropped a liter of milk and the cap had come off and it had spilled on the sidewalk. She went back into the store to try and get her money back or exchange it for a new one, and she carried on at the store for half an hour.

It was also impossible not to know that she was a prostitute. She would get lazy and try to turn tricks right outside of her building instead of going to the strip. The tenants were always calling nasty things out the window to her.

'At least I got a job!' she screamed up at the windows. She was the best screamer in the neighborhood, I think. 'At least I can afford a dryer and don't hang my shit on my balcony. At least I don't do that.'

She was angry with every man who passed and didn't want to pay for her services. She always had crazy insults for them.

'Peewee! Where's your bicycle? You're so cheap, I know you don't ride no car.'

That day she came up to Alphonse looking like she was in some sort of mess. She was wearing a pink and green striped poncho over jogging pants and cowboy boots. The heels on her boots seemed too high for her; she walked like she was climbing up stairs. She looked nervous as hell, as if she was mustering up courage, madly adjusting her bracelets.

I knew that I was going to be incapable of speech for the next few minutes, so I just sat back and watched her talk to Alphonse. She didn't even seem to notice I was there. But that was because she was one of these people who never seemed to be noticing things. Once I saw her washing her face in a water fountain at the park, and there was a whole line of people behind her waiting while she went about her business without a care.

'So this guy, he's like my cousin, right?' Leelee started saying to Alphonse, without saying hello or anything. 'And he wants to stay with me just for a week. I don't want him there, even, okay? I really like my space. You know I have a little space and my space is all I got. So, you know, when it comes to that, fuck right off, right? So that's exactly what I tell him, too. I tell him without beating around the bush because you know that's how I am, right? I don't suffer in silence. I think you for one know that about me. Ha ha ha. You've experienced that firsthand and good or bad, that's the way I am. I can't be no other way. Then my mother, that cunt, calls me up and she's like, you got to do this, you have to let him come and stay with you for a month until he gets his stuff together. You have to do this because he is family.'

'What's this guy like?' Alphonse asked calmly.

'He's a bum through and through. He's always going out with these high school girls. He tells them he's going to marry them and they can move in together and they can move to New York, where he's going to be in that musical Cats!'

'What is he, a dancer?'

'No, I told you what he was, a bum. I don't know where he comes up with these things. They don't even make no sense. He just says them so that he can get them into bed. Because they think that once they sleep with him he's going to take care of them for the rest of their lives, and then they don't have to worry about how they do on their report cards, because they're never going to work. You know, that's what all teenage girls are dreaming about and he takes advantage of it. He totally takes advantage of it. The thing is that he slept with a bunch of girls and their parents all got together so he had to leave town. And the only place that he has to come and live is with me because I got myself a nice place and all that.'

'Well, if you want to put him up, that's your business.'

'Are you sure you're not pissed off? I don't want no friction between you and me. You know that, right? I want everything to be smooth like a locomotive, right, baby, uh-huh!'

'This is fucking delectable!' Alphonse said.

Leelee just stood there staring at him as if she didn't know what 'delectable' meant. She certainly didn't know what Alphonse meant by it. Neither did I, but I was stoned and couldn't really care less what was going on between the two of them. Although when he looked her up and down in a nasty way, that surprised me, a little.

'Where did you get that sweater you're wearing?' he asked her, finally. 'You couldn't have paid money for it. There are too many colors in that sweater. It's like watching a TV set with bad reception.'

'Why would you say something like that?' Leelee said in a pleading and exasperated voice.

'I'm not saying anything, man. I'm just saying that I have an ulcer that I happen to have named Leelee. And it just so happens that this ulcer is a knife in me. Like constant food poisoning that won't leave you alone, until you have to vomit.'

'You're saying that I'm making you sick!' Leelee's voice got really hard and shaky. She took a few steps away, made some semblance of trying to compose herself.

'I didn't say that. I said I got an ulcer that's making me sick. Listen to the motherfucking words.'

'I was listening! You named your goddamn ulcer Leelee! You're mad at me!'

All of a sudden it dawned on me that I ought to give them some privacy. I stood up and looked around, trying to look casual. Instead of going around the bench, I decided that I'd save time and climb over it. My leg got caught going over and I tumbled to the ground. This momentarily distracted Alphonse and Leelee from their conversation. I felt them staring at me as I walked away in that haughty way that stoned twelve-year-old girls sometimes have.

I snuck into the hot dog restaurant that was behind us and sat on one of the stools. I used to be friends with a kid named Marcus whose father owned the restaurant. Marcus and I would come here after school and sit at the back table and play Monopoly. His dad would give us free french fries and pop. We'd beg to mop the floor. Sometimes I'd stop in the restaurant without Marcus and his dad would give me a Coke and let me do my homework at the counter. He never minded me just hanging out there.

The warmth was nice as I stepped in. I put my hair in a ponytail. It made me think of being next to a lion fountain in the park where the water sprayed off and touched you. I used to spend hours at that fountain, sticking my hands under the rush of water that came out of the lion's mouth. I was lost for a few minutes thinking it, but then I realized that Marcus's dad was giving me a dirty look from behind the counter.

'You don't need to be in here,' he said.

'I just came to use the telephone,' I said.

It didn't surprise me that Marcus's dad addressed me

like that. He had probably seen me sitting with Alphonse. When you are a little kid, people don't judge you in the same way. Since I'd turned twelve, a lot of the adults that I knew had started to pretend that they didn't know me. They gave me disapproving looks. This made me feel terrible. I had betrayed them by turning out to be the type of kid that I was turning out to be. I wished that I could stay a cute adorable kid, but I couldn't.

Alphonse was the only one who was different. He'd always ignored me when I was a little kid. It was now that he was interested in me.

'Well, make your phone call and get out of here,' Marcus's dad said, pointing to the back, where the phone was.

I slid off the stool and walked over to the phone ridiculously slowly. I picked up the receiver. I don't even remember if I pretended to put in a quarter or not. I dialed a few numbers.

'Hello, is Martin there?' Martin being the classiest name I could think of. 'Un-huh... un-huh... un-huh... yeah... no... uh-huh... un-huh... okay, bye...'

I walked out all proud of myself. But back on the street the sun hit me and I had to squint and get my bearings. I felt sweaty and dirty again.

I looked around for Alphonse and Leelee, but the bench was empty. I saw them leaning against the bus shelter. They were hugging each other and kissing. She was still sort of hysterical, but his kissing seemed to be calming her down. She was kissing him like crazy and touching his face. I'd never seen two people kiss like that.

'I want to have a baby. You want to have a baby with me, Alphonse? We would have such a good-looking baby, oh my God. What a player he would be!'

I tiptoed by them, heading home. When I was just a few steps away, I heard Alphonse say, 'I want that girl.'

I looked back and Alphonse was staring right at me. I don't even know if he meant me to hear or not. Leelee looked around for a second. She looked past me, to across the street. She couldn't for the world figure out who Alphonse was talking about.

I knew that I should just walk down the street naturally, but my feet started doing a side step that we'd learned in the folk-dancing section of gym class. Then I started just boogying, but I was keeping it low-key so maybe no one could tell that I was flying. Everybody knew that if you were coming down the street dancing, it meant that you were stoned. There really weren't many exceptions. But finally I just couldn't resist anymore and I let myself go. A line of people at the movie theater turned around to look at me as I went, but I didn't mind at this point. I was like a bird out of a cage.

When I turned onto my corner, I saw the landlady standing on the front steps of our building. I was happy to see her. I was hungry and in the mood for some of her cookies, for her conversations that were just composed of smiles. I danced right up to her, but she gave me a quick sour look. Then she turned right around and looked the other way. Her look sobered me up. As I walked up the stairs, everything took on its usual colors and I felt very down. She was the second person in less than an hour who had been disgusted with me.

6

The next day, believe it or not, I was still feeling terrible.
I put my Russian tape in the boom box and turned it on
hard so that I could forget about everyone on the planet.
I felt like never going outside again. Jules came in the
room and started spinning around and dancing to the
music, singing in mock Russian as he knocked things
over. There was such a racket in the room, I couldn't help
but feel better. Jules sat on the armchair and I went and
sat on his lap. He was drinking a bottle of tonic water.
That was his favorite drink. For some reason, he thought
it was good for his health. He shared it with me. When
I'd take too long a sip, he'd hit the back of my head and
I'd hand it back to him. I felt his body rock back and
forth to the music. It felt as if we were in a different
country: a country where no matter how badly you
fucked up, you were still loved.

When I was about six, Jules and I used to ride the bus
to the river and talk about everything. Once he found a
Tintin comic under the seat of the bus and was really
excited because he thought it was a classy comic book
from France. He read the bubbles out loud with a
Parisian accent. I hoped that he loved me as much as he
had then.

The buzzer rang from downstairs. I got up to look out
the living room window and see who it was. It was
Lester. I decided not to buzz him in. I leaned on the
sill, waiting for Lester to give up and walk away.
Unfortunately, he rang again.

'What's the matter with you!' Jules exclaimed, and he
turned off the tape.

Lester and Jules sat at the kitchen table drinking and cooking up a scheme. They spoke in conspiratorial tones, as if it were a criminal plan that only street-smart people with a lot of guts could pull off, but the plan wasn't illegal in any way at all. They wanted to get a bunch of chairs from an old school and sell them in St Agathe. Lester had even legitimately rented out a table at the flea market.

'Chairs are expensive. You can charge practically anything you want for a chair and it will sell,' Lester said, just like he was a tough guy or something.

I started bugging my dad by asking him a lot of questions about his venture. It sounded like the kind of trip that would keep him away for days. I was trying to find holes in their plan and shake their confidence.

'How long are you going for?' I asked my dad.

'As long as it takes.'

'Are you going to leave me money?'

'Yes, I always do, don't I?'

'Who the hell's going to loan you a van to carry these chairs in?'

'I got a lot of good friends.'

'What if kids have written their names on the back of the chairs? Who'll buy them then?'

Jules shot me an annoyed look. He made me a plate of spaghetti and told me to go and eat it outside.

I was the only kid who was punished by being sent to the bench outside on the street to eat my food. Jules knew that I found it embarrassing. People must have found me vulnerable and pathetic sitting there in my orange fur coat with a big glass of milk at my side.

I found a bench close by and started scarfing down my spaghetti. Then I saw Leelee coming down the street in my direction. I put my plate of food in the grass beside me and kicked a plastic bag over it. Leelee was in a much better mood than before. She was moseying down the block, trying to get people to dance with her. Leelee acted so comfortable outside, just like she was right in her living room.

'Somebody give me a goddamn cigarette!' Leelee yelled to no one in particular, looking up and down the street.

Nobody gave her anything. Then she finally spotted me and sauntered over, like a cowboy. She sat down next to me.

'So how old are you anyway?' she asked.

'Twelve.'

'Shit, that's really young. So, what, you don't get along with your parents, do you?'

'No, my dad's always splitting.'

'I could tell that your parents weren't any good. My parents really sucked shit, too. That's why now, when I meet someone who has lousy parents, I can tell right off the bat. It's like a sixth sense. But this guy was telling me it's more like psychic intelligence. What about your mom?'

'I don't know where she is,' I lied, since I didn't want to appear to be too much of a loser.

'You have to track her down! She probably just made a mistake leaving you and thinks that you won't forgive her. So if you went up to her door without calling ahead, or anything like that, I'm sure she'd be happy to see you. I'm sure she'd like cry and all that stuff. Like totally weep over you. Women aren't mean the way that men are. They're full of life and they're like God in that way. Like in the story of Adam and Eve, what nobody says is that the snake is really Adam's dick. He was the one who got everybody in trouble. But he doesn't want to admit responsibility for his dick.'

'Really? Is that what the story's about?' I asked.

'Sure! Isn't it goddamn obvious? If God hadn't made a dick for Adam, we'd still be in paradise. God should have given everybody pussies, man!'

'I guess so. Guys are dogs, huh?' I said, trying to get into the spirit of things.

'I think that Al's okay, though. I think that he really likes you. I can see in the way that he acts when you're around. You make him happy. He won't say it because he's a man and men are totally taught to hide their feelings, but I can see that he's in love with you. And I'm really glad because I can tell that you're a good person. I've met a lot of his girlfriends. He used to go out with this girl Robin and they used to fight like cats and dogs. It was a battlefield around them, literally.'

Robin was a girl who always wore a ponytail and had little eyes. She wore black plastic boots with chunky heels that gave her that white-trash walk. Knowing that Alphonse had dated her made him seem less attractive to me.

'I thought you and Al were going out?' I asked.

'No, he's more like my guru. He helps me through shit. I wouldn't want to ever be his girlfriend because that would really fuck up what we have. So don't ever think that I'm a threat, no way, I would not ever want to stand between Al and a good thing. He would kill me. I'd kill myself. I think I'm too wacko to date Al anyway. He needs someone sweet like you. I think you'd be really good for him, make him calm. You're a quiet little mouse.'

I knew that somewhere, somehow, she was calling me a fool. I thought she was a nice person before, but all of a sudden I wasn't so sure. Then I did something that should have shocked her. I jumped up and I stuck my tongue out at her. She just shrugged. She waved her hand in the air as if to say that she'd tried her best. I grabbed my plate and walked quickly down the street.

I didn't like her evaluation of me. I wasn't some docile kid. I wanted to be a wild child. I'd seen some photographs in a magazine of a girl with long curly black hair and a dandelion behind her ear. She'd been sitting on a motorcycle in jeans and a black leather bra. That's who I wanted to be like. I went upstairs with my plate. When I walked into the apartment, Jules had his duffel bag in his hand.

'I'm going to the country with Lester tonight,' he said. 'We can't let any time slip away with this one. Those chairs'll be gone before you know it.'

After Jules and his friend left, I sat on the couch for a while. Then I got up and went to the bathroom. There was a way that you could take the bathroom cabinet mirror off its hinges. I carried it with me into the bedroom. I set it up on a chair in front of the bed so that I could look at myself naked. I put my hands on my head and swayed back and forth. I decided that I was sick to death of being twelve.

7

The next day, I walked down the street eating a peanut butter and jelly sandwich I'd made for myself. I'd put on this puffy Chinese jacket with goldfish on it that Lester had given me as a present the year before. I hadn't brushed my hair or anything. I had a plastic bag on my arm just in case I should spot some bottles along the way.

I decided to turn in a couple bottles at the corner store in exchange for a cigarette so that I could look like a big shot smoking it. The cigarette was too strong for me and made me feel as if I were breathing in gasoline fumes. Finally, I just held the cigarette between my fingers, letting it burn. I always thought that I would be a natural at smoking. I'd sat in front of a mirror while smoking a pencil crayon and thought I looked very good. One of the things that I wanted to do was to be able to blow smoke rings. I was really just a jackass. I'd never get away with looking sixteen at this rate.

As I walked down the street, I heard some loud music and cheering. I turned and saw the community center parade coming down the street. I had seen posters on some poles saying that they were going to put on something to celebrate something called World Friendship Day. I turned the corner and ran as far as I could from it. Even from afar, it seemed so beautiful to me. I wished that I hadn't given up on that place and had kept going. I should have fought Jules on that, considering that I did on everything else now.

I lingered a little outside Alphonse's building. Sure enough, after five minutes of acting as if I'd lost a key or something, he came out. He was wearing an orange leather hat with his hair tucked under it.

'Look who it is! My pretty little wife. I like what you did with your hair. It's really fancy!'

'Thanks,' I said, sticking my finger through a tangle.

'Come on,' he said, just grabbing me by the hand and pulling me along with him. 'Let's go to the Etoile!'

'All right,' I said, happily. I was bored and in the mood for a movie and the Etoile was one of my favorite places.

The Etoile was a ninety-nine-cent movie theater, the only one we ever went to as I was growing up. It was called the junkie theater because people went there just to have a quiet place to be on the nod. Dealers would come up behind you in the middle of the movie and whisper 'Hashish?' in your ear.

Once when I was there, someone stood up and yelled at the zombie on the screen: 'I'm not afraid of you, you fucking bony bastard. Come on down here and I'll kick your fucking ass! I'll rip your arm out of its socket.'

They didn't put the names of the movie on the marquee out front. It just had the black plastic letters that spelled out 'Cheap movies!!! All day EvEry dAy!!!' There were holes in the greasy carpet, and it was better to remember to go to the bathroom before you got there.

Kids from school went to the theaters downtown, not the Etoile. Most weren't even allowed to go there because someone had gotten stabbed in one of the bathrooms. Jules didn't know this.

I was happy that Alphonse wanted to go someplace that reminded me of my childhood. It made me feel safe. I followed along next to him, wondering if we were on a date. I'd never been on a date before. He didn't kiss me or try to touch me, which was a good thing, because if he had I would have jumped a mile. It would have been like sticking a needle in an electrical socket.

'I know you,' Alphonse said to the woman behind the counter. She smiled back at Alphonse.

'One ninety-eight for you two.'

Alphonse handed her two dollars. He started singing a

song that couldn't have really been a song. 'Bingity, bam, bam.' The woman behind the counter laughed.

He bought me a giant orange slushy from the concession stand. We went in and saw that the movie was halfway through. It was *Repo Man*. They'd been playing this movie for four or five years. There were always a lot of people in the audience, even though they'd all seen it a couple of times. Everyone thought it was really radical and punk rock. They would scream out certain lines with the characters. I'd already seen it three times and I never understood what the big deal was.

Alphonse sat staring at the screen for a while and got a disgusted look on his face. He leaned over to me and pointed out a guy on the screen. He was sitting on a box while eating a can of dog food.

'What do you think of that guy?' Alphonse asked me.

The character started talking about his philosophy about how the human race was started by people from the future that had found a time machine. His name was Bud Light. I shrugged. It was just nice that it was a movie without subtitles or too much cheesy sex.

'Do you find that actress pretty?' Alphonse asked, pointing to the screen. 'I would not go near that woman. Is she supposed to be attractive? Why doesn't she dye her hair or buy a dress?'

'She's a veterinarian, though.'

'What's that got to do with anything? What's the plot of this movie?'

Alphonse tapped the guy on the shoulder who was sitting in front of us. He was a skinny guy with a knit jacket, laughing at a lot of the jokes that weren't funny at all.

'Could you tell me what is the plot of this movie?'

Alphonse asked the guy. 'What is the overall meaning? Because I am at a loss and you look like a very intelligent individual.'

'It's about how these people have no souls in a consumeristic world,' the guy said, matter-of-factly.

'Bullshit,' Alphonse said, leaning back. 'He's just reading that into it. The people who put this movie together wouldn't even know what that meant. I should go ask for my ninety-nine cents back just for the principle. I don't buy this whole scenario. Now who is that suspicious-looking guy supposed to be?'

'That's Emilio Estevez!' I exclaimed.

'Emilglio what? That's not a movie star name. If I was a movie star, I would have a very short name that would be easy to remember. People work all day long—they don't have time to be remembering your long, ridiculous names. If I was an actor, I'd name myself Rap Chip or Tim Tut. Nice and simple.'

'Tim Tut sounds like a Chinese restaurant.'

He started laughing at that a really long time. He lit up a cigarette and everybody around us lit up too, but there was pot in his. He handed it to me and I took a deep drag that almost drowned me. I could hardly speak seconds after I exhaled.

Alphonse looked stoned too. He wasn't paying attention to the movie anymore. He just gazed over; I could tell that he was getting all inspired.

'You know what I wish?' he asked me, softly.

'No.'

'Sometimes I wish that I was the only man left on the whole planet. And then every day all these different women would come up to me and I'd have to give them a little love. Just a little peck on the cheek or a flower or something. Enough to get them through the day. That's the way I was born and that's the way I'll die.'

'I wish I could sing,' I said.

'My mother used to be a pretty good singer. If anybody ever had a wedding, she used to go and sing for it. Then she started getting too crazy to be invited to these things. She'd show up at a wedding in a pair of jeans and snow boots in the summer, holding a bag filled with old cans. She'd want to get up on the stage like that and sing. She got like that after my dad died.'

'How did your dad die?'

'My dad used to be a bum. After he left one time, he sent my mother some counterfeit money for child support. He got killed falling off a city bus or some shit like that. I think that his ghost talks to me sometimes.'

'What does he say?'

'Nothing of any use, actually,' he said, sounding blasé about the whole thing. 'He's just bragging about himself. That's all he ever did. He would come and sit at the kitchen table and talk about how wonderful he was. How fast he could run. How good he could drive a car. How fast he could calculate. One time he excused himself to go to the bathroom, but he just grabbed the television and went out the front door. He is the lousiest bastard who ever lived.'

'But do you still go and visit your mother?'

'You know what's wrong with my mother?'

'No.'

'I don't go to see my mother anymore because she has this cat that she thinks is me now. She's like, "Alphonse, what are you doing on the table? You must be on drugs. I don't like that. Why don't you just come over here and watch television with me?" That's the way she talks to the cat. I get confused as fuck when I'm over there. She liked the stupid name so much that it wasn't enough to call me Alphonse, she's got to start naming every animal Alphonse. We used to have a dog named Alphonse too. I was embarrassed to have any friends over.'

He reminded me of the way I bullshitted when I was stoned. The woman next to us overheard and started laughing. Alphonse smiled at her and continued his rant about his mother. A few other people around us started listening in. It wasn't the type of theater where you paid attention to the film, and Alphonse was on a roll.

'Haven't you ever heard of cheapness being a disease? Well, she's got the worst inflamed case of it that ever existed. One time I broke my leg and she didn't want me to take the crutch from the hospital because it cost money. You know you have to pay three dollars a day or something. She told me just to leave it there and that I could use a hockey stick when we got home. So I was hopping out of the hospital and the doctor was like, I'm sorry but this kid needs a crutch. "No, no. It's okay," she was telling the doctor. "I have a crutch at home that's exactly his size."?'

'How did you get home?'

'Who knows? I had to hop. I started dealing when I was nine years old. It was out of necessity. With the money that I made I bought myself a great pair of sneakers, a dress shirt, and a leather jacket. People didn't even recognize me. They wanted to know me and kiss my feet. My mother said that since I was making money I should start paying rent. She raised my rent every week. She wanted me to pay two hundred seventy-five dollars, and I got hold of a receipt and saw that she was only paying two hundred twenty-two total rent! I would have given her the money if she were spending it, but she just hides it under her bed.'

I smiled. I thought he had put all his cards on the table for me. I thought that he trusted me with his life. I was twelve.

After the movie, we walked down St Catherine Street together. My Chinese jacket wasn't warm enough and I wished I'd worn my fur one. I had a feeling that Alphonse didn't care what I had on. When we were alone, he stopped being funny. He turned and looked at me, all serious. He smiled to the side.

'You really are a special thing,' he said. 'So where do you come from anyway?'

I'd always lived in Montreal, but I didn't want to say that. The only other place I'd ever lived was outside Val des Loups in the country.

'I used to live in a foster home. There was this woman named Isabelle who was really nice. There was one kid there who shit in his pants, and he threw his underwear out the window and they got stuck in a tree branch. Isabelle had to go up there with a ladder and get them out.'

'I could tell that. I could tell that you were a country girl. You're wild, you know. You have your own ideas.'

'Isabelle's uncle one time took us kids for a ride in a pickup truck. One time we went out and we were looking at the moon, and it was just so big and orange. We looked at it for an hour.'

He just let me do the talking. The more I talked about myself, the more I felt close and friendly with him.

'Once we had a dog named Muttley. He would follow me all the way to school. But when my dad went to the hospital, we had to give him up.'

'What's wrong with your dad?'

'He had me when he was really young. He was only fifteen. My mother died when I was little. He had to do everything by himself. He goes out of town a lot. He wanted to be a boxer when he was little, but he wasn't strong enough. He used to have a friend who was a Hell's Angel.'

Jules always told me not to tell people your business, not to tell them your past. He said to keep them guessing. He said that once a person knew all there was to know about you, they'd take advantage of you. Trust nobody, he'd told me over and over. In a way, I'd kept his advice up until just then. I was stoned and felt like sharing all my shit with the whole world. I wanted to be taken advantage of.

Alphonse told me to wait on the street corner while he ran into a store to buy something. It was a crazy Korean store that sold booze and little knickknacks for tourists, even though tourists never came to this neighborhood. Alphonse came out with a big bottle of beer in a paper bag. He opened it with a bottle cap opener from his key chain and took a long swig. He handed me the bottle and it felt enormous in my hands. I felt like a little kid holding a cup. I'd never seen this beer before. There was a beautiful swan on the label. I took baby sips while leaning against the window of the store. I stopped being cold right away. The little figurines in baseball caps were screaming happy things at me. Alphonse took my hand and pulled me to get me to start walking again. The volume button kept going up and down on things. It seemed as if all the sounds were coming from inside my head. Not outside my head. It was the way that mermaids hear things.

The booze made me feel alive. I felt like I was being kissed by every person who looked at me. I reached for the bottle as we were walking and drank some more. I didn't even know how much you were supposed to drink. I wanted to be a heroic drinker and guzzle down as much as I could. I wanted to be one of the girls who walked around the park barefoot with butterflies on their breasts. They were always drinking beer and riding on someone's shoulder.

Five blocks later, I was practically toppling over drunk. I can't remember how I was acting exactly, but I do remember a lot of people giving us dirty looks as they passed by. I sat down on the curb and he had to pick me up. I never exactly knew what kind of drunk I would be. It is the best kind of drunk to be.

'Girl! You can't hold your liquor! You're a wreck!'

We passed a pay phone. He held open the door.

'Do you need to call your dad? Did you need to give him some sort of excuse, tell him where you'll be? Like say you're at some girlfriend's house?'

'No. He's in Trois-Rivières tonight.'

He nodded and let the pay phone door swing shut. He asked if I wanted to smoke up with him. I didn't want to go to his house, so we smoked in an alley. There were drawings in Magic Marker of naked women on the wall and skunks farting.

Alphonse leaned in and kissed me. It was a huge kiss that covered my whole mouth. I didn't know that kissing could make you feel so afraid. I closed my mouth very tight while he kissed me. It felt as if I was suffocating, as if he were holding my head down in the bathtub under water. I thought about that old wives' tale about how cats get on top of you and then swallow your breath. They must creep up while you are sleeping and kiss you passionately.

Although I had kissed a lot of other people, that kiss was really my first. For instance, I had a friend named Clare who begged me and begged me to kiss her toe. I'd done it, but that hadn't been my first kiss. A boy named Daniel and I had blindfolded ourselves with sweaters and had tried to kiss. I'd accidentally kissed him on the nose, but that hadn't been my first kiss. I had kissed a boy after losing a coin toss, and even though I had wanted that to be my first kiss, it hadn't been really. The real first kiss is the one that tells you what it feels like to be an adult and doesn't let you be a child anymore. The first kiss is the one that you suffer the consequences of. It was as if I had been playing Russian roulette and finally got the cylinder with the bullet in it.

Afterward, as I headed down the street, everybody was just walking around as if nothing had happened. Some people even smiled at me as I walked by. They didn't know. How could they know I was a messed-up, ragged, dirty, nasty thing?

I slowly walked up the stairs to the empty apartment. But then I heard the Russian tape playing from our place. My heart swelled up. When I heard that music, I could only think about good things. It made me think of when Jules and I used to walk down to the river. We used to sit there holding tin cans that had fishing line wrapped around them. We'd dig holes in the mud with spoons trying to find worms. And that feeling saved me. I liked feeling like a little kid. I didn't know how long I was going to be able to feel that way. I had a feeling that the rest of me might be something crummy and dark.

I opened the door. The table was covered with food. I was surprised to see him back so soon.

'Baby! You won't believe how much money we made at the flea market! We made a killing!'

The woman next to him had been selling a table full of watches, and Jules had bought me a huge pink one with digital numbers you could see a mile away. He wrapped the plastic band around my wrist, then he ran and turned off the tape player. He came back and picked up my wrist. He squeezed the buttons on each side and all of a sudden the watch began to play a tune. Its metallic little beeps played the most beautiful version of 'Love Me Tender' ever heard on the planet.

'Happy birthday, Baby,' he said.

It was true, the very next day was my birthday and I would be thirteen. He had little gifts for me spread out on the kitchen table. I used to jump up and down and hit the roof when Jules brought home gifts for me. Now the mess on the table looked as if he'd taken apart a robot looking for its heart. I started to cry. Now our love would always be injured in a way. There was a mark on the inside of me that felt as if it wasn't going to go away.

Jules looked at me all destroyed when he saw my tears. They disguised how high I was.

'Things are going to be okay, Baby. Look, I'm going to start making decent money. I'm going to make sure that I go to all the flea markets. And I'm going to get my driver's license back, so that Lester can take a break and we can make twice as many trips. If we make a hundred dollars every three days, we can make a thousand dollars a month. Or if I can sell door-to-door in the country, I could make at least eight hundred a month without even renting a table.'

I stood there as Jules continued to make his calculations. It was as if he was Galileo, absolutely sure that if he just kept doing his math problems, soon he'd have proof that the earth went around the sun. But I didn't buy it. I knew that he was in no position to be calculating the heavens, much less our futures.

Suddenly I realized that I wanted everything to be as it was when I was younger. When you're young enough, you don't know that you live in a cheap lousy apartment. A cracked chair is nothing other than a chair. A dandelion growing out of a crack in the sidewalk outside your front door is a garden. You could believe that a song your parent was singing in the evening was the most tragic opera in the world. It never occurs to you when you are very young to need something other than what your parents have to offer to you.

the milky way

1

Once I auditioned for the school play even though I was convinced I wasn't going to be chosen for any part. I held the script in front of my face and whispered the words. And so, naturally, I wasn't chosen.

There were a lot of things that I had done that I felt funny about. I had let someone give me a homemade tattoo of a tiny moon on my knee with a bottle of India ink and a needle. I'd screamed my head off, but I'd let them do it. I had worn an undershirt in summer, thinking it was a regular T-shirt. I had lain down on a mattress that had been put in the trash and contemplated the clouds. I had drawn a face on an eraser and had named him Marc and had carried him around. I had fed the stray cat that everybody said had rabies. I'd been bitten by dogs twice. I had collected beer bottles in the park and had harassed the corner store owners to cash them in.

These were the kinds of things that you did when you didn't have a mother.

Once my friend's mother had taken us both to the swimming pool. She was wearing a bikini and let us roll the flab on her belly like it was bread dough. I'd never felt anything like that. I wanted desperately to have my own mother whose belly I could poke whenever I pleased.

Jules tried to be a mother, but he'd always kind of fallen short of the mark. He gave me a mount for holding toothpaste that you screw on the wall as a present to bring to a birthday party. For lunch, he'd give me a sandwich that the cheese had fallen out of. He never remembered when it was picture day. If you look at any of my class photos, you will see that I am the messy kid. I also look like I stink in those pictures. A lot of kids get the privilege of looking at themselves through their mothers' eyes. I could only see myself through my own eyes, and sometimes I could barely stand to look.

Mothers pushed their kids to do things. Sometimes even really poor kids that I knew were taken to piano lessons. Nothing like that interested or even occurred to Jules. He figured that he might have to fill out a form, and he avoided anything that involved that. I had never even been able to complete a drawing.

When Alphonse came into my life, it strangely felt a little bit like he was a mother figure. Every good pimp is a mother. When Alphonse spoke to me, his voice always had the same tempo as a lullaby.

Alphonse continued to get me gifts that I couldn't help but like. He bought me a tube of silky moisturizing cream. I liked the smell of it so much that I put it all over my arms. I smelled my hands while I was watching *Last Tango in Paris* at the Etoile. He gave me a notebook and told me that I should write him a letter in it every day and then give it to him after a month or maybe after six months. He gave me a huge amber ring, with a crack in it that looked like a woman dancing.

Alphonse and I went to the photo booth at the subway station to have my photograph taken. It hadn't occurred to Jules to take my photograph in years. He didn't seem to realize that one day I wouldn't be a kid anymore. There would be nothing to remember me by. I climbed into the photo booth and posed with my lips puckered for my little black-and-white glamour shots.

I hid the photographs at the back of my T-shirt drawer, but Jules found them anyway. Jules accused me of sleeping with a pimp. I'm not sure how he figured out that Alphonse had paid for the pictures or that he was a pimp. A lot of people had seen Alphonse and me hanging around together, and anyone could have told Jules. I got down on my hands and knees and swore to Jules that it wasn't true. He kicked me out anyway.

When Jules was mad, I used to sleep over at my friends' houses until he cooled off. But this time he was really angry and called social services and told them that he'd kicked me out of the house. The cops picked me up in St Louis Square. I was stoned and was letting some twenty-seven-year-old guy who claimed to be a wizard cast a spell on me with a stick. When I laughed, I could see my breath, and it looked like the fairies on heavy-metal T-shirts. I was still laughing hysterically when I got into the back of the cop car.

2

At the waiting room of Family Services downtown, I felt as if I were in formaldehyde, one of the little fetuses in jars in the chemistry lab at our school. I'd been removed from my natural environment and brought here to be studied. If someone stuck a pin in my side, I doubt that I would have felt anything. Lots of times when children draw a person on a blank piece of paper, they don't draw any background at all, just a person standing there without any context. That was me.

I didn't know what was in store for me now. They were going to hand me a tumor and were going to ask me to put it inside of me. It is important to hate the people who work in child welfare if you want to protect yourself from their prognosis. You have to think that they are idiots. Because when they say that you are troubled and a delinquent, you need to be able to laugh in their faces.

But I didn't hate them at that moment. The drugs had worn off and I felt awful and low. I would have believed anything they said. I must have had quite a look of desperation on my face when the social worker came out because she looked afraid to say anything to me. But she still managed to communicate that I would be going to the correctional facility. This decision was apparently based on who Jules said I was hanging out with and because I was stoned when they came to get me. I was going that night and I wasn't even allowed to pack a bag. Apparently, it wasn't necessary to bring anything from my sad life along with me.

I rode in the back of a social worker's car out to the country to the correctional facility. The hills around us were covered with bright autumn colors, as if hundreds of little kids' sweaters had been unraveled. The curtain between acts in my life was always a dense forest. It was impossible for me to know what was going to happen when the trees parted. As we turned off the main highway, I looked at the little woman dancing in the amber ring that Alphonse had given me. I thought the little lady in the ring and I were now in some sort of terrible trouble.

*

The detention center was surrounded by a huge fence. I was shocked when I saw it because I realized for the first time that I was being sent to a sort of prison.

The building was a really long hall with rooms off the hallway. There were bars in the windows and alarms on every door leading outside. The floor tiles had a pattern of little stones on them. I tried, for a moment, to pretend that I was walking on the bottom of a lake, but it didn't work. The building was divided into two wings. One was a wing for violent children who had actually committed crimes. These were the children who rightfully hated the world around them and wanted to get even with it. The other wing, to which I was brought, was for children who had run away from home or were doing drugs, things like that. It was for those who turned their aggression inward and weren't actually hurting anyone but themselves. You could easily be sent to the violent ward the minute you showed any sort of hostility toward any of the staff.

I didn't feel any anger, though. I missed Jules and I couldn't believe that he had sent me away. At least I was put on the wing for nonviolent kids.

It's almost pointless to describe the whole month I was in detention. So many weird, unusual things happened in one day, and yet all the days were exactly the same. And apparently, when you have no future, there is really no such thing as time anyway. We only had class two hours a day, and the rest of the time we spent doing strange useless stuff. I found a beetle outside and put it in a pre-scription pill bottle and put it beside my bed for a pet. One boy ate pages out of his math book. Someone shit in the hallway in the back. We spent an afternoon collecting snails and taking them out of their shells. We invented a game where one person would run across the yard while everyone else whipped little stones at him. A boy plucked out all his eyebrows. One boy had a tattoo of a third eye on his forehead; a lot of girls had decided that they were in love with him. He was destined for failure, and so he was someone they really wanted to hook up with. He stuck a fork into a cavity in his tooth on purpose. We wanted to be convinced that feeling bad was a good thing. We were supposed to be streetwise, but we were like little children who only wanted to be.

When it started to snow, one thing we did was to stand outside with no coats on. You had to think that you were a superhero and that the cold could not affect you. It could not even touch you. Or at least that's what I had to do. Your superhuman power was to be able not to feel. Is it there inside of everybody, this self that comes out while you are in captivity? You become the closest approximation of yourself that can tolerate living there.

I never felt so lonely in my life. Jules was in Montreal without me. If I sat and dredged up any good memories of myself and Jules, I would feel absolutely horrible afterward. It was like I was rotting inside. Nostalgia could kill you there. So I stopped myself from having those memories of Jules.

I liked to go to the nurse's office and describe the symptoms of Jules's TB, trying to pass them off as my own. She would tap on my back and chest and put the stethoscope up to my breastbone. I heard my heartbeat through her mind, and it felt wonderful. It was lovely to be touched by a caring adult.

I wasn't the only one looking for this type of affection. There was a social worker who gave haircuts. A lot of the kids were practically bald because they liked the feeling of her cutting their hair and fussing with it so much.

You couldn't get much support from the rest of the staff, however. They had all lost faith in their profession after spending a couple years working in juvenile corrections. You could not make a child with bad memories into a kid with good memories. A really effective social worker would have to be a time traveler who could go back in time and undo the abuse most kids here had suffered. Anyhow, the worst social workers were sent out here to the middle of nowhere. The members of the staff were all sneaky-looking. Most of them seemed to sit behind their desks in a sort of coma. The only ones who were interested in the kids were the ones who were molesting them.

There was a time between nine thirty and ten right before lights went out when the evening shift went home and the night shift had not yet arrived. The only person overseeing our wing was a social worker named Antoine. Now, this social worker was madly in love with a boy named Constance. They hung out in Antoine's office together, until the night staff came. During this half hour the rest of us were left to our own devices. We used to gamble with dice for kisses and pour liquid soap all over the floor.

One night, during our unsupervised half hour, I went out in the yard for a smoke. I didn't like the taste, but I liked to watch the smoke roll out of my mouth, like unicorns. It had snowed for the first time that year and now it was winter. The world got all quiet after it snowed, as though everything and everyone had died. I used to sit out there and imagine that the bomb had fallen. Back then everyone used to speculate on what life would be like after the bomb.

After the bomb, I figured that buttons would be used as currency. Once you traded your buttons for something to eat, you would have to hold your sweater together with your hands. There would be only one lightbulb in town, and you would have to pay dearly to sit underneath it. You would pack your suitcase full of the screws that you had managed to find here and there and move to another city in the middle of the night, hoping it hadn't been hit as hard. At the flea market, you would buy a tape of someone screaming at their wife in the apartment next door because you would miss the sounds of ordinary life.

It would be hard to laugh anymore. You would have to pay a prostitute to tickle you and to read to you from a paperback book of jokes. It would be time for the androids to take over, but they would not have been invented yet. Certain fanatics would volunteer to have their limbs replaced with prosthetic ones.

Before the bomb, your mother embroidered a bird on your pea coat. Once the threads came undone, there were no more birds. Someone would swear they had seen a sparrow, but everyone would have become a liar.

It was hard to imagine that the real world was out there somewhere in the night and that it hadn't all been destroyed. I couldn't possibly imagine what my life was going to be like in the future when I returned to it.

Even though it was freezing out, I noticed that a girl with wet hair had come out in her shorts to smoke a cigarette. She had just taken a shower and the steam was rising up off her hair like a halo. I noticed that she had a cesarean scar on her belly. She smiled at me.

On the way back to my room, the girl with the scar asked if I wanted to go see Ralphy get naked.

'Why's he doing that?'

'Everybody has to go through it. His name was pulled out of the hat this morning.'

I had heard tell of this activity, naturally, but had hoped somehow I'd continue to be excluded from it. She hurried me down to the end of the hall, where we crammed ourselves into a little room. A scrawny boy of about thirteen was standing in the middle of the room with his eyes closed.

Ralphy never spoke to anyone. If the teacher asked him a question, he would just stare back expressionlessly. He whispered sometimes, but you couldn't hear him. He was the person who had most mastered the superhero skill of invisibility. Sometimes when I looked at him, I had a hard time believing he was real, or at least as real as the rest of us. All I knew about him was that he liked to draw spirals in his notebooks, hundreds of them. He had a radio that didn't pick up any signals. A social worker had given it to him as a birthday present because he hadn't gotten a present from anyone else. He sometimes walked around the yard with the antenna straight up, trying to stumble across a sound.

'Start already, Ralphy,' someone said.

Ralphy started to sway his skinny hips back and forth. He put his hands in the air and started to pull his sweater off. It felt as if there was a dove fluttering around under my jacket as I realized he was really going to take off all his clothes. Some of the kids cheered. Others just sat there calmly, as if not even this could make them feel anything.

Finally, Ralphy was left wearing nothing but a pair of stretched underwear around his hips. When he shook them quickly, the underwear came down little by little until they finally slipped down around his ankles. The only thing that Ralphy had on now was a house key hanging from a shoelace around his neck. I thought he was pretty, but I noticed that the other kids could barely stand the sight of him. He reminded them too much of themselves. You looked at his ribs sticking out and his stretched-out underwear around his ankles and you shuddered and wondered, Is this what I've become? This was the type of thing that might happen to you in an anxiety dream. That's what happens when no one is able to look after you. Terrible, absurd, and humiliating scenarios are no longer the stuff that dreams are made of.

'You'd never make a dime stripping, Ralphy!' an older kid yelled. 'Who would want to look at your sorry ass?'

Everyone laughed hard, as this joke distanced us from Ralphy's predicament. He kept his eyes closed and stood still and naked. And he really was as naked as the day he was born. God had created us without clothes, but it was still a horrific thing. I looked at every part of Ralphy. I noticed that he had a cut on his knee. Someone should kiss it better, I thought. He was covered with invisible wounds that would never really heal.

Suddenly, the bell that signaled that we should return to our rooms sounded. We ran out of the room as Ralphy hurried to get dressed. I walked down the hallway alone. It was better to keep to yourself here, I figured.

I shared my room with two other girls. The lights went out and they both scrambled under their covers and went to sleep. The day before, one of the girls had informed me that the best way to get out of here was to attempt suicide and get taken to the hospital and escape from there.

'It's a risk,' she said, 'but it's totally worth it to get out of this toilet bowl.'

Other children had offered me other possible ways to escape that didn't seem too viable, since they were still in here. I changed into the white men's pajamas with enormous butterfly collars that I'd been issued. They were too big, but I didn't care. I pulled a paperback book out from under my mattress and examined it lovingly. This was how I escaped from the prison.

I'd been carrying the book around in my pocket for the past couple weeks. I felt so lucky that I happened to have had it when I was picked up. It was a copy of Réjean Ducharme's *L'avalée des avalés*, *The Swallower Swallowed*. It wasn't one of Alphonse's presents; a girl in the park had given it to me. She said that someone is always given a copy of *L'avalée des avalés* by someone else and that you can't buy it. It was the story of a young girl who was at once enraptured and furious with the world.

I had always liked reading, but lately I had started reading in a different kind of way. When I opened a book now, I was seized with desperation. I felt as if I was madly in love. It was as if I were in a confession booth and the characters in the book were on the other side telling me their most intimate secrets. When I read, I was a philosopher and it was up to me to figure out the meaning of things. Reading made me feel as if I were the center of the universe.

I lay down on my bed and flicked on the tiny nightlight next to my bed. Although it only gave off the smallest puddle of light, my eyes slowly adjusted to the darkness and the words became clear.

Tout m'avale... Je suis avalée par le fleuve trop grand, par le ciel trop haut, par les fleurs trop fragiles, par les papillons trop craintifs, par le visage trop beau de ma mère...

It was impossible to say that I was pitiful after I had read *L'avalée des avalés* for an hour. I put the book under my pillow and turned off the light.

It was necessary to have a black chalkboard to be able to see the words written on it in chalk. The stars are always up in the sky. You just can't see them during the day until the sky becomes dark. Then when it is perfectly black, they feel less vulnerable and out they come. To see the stars properly, you have to be out in the country where there are no streetlights or lights from apartment windows. When you stood outside the detention center, it was almost shocking how many stars were out there. This is where they were all sent to. So that nobody could see them but one another.

3

One night, the girl with the cesarean scar came up to me in the cafeteria and told me that it was my turn to take my clothes off. Everyone stripped when their name came up. Once a boy named Bing had refused to go to the room to strip. Everybody ignored him now and wouldn't even look at him in the cafeteria. He sat in his black T-shirt looking sadly out the window. It was the only rule the kids had invented. It gave us a sense of power over at least one aspect of our own lives.

I had been dreading my name coming up, but I was glad to be able to get it over with. I had decided that when it came my turn to strip, I would keep my eyes open. I wouldn't shut them as Ralphy had. I would act as if it was nothing for me to take my clothes off. I would not crack on the scaffold; I would go to my hanging with dignity.

About thirty kids crammed into my room at nine thirty and whispered harshly for everyone to shut up. We couldn't really play music during the strip shows, as it would attract the attention of the staff. One boy named Julian had taken to humming during the performances, and I listened intently as I started to unbutton my flannel shirt. It didn't make me feel any better about taking my clothes off. It wasn't my fault, and it wasn't the boy's fault either. It wasn't any of our faults.

I took off my undershirt with the yellow and red flowers on it. I didn't even own a bra. I thought for a moment that this would cause an uproar, that everyone would start screaming with laughter. Everybody got quiet when they saw that I was shaking. I could hardly get the button of my jeans open because my fingers didn't seem to be functioning. My whole body was acting as if it was very cold and I'd just stepped out of the swimming pool. If someone blew on me, I would turn into ice and break into a million pieces.

Then as I took my underwear off, I closed my eyes. And I realized why Ralphy had closed his eyes. It was because he was praying. I was praying that someone would come up and wrap their arms around me and hide my nakedness. I wished and wished in the darkness that I was not alone, but no one came. I remembered that little boy Zachary from the foster home in Val des Loups who always believed that his mother was coming to get him. Right at that moment, I knew exactly what he felt like.

The bell rang and the humming stopped. I heard

everyone running out of the room. I opened one eye, and even with one eye I knew that things were different for me now.

It is a fact that things always get worse for children after a stint in juvenile detention. Being there does something to you morally. When I left a month later, I felt much more vulnerable. I was like one of those baby birds that fall out of their nests in the spring and are virtually impossible to rescue; they need an amount of attention that no one can give them.

I was supposed to be able to leave right before Christmastime, but the social worker informed me that Jules was sick and was going to be in the hospital for a couple nights. Jules usually got sick at the beginning of every winter, but we'd always managed to spend Christmas together. As long as I could remember, Jules and I had had our Christmas dinners at the soup kitchen at the Mission on St Laurent Street. Last Christmas they had served a plate of turkey and french fries with white bread and all the Pepsi Cola you could drink. Jules never got me a Christmas present because they had a bag of donated gifts for the children there. As I unwrapped mine, Jules and I would both hold our breath, equally excited to see what the present would be.

Big deal, I thought, determined not to care about missing such a paltry affair.

The children who weren't allowed to go home were all eating dinner in the cafeteria with their parents or second cousins or whoever had come to visit them. A social worker invited me, but I asked permission to stay in my room. I lay in bed reading a book on formal wear in Edwardian England that I'd found in the broom closet among the donated books that they referred to as a library. Their book selection consisted mostly of Harlequins and outdated science textbooks, so this wasn't too bad. I turned to the page on decorated buttons and tried to ponder their beauty instead of my own loneliness, trying to will myself into being a sociopath.

I met with the social worker my last afternoon there. She had a walleye. I had this terrible habit of turning to see what she was looking at. She told me that I was going to be able to go back to Montreal to live with my father. I left the detention center with only a plastic bag that had my paperback book in it. It was strange. I had no idea why I had been there, or what had been the point, exactly. I wished she would have explained it to me and pointed out to me how I was more suitable for society now.

She did tell me that she thought my dad was too young and immature to offer me much guidance in life and that he was still trying to figure things out for himself. This added to my confusion, making me wonder if it was because of me that Jules was kind of a fuckup. He had to take care of me when he was fifteen instead of going to school or traveling the world or finding a career. Maybe it was me who dragged him down and not the other way around.

We just sat in silence after she said that. I pointed to the door to indicate that I wanted to leave, and she nodded. I walked to the front door of the detention center, a free person, I suppose.

I remembered one time when my dad and I had gone to a flea market on the other side of the river, right after you took the city bus over the giant Jacques Cartier Bridge. We stopped to watch a man emptying boxes of doves from the back of a truck into a bigger cage. He reached his hand into the smaller cage and transferred the doves into the big cage one by one. They looked so soft. They were the color of a cup of coffee that had been filled with too much cream. They stood on the newspaper muttering prayers under their breaths. All of a sudden one of the doves burst out of the man's hand like a magic trick. The dove circled around our heads crazily for a moment, as though it were an idea or a thought bubble and couldn't decide who it belonged to. Then it flew up into the sky and was lost against the clouds.

'That little guy had so much balls!' Jules cried. 'Did you see him just get the hell out of there! He'd been planning it all along. Don't tell me that bird isn't a master criminal.'

The owner of the doves looked at Jules as though he was completely out of his mind.

playing grown-up

1

Jules showed up with his friend Lester to pick me up. Jules didn't say a word to me as we drove to the city. Lester coughed uncomfortably once in a while, but that was all we had in the way of conversation. Lester dropped us off in front of a building I recognized, with glazed white bricks on the facade. It was just another building in the long string of lousy places that we had lived in. Still, I was surprised that we'd moved here. It was so bottom of the basement. Only welfare cases and junkies ever seemed to live in this building.

The white bricks still managed to give the impression of being really dirty. It was called the punk rock building because a bunch of punk rockers lived in one of the bigger apartments. They would stand in the doorway in their pajamas. There was a sign in the lobby directed at them that read DO NOT BUM FOR CHANGE IN THE LOBBY. On the first of the month, a crowd of eighteen-year-olds waited there for their welfare checks. They hopped up and down and danced a little jig when they saw the postman coming.

One of the punk kids used to stand outside the building with a guitar and do really ridiculous versions of popular songs. He couldn't sing at all. He strummed his guitar so hard that it sounded like a pot lid falling on the ground. I always wished I had change, so I could strike up a conversation. Once I returned some beer bottles and gave him the change, but he still didn't really acknowledge me. It made me feel terribly lonely.

I couldn't look Jules in the eye anymore. I couldn't get it out of my head that he was a rat to have sent me to juvenile detention. We just kept to ourselves, even when we were on opposite sides of the breakfast table. Jules looked at me one morning, shortly after I'd returned, and his face trembled and turned red as tears rolled down it. There was part of me that thought he was faking. He kept on crying and I started to feel deeply crummy. I felt bad for Jules and wanted him to be happy.

'It's okay,' I said. 'Don't worry about it, Dad.'

I had liked my very first social worker, Corey, who was assigned to me after I got home. She put makeup on her face to make it white and smelled like baby powder. She had black hair that was teased up in random directions. I thought she must be mad to think that her hairstyle looked good. It made her endearing. She always brought me broken toys, which made me so sad I couldn't speak. I'd get all choked up when she put her arm around me.

Then one day I had a new social worker, a slim Indian man with a British accent who took notes all the time. I was in shock. What a fool I was. I realized that I had thought Corey loved me, but she hadn't even said good-bye.

After that, I had a string of different social workers. I didn't understand how it was that I couldn't have the same social worker for a few weeks even. They often got my file mixed up and thought that I had gone to juvenile detention for being a prostitute. All I had done was date a pimp.

I didn't even know where I was supposed to go to school. A well-dressed and intimidating social worker came over and explained the situation to me. After I was in detention, my regular high school didn't want to take me back. I was considered a system kid, and they didn't have the facilities to deal with a system kid. That was just their policy and had nothing to do with me.

The social worker had arranged for me to go to a high school that had a special program for delinquent kids who weren't good at school. It was a school called Regent Academy, although it was known throughout the neighborhood by a different name.

'I have to go to Bobo Academy?' I said in disbelief.

'There are some good students there who go on to graduate. There's a regular high school program. You'll probably be happier in the remedial class. They have a lot of life skills classes that teach you things that'll be more suited for everyday experiences.'

'Like for English we would write a grocery list?'

'Exactly. Or I saw one project where the kids wrote personal ads. I thought that was really neat. In math, you learn to organize a budget.'

'I don't have any money.'

'See! Having a budget might turn that problem around.'

I didn't bother explaining that I'd been on the honor roll at my last school. That I had to go to a program for kids who had learning disabilities just made me sad beyond words. When I got sad like that, I was struck dumb. It felt as if I'd never be able to speak. She kept asking me questions, but at this point, I couldn't say a single word.

'Is there something wrong?' she asked me, all matter-of-fact, when she noticed that I was crying. I shook my head. 'Then why aren't you talking to me?'

I shrugged. She said that I had to go to see a psychologist on Fridays to figure out what was wrong with me. If I didn't show up, she'd call my dad and I might have to go back to the detention center.

It was late January and winter now. The sky was the color of lightbulbs that weren't lit. There was something frustrating about it. The city always looked like it was just about to get dark, as if the day was always over. Even first thing in the morning you had the feeling that you were running out of time and could never accomplish anything.

It had snowed the night before, and as I stepped onto the front steps of the building, everything seemed so clean, as if the world had finally tidied up after itself. I noticed some bird footprints all over the light layer of snow on the sidewalk, making it look like a Chinese menu. I set off knowing I wasn't the first one to ruin the pristine snow. My feet made a sloshing noise as I walked, as though someone was sucking their teeth at me.

I found out right away that Bobo Academy was run by system kids. They wouldn't let any of the kids in the regular stream sit on the school steps with them. They wouldn't let them wear Ozzy Osbourne or Metallica T-shirts or any other heavy-metal band pins. They weren't even allowed to talk about liking them, for that matter. They weren't allowed to wear black jean jackets or fedoras. They weren't allowed to come out and try to bum a cigarette.

The system kids at Bobo Academy were proud of being messed up. There was a hierarchy there and they were somehow at the top. In moral religious education class on my first day, the teacher was fifteen minutes late. The kids sat around bragging loudly about their mental disorders, diagnosing their own conditions. As if they didn't have enough problems, they had to insist that they were mentally ill. Being manic depressive seemed to be regarded as romantic.

'I'm bipolar.'

'That's nothing. I have manic depression. I have it hormonally. My dad had it and his dad before him. I'm just not taking pills for it, either. It's our way.'

'I'm schizophrenic. But only mildly. It might get worse. I'm passive aggressive.'

'Passive aggressive! That's not a disease!'

'Wait, it's something. I can't remember what the doctor said.'

'I'm suicidal.'

'So, I attempted suicide.'

'You did not.'

'I did so. Toby found me.'

'You scratched your wrists. You didn't even slice them open. They weren't gushing blood or anything.'

'It doesn't matter how successful you were. Just trying counts as having attempted suicide.'

'You just did it for attention. Because you knew that I was going to be back with the pizza in like one minute.'

'Fuck you. You don't understand anything about it.'

The girl who claimed to have attempted suicide stood up and stormed off. It was a real blow to your self-esteem to have your suicidal tendencies challenged. She kicked the door of the classroom open, and it smashed into the teacher. She got suspended for that.

At lunch that day, I sat with a gang of kids from my class on the school steps. They were all wearing flimsy clothes, as if freezing to death was the least of their worries. They were talking about the correct ways to beat other people up.

'If you hit the guy at the bottom of the nose, that can kill him,' this guy Kevin told me. 'You have to hit one eye and then the other to totally disorient him. Give him two black eyes. That's my calling card. If you see a guy walking down the street with two black eyes, you know him and me tangoed.'

Later I learned that Kevin was famous for having demonstrated a punch on himself and breaking his own nose.

They spent the lunch hour telling stories about people they had tried to murder. Once you started telling these kinds of stories, you couldn't talk about anything else. Everybody shut up and listened closely. It was like preaching the word of God. You could stand on a milk crate and tell these stories and all the system kids would gather around to hear them be told.

'Do you have any good stories from juvie, Baby?' Kevin asked me.

'I used to share a room with a girl named Simone. Her brother ripped off some drug dealers. So they found him and they buried him alive in his underwear. His mother had him cremated and she kept his ashes in a shoe box under her bed. She kept the blinds closed and lay there. That's how come Simone ended up in detention, because her mother let her run around all night. One time her mother came to visit her. She was running up and down the hallways looking for Simone. She came into our room and she begged Simone to take off her shoe and her sock. Then she counted Simone's toes. When she saw that Simone still had five toes, she was all happy.'

All the kids were quiet. They looked at me, as if they were trying to recognize who the hell I was. I sort of felt as if I'd done something mean to them.

I said good-bye and quickly headed down the stairs to the technical drawing class that was in the basement of the school. I sat down at my desk and, along with the other students in the class, took out my rulers and graph paper. For the next hour we tried to reconstruct and make sense of the universe. Luckily, most of our designs always ended up in the wastepaper basket. Lucifer was probably sitting there in the guise of one of these children, making his cryptic ambitious blueprints. He was the one child who still believed in evil. He was the one who hadn't figured out yet that it brings you no joy at all.

2

After a couple of weeks at that school, it felt as if I'd been there forever. As for Alphonse, whose gift had gotten me into detention in the first place, I assumed that he'd forgotten who I was. I was coming home from school when I finally saw him. He was wearing a white down-filled jacket and had a skullcap over his dreadlocks. I'd forgotten how well built he was, since I'd just been hanging around with scrawny high school kids. His blue eyes were bigger than I remembered too. I felt embarrassed about the way that I looked.

I was wearing a black knit cap with yellow stars on it and my fur coat and these awful green moon boots. Jules had destroyed everything I owned while I was in detention. He said that he couldn't be sure what had been given to me by the pimp and that he couldn't take any chances. He'd even destroyed my old gym uniform. Why would a pimp buy me that? I was stuck wearing the dorky secondhand clothes that my social worker brought over. I thought that my ugly clothes probably made me look even younger than thirteen and that Alphonse would be turned off for good.

I didn't know how I felt about him, but I did know that I wanted him to like me. I couldn't take the shock of seeing him. I put my hands over my face.

'Don't be like that,' I heard Alphonse say. 'Let me see your face. I missed you. I thought about you every day.'

I smiled at him through my hands and he smiled back. He had this way of making only one side of his mouth smile that always made me feel like a silly little adorable kitten. He leaned in so I could feel his breathing against my ear. I wasn't sure if I actually heard what I think I heard. I was afraid later on that I might have imagined it, because it was what I had wanted to hear so badly.

'You belong to me,' Alphonse had whispered, and his breath warmed the whole side of my face.

I knew what all the hubbub about commitment was. I wanted desperately to belong to someone. It didn't really matter who. Suddenly it seemed as if everything in the world was going to be all right.

I met Alphonse after school at a tiny arcade. There were little tables in the back where you could sit and drink Cherry Coke for a couple hours with no one bugging you to move along. The place was so small that I walked back and forth and up and down the block a couple times trying to find it. There were eight crummy hot dog shops on that block, so it was hard to establish any landmarks. In the arcade, Alphonse and I played a game where you held a really big black gun and fired at people on the screen. I screamed out loud whenever I hit anyone.

Afterward, as we were walking down the street, I showed him a handstand against the side of a building. We stopped outside the strip joint. There was aluminum foil in the window with pictures of nude dancers tacked onto it. Standing outside in the cold, it seemed impossible that anyone could ever be as naked as the girls in those pictures. Alphonse and I pointed out which strippers we found the prettiest.

'I thought that strippers were supposed to be ugly,' I said.

'These are guest stars. The ordinary girls are pretty ugly and they have weird tastes in music.'

I went over to his house. I took off my winter clothes and sat in my jogging pants and yellow T-shirt. He made us a big plate of spaghetti, sprinkling pot liberally into the sauce, and it was the best I'd ever tasted. He put on a Nina Hagen record and turned it up hard. He'd always liked women singers who sounded like men.

'She just totally rips me up inside,' Alphonse said, slouching next to me on the couch. 'She opens up all my old wounds. Feel my hands. It makes my blood run cold, I swear to God.'

Alphonse started making these plans for us to go to New York City to see Nina Hagen in concert someday. He said that we could live in a little hotel room there and become alcoholics. It was the most beautiful plan I'd ever made with anyone. I didn't know you could make plans like that.

We lay down quietly next to each other on the bed, listening to music. It was putting me under a spell, and when Alphonse put his hand out to me, I held it. Then he rolled over and moved on top of me. It shocked me when he took his shirt off. I'd never realized how big he was. When Jules took his shirt off, the shock was how skinny he was. The boys at the swimming pool always looked so much tinier and littler when they took off their shirts and stood there with their toes turned in. Alphonse seemed like he was in a whole other league of human beings than I was. He looked about the size of three of me. I couldn't even imagine how it was that he was on top of me and not squashing me to death, but he wasn't heavy. Although each part of me was able to move, I was still pinned down. I wasn't sure what part of me was pinned down or how I was pinned down. We had become a part of each other.

I hardly even touched him, but it didn't seem necessary. Somehow every part of me was being touched by him. Every part of me was full of him. I couldn't move a finger on my hand or my knee without squishing against him. I felt helpless. He sucked on my fingers and then he held my hand up against his face and licked my palm. My whole body seemed wet.

He put his hand on my side and then slid his hand right up to my breast. I was stricken by panic for a second. I thought he was going to be freaked at how small my breasts were. They hadn't even really started to grow yet. I had to look sideways in a mirror to notice them, and even then I thought that maybe I was just imagining their existence. But Alphonse moaned with delight touching them and suddenly I felt relaxed and at ease. He lifted up my shirt and put his mouth on my nipple. It sent waves through me, soft ones, and I hoped everything else would be soft the same way. He took my shirt off. Then he raised himself up and looked at me lying there between his legs.

'God, you are so pretty,' he said.

After he said that, his kisses began to feel good. They were like tubes of lipstick being crushed against my mouth. I took comfort in his kisses. They were so soft now. They made me smile. His lips tasted like my tears, so I realized that I was crying. They were like kissing baby's feet. It was as if little babies were stepping on me.

He turned off the light before making love to me. His room was dark like a grave. When I closed my eyes, it wasn't as if he was on top of me. There was just a weight. I was making love to the Invisible Man. It felt like something terrible had happened to me and he was comforting me.

As I walked home, the line of gray buildings seemed to be shoved together like the letters cut out of a newspaper and stuck together on a ransom note. The sky was the color of an X-ray of Jules's lungs that used to be tacked to our wall. A well-dressed teenager yelled at me from across the street that fur was murder. That happened a lot, but now it really made me want to kill myself.

When I got home, the apartment was empty. I peeled off my clothes and walked to the bathroom naked. I felt as if my insides were cold. I turned on the hot water and stuck my hand under it, waiting to feel warm-blooded again. I looked in the cabinet mirror and told myself that it didn't matter. So I believed my reflection, since there was no one else telling me what to do. I filled the bathtub with hot water and the mirror became fogged up and I couldn't see myself in it anymore.

Early the next morning there was a knock at the door. It was a postman with a registered letter addressed to my dad. Jules was still fast asleep so I signed for it and opened it up in the kitchen. It said that we were behind in the rent and if we didn't do something to rectify the situation they'd take action to have us evicted.

I looked around and realized I would be glad never to come back to this place. What unsettled me was that Jules hadn't been paying the rent. I hadn't even realized this. Jules always tried to pay the rent. It was only when things were really bad that he couldn't. That we were actually getting evicted must have meant that things were at their worst. I had been so busy with destroying my own life that I hadn't realized he was doing the same with his.

I should have noticed the signs that he was heading for the street. He didn't eat anymore. He smoked all the butts in the ashtray in order to get one last puff out of them. He spent practically the whole night in the bathtub. He started collecting things that had no apparent value. He brought home a ceramic teddy bear with balloons; he washed it in the kitchen sink and put it on the coffee table in the living room. As I looked at it now, it was so ugly it broke my heart.

I realized that he'd been sad. When he was depressed, he acted as if he were deaf, as if he couldn't hear what was around him. He distanced himself from the world. He started to have the habit some homeless people have, of standing still. You see only the beautiful things when you stand still. You only see things that you don't ordinarily notice. The birds are the prettiest things, I imagine.

Jules always owned a tin of tiger balm. When I was little, I accidentally kissed him one day after he'd applied it to his neck. It felt as if I was being slapped in the face. All my sinuses were immediately opened up. He used to rub the balm on his knee for hours. He did this because there was something wrong with his circulation, he said, which was why he was always so cold. Tiger balm was the perfect cure for all ailments that were hard to believe in, that you couldn't see the doctor about. Since he always smelled like tiger balm now, one could only assume that he was trying to treat some very deep wound.

I hadn't known because we'd been so emotionally distant lately. A week before, he had been singing a song in the bathroom when I got home. I wanted to ask him what song it was, but we weren't really on speaking terms. And to ask someone what they were singing was a deep question that could lead to all kinds of other concerns. So I didn't.

I was hurting Jules and Jules was hurting me. Except for our conversation and our love, we were losers. We were both just lonely drifters. I didn't even care what happened to me since he was being hurt too.

I put a boiled egg and a can of ginger ale from the fridge in a plastic bag and headed off for school. I hadn't washed and I smelled different, as if I was being followed down the street by someone else. If I was two people, I would have parted ways with myself at this point.

I crossed the street without even looking, and a bunch of cars honked hysterically. I didn't care. If you added up all the times I'd fallen off monkey bars and the like and come out unscathed, you'd have to agree that my chances for survival were incredibly high. I felt different in class. I suddenly didn't feel as if I was friends with anyone there. I could no longer be afraid of the things that children were supposed to be afraid of.

For the next few weeks, I fooled around with Alphonse a bunch of times. I was sitting on Alphonse's bed this time wearing only my Cinderella undershirt and a pair of underwear with sailboats on it. The underwear were like three years old. There was a hole in the butt.

'You should be ashamed to go around in those,' Alphonse said.

I shrugged. I just didn't like fancy underwear anymore. They had got me into trouble. It was one thing that I was always going to refuse to wear. I got funny when Alphonse wanted to make love. I curled up, got under the sheets, and crawled all the way to the bottom of the bed. He yanked me back up and pinned me down on the bed. I closed my eyes tight.

'Why do you close your eyes when I touch you?' he asked.

I shrugged. I opened one eye and looked up at him. Then he kissed me and I closed my eyes right away.

'I want to know what you're thinking about. Whatever it is, I can do it for you. Are you thinking about white horses, whatever? You can tell me.'

Of course, I hadn't been thinking about white horses. But it seemed like a nice thing to be able to think about while having sex. I tried to think about white horses as he ran his hands up and down me. The more he touched me, the more beautiful the white horses started to seem in my mind. They were doing fancy tricks and wearing those pink and blue bridles with gold buttons. They were just like the ones I had seen at a circus when I was little. I forgot all about Alphonse as I dreamed about white horses under circus lights with ladies on their backs.

Then Alphonse exclaimed suddenly that I wasn't getting into the sex at all. So I had to get rid of the horses and think about dirty ugly things, which were the things that turned me on for some reason. I thought about being raped in an alley. That made me come. As usual, I felt guilty about having fantasized about that and I felt lousy for a few minutes. I lay there as if I'd been shot.

My favorite part of sex was afterward. We lay on the bed after making love and he just gazed at me and marveled at my naked body.

'Do you ever notice how when you walk down the street, everybody turns around and looks at you? That's because you're the prettiest girl in the neighborhood.'

'I am not!'

'Yes, you are. You're better looking than those girls in the fashion magazines you read even.'

Alphonse's compliments weren't like the lame compliments that the social workers gave me. They had a cue card tucked away in one of their pockets with compliments that they were supposed to give me. Some of them had used the exact same lines on me.

'You're a very strong person,' they used to say. 'You can make something out of yourself if you want.'

After Alphonse noticed that I was beautiful, it seemed as if everybody in the world noticed it too. I was still afraid of the dark and I still dressed like a dope, but after I turned thirteen and got tall, things started to change for me. One time in the bathroom at a McDonald's, the guy in the next stall peeked over the top at me. When our eyes met, he jumped down and scurried away. I had the same sensation that I used to get when I peed in the swimming pool.

The lowlifes said really dirty things to me after I turned thirteen. The younger bums would come over to me with their cups full of change. First they would ask me if I had any change to spare. When I said no, they would start the dirty talk. They asked me loaded questions. 'Do you want to come over to my apartment? I can teach you some sex moves.'

I acted like I'd won the lottery when anyone bought me a Coca-Cola at the Burger King. A man with a beard, a green army jacket, and a fedora put his skinny arm around me at the park. He bent all over the place like spaghetti when he walked. He reminded me of how cartoon characters walked after they had been run over by a steamroller. He had a scrawny German shepherd with him that I was playing fetch with. The guy kept begging for a kiss, so I finally let him kiss my cheek. It was like a slug on my skin.

Thinking that certain people were scum was a defense mechanism I didn't have. Why would anyone kiss a boy who had scabs all over his hands and a tattoo of Porky Pig on his neck? I could have told you back then.

I hung out with Alphonse almost every day. Jules didn't notice. He had just decided not to see what I was doing anymore. A lot of kids from my school had parents who did that too. They pretended that when we were outside, we were in a cardboard box with the controls for a rocket ship drawn in crayon on the inside. We couldn't actually fly to the moon in that ship, they believed. I knew Alphonse was a pimp and that sooner or later I was going to have to turn a trick. For some reason it seemed as natural as growing wisdom teeth. I didn't even question why I was going to have to. I wanted to be brave. I didn't want to be afraid.

Alphonse had some other girls who worked for him. Two of them who lived together never spoke to me. One of them went by the name Baby. She got all upset that my given name actually was Baby. One day she came up to me and told me that I should change it.

'I came up with Baby first,' she said. 'I've been using it since before you were born.'

'I'm not going to change my name. It's on my birth certificate!'

'Man, I hate these fucking little kids,' she said, looking up at the sky. 'Don't you have a curfew?'

'It's four o'clock in the afternoon.'

'Then go home and do your homework.'

Everyone within earshot laughed at that one.

Leelee still spoke to me, though. She thought she was smarter than me and always wanted to give me the lowdown on things. It was ridiculous, really. She came up to me one day and wanted to sit down and have a long talk. She bought us both coffees, although I couldn't even stand the taste of it. Leelee got me to sit down on a bench with her at an outdoor café by the skating rink. She was wearing a skinny, gold scarf that seemed to wrap around her neck about twenty times.

'Things used to be a lot different between Al and me,' Leelee said.

I started fidgeting nervously. I knew I was in for a long stupid speech, and I was impatient for it to end already. My butt was cold.

'He used to like me a lot more,' she continued. 'But now you're his favorite. Sometimes I think that I'd like to see you gone. Just vanish. I mean if you ever wanted to get out of this town, I'd help you. I'd loan you some money. You know it wouldn't even be as if I was doing you a favor, because in a way it would really be as if I was doing myself a favor.'

I nodded in an exaggerated way because I knew she expected some sort of thanks for being so goddamn honest. This unfortunately caused her to elaborate.

'I'd be able to get these hateful thoughts out of my head. Always thinking about putting rat poison in your coffee – crazy, crazy, crazy shit like that – I'm not even kidding. Not that I'd ever do it. Because I'm not like that by nature. No way! Not one little bit. I'm like truly a spiritual and good human being. Like all that stuff about helping your neighbors out and all that – well, I don't go to church – but I really do believe in that. I really do!'

I'd had enough by this point. I took a sip of coffee for politeness but let it drool out of my mouth onto the sidewalk. Leelee didn't even seem to notice, though. She was too busy appreciating the wisdom that was coming out of her own mouth.

'Fuck, there are supposed to be six people in your life that mean anything to you,' she continued, as if I was interested. 'And I think you might be one of them. It's just that Alphonse and me used to have some great times in bed. Now he doesn't even want to touch me. He doesn't feel anything physical when he's around me. He's just too busy crying his eyes out when you're not around.'

She looked like she was trying to make herself cry. I thought she looked downright pathetic. I used to admire Leelee because she had a tattoo of a butterfly on her wrist. Now I just wanted to avoid her. I missed how I used to think of her as some sort of free-loving, stylish adult. Now she just seemed like a skinny tramp that Alphonse didn't even want to touch anymore. She was the only person who'd fallen out of grace for me. Eventually everyone would fall one by one like stars dropping out of the sky, leaving me standing in the dark. But during those first days of delinquency – there's nothing that ever tastes sweet like that – most everyone still dazzled my eyes.

3

One afternoon, when I was over at his apartment, Alphonse started talking about how he was going to give me a hundred dollars to go down to the Spanish Social Club and sign up for flamenco lessons. The Social Club was in an old ballroom. I could hear the dancers stamping their high heels on the floor from outside on the street. Every time I passed by, it seemed as if the building had a heartbeat.

Alphonse had made up a plan where we were going to tour Europe. He would be the ringmaster and stand out on the street corner and announce when my show was about to begin. He would set up a wooden box for me to dance on, and all the world would adore me. He had a pretty travel book of Spain that he would open up on his lap and stare at. I bought a Spanish- English dictionary and tried to learn a few words a day, as if I could learn the language that way. Alphonse said that when I learned the language, I should teach it to him. Anything seemed possible to me at the time.

'You've got to make some money, girl, so we can get

our asses to Europe. It's nice to be rich. Fuck this poverty shit.'

'Okay,' I said, brushing it off.

'Okay. So go out with Leelee. She'll show you where to hang out and all that shit. You two get along, right?'

'No! She just talks and talks and I feel rude to just stand up and walk away.'

Alphonse just left it at that. One day soon after, I was walking home from school by myself. I was wearing my gym uniform under my fur coat because it had been my last class in school and I'd been too lazy to change out of it. I stopped to wait for the bus that would take me to my building.

Alphonse came up out of nowhere and grabbed my hand. He walked a little ways with me. This was unusual because I'd noticed that Alphonse made it a point not to touch me in public. He would never do something like hold my hand. We always walked apart on the sidewalk. When people passed, we let them go right through us instead of around us. That day he held me close to him.

'Get into that brown car,' he said suddenly.

Alphonse pushed me toward a brown car parked on the side of the street. I twisted around and Alphonse's hand came off my wrist. I stood a couple feet from him.

'No, I hate brown cars. What kind of dope would buy a car the color of shit?'

'What the fuck are you being crude for? You know you're a lot of talk. Don't be something ordinary. You're special. You're the best. You're better than all that.'

'Whatever,' I said and held up my hand.

'He just wants to have a few words with you. He just wants to give you a lift home. Remember how you said you liked to hitchhike last night?'

The night before, I'd had a glass of wine with Alphonse and I had started talking about how I was the greatest hitchhiker in the city. According to my tale, when I put out my thumb, cars smashed into each other trying to stop for me. I claimed that I hitchhiked everywhere. Actually I'd only hitchhiked once. Someone had offered me a ride home while I was in the pouring rain. I'd been so afraid the whole time, even though it had been a woman who'd picked me up.

I bent down to take a look at the guy in the car. A man with brown hair and a long face leaned over and smiled. He looked ordinary enough to me. All adults looked the same. There were no doves with their heads bitten off or chain saws in the car, so I guessed it was safe to get in. Suddenly I wanted to see what the consequences would be.

My whole body was resisting, even though I told it not to. It was like once when we tried to put my friend Miro's dog in the water. All the other dogs were in there having such a good time, but Miro's dog kept scrunching up and twisting his body every time I lowered it near the water. I kind of felt like that dog. I felt like crawling right back up Alphonse's arm and jumping out of the car window.

Alphonse shut the door for me. I waved good-bye to Alphonse, as if I were going on a holiday. As the car drove away, I continued looking out the window.

'You can take me to St Christophe Street,' I said.

He turned the car toward the overpass. I felt a little comforted, seeing that he was going in the direction of my house. I wanted to ask him to drive faster, but I didn't know him, and that's not the kind of thing that you can ask a total stranger. We crossed over the overpass that went over the neighborhood. All I could see were the church spires. They looked like a group of hobgoblins going off to war. For a second I started to believe that this guy was just going to give me a ride home.

'What's your name?' he asked.

'Diana,' I said, not wanting to have a conversation about how unusual and cute my name was. I didn't want him to have anything to do with my name. All of a sudden it seemed precious to me. I thought I would stab that other hooker if she kept using it.

'Diana. That's lovely. How old are you?'

'Fifteen,' I lied.

'Wow! You're a brave little thing, aren't you?'

I shrugged and smiled at the window but not at him.

'I want to have sex with you,' he said suddenly. 'I'll give you a hundred bucks.'

'No,' I answered, not even looking at him, looking straight ahead.

My heart started beating really quickly. It made me nervous, like watching a toddler knowing it was going to trip. I wished my heart would knock it off.

'Come on. I really like you. You're beautiful.'

'Well, you can look at me then,' I said, hoping that sounded witty and tough and would make him back off.

'If I pull up behind that school, could you take your shirt off? I'll give you fifty bucks if you take your clothes off.'

I didn't say anything. He pulled into the parking lot of a closed factory, leaving the engine running so that we wouldn't freeze to death. There were vines everywhere because the factory had been closed for a long while. They were brown and gnarly and naked. They climbed up the fences and the telephone poles. They climbed along the electrical wires and along the telephone cables, going as far and as high as they could. I thought about climbing up one of those vines just like Jack and the Beanstalk. I could steal myself a golden goose that laid eggs and a golden harp that would play and sing whatever song I wanted it to. I would request 'Angie' by the Rolling Stones. I liked that song.

I was lost in my reverie, hoping he wouldn't interrupt me and just change his mind and drive me back to St Christophe Street. Instead, he handed me a fifty-dollar bill. I took it quietly and stuck it in my boot. He got out of the car and got into the backseat. I climbed over the front seat and sat next to him, deciding to get it over with. It all seemed out of my hands, somehow. It had to be done and money was money. He reached over and started fumbling with my gym T-shirt. I lifted it up under my coat and pulled my jogging pants down to my boots. I couldn't take the boots off because the money was in one of them and it would get lost for sure.

We sat next to each other in the backseat while he nervously touched me here and there, as if he was pointing something out. I squirmed myself into a horizontal position and he got on top of me. I didn't really know how you were supposed to ask guys to put a condom on, so he didn't use one. I didn't really know what I was doing, and I was worried I would somehow get broken in the messy position he was banging me into.

I think my body went numb from lack of circulation because I didn't feel much. Every time I'd had sex before, it had been kind of painful. That time I didn't feel a thing. It was hard to believe he was even inside me when he was there. I didn't know it was over until he started buttoning up his pants.

*

He dropped me off at St Christophe Street and sped away. I took the condom that Alphonse had given me and dropped it down the sewer. It was yellow and I knew that Alphonse was going to look through my things to see that I had used it. It didn't seem to me as if Alphonse could possibly know what exactly went on with me and that guy. I felt that if he knew he wouldn't be attracted to me anymore. I knew logically that Alphonse was wise to what had happened between me and the john, but it was still hard for me to grasp. It was still a little hard for me at that age to even accept that the rest of the world was having sex.

When I got back to my apartment building with the white bricks, I stood there a bit, just looking at it. Nothing had changed. The universe looked exactly the same.

Jules hadn't come home from work. He was probably going to be out late, selling quilts in the country. The same circulars were lying in front of the door as when I had left that morning. The bowl that I'd eaten my cereal in was still there, warm milk pooled in it. The radio hadn't changed stations. Jules's jacket had fallen off the hook when I had grabbed my own, and it was still there, lying on the floor. Not even an earthquake could pick that up.

I put the money in a wooden box for Cuban cigars with a sparrow smoking a cigar on the lid. I slid it under my bed. I stank differently. I didn't smell like myself. I smelled like cigarettes and somebody else's hands. It started to get dark in the room. Usually when I was alone in the house during the evening, I had to turn on every single light, but I just didn't care that night. So what if a hand came out from under the bed and grabbed me?

That would be nothing. They say that certain things are going to be terrible and that they are going to destroy you, but they don't. I sat on the side of the bed. It was as if my soul had been frozen, and I waited for it to thaw, in order to get on with life.

The second time was much harder. Alphonse introduced me to a short man with black curly hair and a kind face. We walked down the street together.

Most of the buildings were two stories around there, and the first floors seemed to have a lot of trouble holding up the second floors. There was a hotel on the second floor of a building, up on top of a tattoo parlor. We had to walk up a stairwell whose walls were painted black. The word 'Fuck' was scratched into the black paint over and over again. Fuck seemed to be the only constellation in the night as you climbed up those stairs into the sky.

Inside the room, there were paisleys on the wallpaper. They were like the made-up eyes of silent film stars. A couch the color of an orange tennis ball with brown shepherdesses on the print was in the center of the room. It reminded me of Christmas wrapping paper. He told me to take my clothes off. I made my clothes into a little pile like I was at the doctor's office. I held them in my hand waiting for him to tell me where to put them. When he didn't give me any instructions, I sat down on the couch and put them next to me.

It seemed like a terrible thing to sit on a couch undressed. I'd never done it before and it seemed un-natural. It was an uncomfortable, scratchy couch, too. I couldn't lean back on it. I just sat up all proper, as if I had a glass of lemonade in my hand. He got undressed and came to sit next to me. He turned toward me and put his arms around me. It was difficult to hug on the couch. It was like when puppets try to hug but can never really get their arms around each other properly.

I didn't mind kissing. I guess I considered it being polite. It was strange to put his fingers in my mouth because he bit his fingernails.

He had a large bottle of beer with him in his bag. He made me drink it. I drank it so quickly that I had trouble keeping my balance as I walked to the bed. I was glad to lie on the bed. I pulled the sheet over my head, feeling that he would never find me under there. The bed seemed to be tilting all over the place like a raft. I felt seasick. He lifted the sheet.

'Cuckoo,' he yelled and I laughed in surprise.

I didn't want to sleep with him. I told him that I had changed my mind about the whole thing, although I didn't offer to give the money back. I just lay on the bed with my legs crossed really tight.

'You can't go inside me,' I said.

He got on top of me and rubbed against my belly. I kept my head turned toward the wall, as if he was trying to pick me up on a city bus and I was ignoring him. He sounded like he was crying when he talked.

'Oh, you're so pretty, so sweet, you're mine. You're mine.'

It was like he had just dragged me naked out of a river and had fallen in love with me. Afterward, he lay on the bed next to me, looking as sad as I was.

'You never did this before, did you?'

I lied and shook my head.

'How old are you?'

'Thirteen,' I said.

I often lied about my age to people. When I said my real age, they would laugh and tell me to get lost and go play soccer in the park. This guy, however, started to cry. He begged me to come home and live with him. He said that he had been in a group home when he was little and knew what I must be going through.

Once I was outside on the street and alone, I sat down on a chair with a blue-and-gold linoleum seat on it that was sitting right out in the middle of the sidewalk. Objects sometimes got misplaced like that in the winter. This chair could be on the sidewalk for months because no one would want to go through the trouble of moving it until summer. The buildings across the street all had little storefront windows filled with colorful things. They were like a row of Easter Seal stickers. I felt very sad, hollowed out. I started thinking about every bad thing that I had ever done. I started thinking about the time I stole some bus tickets from a friend of mine. I thought about how I had told a boy to fuck off when he wanted to go out with me. I wished that I was on the badminton squad. I wished that I had friends who lived at home and who were worried about their science projects and who had boyfriends who played on the football team, even though my school didn't even have a football team.

The snowflakes came down like little bits of news-paper. The night was a typewriter key that got stuck and kept punching all the letters on top of the others until all that was left was a black blob. No word, no letter, no message in the night for me.

I had the habit of walking down the street crying. Crying is contagious and that guy had got me started. Sadness fit me like blue jeans. Sadness fit me like a hangman's noose. It crawled on me like an electric blanket and it was hard to resist its warmth. I tried to straighten myself up when I saw Alphonse. I gave him all the money; I didn't even wait for him to hand me back a couple dollars.

He didn't seem affected particularly by what happened to me. He kissed me sweetly and acted as if I was mad to be upset.

We walked down the street together, and he suggested we go into the public greenhouse to get our minds off things. The greenhouse was a miniature glass cathedral filled with exotic flowers. There were birds made out of cloth with lights inside them hanging from the ceiling. Alphonse took a bottle of rum out of his jacket and gave me a sip. I felt myself warm up and start to be happy despite myself. The flowers were so pretty. I don't think anyone had pointed out how pretty flowers were since I was little.

We went into the little room at the back of the greenhouse whose walls and floors were covered with white tiles. There was a pool in the middle of the floor with huge goldfish swimming around. The ground of the pool was covered in pennies that represented hundreds of unfulfilled wishes.

'It's going to be all right,' Alphonse whispered.

Because of the acoustics, his whisper filled up the room entirely, like a fur coat that was too big and hot.

That night the apartment seemed to have shrunk. The ceiling was practically touching me. The house was a drawer in a dresser. When I woke up in the morning, it felt as if I had been beaten up. I was tired and there was a bullet in my stomach, I was so hungry. I was almost ashamed to look at myself in the mirror.

There was a tin geometry set on the kitchen table. Jules had been carrying it around lately; I'd noticed it in the pocket of his jacket a few times. I thought it might be a gift that he was afraid to give me. Maybe when he gave it to me, everything would get better between us. I picked it up and opened the lid. My heart skipped a beat and I almost dropped the tin. His works were inside the geometry set: a hypodermic needle, a Q-tip, a cigarette filter, a spoon, and a lighter. I had found his works by accident before, so I wasn't sure why I was so shocked. It was as if I had opened the tin and found something living and frightening in there, like a bunch of cockroaches.

I didn't know what to make of him doing drugs again. I wished I didn't know at all. I was so confused by things that nothing quite seemed real at that moment. It wouldn't have surprised me if the spoons in the utensil drawer started crying and needed to be rocked to sleep.

Alphonse and I sat on either end of a row of benches on St Catherine. If anyone stopped to look at me, he waved them over to talk to him. I found it cold and boring and hard to sit in one place. I took my knit hat off and leaned forward and gave my head a really good itch. That was one of the best feelings and made winter worthwhile. I blew my nose about a million times.

I started thinking about what happened to you if you slipped through the ice this time of year. I had a friend at school who was always talking about what would happen to you if you did. I had never known anyone who had fallen through the ice in the winter. I imagined what my face would look like under a layer of ice with other children skating over it. I forgot all about why I was sitting there. Children are distracted so easily.

I didn't even feel like a prostitute. A prostitute stands there all night looking for people. A prostitute wears a sparkly silver jacket and high heels, not a tacky winter hat and snow boots.

But I always had offers. I believed at first that no one could possibly even imagine why Alphonse and I were sitting on that bench, but they did. There was something about me that made it obvious what I was doing. I never even got used to the propositions, though. I had a minor heart attack every time a guy came up to me and suggested that we go off someplace alone. It was like a bump in a ride on a roller coaster.

It happened once when my friend Jeremy and I were fooling around in a pile of snow. He tripped and fell flat on his stomach on a mattress that had been put out in the trash.

'Bedbugs!' I screamed, laughing. 'You got fleas in your pants now. The person who owned that bed had herpes!'

Jeremy was grabbing my boots when I noticed a guy with blond hair and a bomber jacket waving at me from his car window.

In the motel room, the blond guy wanted me to stand up against a wall while we did it. I had to stand on my tippy toes and hold myself up by pushing on his shoulders, like I was trying to see something passing by in a parade. I doubted that we would ever be able to fit together and have sex, but he managed it. I kept almost falling over and he had to stand me back up.

I wish at least Leelee had told me about some of these details. I never knew what to do. I knew that I was probably a bad lover. I felt guilty that I was wasting their money. I thought that I would do a better job the next time, but I never did. It was always awkward. I refused to do different things on different nights. I always refused to give hand jobs. They seemed to take forever and I never knew how to do them properly. They were like, 'Faster, slower, harder, faster, no, slow.'

I never made any noises. I never said anything dirty, even when they begged me. I was terribly shy. I begged not to have to be on top. I didn't know why anybody would have sex with me because my breasts were so small. I felt like the Wicked Witch of the East lying under Dorothy's house with my legs jutting out.

When I was done with the guy with blond hair, I felt as if I had to get out of the room immediately. It was as if there wasn't any oxygen left in the room. I hurried to get all my clothes back on, but I couldn't find my glove. I ran around the hotel room for ten minutes looking for it. Alphonse had bought me a pair of black gloves with red hearts knitted into them that I was crazy about.

'Look, did you hide it?'

'No, I swear. Maybe it's under the bed?'

'You're hiding it. I better not find out that you're hiding it.'

I ran down the street crying and cursing. When I got home, I found that my glove had been in the sleeve of my jacket the whole time.

I gave Alphonse all the money I made. Since I would have been scared to death to do it without him, I figured he deserved the money. He insisted on giving me back a little money each time, and five dollars was more than I needed anyhow. I liked being able to buy my own cigarettes, even though I still couldn't figure out how to smoke them. Each time I lit a cigarette, I thought it was going to be great, but it left me feeling grimy and gave me a bellyache. I must have smoked in a past life when I had a bigger and tougher constitution, when I wasn't such a little girl.

I bought myself a paperback Agatha Christie book with the rest of my change. I walked down the street reading it. A wet snow started to fall from the sky. Whenever a raindrop fell onto the page, the paper changed its shape and moved toward the raindrop, like a face reacting to a kiss.

On the way home I saw on the marquee that there was a Celine Dion impersonation contest going on at the Metropolis Club. The high-pitched voice of a man singing 'Where Does My Heart Beat Now' floated out onto the street. I tried to get in, but the bouncer told me to go back to nursery school. It seemed ridiculous that I couldn't go into a club after all the shit I was doing. What was even more absurd was that I had to go to school the next day.

The truth was that even if Alphonse had encouraged me to, I couldn't stay out late at night turning tricks. I wasn't allowed to miss school without a bona fide reason. My social worker checked my weekly progress reports that kids in the remedial stream were handed on Fridays. She'd warned me that if I started missing school, I'd have to go to detention. I sure as hell wasn't going there, and Alphonse didn't want me going there either.

I explained all this to Alphonse one night in the park. He wanted me to come over in the morning on a Wednesday and spend the day with him. I was embarrassed that I had to remind him I was still in high school. But then I told him a funny story about a boy in my class.

This boy named Jamie had brought a bag of magic

mushroom crumbs to school. He said a drug dealer had
sold them to him for a great deal. He gave them to some
kids, and they all said that the crumbs were bunk and
totally not effective. But Jamie walked around all day
thinking he was high. He sat next to me at lunch on the
school steps, trying to figure out if he was hallucinating
or not.

'Do you see that guy with a cowboy hat across the
street?'

'Yes.'

'Shit. Well, do you see that couch over there in the
garbage?'

'Yeah,' I said. 'I see that too.'

Alphonse laughed his head off when I told him that
story. He liked when I told him stories about how
retarded the kids at my school were. It reassured him that
I wasn't interested in them. These stories were like decla-
rations of love to Alphonse.

'I don't know how he lets you get away with it,' Leelee
cried as she saw me walking home. 'I work every night.
It's because he knows that you're thirteen, I guess. You
got so many years in you still. He doesn't want to scare
you away. I hate when he puts his hands on me. Your
little period of grace isn't going to last forever.'

4

Alphonse fell asleep one evening after we fooled around,
even though it was only six o'clock. I walked into his
kitchen and poured myself a big mug of chocolate milk
and cut myself a piece of cake. Alphonse always had
good food in the fridge. I sat at the kitchen table in my

underwear and undershirt, with my bare feet on the cold floor. I took out my schoolbag from under the table and took out my notebook and a ballpoint pen. I had an essay for English class I was looking forward to writing. I was probably going to be the only one in class who handed it in on time. It wasn't hard to have the best mark in that class. The girl next to me told me that she would never write in cursive because it reminded her of pubic hair.

I'd always just been good at schoolwork. It was the simplest thing, like wanting something that was in a store window and having a pocket full of money.

My schoolwork of late wasn't particularly challenging. In moral ed. class, we had been working on our family tree for an entire month. The girl who sat next to me claimed that she was a distant relative to Jimi Hendrix.

One Monday the teacher announced that we were moving on from our family trees to a new topic. We were going to be studying cults that week. The teacher rolled in a VCR to show us an interview with Charles Manson from prison. Everyone lost their minds with excitement. A few of the kids owned Charles Manson T-shirts. The whole class started chanting, '*Charlie, Charlie, Charlie,*' thumping their fists on their desks.

Then a funny thing happened that wasn't supposed to happen to a kid like me at all. I was called to the office on the intercom. At the office the guidance counselor held up my report card. I had received a ninety-six average. She told me that I was being put in the regular stream. I didn't know what my friends were going to say, but I didn't care. I had never been singled out at school or anywhere else for any sort of achievement. I was happy.

I went to the science class on the second floor, which was to be my new homeroom. The teacher told me to go and sit next to a boy named Xavier, who would show me around the school. This was a bit silly since I'd already been going to the school for three months. The regular kids were on a different floor from the system kids, and we never intermingled, so a lot of the kids seemed to look at me as if they'd never seen me before. It really seemed as if I was getting a fresh start.

Xavier was the only kid in the class who didn't have a partner. Everyone started snickering when I sat down beside him. He was skinny and looked small for his age. He had messy black hair and a perpetually surprised look on his face.

With his fancy black ink pen, he wrote down everything the teacher said. The teacher started telling a story about how his boat had almost capsized when he was on holiday, and Xavier wrote that down in his notebook. He highlighted certain sentences that he had written down, selecting from a pile of yellow, pink, and blue highlighters. I enjoyed watching him take notes. It was like being at a really busy office.

He showed up in English class without his notebook. He told the teacher that he had become a Buddhist and Buddhists don't take notes. He gave his English report on *Animal Farm* in an English accent.

I saw him later that day in the cafeteria, listening to a Walkman and swaying to the music with a scarf wrapped around his neck. He was waving his arms around as if he were conducting an orchestra.

'What time is it?' I asked, just to make conversation.

'Midnight.'

'What?'

'It's midnight in Tokyo.'

'Well, here, on planet Earth, what time is it?'

'Three o'clock.'

'Thank you.'

'Can I have your coordinates?'

'What does that mean?'

'Can I have your phone number and all that?'

'Okay.'

Xavier got caught drawing a portrait of me in math class. The teacher held it up for everyone to see, and they all laughed and laughed. He held his head up because he didn't care at all. He was different from my friends. I liked that he was immature and that he seemed naïve, as if he was actually acting his age. He didn't have a chip on his shoulder. We had caught each other's attention. Who knows why? We were probably the most different kids on earth, but I felt like we were the same and so did he.

In science, we were going to be studying different kinds of rocks. We were supposed to collect a bunch and bring them into school the next day so that we could examine and discuss their properties. Xavier and I were partners. I figured that everybody was just going to pick up rocks on their way to school the next morning. Xavier, however, was all gung ho about going to the park by the river and collecting a variety of stones.

I sat waiting for him on the picnic table outside the school. He came up to me and asked if he could see my hand. He took out a felt-tip pen and scribbled on one of my fingertips. Then he held my finger and pressed it down on a piece of paper. He explained that it was necessary for him to have my fingerprint on file. He didn't say why. All I knew was that it had felt good when he was squeezing my fingers.

We headed to the park. He had a bread bag filled with Oreo cookies that his mom had packed for him for lunch. We walked down the street eating them.

'I live down that street,' he said, pointing. 'Look! It's my cat.'

Sure enough a cat came sauntering toward us. It had gray matted hair and crooked eyes. It was the ugliest cat I'd ever seen.

'That is the ugliest cat I've ever seen,' I said.

'No, it isn't. He's a Persian. He's a rare breed!'

'It's rare because nobody wants a cat that looks like that.'

'But doesn't it look like it has a lot of personality? We found him at Old Orchard Beach. Do you go there on holiday?'

'No, that doesn't really appeal to me.'

'Why not! It's so much fun. We go a lot. We build these bonfires on the beach that are really neat. We had the biggest one last summer.'

'My dad and I built one by the river last year, and all these kids were helping out. They started putting garbage in. And the plastic was letting out all the toxic fumes.'

'What does your dad do for a living?'

'He's a spy.'

'Wow! That's so neat. My dad's an accountant. I think he should have been an architect, though. Do you ever do models? My dad and I put one of those pirate ships together. It took us five months. I'm surprised it didn't drive us crazy.'

It was unusual to hear someone talk about their parents like that. Most of the kids I hung with only mentioned their parents when they were telling anecdotes about mean or crazy things that they had done. It made me feel very peaceful when he told nice stories like that about his parents.

When we got to the park, Xavier reached into the pond to try and find some smooth stones. He wanted to show the effects that water had on stones over time. He rolled up his coat sleeve all the way, almost to his armpit. He stuck his arm in and shrieked from the cold. His sleeve had still managed to get wet.

'I should be wearing my rubber gloves,' Xavier screamed. 'It's all spongy down here. It's like walking on dog poo. In Old Orchard Beach I found a starfish, and we kept it in our cabin for a couple days. It was beautiful.'

Xavier sat Indian style on the stone embankment of the pond next to me. He opened his palm with the stone in it and we both stared at it. It was pretty and smooth, but who knew what it was going to look like once it was dry.

'We should cover it in transparent nail polish so that it always looks shiny like that,' I suggested.

'This is a beautiful rock. Some people give their rocks names.'

'He looks like a Frederic.'

'That's a nice name. Let's put each one in a separate Kleenex box and label them not only with their scientific name but also with their common name that we choose for them.'

'Okay.'

'All right.'

I noticed a snail with a yellow and black shell hibernating next to the embankment. We both got down on our hands and knees to look at it.

'I love snails,' Xavier said.

'Me too,' I said.

And I realized that up until that moment I had totally forgotten how much I liked snails. How dark and nasty they were, like a black eye. We sat there waiting for the snail to come out of its shell. I looked at Xavier, and it felt as if we were sitting there naked. It felt very intimate.

Xavier put the snail in his pocket. He thought that it would breathe better in a cloth environment than in a plastic one. He said it would come out of hibernation if he put it next to the radiator.

'This goes into the project. A wandering rock. Do you want to come over now and label the boxes at my house? We have a label maker.'

'No, I have to meet a friend of mine. We're going out to see a movie.'

'Okay then. That's cool. Remember to sit through the credits at the end of the film.'

'Okay.'

'Very important, you know.'

'Okay.'

'Promise you will.'

'I swear to God, I will!'

I laughed and we both turned to walk in opposite directions.

Xavier called out for me to come back and see something. He pointed to the bottom of the fountain and then stuck his hand in the water, yanked something out, and displayed it in his red and trembling palm. It was a plastic figurine of a zebra that some little kid had dropped in there. Xavier held it up for me to see, as if it were a miracle.

'I read that no two zebras in the world have the same stripes,' I said reverently.

I knew all about wild animals, even though I had never even been to a real zoo. He handed it to me before we parted again.

I was taken aback that he would just give me such a cute little figurine without any hesitation and without wanting anything in return. No one had given me a toy in so long. I used to have a row of plastic animals that I kept on the windowsill and that Jules and I would play with together. Back then, I didn't believe it was Jules and me making the voices of the animals, but that they just spoke themselves.

As I was walking away, I took out the zebra and held it up against my ear in order to hear what it had to say.

'Hello there, Baby,' the zebra said.

The sound of his voice was so sweet to my ears.

It suddenly dawned on me how late I was to meet Alphonse. We had planned to meet at the four o'clock showing, whatever it was. It was already four thirty. I put the zebra back in my pocket and ran down the street in a really good mood.

I got to the front of the movie theater and Alphonse wasn't there. I didn't even have enough money to get in. I hadn't turned a trick in weeks. I counted my pennies and nickels on the counter, and they came up to eighty cents. Ninety-nine cents was the adult fare, but if you were thirteen years or under, it was only seventy-five cents. The guy at the counter didn't believe that I was thirteen for one second.

'When's your birthday?'

'November the nineteenth.'

'What sign are you?'

'Scorpio.'

'Bullshit! You look like a Sagittarius.'

'Please, please just let me in.'

'I'll let you in if you give me that pin you're wearing on your jacket.'

I took off the pin on my fur coat that said 'Fuck the Sex Pistols'. The pin had been getting on my nerves lately. Every time I wore it, my dad would make me stand in front of him with my eyes wide open for two minutes. He figured that if I wore a pin like that, I must be getting stoned. I gave the cashier my pin and he waved me past.

'Take your pennies,' he called back to me. 'You'll need them to eat tonight.'

I ignored him and pushed open the door to the theater. I ran down the aisle between the seats, looking at the heads and trying to spot Alphonse, then ran up the stairs to the balcony. I tripped on the carpet, which was rolling up at the ends.

'Hey, that's a nice trick. Can you teach me that?' a stranger whispered.

Alphonse was sunk into his chair, watching the movie. I crawled over the chairs to get to him from behind. I climbed into my seat like a monkey, and one of my boots came off. When I slid down next to him, Alphonse didn't turn around to look at me. I just sat there straightening myself up. Then I relaxed and tried to focus on what was happening on the screen. I realized, to my dismay, that the movie playing was *Blue Velvet*. I hated that movie. It creeped the hell out of me. Creepy movies were unfortunately very popular at this theater. I used to like to talk a lot during this movie to distract myself from what was happening in it: a naked nightclub singer kept prisoner in a terrible little suburban apartment.

Then Alphonse reached over and took my hand. He

guided it between his legs, and I had to rub there during the movie. I hoped it would make up for having shown up late. He leaned his face into mine and we started kissing. Kissing him while *Blue Velvet* was playing made me feel as if I were kissing the people who were in the movie. Eyes closed, I could hear the characters whispering deranged unwholesome things. I felt dirty and uncomfortable, but I didn't want to upset Alphonse by pulling away.

When the movie was over, I told Alphonse that I wanted to sit through the credits. He absolutely refused.

'Are you planning on writing each and every one of them to tell them how bad their movie is?'

'No.'

'Then why do you need to know their names?'

'I don't know. I just like to watch the credits. They're important.'

'You hate this movie! Why do you want to read the credits?'

'Why'd you choose this film if you knew I hated it? Besides, I read the credits of all movies, even when they're bad.'

'You loved *Drugstore Cowboy* and you didn't need to read the credits when the movie was over.'

Alphonse and I had seen *Drugstore Cowboy* a little while before, and we'd gotten along very well the week after. I kept pretending to be the main character's tough sexpot wife, and I started shoplifting chocolate bars from the pharmacy. Alphonse found it adorable when I shoplifted. I followed him out of the theater, nervously, wishing that he'd stop being mad at me and go back to thinking I was cute. We walked down the street, and since he didn't say anything, I started whistling.

'Where were you?' Alphonse asked, angrily. 'Hanging around those doofuses from your school? You want to end up like them? The whole gang of them are going to end up with rotten teeth and tattoos on their necks.'

'Okay,' I said.

He stopped suddenly and simply glared at me. I leaned against the blue tiles of the Chinese Laundromat, a little bit like a cornered rat.

'Okay?' he responded, sarcastically.

'Yeah, okay,' I said.

'What does okay mean?'

'That they'll end up with rotten teeth and tattoos on their necks.'

'Are you trying to fuck with me, Baby? I hope to God that you are not.'

'I'm not!'

I didn't know if I was fucking with him or not. I didn't even know what that meant.

'It's not my fault that you don't believe me,' I said.

'Don't believe you! You didn't even tell me where you were! You didn't even give me the benefit of an excuse.'

'Well, you see…'

'Don't, Baby. Don't shit on what we have.'

I just kept quiet. This whole conversation was over my head. Whatever I said was going to upset him. I was glad to be able to leave and head home. I wished that there was an easy way to get out of ever seeing Alphonse again.

When I reached our building, Jules was sitting on a bench next to another man. They were both stoned. The man he was with was wearing a baseball cap with a dolphin on it, a baseball jacket, and white track pants with dark blue stripes on them. Not many junkies dressed in jock clothing, so some of them used it as a

257

disguise. He had an empty plastic bag in his hand. They leaned against each other, supporting each other so that they didn't fall over. One of his friend's sneakers dangled from the tip of his toes like a slipper. Jules's mouth was opened halfway, as if he was pronouncing a syllable. His friend's eyebrows were raised as if he was very interested in a new idea that Jules was putting forth.

What could Jules do for me now?

5

I liked being in the gifted class because the work was actually challenging and enabled me to get my mind off of life for the afternoon. We'd had a lecture on Dostoyevsky that day and it had put me in a good mood, by virtue of being thought-provoking. Xavier came running after me on the way home. He slipped and fell backward onto the ground. I could tell that Xavier was one of these people who were genetically predisposed to slipping on the ice. He got up quickly, blushing and wiping himself off. I smiled to make him feel at ease.

'Was the film you saw good?' he asked me, still flushed.

'Not really. Actually it was probably good. But it made me feel bad.'

'I love movies that do that! I'm going to make films when I get older. I have an artistic temperament, which is really a tragic thing. It means that I'm going to be miserable and go insane probably. I've already decided how I'm going to kill myself. My death will be my final work of art. I'm going to film myself in the bathtub overdosing on opium.'

'I would load myself up with painkillers,' I said.

'Morphine or whatever they give soldiers so that they can't even feel when one of their limbs has been chopped off. Then I would jump off a tall building. Just so I don't have to feel all my limbs and neck breaking.'

'That's so nice. That's the prettiest way to die.'

'I'd jump off an opera house in Paris.'

I'd stolen that from Perry, a boarder who had rented a room in an old apartment of ours a couple years before. Perry used to have a black-and-white photograph of the Paris Opera on his door. He said that when he saved enough money, he was going to go to that building and throw himself off it. He had a jar for money especially for that in his room. It only ever had some dimes and nickels in it and pennies. He would gather them all up and spend them on cigarettes.

'I'm never going to be able to afford to kill myself!' he used to scream from his room completely out of the blue, when the house was quiet.

He had these great offstage moments that really made me laugh. I smiled thinking about him.

'You look really pretty when you smile,' Xavier said to me.

I was glad he thought I was pretty and that he liked me. When older men told me I was pretty, I always felt as if they were up to no good.

We walked home together again. This time just because we wanted to and not because of a science project. Instead of going our own ways, when we got to St Christophe Street, we sat down on a wooden bench that was on the corner. The bench was totally lopsided, as if it was made to go on a hill and then got put on this corner by mistake. It was a very popular bench. Hardly any kid could walk by and resist the temptation of sitting on it. Xavier sat at the lower end of the bench and I perched at the top, but I slid down and sat leaning against him. It was impossible not to.

'This is my favorite bench,' Xavier said. 'See if you can push me off. I'll bet that you can't do it.'

'All right, you're on,' I said. 'But I warn you, I'm much stronger than I look.'

I started pushing him. He held himself on the bench. I liked squeezing my body against his. We just sat there pressing up against each other. I wasn't really trying to push him off.

'Forget it,' I said, laughing, 'I can't do it.'

'Oh, you lose the bet!' he squealed. 'Now I get to decide what I win.'

'I don't have any money. I'm flat broke.'

'I don't want money.'

'Well, what do you want?'

There wasn't even a point to me asking him, actually. I knew exactly what Xavier was wishing for. We both wanted the same prize. I was glad that I hadn't won. He was the one who was going to have to ask me for a kiss. Xavier didn't say anything, though. He just stared at me with his face close to mine. When two people are thinking the same thing, it sends a charge through your whole body. My veins were telephone lines with people laughing and screaming through them.

I wasn't wearing any gloves that day. Now Xavier took off his own and shoved them in his pocket. He put the tip of his finger on my knee, testing to see if I would move away. I didn't move a muscle. Then he put his whole hand on the back of my hand. I turned my hand over so that my palm was flat against his palm. Then we held hands.

And my heart felt so big. I just wanted to hold hands forever. This was like a promise, an agreement that we wanted each other. Holding hands meant that we each thought the other was perfect. For whatever reason, we'd rather hold hands with each other than anybody else in the entire universe. It was sweet because it meant that so much good stuff was going to be following. After we held hands, we were girlfriend and boyfriend.

I realized that this was the first boyfriend I'd ever had. Despite whatever else had happened to me, this was a brand-new and wonderful thing.

Now that he was using again, Jules basically didn't care what I did anymore. The one single advantage of having a negligent parent was that you got to hang out and do what you wanted when you wanted. There was a very small period of glory when all the other children are jealous of you. And now Alphonse was ruining this for me. He wanted me to come to his house after school every day and not dawdle on the way. He didn't push me to turn a trick very often, but he still set it up every few days. He said I should live with him, which bugged me. I didn't even like the idea of him being able to boss me around twenty-four hours a day.

I started skipping going over to Alphonse's after school to be with Xavier. He walked me home every day. He did some really nice things while we hung out. One time he serenaded me in made-up Spanish. He held my hand when we got to the street corners, as if I was a little kid who was going to dash out into the traffic. When he saw the coast was clear, he let go of my hand and let me cross.

His mother made him good lunches, and he always

shared them with me. He had a book of jokes and would sit next to me in the cafeteria and read it to me as if it were a novel. A girl handed me a paper on my way to sit with Xavier. It was a petition signed by about twenty-five kids saying that they wanted him to change his hair-style. I threw it in the garbage before I joined Xavier. None of the other kids ate with him, so we were left completely alone, which I found very pleasant. One lunch, he brought me a handful of mints. He had gotten them from a restaurant he'd eaten at the night before with his family.

'Here! Here! Eat up! You need these for your health. Yum, yum! Fatten you up!'

I'd become less tough since I had started hanging out with Xavier. I started doing weirder things, that was for sure. I went outside my building after supper to feed my leftovers to the pigeons. I could recognize some of the pigeons and I named them.

'You are Pablo. You are Antoine. You are Marco. You are Bonbon. You are Jesus.'

I had a box filled with pigeon feathers. Jules would be hysterical if he saw them. He claimed that pigeon feathers were poisonous and could kill you. But he had stopped going through my things. I flitted one in the air in front of me as if it were a paintbrush. It made the sounds of birds in the sky.

Xavier swore that he would never touch another woman as long as he lived. We had started kissing. At first, we'd lean forward and just peck each other on the lips nervously and quickly. It was like being at a petting zoo. You put your hand out for a deer to eat the grains on your hand. I liked that I was the only one who had ever kissed him. I knew that he really appreciated my kisses. He wasn't that good of a kisser, though. He used to kiss me too hard. One afternoon, he pressed his lips against mine so hard that he ended up pushing me up against a wall.

We'd only gotten as far as you can go while hanging out in alleys and on street corners. He tried to put his hand down my pants, but my belt was too tight. Then he stuck his hand under my shirt and I screamed from the cold. He rubbed his hands together vigorously until they were a little warmer and then slid them under my jacket and my shirt.

'You don't wear a bra?'

'No.'

'You still wear an undershirt?'

'So.'

'I still like your breasts. They feel nice. Can I look at them?'

He pulled the collar of my shirt and looked down.

'You're retarded!' I yelled.

I slapped him in the face with my mitten and we both laughed.

Really I was nervous when he put my hand near my belt buckle. I acted as if touching someone else was all new to me too. I never even considered telling Xavier about how I turned tricks sometimes. I had no trouble having a double life. All teenagers start leading double lives anyhow; mine was just a little more extreme.

'Don't forget to practice your lines tonight,' Xavier warned as he turned to head home.

'I won't,' I promised.

Xavier and I were supposed to put on a scene from a Molière play for French class the next day. It was the first time that either of us had ever had to memorize lines from a play. He had his mother buy him a set of highlighters, specially for the occasion. He had written the words to his monologue on a Bristol board and thumbtacked it to the wall in his room. He forced his brothers to read my part in the evenings.

That night I met with a guy named Harvey in a hotel. I had started meeting him there every Thursday night around five. I sat at the edge of the thin mattress naked and whispered the words of the play under my breath. '*Voleurs!*' I whispered quietly so that Harvey wouldn't hear as he took off his clothes. I certainly had less of a support system than Xavier, more distractions and more obstacles. But it was all right. It didn't seem to affect our relationship. The next day, we both knew our lines perfectly and the teacher gave us an A.

Once I wanted to read Xavier some poems from a book I'd taken out from the library. We walked to my building, but I wouldn't invite him up to our ugly apartment. I left him down on the street and ran up to my apartment to get the book. When I came back down, I saw that Jules had come home. He was talking to Xavier outside. I really didn't know what to make of it. I never considered how he would feel about me being with Xavier. I had been keeping my life so separate from him. I watched them from the window in the front door.

They both seemed to be fascinated by a skunk that was waddling down the street. Xavier was telling Jules that baby skunks didn't have any spray. Jules said if you raised a baby skunk with a cat, it would think it was a cat. I think he got that idea from Pepé Le Pew. Xavier said they liked strawberries. Jules said they particularly liked our garbage.

Jules was wearing a long pea coat over a suit. He'd

been sleeping in that suit since the day before. I always found that he looked completely removed from the everyday world when he was wearing a suit and hanging around in the park. The bums in suits were always the craziest. Xavier wouldn't know this, though. He probably thought that Jules was coming home from a business meeting. I walked out of the building and up to them. I waved to Jules and introduced them quickly. Then I gestured for Xavier to come on along.

'Good-bye, sir,' Xavier said to Jules.

As we were walking down the street, Xavier told me that Jules was good-looking for a dad. He couldn't be good-looking, I thought, because he had never had any girlfriends. 'He's just young for a dad actually,' I suggested, but Xavier disagreed. I smiled.

If Jules was the type of person all the time that he was in Xavier's eyes, then things would be okay for him. Then again, if I was the type of person all the time that I was in Xavier's eyes, I think I'd also be okay. Wouldn't that be a nice life? Xavier wasn't put on earth to witness the bad things like Jules and I were. He had been put here to notice lovely things, things that God had created and no one had any complaints about. Leaves turning red in autumn. How when the tide goes out, the shells are left on the shore. I was put here – Jules and I were both put here – to see sadder things. We had to stand in the rain and explain why the world was a lovely place.

That night, Jules called to me from the other room while I was lying in bed.

'Hey, cookie? I liked your friend. What was his name? Xavier?'

I didn't answer. I didn't know what to make of his words to me anymore. I crawled to the end of my mattress and up against the wall. If was as if I was avoiding his words. I didn't like at all that he was making his voice sound like we were getting along.

When I was younger, Jules would always feel really guilty later in the night for having yelled at me. He'd call out to me from his bed in the other room, apologies and compliments hanging in the dead air.

'I like that drawing that you brought home from school. That was beautiful!' he'd say.

'It's all right. I'm not mad anymore!' I'd call out.

'I'm sorry I yelled at you. You're a perfect kid.'

I used to like our conversations through the wall. I'd run my fingers over the designs on the wallpaper while he said nice things. I suddenly wanted to call something back. I almost had to put my hand over my mouth to stop myself. I didn't want to reassure him.

Things were different now. I wasn't just going to forgive him for not taking care of me during the past year. Instead of saving me, he had rejected me. If he hadn't sent me to a center for rejected children, I wouldn't have become such good friends with Alphonse. I would be a virgin. I needed to be angry at someone other than myself. Being angry at Jules kept my head above the water. Only when I was done being unhappy with that would I let him be done being unhappy too.

So I didn't call back and Jules was quiet. From the way that people have always talked about your heart being broken, it sort of seemed to be a one-time thing. Mine seemed to break all the time.

I only went over to Xavier's house for the first time after we'd been going out for three weeks. He begged me to come, taking my hand and pulling me toward his home.

I gave in finally. He still insisted on holding my hand the whole way so that I couldn't dart away.

We took a shortcut through his alley. There was ice all over the ground, with dirt and sticks and crushed Coke cans frozen in it. I fell over about three times on the ice. Xavier kept catching me and then falling on top of me and howling with laughter. My palm was cut and bleeding by the time we got to his house, but it didn't bother me at all.

Xavier's house had yellow clapboarding all over it. That was something I loved because Jules and I had stayed in a hotel by the sea once with clapboarding. I mistakenly thought that all houses by the sea looked like that. I looked at his house and thought of the ocean and waves and seagulls, and it made me feel good.

'My dad's back from his business trip!' Xavier shouted, pointing to one of the cars in the driveway.

I had always lived in apartments, so I thought that all houses were enormous inside even if they looked quite small outside, but Xavier's house was tiny. There was wallpaper with green leaves all over the walls that made it look even smaller and cozier.

There seemed to be hundreds of coats and boots in the entrance. Xavier hung both our coats together on a hook and we walked in. His parents were lying squashed next to each other on a couch in the living room that was off the kitchen. His two brothers were upstairs in their room, and from the pounding they just seemed to be running around in circles. After introducing me quickly to his parents, Xavier led me upstairs. He was the oldest, so he had his own room. He closed the door to his room, but the walls in the house were very thin and it sounded as if everybody in the house was still in the room with us.

How I liked that! All the voices and spoons falling and everybody getting on each other's nerves!

I took a look around Xavier's room. His bed wasn't made. He had a gym award tacked to the wall. Next to it was a project we had made in art class. It was a sunset made out of a bunch of ripped-up yellow and orange tissue paper. I didn't know that anyone kept these projects. Seeing that made me wish that I hadn't thrown out all of my own. I remembered that I had drawn a bird with a top hat in grade five that I wouldn't have minded seeing again.

Xavier put the hook on the door, but he didn't seem to think that would do the job, so he pulled his desk over and then a chair. I sat on the side of the bed watching him. He pulled on the doorknob hard. When he seemed satisfied that nobody was going to be able to get into the room, he turned and dove, all the way from the door, onto the bed. He knocked me over. We were both lying next to each other now.

'Goddamn!' I screamed.

'I'm sorry, Baby,' he said. 'Can I ask you a personal question?'

'No.'

'Please.'

'Nooo…' I whined.

'I'm going to ask you one anyway.'

I put my hand over my ears. I suddenly had a crazy foreboding that Xavier would ask me the right questions, that he would ask about Alphonse and the johns. He wrestled me down on the bed. He grabbed both my hands and pried them away from my head. He pinned me down and sat on me.

'Just for once. I need to tell you about my feelings.'

'No.'

'I want you to be my girlfriend.'

'Look, why do we have to have a name for it?'

'I think that there's a really good energy between us both.'

He started pointing from me to him and then from him to me, over and over again. He had a questioning look on his face as he waited for me to agree that there was good energy between us. I didn't say anything. I didn't want to admit anything.

I had never actually called anybody my boyfriend. My dad had advised me against having a boyfriend. He told me that the jealousy would just kill me. He said that when you are in love with someone, you want to follow them to the bathroom. He said love just makes you pathetic.

'Yes,' I said. 'I'll be your girlfriend.'

'Great!' he exclaimed.

We lay on his bed quietly for a bit. We pushed our bodies gently against each other. We kissed for twenty minutes until we were all kissed out. I took the ends of his shirt and pulled it off over his head. He had a big birthmark that was shaped like a heart below his collarbone. I put the tip of my finger on it. But he pulled my finger back down quickly. I felt like going all the way, but Xavier was too scared. I just pressed my chest against his to feel his heart racing really quickly. I liked it much more than sex.

We just kept kissing each other. Each kiss made my heart beat quickly. We were surprised by every one. No kiss was lost or was insignificant. I had as little experience in kissing someone that I really liked as Xavier had. Alphonse used to kiss me all the time, and I just kissed him back, almost to be polite. I had become numb and desensitized to it. His kisses didn't disgust me the way they had at the beginning, but now they bored me to death. I was always impatient for him to knock it off.

Downstairs Xavier's brother was having a temper tantrum. His mother was making one threat after another. She kept repeating his name over and over as she threatened him.

'Benjamin, don't you dare talk to me that way. Benjamin, it's time for you to change your attitude, mister. Benjamin, look at me in the eye politely when I'm talking to you.'

What it must be like to have your mother scream your name so many times in the space of a minute!

'That was the first time I did anything like that, okay?' Xavier said.

'Okay,' I said.

We lay under the sheet holding each other until his dad called him from downstairs and we hurried out of the bed.

'That was really cool, huh?' Xavier whispered as he moved the barricade away from his door.

We ran downstairs together. His parents asked me about a million questions because I was the first girl that Xavier had ever invited over. They said that he talked about me all the time.

'Where do you live, Baby?' his mother asked me.

'East on Christophe Colomb Street.'

'Oh, there are some beautiful houses there.'

I didn't tell her that she was thinking of the houses above Sherbrooke Street and that I lived below.

'And Xavier tells me that you live with only your dad?'

'Yep.'

'Wow! He's really a courageous man. It's not often you see a man raising a kid all by himself. But he did a great job with you!'

'Thanks, but I'm not that great.'

'Xavier tells me that you scored a hundred percent on the geography test.'

'Yeah, but it was multiple choice, so it was easy.'

'You're so modest. See how polite she is, Xavier. You should learn from Baby.'

Xavier's cheeks were red. He kept grinning ridiculously for no reason whatsoever. He would turn and face the wall to avoid having anyone look directly at him. His parents didn't seem to notice anything was unusual with him, though.

His mother took a picture of me even though I warned her that I looked terrible in pictures. She said that I looked like a movie star. That was my favorite compliment ever.

I always found sex painful physically. I kept hoping it would stop hurting, but it didn't. It wasn't that way when I was cuddling with Xavier. Fooling around with Xavier was like climbing into a hot bath. It was like popping a piece of orange into your mouth.

6

The next time I went over to Xavier's house, we didn't even fool around. Xavier took a loaf of bread and a jar of chocolate spread out of the fridge, and we went onto the covered back porch to eat it. We sat on the old couch out there and listened to a tape of his cousin singing. Philip sang at weddings and things like that and had made

himself a promotional tape. I didn't think there was anything wrong with it, but Xavier almost choked himself
laughing when he listened to it. We ate almost the whole
loaf of bread.

We started putting together the ingredients for bombs:
baking soda, water, and plastic Seven-Up bottles. We
both put on swimming goggles, set up the bombs in the
middle of the yard, and then ran and crouched down by
the porch for cover. Each bottle made a beautiful, hard,
perfectly catastrophic noise. The bottle lay on the
ground, ripped open like some sort of exotic flower.
After our last bomb exploded, Xavier and I just lay on
the ground. One of Xavier's cats came tiptoeing all confused over the scarred battlefield.

They had three cats in their house, which were named
Roland, Harold, and Arthur. The cats were always on the
tables. They would jump up onto chairs that you were
about to sit on. I'd never cared about cats until I started
hanging around at Xavier's house. Xavier and his whole
family were madly in love with their cats. They took pictures of them, and they laughed when the cats had funny
expressions on their faces. Harold was supposed to be an
existentialist because he spent most of his time under the
bathtub. Arthur was supposed to be absentminded but
generous and sweet.

I crawled over to Arthur. I picked up the skinny cat
and held it in my arms and declared my love.

'Poor little shit head. Poor wee little shit head.
Nobody loves you.'

Xavier put his hands out for the cat. He wanted to
declare his love to the cat also, so I gently passed Arthur
over to him. We whispered to the cats until it was supper
time and I had to go home.

Alphonse didn't have any problem with me having sex for money. When you're young, sex doesn't mean as much, it isn't sacred. Children make the best prostitutes because they're the most perfunctory about the whole encounter. The whole act is like a dare, like kissing a frog or something. It's nasty while it's happening, but you forget about it soon afterward. And sometimes it isn't even that nasty. Whatever it is, it's so far from love, it was easy for me to understand why Alphonse never got jealous when I was with a trick.

I knew, on the other hand, why Xavier would make him jealous. When I hung out with Xavier, I didn't want anything to do with Alphonse. I didn't need him. When Xavier and I would eat toast with melted peanut butter in the rain, I was happy and didn't even mind being motherless. I didn't mind being a child. And like any child, I preferred the company of another child.

When I got home that day, I noticed there was a letter with no stamp on it for me in the mailbox. It was from Alphonse. I felt terrible when I saw that letter. I felt as if I had only been pretending to be an ordinary kid lately. It was time to face the facts, I thought as I opened up the letter.

There was a single piece of a puzzle inside the envelope. Alphonse was trying to be mystical, and usually I really liked when he did weird enigmatic stuff like that. But I wasn't interested now in what Alphonse was thinking at all. I threw the letter in the wastepaper basket in the lobby of the building. And just like that, I realized that Alphonse meant nothing to me anymore.

I had been avoiding him for the past couple weeks. I hoped that Alphonse would simply figure that things were over between us and stop coming around. After all, he did have about five other girlfriends. Seeing the letter, I realized I was wrong. He must be desperate to see me if he was venturing near my building. No matter how scrawny Jules was, Alphonse was worried about ever running into him. In fact, Alphonse was probably the only person in the world who was afraid of Jules.

The next day, I walked to school feeling nervous. I looked around every corner, expecting Alphonse to be waiting. I was really being paranoid, as he never got out of bed that early. Still, I was relieved when I finally got to school.

It was on the way home that he got me. A dark burgundy car pulled up when I was a half block away from my building. Alphonse got out of the car and quickly came around toward me and pushed me inside the car. I had planned on spitting in his face and saying some vile things to him. But instead I found that I liked the feeling of being abducted. I found it sort of exciting and suspenseful, almost. I'd been fantasizing about being kidnapped and raped since I was nine years old. My head hit the top of the car as he shoved me in, and my heart beat happily. I hoped it would leave a big bruise on me. I realized that the situation called for being somber and not excited. I sat in the car very quietly, not saying anything.

'Whose car is this?' I asked, but he chose not to respond.

I had no clue if he was angry with me or what. I followed him up to his apartment. He had spray-painted 'I love Baby' in red in the lobby. I didn't know how this relationship had become one-sided, but it had.

Alphonse made me sit next to him on his little leather

love seat. He was too close to me, and I felt as if I was suffocating. He took out a picture of me from his wallet. When I saw the photograph, I felt myself flinch. I hated looking at pictures of myself. I always perceived myself as being really tough and fashionable and foxy. When I saw myself in pictures, I was always shocked by what a skinny, scrawny nerd I was. In the photograph, I was leaning against a car with my hands shoved deep in my pockets. My hair was a mess and my shirt looked two sizes too big. I looked about nine years old.

'I realize that I freaked you out,' Alphonse said. 'I know the way that I feel about you is so heavy. I don't love the way that other people love. I was just born with so much love; it's like a burden to me. I shouldn't make it a burden on you just because I've fallen in love with you. I found this photograph the other day. I took it when we first started hanging around together. I looked at it and I realized, this girl really loves me! She really loves me! But it's my fault. I pushed you away by being too intense.'

'Okay,' I said.

'So I want things to be okay between us again. I don't want there to be any bad blood.'

'Okay.'

'Okay! 'Cause you know I'm crazy 'bout you. I bought you something.'

'You did!'

I was a very shallow person. I felt like jumping into Alphonse's lap when he said that he had a present for me. Alphonse always gave me the coolest gifts. Once he gave me a red fake fur scarf that made me feel like a Russian princess. The girls in my school were jealous of it. He bought me things that only adults could afford.

In a way his gifts were way cooler than Xavier's.

Xavier gave me paper clips that were twisted into stick figures and stuff like that. Once, he'd given me a stone that he thought had a crack in it that looked like a smile. I kept Xavier's gifts on my dresser at home, and my dad was always mistaking them for garbage and throwing them out. Anyway, it's a terrible thing, but I wasn't thinking of Xavier at all when Alphonse handed me a pink paper bag.

I looked inside and saw a skinny kind of pocketknife. It had a thin blade that swung all the way around, the way insect wings did.

'You know what this is?' he asked.

'No.'

'It's a butterfly knife.'

'Is that really what it's called! A butterfly knife?'

'You're only interested in the name. Not the thing!'

'I love the word "butterfly."'

'I know you do. But that's only part of the reason why I bought this for you. I bought it for you 'cause you fit it in any pocket and hide it. No one will spot it. You can just whip it out and cut the guy who's bugging you in the face.'

'Won't I go to jail!'

'Well, don't cut his fuckin' throat or nothing. No dickwad's going to call the cops after he's just banged a thirteen-year-old.'

I held up the knife and spun the blade around, trying to figure out exactly why it was called a butterfly knife. I was pleased with it anyway. I swore to myself that I would get a tattoo of a butterfly on me before I turned fourteen.

'I like taking care of you,' he said. 'You like taking care of me?'

'I guess so.'

He leaned over to kiss me. I closed my eyes as tight as I could, and I leaned in to kiss him. It was then that I started thinking about Xavier again. I wished that Alphonse was as small and skinny as Xavier. Xavier and I wrapped around each other perfectly. With Alphonse it felt as if he were drowning and was taking me down with him. It seemed as if the bus had stopped really quickly, and his body had rammed against mine in the aisle.

As I was sitting on the floor by the front door putting on my boots, Alphonse squatted down beside me.

'You're not seeing anyone else, are you?'

'No,' I answered, concentrating on tying my shoelace as if it were a calculus problem.

'Because you know I couldn't take that, right?'

'I'm not seeing anyone.'

'I'd fucking want to kill you.'

'Jesus Christ!' I screamed, picking up my schoolbag. 'Lighten up, would ya?'

He smiled as I patted him on the head and ran out the door.

I didn't listen to Jules anymore, I thought as I hurried down the street away from his building, so why should I listen to Alphonse? I was terribly annoyed that Alphonse was trying to tell me what to do. I walked down the street, happy, thinking that I could do whatever I wanted. I didn't need to turn tricks because I didn't mind being flat broke. I'd been broke since the day I was born. Alphonse was the fool who needed money all the time. Let him find some other way of getting it, I thought defiantly. Still, I knew that I'd best stay out of his way.

*

I continued seeing Xavier as if nothing had happened. I made sure to try and stop by Alphonse's house a couple times a week. I told Alphonse that I had exams and I would be really busy for a while. I told him that if I got anything lower than a B, I might have to go back to detention. That was, of course, a lie. Alphonse seemed to want to believe anything in the world other than the fact that I had a boyfriend.

About a month after my abduction, Xavier and I were walking home, as usual. I picked up a stick and was swinging it around. It was a habit from childhood that I hadn't been able to shake. We stopped at the library and went down to the children's section. We sat across from each other at a table that was too small for us, as we couldn't fit our knees under it properly. Xavier was experimenting with the punk rock look that day. He had pushed all his hair back with gel and was wearing a tight black sweater with holes in it that he had cut himself with a pair of scissors. He took his notebook out and looked in it, seeming preoccupied with something.

'You have to promise me that you aren't attracted to any boy, other than me,' Xavier turned and said to me.

'All right,' I said, putting down my own math notebook.

'Do you mean it?'

'Yes.'

'I made a list here of all the boys in our grade,' he said, showing me his notebook. 'I would like to go through each of them with you so that you can fully consider whether or not you are attracted to them.'

'No.'

'Please. It'll only take a second.'

'Fine. Hurry up, though.'

'Gordon Baxter?'

'Who?'

'Peter Campbell.'

'Who's that?'

'You know. That blond kid who rides the BMX.'

'No.'

'Gary Wheeler.'

'Which one is he?'

'He looks like Mel Gibson.'

'I've never even seen him before.'

'He sits right behind us in science class and you don't know who he is?'

'Maybe. I can't picture him, though.'

'Well, I guess that means you're not attracted to him, right?'

'Right.'

'Those were the best-looking guys. The ones I was worried about!'

'Well, you don't have to worry anymore then.'

The lights turned on and off, signaling that the library was closing.

'Damn!' Xavier shouted. 'I was having such a good time.'

We headed back outside and started walking homeward.

'I have to go down this street now,' he said meaningfully when we got to his corner.

When we got to the street corner where we parted ways, Xavier and I always took our sweet time saying good-bye to each other. We were addicted to kissing each other. We would kiss in shock, as if we had two buckets of water dumped on our heads. We would kiss sadly, as if the dog was lost in the night. We would kiss like cockroaches headed for the cracks. One time we decided to see if we could set some sort of record. We stood there like hens pecking grains off the ground. We kissed each other fifty times, but then I started to get dizzy, so we had to knock it off. Once, on a particularly cold day, he had kissed me with his ski mask pulled down over his face. It was like all that existed of him was that kiss.

We faced each other now and held each other's hands, swinging them back and forth. Then we started playing mercy and squeezing each other's fingers really hard. We yelped and kicked at each other's ankles.

Then a small white bird feather floated through the air between us. If you caught one of those in your hands, you got a wish that would certainly come true. It was much more reliable than eyelashes. Xavier and I jumped up and down trying to snatch it while pushing each other out of the way. It sailed down to the ground and landed gracefully on the sidewalk. We both dove after it. Xavier captured it and held it down under his cupped palm.

'I have it. I have it!' Xavier cheered.

As I was getting to my feet, I almost fell right back down again. There, standing across the street, was Alphonse. He was staring right at me. Once I met his gaze, I couldn't drop it. I turned to look the other way, and when I looked back, he was still staring right at me.

I jumped to my feet. My heart was beating so fast that the goddamn thing was choking me, jumping right into my throat. I had been hanging out so long with both Xavier and Alphonse and we'd never bumped into each other, so I assumed that it was somehow impossible for either of them to occupy the same physical space at the same time.

Xavier stood up too, oblivious that anything was going

on. He held the feather in his glove and was taking his time making a wish. I was scared that he was going to spend all day deliberating on his wish. I leaned over and wiped the feather off.

'Hey!' he yelled. 'Why'd you do that? I was about to wish for something really nice.'

'You should have wished that we were invisible.'

'Anyhow, we don't have anything now. I was wishing for world peace, you know, and now you've messed it up for everyone just because all of a sudden you're in some sort of mood. Very self-centered.'

I turned around and took a few steps away from him. I hoped Xavier would also do an about-face and head off in the opposite direction. I needed him to walk away so that I could walk over to Alphonse. I knew that Alphonse was probably getting madder by the second waiting for me. When I turned around, Xavier was still standing in the same spot. I knew that he was waiting for his good-bye kiss.

'You can't go no place without giving me a kiss,' he said, smiling.

He put out his arms, just like a toddler waiting to be picked up and hugged to death. Now I was really terrified.

'I'm in a hurry. I can't give you a good-bye kiss today, okay? I'll owe you one for tomorrow,' I pleaded.

'What are you talking about?' he said, looking confused. 'A kiss takes approximately point five seconds. You could have done it already. It took you like ten times as long to explain how you didn't have time to give me a kiss than it would have to just give me a kiss.'

I knew that there was no way I was going to be able to get away with not kissing Xavier. I leaned in and gave him a sloppy kiss on the lips. He jumped back and pretended to be electrocuted. This was his new thing. He walked off down the street all shaky and crooked, as if he were still experiencing the effects of electric shock. When he turned the corner, I walked across the street toward Alphonse. I looked at the ground. I wished I had telepathic powers and could make Alphonse think that he hadn't seen what he'd just seen.

'What the fuck was that!'

I shrugged. He took my hand and dragged me down the street and pushed me up the stairs, I looked at my wrist. I hadn't felt any pain, but there was a red ring where his hand had been squeezing. The sight of it made me want to sit down and cry. I ran up ahead and waited at his front door. I stood to the side as he unlocked it. When he flung the door open, I ran inside ahead of him. I didn't know where to go. I just stood there, like a fool, I guess. He pushed me hard toward the bedroom. I fell on the ground and skinned my knee on the carpet. Before I could even feel it, he picked me up and threw me onto the bed. He held down my hands and sat on me, pinning me down. I was afraid he was going to spit in my face, since his hands weren't free to slap me.

'Who was that kid?' he demanded.

'He's best friends with my cousin. I have to hang out with him.'

'You're lying.'

'My dad's best friends with his dad.'

'I don't believe that. That's a lie.'

'My dad likes him so he lets me hang out later at night if he thinks I'm dating him.'

'I guess that sort of makes sense, but it's still nasty.'

'I won't hang out with him anymore. He's a virgin so I don't have to sleep with him.'

'Has he seen your breasts?' he asked bitterly.

'No! He's a baby. He just likes to kiss good-bye.'

'I want you to stay away from him. You're my lady and it looks bad. What are you doing to me?' He sounded like a little boy. 'Now I have to walk down the street like a fool. How many people I know have seen you with that little bastard? I feel like packing up all my bags and getting the hell out of here. I'm so fucking cool. Did you see that little pipsqueak that you were with?'

'Okay.'

'Fuck you with your okays, Baby.'

'Okay.'

'Don't push your fucking luck. I forgive your ass now. Let me just say for the record that that was the saddest-looking kid I have ever seen, and I don't know how you could kiss him. You! Who pretends to be so goddamn fussy all the time.'

I lay there staring at him, not knowing what to say about my love for Xavier. It was much too dear for me to explain it to him anyhow. It would be like giving your pet mouse to a cat. I was also afraid that if I explained to him what I liked about Xavier, he would just say something to prove how idiotic I was. Even the stupidest adult was a better debater than me.

Alphonse looked at me tenderly. He reached over and started playing with my hair. Love made his eyes go the way that junkies' eyes went: all welled up with tears that are never going to fall.

I told Alphonse that I had a meeting with my social worker. He rolled off me and just lay on the bed, staring at the ceiling. I flipped off it, almost hitting the floor again, and ran out the door. I decided that I was only going to see Xavier from now on. To hell with Alphonse.

As I was leaving his house, I kicked one of his boots down the stairs and left it there.

There was a surprise warm day. You still had to wear a coat, but the snow miraculously thawed by noon and everyone was out and walking the streets. I should have stayed inside with Xavier, but he wanted to take advantage of the weather to ride his bike. As we doubled down St Dominique Street on a bicycle, it was my turn to sit up front and pedal. Xavier had his arms around my waist too tightly, and he kept screaming about how his ass hurt. How could we not be noticed by the entire city? He sounded like a dog that had been hit by a car. We passed rue Napoleon. I knew that Alphonse and his friends used to meet at a small club on this street during the day. I had a crazy urge to turn down it, and so I did. As we approached the club, I began to feel nervous, as if I was going to pee myself. I could see a small crowd of black men gathered out there, and among them I could easily make out Alphonse, with his red hair and turquoise coat. Xavier kept his arms wrapped around me, alternately singing and moaning loudly in pain. He started to tickle me, and I flinched so suddenly that we crashed on the side of the curb.

Alphonse and all his friends turned to look at us, mangled up with our bicycle on the sidewalk.

'Quick, get up!' I yelled to Xavier.

'No, my butt's broken. I need to lie here for a while.'

'Come on. There's someone coming to kill us. Hurry! Hurry!'

You might have thought Xavier was too old to play this game, but he was not. He untangled himself from the bicycle, screaming, 'They're coming! They'll torture us!' He got on the front of the bike, yelling at me to jump on. I climbed behind him and put my hands on his shoulders. After a few false starts Xavier managed to get the bike upright and going. The whole time we were screaming because our imaginary enemies were coming closer. They were practically on us.

Xavier cycled us right past Alphonse. I'd never seen Alphonse look so pissed off, and it gave me a rush of strength. I yelled loudly to Xavier that our enemies had dogs and that they were now at my feet. I knew that I was offending Alphonse's dignity by ignoring him and acting like such a child, but I wanted to do much more than that. I wanted Alphonse to know for sure how I felt, that I thought he was a worm. I turned back and flipped him the bird. I wasn't smiling either. Alphonse and I stared at each other, deadly serious.

7

I was in my bedroom when I heard a crashing noise in the living room. I walked in to find that Jules had knocked three lamps off the coffee table. Lately he had started picking up every lamp he found in the garbage. They lined his bureau and the floor. When he learns to make them all work, I thought, his room will be filled with so much light.

He was wearing a big blanket with a hole cut in the middle of it over his head. That's what was making him clumsy.

'Oh, no!' I said. 'You're going to be one of those guys who wears a blanket on their heads.'

We both started to laugh at that. I helped him set the

lamps back up, and I realized that I didn't feel like being alienated forever from Jules.

Later that night some kids I knew from remedial stream came by my building. They started hollering my name from the sidewalk down below. I leaned out my bedroom window to see what was going on. Zoë waved at me.

Zoë had been working on her fucked-up image a lot during the past year. She didn't look thirteen anymore. She had big boobs and wore a tight black plastic jacket to accentuate them. She bleached her hair and wore giant leather boots everywhere. She was the most popular girl in our circle of juvenile delinquents. She wouldn't hang out with anyone who wasn't a badass poor kid. For some reason, she always insisted that she was my best friend. Maybe it was because my apartment was filthy, I didn't have a mother, and my dad fell asleep on benches. She had made being down-and-out into a religion.

She thought the same things about me that Alphonse had thought. He thought he had chosen the perfect girl when he had seen me in the park with a black eye. He must have thought that I was so mature. He must have thought that I was sad and sweet and vulnerable. But he had chosen wrong. I wasn't like that at all. There was a part of me that was smart and original and nerdy too.

When I thought of my old friends Linus Lucas and Theo, I realized they were not really criminals either. They were like me. We were just acting out the strangest, tragic little roles, pretending to be criminals in order to get by. We gave very convincing performances.

I put on my coat and my running shoes. I decided against my moon boots since these kids hated anything practical like winter boots more than anything else in the world. Since we'd be riding in the car, I didn't think it made much of a difference anyhow. Zoë pointed proudly at her girlfriend Cherie's new car. It was a big blue embarrassing Chevrolet that was impossible to park. The leather seats were wide and made it feel as if you were sitting on a couch, which was nice. There were a bunch of kids crammed in. I smiled down at Zoë and all of a sudden I wanted to squeeze into the car with all of them.

Alphonse wasn't the only person who didn't like me hanging out with Xavier. None of my remedial friends were very fond of the idea either. I'd just stopped hanging out with them altogether. In truth, even though I was one of them, I was a little relieved to get far away from them. I was tired of their superiority complexes. Maintaining a superiority complex, especially when you were a loser, took a lot of mental effort and denial.

Zoë's new girlfriend, Cherie, the loudest girl on the planet, was behind the wheel. She was playing with Zoë's curls as she drove. There were three boys in the back; one of them was a kid everyone said was cute named Greg. Zoë had implied for months that Greg and I would be perfect for each other. She motioned for me to sit next to him. I climbed over the laps of the two other boys and sat next to Greg in the backseat, just to make everybody happy.

Greg was sitting next to the window smoking probably his fiftieth cigarette of the night. The tips of his fingers were so yellow that you would imagine he colored them in with a marker or something. Cigarette burns speckled the front of the black sweater he was wearing under his black leather jacket. He had the word 'Hell-raiser' written in ballpoint pen on his hand and a big ring with keys on it hanging on the belt loop of his jeans. I wasn't sure exactly how that was supposed to be cool.

Greg wore his black hair so long in the front that you couldn't see his face. His brother had given him a pair of hand-me-down combat boots that were three sizes too big, but he desperately wanted a pair, so he wore them anyway. When he walked, it seemed as if he was walking on the moon, or stepping over puddles. It got so that he started walking like that even when he wasn't wearing them. I saw him walking on the moon at the swimming pool in his bare feet once.

Everybody in the bobo stream used to talk about how good-looking he was. He was considered the intellectual in our group.

'He's mysterious. I would sleep with him in a heart-beat if I liked guys,' Zoë had said to me. 'He'd be perfect for you because he's super smart. He's like a genius, but he still hangs out with us. That's so cool.'

He had a motorcycle magazine with a section that had drawings of the devil on it. He always carried it around in his back pocket so he could pull it out and comment on the artistic merits of the drawings.

'This one is really quite good because of the details on the wings. You see that? This one is very sloppy because the face has really bad proportions. Look at how small his hands are. These were probably done in watercolor and not airbrush. Only real slobs and people who haven't even been painting very long don't use air-brush.'

Zoë thought he was on the straight and narrow and that he was going to grow up to be a lawyer or something, but she just didn't know anyone who was straight to be able to compare him to. There were many oddball things he did that kids from straight families didn't do. For one thing, he hung around with this old guy named Bertrand who drove a limousine. Bertrand would pass by his house, pick him up, and just drive him places. They would go grocery shopping together in the limousine or drive over to stare at the river. And he had a huge scab on his arm that he used to pick at with a knife. This really grossed me out. Zoë told me just to not think about it when I was with him. Greg pulled up his sleeve on the arm that didn't have the scab on it as a conversation starter. He peeled off a Band-Aid to reveal a tattoo of a laughing skull with a top hat on it.

'I didn't know when I got it that it was a Hell's Angels tattoo. If the Hells see me with this tattoo...' Greg said while staring at me expressionlessly, 'they're going to take a knife and cut it right off.'

He put the Band-Aid back down. He had to rub it to try and make it stay on, but there didn't seem to be much glue left. He must have been peeling it up all night to show people how he was hiding it.

I wasn't drinking, but everybody else was. I wasn't in the mood, and I wanted to be able to do my homework later. Zoë parked the car on a dark little street by the river. They were all getting louder the more they drank. Inspired by Greg's revelation about the Hell's Angels, they started telling stories of their own.

'There's this guy named Pierrot. He was selling laundry detergent instead of cocaine to the Hells. So as a punishment his left hand was chopped off, and then he was rammed into a washing machine.'

'I heard there was this Hell's Angel and he used to go to the river fishing every day. So one day, I went up to him and said, like, shit, don't you know that the fish are so polluted in this river that you can't eat them. Then he tells me that he only catches big ones so that they can give him blow jobs. He said it was like the best head ever. They suck you off as they die.'

Everyone started screaming and convulsing with disgust at that last tale. I knew a few Hell's Angels who fished down at the river because my dad and I used to go down there every Sunday to fish. We mostly only caught tiny little fish that bit kernels of corn if you put them on the end of your hook. There's no way any of those fish could fit anything bigger than a pencil in their mouths. Some of the guys brought their fishes home to eat. But anyway, the fish were long dead before they would be able to get them home and take them to bed. That Hell's Angel must have been pulling his leg.

'Baby, you're so quiet,' Greg said suddenly.

'She's shy. Leave her alone!' Cherie screamed from up front.

'I didn't say there was anything wrong with being quiet,' Greg said. 'I like it. She's thoughtful. I like people who think a lot. And then when they talk to you, you feel much more special.'

I didn't know what to say. I wasn't particularly quiet anyhow; I just didn't really feel like making an effort to say anything. I had a bad habit of wanting people I didn't like to like me. Tonight I just didn't care. Since the car had parked, everyone was depressing me.

'Are you seeing someone?' Cherie asked.

'Of course she's seeing someone!' Greg interjected. 'If you're that cute and you don't have a boyfriend, it means you're a real bitch. So personally I think it's a good thing when I meet a girl and she tells me that she has a boyfriend. It means that she's tested and true.'

'She's dating Xavier,' Zoë said.

I felt myself go all red when she said that.

'Who's Xavier?' Greg asked, turning to me, again without any expression on his face.

'That kid who rides the bicycle with the lobster heads on the handlebars and wears a lab coat,' Zoë said, her voice dripping with disdain.

'I've seen that kid!' Cherie shrieked. 'Oh, my God! He is so weird.'

'He's always having garage sales outside his house in the summer,' one of the other boys in the back said.

'That guy is not your boyfriend!' Cherie bellowed. 'I thought he was nine years old. I really thought he was. Isn't he too young for you?'

'Baby looks older than she is,' Zoë said.

'How old are you, Baby?' Greg asked.

'Thirteen,' I said.

All of a sudden, without saying where I was going or good-bye or anything like that, I climbed over Greg and out of the car at a red light. I heard Cherie laughing hysterically as I sloshed down the slushy street. Zoë got out of the car and called after me.

'Fuck you, Baby. Don't you come crawling back to me. You're no friend of mine. You're a stuck-up bitch!'

'Fuck you back!' I screamed. I didn't know what the hell was up with me. I thought I was having some sort of personality crisis. I used to love riding around with kids, and now it didn't do anything for me. That was pretty confusing. I just wanted to be a good kid. I didn't want to sit drinking beer in a car with a bunch of teenagers who were going to be in grade seven for the next four years, who talked about stuff you would see on the cover of the tabloid newspapers. I wanted to be able to go home like Xavier did at the end of the day.

I walked down the street, a broken lonely East End

street. The air smelled like the river. Night always seemed darker the farther east you went. I realized that in the course of the day I had told everyone to fuck off. The only friend I had left was Xavier.

I went home, but the front door was locked. I banged on the door, but Jules didn't answer. I put my ear up against the door for ten minutes before I was satisfied that he wasn't there. There were two locks on the door: one that I had the key for and one that I didn't. Sometimes when Jules was mad at me, he locked the second lock. If I didn't come home by midnight, he locked it. If I was out past midnight, it meant that I was whoring around and I could do it on someone else's time. He said that if he locked me out, no one could accuse him of having made me a delinquent. It was only ten thirty, and my curfew wasn't until eleven. I didn't know what I'd done this time. Just lately, he'd started locking it more and more. Sometimes he locked it if he was going out of town and didn't want the social worker to show up and find me there alone. Whenever he locked me out, I'd go spend the night at Zoë's. Her mother was always in a daze and let anybody sleep over. Zoë had a big double bed. It was where all the kids went when they were having arguments with their parents or they'd been kicked out. Sometimes I was happy when he locked me out because I liked sleeping at her house.

Lying next to other kids, sleeping in their T-shirts and underwear, was so comfortable. Everybody's legs were cozy and warm. If you were having trouble falling asleep, all you had to do was turn your head to the side and talk to the person lying next to you until you drifted off. It was nice to be woken up unintentionally. We all started having the same breathing pattern as we slept. That's how we were meant to sleep: a bunch of children all jumbled together in a softly breathing heap. I had such nice dreams there some nights that when I woke up I thought I must have borrowed the dream from some other child in the bed. Once I dreamed I was standing on a pier at a lake. The wood under my feet was warm and soggy, and the air was blue and filled with gnats and dragonflies. I had a butterfly net and I was dipping it in the water, trying to catch fish. I'd never been to such a pier. It must have been some other kid's dream for sure.

I stood leaning against the door for twenty minutes, kicking myself for having cursed at Zoë. Why had I done that! Everyone in the car was probably going to sleep heavenly over at her house, and here I was, stuck in a stinking hallway. I started banging on the door, hoping that I could kick it in. I thought that I would sleep in the hallway, but the landlord came out in his gold-colored crumpled pajamas and told me that I couldn't do that, for some stupid reason.

'Can you get the key and let me in?' I asked him.

'I don't have the key for that top lock. If I did, in a week you'd say that I stole your television.'

8

'You look good tonight!' someone called to me from their car.

Fooling around with Xavier was so much different from being with tricks. Xavier and I climbed all over each other like we were on the monkey bars. He'd start singing a Led Zeppelin song while we were making out. He'd sing *ba dad ba dum* while pulling his sweatshirt off, then swing it around his fingers as if he were in a strip show. It was quicker too, and I liked that, how it never seemed long enough. I pretended that my plane was leaving to Russia and I had to kiss him good-bye quickly before the KGB burst in. We were always laughing.

When I had sex with a trick, everything seemed as if it was happening in slow motion. Each movement seemed more tedious and distasteful than the one before. Each time it seemed to last for three hours or something, even when it was only half an hour. It felt as if my life was passing me right by while I was hanging out with them.

I had been determined to never see him again, but still the only person I could think of going to right then was Alphonse. So much for my resolution, only a few hours earlier, to be free of him. Unfortunately, he was the most dependable person in my life.

I walked quickly to his apartment building. The cold was being sneaky and disgusting. It was getting down into my ankles and my neck. I wished it would leave me alone. I decided to run down the street, to keep warmer. I wasn't sure what reaction I was going to get once I got to Alphonse's, or how I was going to act toward him. I knew it was going to be bad, but knowing this made me feel as if I was magnetically drawn to his place. I ran up the stairs, almost curious to see what would happen to me now. Our hearts are never ready for these types of confrontations. I started feeling hyper because my own was beating so hard. The sound of my shoes on the steps seemed to make terrible and tremendous noises, as if I were an angel coming up the stairs. I looked down at my feet standing on the black tiles with golden specks. I was struck by the feeling that if I jumped up and down and just didn't stop, the building would just come apart.

When he opened the door, I saw right away that Alphonse was positively stoned. He looked as if he had just been drowning himself in the bathtub and had achieved a higher consciousness. As he stood there staring, I started to laugh. I decided that I was the one who was going to do the reacting.

'Look who it is!' I screamed. I flung my arms around him. 'Look who it is, buddy! It's me.'

'Baby, chill out,' he said, backing up. 'I hate when you get all crazy. What are you doing here, showing up like this? You don't have much fuckin' pride, do you?'

'I need a place to stay.'

'Get inside, then. Come on. I can't lie. It's good to see you again.'

I followed him into the living room. He walked slowly and at one point stumbled sideways against the wall. The radio was on, so I took off my fur coat and started to do all kinds of modern dance moves. He tried to get out of the room to walk down the hall, but I blocked his way by doing some martial arts stuff. Alphonse fell back onto the living room couch. He sat there looking up at me.

'We're going to go through this again?' he asked. 'I hate this side of you.'

Alphonse couldn't stand when I was excited and crazy. Once I pretended I was an android who had run low on batteries. It took us half an hour to walk three blocks. Another time I pretended that I was speaking Russian. I liked the sound of my accent so much that I kept going on and on even though he begged me not to.

'Who's your daddy?' I yelled, slamming my hand down on the shelf. A glass vase fell off and smashed onto the ground.

'You're destroying shit, Baby! Look what the fuck you just did!'

'I'm sorry! I told you I was sorry.'

'You didn't say you were sorry. I can't even think properly.'

'I'm sorry, but I just wanted to know who's your daddy.'

'So how come you need a place to stay?'

'I'm the one who's going to be asking the questions tonight, mister. You had better answer my question before I answer any of yours.'

'What the hell is your question?'

'I want to know who is your daddy?'

'What the fuck are you talking about?'

'*Who's your daddy?*'

'Baby, you're…'

'Who's your daddy!' I yelled at the top of my lungs. 'Who's your daddy!'

Alphonse jumped up, grabbed my arm, and started pulling me down the hall. It surprised me how easy it was for him to move me. For a minute, I'd forgotten that Alphonse was literally the size of two of me. He pushed me into an opened closet in the hall and slammed the door shut. I stumbled over the boots and boxes on the floor and fell down.

'Now count to fucking five hundred and come out when you're ready to act like a normal human being. Jesus! Let's both get ourselves collected.'

As soon as he closed the door and I was left in the dark, I felt extinguished, as though I was a fairy and a child had stopped believing in me. One of the worst things in juvie was that when you had broken a rule, they made you go into 'backup'. You had to sit in a tiny white room for up to two days. One boy had been in there for yelling too loudly that someone had stolen his motherfucking Pepsi. I'd gone in there once for threatening to murder a girl named Michelle in her sleep. I tried to explain that it was just an expression, but nonetheless, I had to spend twenty-four hours in there. I'd developed a nervous tic in backup, where I'd put my head down on my shoulder three or four times in a row, and I was still working on kicking it. It came out when I felt anxious. One of the reasons I wanted to stay out of detention was to avoid backup. Now, here I was on the outside, locked up again. The injustice of my lot in life hit me hard all of a sudden.

'I don't know what the hell to do,' I whispered to myself. 'I don't even have a home.'

I figured that I'd come to the realization that Alphonse had wanted me to. I knocked gently on the door, but there was no response. I squeezed my mouth in the crack under the door and begged him to let me out, but he didn't come near. I started kicking the closet door with my running shoes furiously, but it was futile. I could have banged on the floor to get help, but there was only a pet store downstairs and it was closed. Besides, what help would I get in the end? If the police came and found me in this predicament, I would be punished severely. I'd be in detention until I was fifteen, at the very least. I sat right down on a pair of boots as though I was sitting on a curb waiting for a school bus.

A social worker told me that the point of backup was that we were supposed to reflect on our situation and how to improve it. But I never thought about my actual life while I was in backup. I would think about anything else. Adults reflect on ugly things and come out of jails more brutal than they went in. A child's mind is like a bird trapped in an attic, looking for any crack of light to fly out of. Children are given vivid imaginations as defense mechanisms, as they usually don't have much means for escape. The minute I heard them lock the door, I'd lean against the wall and start daydreaming. Once you started daydreaming, it was like being hypnotized.

The closet was different than backup because there was no light in there. It was completely dark. I didn't want to imagine anything because I would confuse it with reality. If I fantasized about owning a pigeon coop, the whole closet might suddenly be filled with pigeons. It seemed entirely possible.

I tried not to think or imagine anything, to just keep my mind a blank, but the dark started imagining things for me. It started imagining there was a hole underneath my feet. It started imagining there was a man sitting right next to me, looking at me with terrible zombie eyes. I didn't dare move because I might touch something very scary that the dark had imagined, like the face of a wolf.

I don't know how long I'd been in there when Alphonse opened the closet door suddenly. I just sat there with my hands over my face, shielding my eyes from the light. I wished he had warned me or knocked on the door. Jules used to do the same thing, turning on the light in the middle of the night when he had something to say. After a few seconds, I squinted and lowered my hands and took a look at Alphonse. He was wearing a big bulky sweater over some underwear and had a spatula in his hand. He looked really stoned.

'Hey,' I said.

'Christ, I almost forgot about you in there. I'm sorry. I was only going to leave you in there a second. I just sort of wanted you to cool out.'

'I think I'm going to go now.'

'What are you talking about? You can't go home. You're going to live here. I'm making dinner now.'

Alphonse laughed as he helped me up. I went to the bathroom and peeked into the cabinet mirror. I was a mess, but that was nothing new. I never spent any time grooming myself, and as a result, I always looked like a kid that had just fallen off a seesaw. I picked up Alphonse's hairbrush to try and fix myself up. I had to comb a little dreadlock out of the back of my head because it had been a long while since I'd bothered to even attempt to brush it. I tied my hair in a ponytail on the top of my head. I put on some makeup that he had in a box in his drug cabinet and was always encouraging me to wear. I stepped out of the bathroom feeling like a different kind of person: tougher but empty.

I sat down on the living room couch and tried to feel right about being there. I tried putting my hands behind my head and then underneath my butt. I tried lying down but sat back up quickly. I even tried sitting upside down with my legs straight up the back of the sofa. I was twitchy, like all my instincts were telling me to get the hell out of there.

I heard him start singing in the kitchen. Once he told me that if he had one wish in the world, it would be to have a better singing voice. I thought his voice was really good though, or at least that he sang better than anyone else I knew. Now he was singing 'Desperado', which was one of my favorites. That song had a funny way of reminding me of places that I'd never been to, places that I'd seen in the pages of *National Geographic*, places that I might never actually get to.

I put my feet up on the coffee table and stared at my

running shoes. They looked like the shoes someone would be wearing when they were dragged, murdered, out of a lake. I remembered the story Jules told about how they'd taken his shoes away at the hospital so that he couldn't escape. That's when I realized I had my shoes on and they were all I needed to get the hell out of there.

At the detention center, kids were always making dummies of themselves. This was considered the first essential step to escaping, as it would give you time to get far away from the building before your flight was even detected. This was often the only step kids took. It was a lot less risky than actually trying to sneak out of the building. So everyone labored at their dummies, stuffing nylon stockings full of toilet paper. There was often a shortage of toilet paper because of this activity. There was a half-baked dummy in almost everyone's room, stored in the closet or under their beds. Staff were always finding and dismantling them.

Sometimes you would feel staff putting their hand on you in the middle of the night, making sure that you were real and not a pile of clothes masquerading as a human. It made me feel reassured when they walked off satisfied. Yes, it was a real child lying under the covers.

I called out to Alphonse that I was going to lie down. I walked into his bedroom and quickly tucked some pillows under the cover and positioned them in the shape of a sleeping body. This probably wasn't even necessary. But it felt symbolic, as if I was leaving part of myself behind. The part of me that had been with Alphonse was fake.

Even while he was at his best, singing 'Desperado', Alphonse didn't come close to Xavier. Xavier made me feel happy and intelligent. With Alphonse I was just a jerk with a ponytail who wasn't going to see or do anything in this world! I put on my fur coat and pushed open the window and crawled right out onto the fire escape. The fire escape was slippery as hell. I held on to the freezing railing and stepped slowly and carefully down to the street.

As I dropped to the ground and started walking away, I whispered the words to 'Desperado' under my breath, just to calm myself down. At first, I didn't realize I was singing the song, but when I was half a block away, the sound of my voice got louder, and I couldn't help but hear it. After three blocks, I felt completely rid of Alphonse and I started singing 'Desperado' loud enough that passersby turned their heads.

Since I had no curfew, the night seemed to have entirely different dimensions. It seemed almost as if flight was possible. And if not flight, then at least jumping out of a window.

I was on the corner of Sherbrooke Street not knowing where to go. It started to snow and I watched the flakes light up like millions of tiny fireflies in the streetlights. Sometimes when you are standing still and it's snowing, you think that you hear music. You can't tell where it's coming from either. I wondered if we all really did have a soundtrack, but we just get so used to it that we can't hear it anymore, the same way that we block out the sound of our own heartbeat.

I experienced a cold shock of freedom. I could go anyplace now and do anything I wanted, which I could do before, I guess, but now there would be no guilty feelings. That's what I thought, at least. I decided to go and see Xavier, as he had just suddenly become my only friend in the world. I thought he'd help me out. I thought that I could sleep in their garage and Xavier could bring me cream cheese sandwiches.

I hurried down the street to Xavier's house. I decided not to knock on their front door. Instead, I crawled over the back fence. I stood under Xavier's window and started throwing snowballs up at it. I jumped up and down on my tippy toes. That was a kind of prayer that I used to do back then. Finally his window opened and he stuck his head out, looking utterly disoriented.

'What are you doing there!' he whispered.

When he whispered, he always whispered louder than he spoke. I gestured angrily for him to come downstairs immediately. He left the window and in a few minutes came out his front door. He had his cat, Roland, in his arms. He said Roland needed some air anyhow. The cat wriggled free and Xavier laughed. He was wearing his seagull pajamas under his winter coat, and he had on his mother's furry pink boots. He then noticed all the makeup that I had put on.

'You look pretty,' Xavier said.

'Thank you,' I said.

'Really, really, really pretty.'

'Thank you.'

'It's eleven o'clock. What are you doing here?'

'Can I come in?'

'I'm not allowed to have anybody over after ten o'clock. That's my mother's number-one fascistic rule. We can hang out tomorrow, though.'

'I'm not going to school tomorrow.'

'Why not? Where are you going?'

'I can't go home tonight. My dad locked me out.'

'What! How could he do that to you? He can't do that. Call the police.'

He took both my hands in his hands. I loved so much when he did that. I had seen mothers take their children's hands like that and ask them what was wrong. Maybe he had learned it from his mother. I was glad that I had come here. He always cheered me up just by making me feel I was a part of his world instead of just my own.

'I just can't stay at my house anymore. Can I sleep in your room?'

'Are you crazy? My mother doesn't even think we should be left alone in the same room together anymore. She says that things can go too far and that we might not even have control over them ourselves. Can you imagine her talking to me like that? I want us to always, always be together. For the rest of our lives.'

'Well, can you ask your mother? Otherwise, I'm going to end up sleeping on the street.'

'What!! Are you crazy!! Are you certifiably mad! I won't let that happen. I'll go tell my mother that you're going to stay here. You'd better wait here, though. In case she says anything stupid and embarrassing.' He scooped up the cat and went back inside.

I might as well have gone with him, as I could overhear the conversation.

'What is Baby doing here at this hour?' his mother asked.

'She's my girlfriend!'

'This isn't right. Does her father know that she's here?'

'He doesn't care where she is. She has to stay here.'

'I'm going to call her father.'

'Nooo! You can't do that. You're ruining this for me.'

'You can't interfere in this, Xavier. I don't think you should be spending so much time with her either.'

As I started to walk away, Xavier came running out after me. He had put on his own boots and had a plastic bag in one hand and Roland under the other. His mother came out of the house after him. I tried to wipe my pink lipstick off, but it wasn't any use. I didn't like how she was looking at me. The way she looked at me made me feel naked. I felt as if I was stripping at detention all over again.

Then his father came out. He was wearing his slippers and pajamas but was looking serious as hell, as if the cold couldn't possibly bother him. He walked over and just picked Xavier up in his arms and carried him inside, as though he was a little kid. And I realized that he was only a little kid, really.

'Baby, I love you,' Xavier called after me.

I headed back to St Louis square. I still had chosen Xavier, even if I might not be allowed to ever see him again. I chose Xavier, but I still had to go back to Alphonse's so that I could have somewhere to stay that night. I hurried down the street, pulling out my butterfly knife and unfolding the blade. I whispered harshly at the air in front of me.

'Motherfucker. Don't mess with me.'

I didn't know who I was supposed to be swearing at. I guess I was threatening my own shadow. I couldn't really hurt anybody but myself. I held out my skinny arms and noticed what a weakling I was. Who in this world was afraid of me?

I wasn't paying attention to anything as I walked along. I was trying to have very little to do with reality. This might be a good tactic while you are in heaven but not on earth. I stepped off the sidewalk and slipped on the ice. I splayed across the ground like a handful of change. I scraped my knees and my palms and my chin, and the knife went skittering across the street.

You can only imagine what a wreck I was when I finally showed up at St Louis Square, bleeding everywhere. First, I wanted to buy some hash oil. It only cost three bucks, and the dealer who sold it in this park always let me borrow his pipe. Smoking it always made me feel like a fat drug pusher in a cheetah-skin coat I'd seen on the cover of a reggae album. Yes sir! It made me feel spiritual. Maybe I could just find a good bush to sit under and close my eyes and think about birds with long colorful tails that swirled all over the place, like the ones on Chinese tea tins. In St Louis Square there were always a few adults who called themselves Steppenwolf or Jonathan Livingston Seagull. They would sit next to you and talk about how they were a sort of messiah all night long. That was a good thing, as I had no desire whatsoever to be alone at that moment.

When I got to the park, I spotted Alphonse right away. He was talking to a drug dealer who was leaning against a skinny tree. Alphonse nodded to me and the drug dealer skittered off. Alphonse walked up to me, with his head tilted to the side. He always did that when he was curious about something. I used to think he was especially handsome when he did that.

'I don't know why you're standing there so calmly. I was looking for you. I am seriously going to kick your ass.' Since he was still stoned, he didn't sound that threatening.

'Look, I just feel all freaked out and lonely tonight.'

'Are you okay, sugar?' he asked me. 'Somebody mess with you?'

'I fell down.'

'Where the fuck did you go? Did you tell me you were going out?'

'I said I was going for a walk.'

'Bullshit. I don't even remember. How the fuck did you fall right on your face?'

He laughed and put his arms around me and kissed me on the top of the head.

'Poor baby,' he said. 'Come on. Let's go home, okay? Let's get stoned and lie in a hot bath. With some nice-smelling salts. Then we can just cuddle for the rest of the night. But seriously, if you fuck around one more time, I'm going to slap your ass, okay?'

'Okay, okay,' I said.

I held on to his hand as we walked up St Denis Street to his apartment building. It was after midnight and it was okay for us to hold hands and walk down the street as a couple.

'I'm sorry I locked you in the closet,' he said. 'I was just stoned. I'd like you to live with me as long as you want. You don't even have to work. You're just a little kid. You need time.'

He looked at my hand and noticed for the first time that it was scratched. He moved me under a streetlamp and tilted my head up all Greta Garbo–like. He ran his finger under my eye and then along my neck. The side of my neck felt really sore when Alphonse touched it. He had a surprised expression on his face, although those marks were probably from the fight I had had with him.

'You're hurt?' he asked.

I nodded and felt the back of my throat trembling again. Alphonse put his arm around me and we walked quickly to his building. The doors of the lobby seemed like the most inviting doors in the world. Once we got inside, he bent over and picked me up. It was amazing how easily he carried me. It seemed as if he could change the rotation of the earth if he really wanted to.

Once, when we were alone in his house, Xavier had tried to carry me from the couch to his room. He ended up tripping over the coffee table and knocking my head against a lamp. I knew that Alphonse could pick me up and rock me like a baby. All of a sudden the idea of being with a grown-up man seemed appealing, not scary. In a way, I was a little bit glad that I was going to be unfaithful to Xavier tonight. It was a way to get back at the way his parents had looked at me.

Alphonse deposited me in his bed and then left me to go to the bathroom. He had put on a record of a French singer that I'd never heard before. I lay listening to her tinny, high-pitched voice. She had the most beautiful voice in the world. She was so sweet. I imagined her on a cobblestone street in a little tiny black dress and the sky filled with white pigeons all around her. I wanted to kiss her.

'You've never done heroin, have you?' Alphonse asked me.

The minute Alphonse said those words, my guardian angel started humming and circling around me happily. I could feel her there, getting excited. Some guardian angels did a terrible job. They were given work in the poor neighborhoods where none of the others wanted to go. Every delinquent kid had one of these miserable angels who made sure that they made the worst of every situation. These angels loved when people did the wrong thing or took risks. You can't have that many bad things happen to you without some sort of heavenly design. I had never felt my angel jump so quickly to work as when she heard the word 'heroin'. I guess she'd been waiting a while for someone to say it.

christmas

1

I didn't go home the next day or any day after that. Instead, I stayed with Alphonse and continued to get high. As far as I could tell, it was true that you got hooked the first time you used heroin. I was stoned right down to my bones most of the day.

When I was stoned, I wasn't cold or sad. I saw things in a lovely way, where everything was brand-new and meaningless. I found a marble on the ground, and when I held it up in front of me, I noticed that inside there was a tiny horse stuck in a rainstorm. A white pigeon sat next to me and began flawlessly conjugating French verbs. The dead flies on the windowsill were keyholes that had left their doors. I held a cricket in my cupped fist and examined it carefully. I discovered that a cricket was nothing but a safety pin that believed in God.

As soon as the drugs wore off, the universe went back to being the way it was before. Each time I came down, I made a secret promise to myself that I would feel that way again soon.

It was amazing how I became a bum so quickly. I went down to the bus station to pick up some cigarette butts off the ground and smoke them. I exhaled swans and white sheep. I stood in the same spot for about five minutes because there was no reason whatsoever to move. I started to laugh. In a way, being a bum was an attempt to feel good. It was about feeling low-down like a dog because they are less complicated than humans.

I never thought I would end up doing heroin. I don't think I did it because of Jules. I think we both did it for the same reason, though: because we were both fools who were too fragile to be sad, and because no one was prepared to give us a good enough reason not to do it.

In any case, I never thought of heroin as a terrible, frightening thing. I remembered how Jules loved me best when he was stoned. That was still my main idea about junk somehow. If there was an alphabet book for little street kids, on the page where it said *H is for heroin*, there would be a picture of Jules smiling.

Alphonse and I had moved out of his apartment. We were staying in a hotel on St Hubert Street, a little street off St Catherine. There was a row of old and beautiful four-story hotels on this block that were each painted a different color. They could have been some of the most expensive real estate in the city, but their location made them seedy. The street was surrounded on all sides by areas where prostitutes and drug dealers did their business all day long. If you walked along that block at night, you would change colors because of the neon signs over the doors of each hotel. They all had names like the Lily or the Oiseau Bleu. These were names from another time. No one would have the audacity to name a hotel something like that now, as this was the ugliest age of all time. The clerks never asked questions when anyone walked into these hotels. They certainly didn't have a problem at the Licorne when Alphonse and I moved in with a couple suitcases and a pillowcase filled with my clothes and some paperback books.

It was right after we moved into that hotel that Alphonse started doing way too much drugs. He lay in bed naked for long hours at a time. I couldn't get his attention or get him to say anything affectionate to me when he was stoned. Talking to him was like trying to have a conversation with a drowned corpse at the bottom of a pond. He acted completely different than Jules used to when he was high. But then again, Jules had a cheap addiction compared to Alphonse's. Some people can live with heroin in a sort of on-and-off relationship for years. They can get by on ten or twenty dollars' worth a day and go through withdrawal eight times a month. Once Jules went through withdrawal while we were at the hot dog restaurant. He was trembling and sweaty for a couple hours, but he managed to read a comic book and drink five glasses of Coke at the same time. Alphonse, on the other hand, needed a hundred dollars a day for junk and couldn't do without it. I had never seen him go through withdrawal and had no desire to, either.

I had to turn tricks every night now. Since I'd started living with Alphonse, he had a shorter temper and didn't cut me any slack in that department. I had to go meet him straightaway with the money at the end of the evening. I wasn't allowed to stop at the arcade or the comic book store. There were more rules living with Alphonse than there had ever been living with Jules. Jules didn't know the difference between right and wrong, so he was never sure if he should, or if he even morally could, punish me. It was impossible for Jules to even send me to bed without feeling guilty. Alphonse, on the other hand, had rules that I was always crossing.

One night I put my sneakers on the radiator to dry. Alphonse found this revolting and said he couldn't take my filthy ways anymore. He told me that I was white trash and he slapped me, which left an imprint of his hand on my face for three days. It made me sick to my stomach thinking about why I'd been slapped. Slapping is never a good thing, but there should at least be some sort of legitimate reason behind it, like an exclamation mark needs to follow an exclamatory sentence. I remembered the teacher who'd made fun of me for doing that. You can't just put an exclamatory sentence anywhere!

Since Alphonse spent all the money I made on dope, we were broke. I didn't really mind that, as I was so used to poverty by now. But I got really pissed off when he yelled at me for wasting four dollars on a John Le Carré novel I'd bought at the drugstore. I couldn't even look at him for the rest of that afternoon because I thought he was so cheap. Sometimes I went without a meal, too. One night I hadn't eaten and I went to the store and tried to pay for a carton of chocolate milk with the pennies and nickels that were hanging around the hotel room.

'I'm not going to count that shit,' the guy at the counter told me.

'Come on,' I said. 'Please.'

Alphonse only gave me a flimsy cut of the heroin he bought, and I never seemed to get high enough. I had to wait in the hotel room while he went out and scored. I hated that. Anticipating the dope would make me start going through withdrawal. It made me feel like an insect had crept into my ear and was crawling around under my skin. I felt crushed when I sat still, as if someone were squeezing me between a bureau and a wall. I got uncomfortably hot too, like I was standing under a bunch of lightbulbs.

To kill time while I was waiting for Alphonse to score, I would come up with ways to murder him. My best idea was to drop a jar of frozen tomato sauce on his head. People often kept frozen foods on their window-sills in the winter. No one would suspect it was anything other than an accident. This one night, I pushed the bed aside and drew a pentagram on the floor with a piece of cockroach chalk and wrote his initials in the middle of it. I prayed for Satan to strike him dead before pushing the bed back and continuing, unsatisfied, to wait for him.

As soon as I heard him open the door, I stood up on the bed, pointing at him. 'Where've you been!' I yelled. 'I've been waiting a whole fucking hour!'

He smacked me hard and I fell off the bed. I didn't even know where any of my limbs were until they smashed against the ground. My head hit the radiator and I rushed to put my hand up to the sharp pain. Jules had always warned me that if your head hit the radiator, it would surely crack open. I was stunned to find mine still in one piece.

I didn't think I deserved to be hit for yelling at all. The injustice of it made me start to cry. I didn't want to let Alphonse know that he had made me cry, but it's hard to hold it back. One time I tried to keep my head under the water in the bathtub to see if I could drown myself. It was likewise practically impossible.

I gave up on trying to exercise restraint and sat in a ball on the floor, crying and imagining alternatives to my life. I planned to go to Hollywood to become an actress. Then I changed my mind and decided I was going to live in the desert outside Las Vegas. I briefly considered getting a job as a traffic cop. All these wild escape routes opened themselves up to me when I was angry.

'You're a crybaby,' he said after he shot up. 'It's not a bad thing. One day you won't cry anymore, and I'll always be poking and pinching you to see you cry. Your eyes look so blue when you cry.'

He handed me the syringe with what was left of the dope in it. There wasn't much, but it was enough to make all my anger dissipate. As soon as I was high, I couldn't even remember what my escape plans had been. I wasn't upset that Alphonse had slapped me ten minutes before. It all seemed to have been make-believe, the way that a magician's assistant is cut in half and then magically steps out, looking lovelier than ever.

The next evening, I put on my winter clothes and went outside. It always seemed as if it had been winter forever. The windows of closed stores were plastered with posters for unknown French bands. They flapped around like a flock of seagulls. The only birds were the ones on the mannequin's polyester shirt. It was just getting dark. The lights were just coming out, like when you lay bread out on top of the water and the fish come out one by one, but slowly.

My running shoes were already wet after five minutes of being outside. It's harder to pick up a trick when you're wearing a yellow pom-pom hat, as you just looked like an ordinary kid and it hid your good looks. But it was simply too cold to go without a hat. I pretty much had a lot of regulars anyway. That was the only point in my life when everyone I met was falling in love with me. It was because I was so young, I think. It's like at the pet store –

everyone wants to cuddle a kitten more than they want to cuddle a cat.

Despite my lifestyle, I could still be pretty immature. I always asked little kid questions. I couldn't help it, as I was curious.

'Do you have any idea what a mockingbird looks like?' I asked a trick once. 'Is it a real bird or something mechanical?'

My breasts were still too small for bras. I went into an Outreach Center to get some birth control pills and condoms, and a social worker gave me a plastic bag with boys' underwear that were covered with little fighter jets from the Second World War. So far, I'd had no complaints about them from customers.

Like this one guy, Marcel, held my hand and touched a phone number that I had written on my skin in ballpoint pen, as if it was the most beautiful thing he'd ever seen. He kept fondling my bracelet that was made of tiny monkeys holding hands. I had gotten it for a quarter from a vending machine. I always hoped to get a rubber crazy ball but ended up with cheap jewelry.

I didn't know if there was anything different between men who chose to be with younger prostitutes and those who didn't. They were the only men I knew, and because of them I didn't have a very high opinion of adults. I didn't think there was any point in going to school or having a career. The adult world was filled with perverts, so it hardly seemed like something worth preparing for.

That night, I was waiting for a trick named Harvey on the corner of St Catherine and St Dominique. He had a crooked nose that looked as if it must have been broken at some point. I spent most of the time with him wondering what he would look like with a straight nose. He finally showed up about ten minutes late. I threw my hands up in the air, as if to say, What the hell?

We walked together over to the Hotel of the Stars. The outside was whitewashed cement, and people were always autographing it and drawing pictures on it with ballpoint pens and markers. I noticed someone had scribbled the words 'Fuck the Police' in ballpoint pen on the wall. Suddenly, the words seemed to crawl several inches over, as though they were some sort of insect. Sometimes I wouldn't even know when I was stressed out anymore until something weird like that happened.

The reason this hotel was called Hotel of the Stars was because there were some signed photographs of actors, who I'd never even heard of before, in the lobby. It wasn't fancy anymore. Harvey paid for the room through a little slot in bulletproof glass. There was a microphone. You'd shout into it, but they never heard you because it didn't work. You had to lean your face down and talk through the money slot.

I knew the girl working at the desk. Her name was Aileen, and she had a crush on Jules that he never recip-rocated. He used to call her Boney Bones behind her back because he said she had no figure. To win him over, she was always trying to act as though she was my mother. She would run up to me and tie my shoelaces in the middle of the sidewalk and do other ridiculous things like that. She was all right, though, and I'd stop by the hotel sometimes just to hang around with her a bit. She was always touching me, which I really liked. When she played with my hair, it tingled and felt like the roots were falling out. And she had given me my new favorite T-shirt that said 'Kiss me I'm Polish'. I thought it was pretty damn funny.

Right then, however, I tried to avoid eye contact with her. I gave her a glance that indicated that she should shut her mouth and not bother me right now. She just looked at me blankly, making as if she didn't recognize me.

I couldn't help but hop along the patterns in the tiles on the way to the room.

'I think these tiles are the steps to a Viennese waltz,' I shouted.

When we got to the room, I took my winter clothes off. My pockets were filled with Tic Tacs and other tiny things that fell all over the floor. When I took off my hat, it seemed that I'd been sweating. I looked in the mirror, and my hair stood up like a wet cat that had been dragged out of a well. I had a cord with the key to the hotel room around my neck. It also had the keys to my last two apartments on it, even though I didn't have any magic shoes and wouldn't be returning to them anytime soon.

Harvey switched off the overhead light and turned on a lamp on the night table that had a net of plastic chandelier beads as a lampshade. Each bead was like a penny catching the sunlight. The candles made everything the color of stained glass, the color of a brand-new tiger tattoo.

'Do you need to get ready?' he asked me.

'How do you mean?' I asked, genuinely confused.

'Do you want to dance for me?' he asked.

'Without any music?'

There was a clock radio on the night table that he turned on. He held me in his arms and we started dancing. I remembered the songs that Felix used to sing into his tape recorder. It's funny, but if I could have chosen any songs in the world to listen to right then, I would have chosen his. Harvey and I continued dancing when the radio announcer came on and started talking. I wasn't sure whether I should stop or not. He didn't seem like the type of person who really even understood what music was. Finally he stopped and he looked at my face.

He kissed me. The kiss sat on my face like a real physical thing. I could smell the kiss sitting on my face. I almost recoiled from him. Lately, I hated being kissed so much that I was wondering how much longer I could possibly bear it. It was hard to imagine not charging anyone to touch me. Then I remembered how I used to feel when I touched Xavier. I liked when we would be next to each other in class and knock our feet against each other's. I liked holding his hand. I liked when we would take off our shirts and draw imaginary tattoos on each other. I wondered if he had been looking for me.

Because I was thinking of Xavier, I almost smiled when I took off the rest of my clothes and climbed into bed.

Afterward, as I laced up my running shoes, I realized that I couldn't stand to work anymore that night. I usually met Alphonse at the Vietnamese restaurant at nine. It was only six o'clock now and he would have expected me to turn at least another trick by then. It was Friday and he always hung out with Leelee that night, so I wanted to enjoy the time alone. I wanted to maybe go to the bookstore and read for a bit.

I leaned against the door with my clothes on and looked at Harvey. He was still in bed, looking at the ceiling and waiting for me to leave. He always liked to be alone in the room a while after we were done.

'Hey, Harvey boy,' I said, trying to sound cute.

'Yeah,' he said, looking at me.

'Can you pay me for the next time too? I didn't get any presents for my sisters, and I'm going to see them tomorrow.'

'You have sisters?' he asked, surprised.

'Yes. They're little, they live outside the city. They both have birthdays in the same month.'

He looked sad when I mentioned my little sisters. I knew he would somehow. He was very sentimental, and thinking about my family was probably more than he could deal with.

'Okay,' he said and nodded. He pulled out a couple extra twenties. '*Have a nice trip then.*'

I snatched the money and hurried out the door. I ran down the hallways and stairs as fast as I could, just for fun. I was feeling pretty proud of myself. I still really liked the feeling of sticking it to Alphonse. I was skidding across the marble lobby floor when Aileen called out to me from the money slot.

'Baby!'

I stopped and stared at her.

'Yeah?'

'I wanted to tell you that Jules was around here asking about you a week ago.'

As soon as she said the name Jules, I felt like a coat that had just been pulled off its hanger and hit the ground. I felt like collapsing and just lying on the floor until my heart slowed down. Instead, I just leaned against the wall for support.

'What'd he say?' I asked, cautiously, not really sure I wanted to know.

'He wanted to know if I'd seen you.'

'You're not going to tell on me, are you?'

'No, I'm not going to tell on you. I was just passing a message that your father was asking around for you, and he seemed very interested in knowing where you were.'

'And...' I said, annoyed.

'And he's staying at the Mission Shelter if you want to get in touch with him.'

I looked her straight in the eye. She tried to look at me tenderly, but I refused to respond to her pity. Suddenly I was very angry with her. Her telling me that Jules was looking for me had upset me very much, and I wanted to take it out on someone.

'Oh, yeah! Oh, yeah!' I said, sticking my face near the slot. 'Jules doesn't like you whatsoever. So get over it!'

I kicked open the door of the hotel and stormed out. I would have liked to take out my aggression on Alphonse, but I couldn't. As I walked down the street, I imagined slapping Alphonse over and over again in the face.

It made me sick to my stomach with guilt to think about Jules. I missed him, but I was too afraid to go and see him. I couldn't handle the idea of him being angry with me. I couldn't even imagine how mad he could get at me for something like this. Each day made me feel a little worse because it was another day that I had gone without seeing him. It seemed more and more impossible to ever go home. I wished that he hadn't laughed the last time I'd seen him. I would think about him laughing, and it would make me want to die. That day, I hadn't thought about him for a straight eight or nine hours. I could have strangled Aileen.

I missed the way that Jules used to kiss me. I missed being kissed like a baby. Once he tied me to a chair with a skipping rope so that I couldn't move, and he kept kissing me while I screamed and begged him not to.

When I was really unhappy, I realized how much that street stank. It smelled like rats and beer. My body felt dirty, as if it was covered in too many fingerprints. The wind was a man with a lisp talking about people who had stabbed him in the back. I hurried to get home and escape him. The moon was a child's face squeezed against a screen, yelling curses down at us.

Then I remembered the solar system that Felix and I had built when I was living at his house. I started thinking about a moon we had made from papier-mâché. We were going to paint it, but we had decided that it was beautiful just the way it was. I wished that was the moon that was up in the sky. I wished the universe was innocent again.

I decided at that moment that I wanted to get high. Actually, I wanted to get really high. I wasn't going to wait for Alphonse to give me an infinitesimal hit; I was going to score the stuff myself.

Alphonse never introduced me to his drug dealer because he wanted to make sure that I'd give him all my money to score. People were ridiculous about giving up their dealers in general. They acted as though it was an important business partner, or a secretary of state or something. The drug dealers in this neighborhood were all white, and they all had bad haircuts. They tried to look punk but came off looking more like cats with mange. Just like squirrels in certain areas take on certain characteristics, so do heroin dealers. The biggest jackasses in the world dealt heroin in Montreal. The guy who tried to sell you a vowel on *Sesame Street* was more menacing.

I did know one dealer, who I'd met on thirty or forty separate occasions: Jules's old drug dealer. Stacey was a squirrelly kid who rode his bicycle with a dog on a leash.

But the dog wasn't even obedient, and it always pulled Stacey right into the traffic. Jules couldn't stand him because he was always telling a story about how he had slept with Patti Smith. Jules said it was just plain crude. He was always at the Electric Bumbum after five o'clock every night.

The club was only three blocks away. It took up half a block on St Catherine. There were monsters and UFOs painted on the wall out front, and inside was a huge sprawling bar. You could walk around in there for half an hour before anyone who worked there found you and carded you. Early in the evening like this, they hardly cared anyway. I walked up a narrow staircase and found Stacey sitting in front of an empty stage. He stood up and hugged me when he saw me.

Despite having known me since I was nine years old, Stacey wasn't at all freaked out about selling me dope. The heroin was in a folded-up lottery ticket, as it was done back then. The tickets had the same little squares as were on the answer sheets on our end-of-year exams. He offered to buy me a beer. He said I had to stay at the table with him for a little bit so that it wouldn't look suspicious. I hardly thought that was necessary since we were the only people in the room.

'Hey, did you know that Sherlock Holmes was a junkie?' he asked me.

'Mmmhmm,' I said, politely but unenthusiastically.

Some junkies had an obsession with listing off historical heroin addicts. I didn't want to get stuck having to sit there and have a conversation with Stacey for the next hour, so I decided to cut it short.

'I gotta split, okay? I'm underage. They'll throw me out on my ass?'

'No, it's okay. No one cares. Come on, have a seat. Keep me company.'

I waved and walked away. You had to be that way with heroin dealers. They possessed the worst aspects of a child that you don't want to have anything to do with: neediness and loneliness. Who needed it?

I went into the bathroom on the first floor. There were twelve stalls in there with peach-colored doors. Since the bathroom was empty, I took a syringe out of my pocket and quickly filled it with a little water from the tap. I walked to the one at the end, where I could have the most privacy. There was a framed photograph of a mermaid on the wall of that stall, advertising soap. Public bathrooms were often good places to shoot up in because the fluorescent lights made your veins stand out as much as the phone numbers scribbled on the wall with blue pen.

I sat on the toilet lid and took my works out of my fur coat pocket. I cooked up the dope by mixing it with the water in a spoon I carried around. I cooked it with a lighter that had a sticker of a moose on it. Then I stuck a tiny bit of a cigarette filter in the spoon and stuck the tip of the needle through it and pulled the plunger until the tiny creamy mixture had climbed into the syringe. I pulled down my pants and shot the dope in my thigh. That's where Alphonse had suggested that I shoot up these days so that it would be less noticeable. I hadn't cooked up all the dope because I wanted it to last through the night.

Before I'd even pulled up my pants I started to feel the effects of the heroin. It hit me even harder than it had the first time I had used. This dope was different. I could hear the sound of my own heart beating. The woman in the picture began combing her hair. I whispered the word 'Shit' and it came out of my mouth in calligraphic letters, like in a cartoon. I looked up at the ceiling and noticed a toy seagull fluttering around up there. It was a Styrofoam seagull with real feathers for wings that Jules and I had hung on our door for three Christmases in a row. 'I know you,' I said, pointing to the bird. Again my words came out of my mouth in fancy white letters. I decided I'd better keep my mouth shut. I was way too stoned.

I stepped out of the stall and went over to one of the mirrors and looked at my reflection. The snow that week had made my hair look curly and the heroin was making my eyes bluer. I decided that I looked particularly pretty. I was really excited about how good I looked, and it occurred to me that I would like Xavier to see how pretty I was too. Right then, feeling like a brave soldier, I decided to go see Xavier again.

I went out in the snow and started walking in the direction of a music studio where I knew that Xavier took piano lessons every Friday around this time. The studio was above a car dealership, and you entered through a glass door that led to a narrow staircase. I went inside and sat on the stairs. I could hear someone playing piano slowly and badly. It might have been Xavier, but I wasn't sure. I was staring at the brown and white tiles, slowly hypnotizing myself. My head gently fell off my neck and rolled away. I heard my name cried out in a terribly joyful way.

'Baby! I can't believe it.'

'Hey,' I said, standing up.

Xavier ran down the stairwell to meet me. Between his winter clothes and his piano books, he made a lot of noise. He sounded like an orchestra shuffling into their seats. It was so good to see him I felt like lying on the ground laughing, the way the bums do. We grabbed each other's hands instinctively.

'I tried calling you, but your phone wasn't working. Then I went by your apartment and *you had moved*,' he said, emphasizing the word as if it was the craziest thing that any child could ever do.

'Yeah, I moved.'

'Did you try calling me? My mother wouldn't give me the messages if you did. I'm not allowed to hang around with you anymore. My mother went and spoke to the guidance counselor at the school. They told her that you were a troubled kid and from a broken home.'

'I don't come from a broken home! My parents weren't divorced. My mother died,' I shouted, genuinely insulted. 'So much for confidentiality. I can't believe she told your mom that. I should sue her.'

I was trying to play it cool. For the past year, I'd known that I was from an unstable home, but I desperately didn't want Xavier to know it. He was the one person on earth who didn't know about all that stuff.

'I told them how nice your dad is,' Xavier insisted. 'They were considering changing my school until the principal phoned and said you'd run away.'

'I'm living with my uncle,' I lied. 'He's a salesman. I'm going back to school soon. It's perfectly legitimate.'

That was a stupid thing to say. Only lowlifes claimed things were legitimate, classy, or exclusive. But Xavier didn't seem to notice; he just nodded solemnly.

'I don't care what anyone says, Baby. They're all ignorant. You are like my favorite person on earth.'

'Really?'

'Yes!'

'Well, I like you an awful lot too.'

'Where do you and your uncle live?'

'I'm staying at this hotel. Over off St Catherine Street.'

'A hotel. Like the Holiday Inn?'

'No! Not one of those big tacky ones. I'm staying in a European-style hotel, where poets and stuff stay. You know... on St Hubert.'

'Oh... those buildings. I always wondered what they were like inside.'

'We're not going to be staying there very long, though. We're going to move. I just live three blocks away. We could meet sometimes after you finish school.'

'Can I see where you're staying?'

'I don't think so.'

'Please. I want to go over for like five minutes.'

I think the drugs were messing with my reasoning skills. I'd made one successful dare by coming to see him, and I wanted to make another one. It was half past six and there was still loads and loads of time before Alphonse came home. Although the thought of bringing Xavier up to the room made a cold tremor run through me, I was stoned enough to think I could somehow get away with it.

We opened the door of the music building and walked side by side to the hotel. As we walked up the stairs of the hotel together, he craned his head all over the place, looking around. He found it fascinating and new. I was happy to see that he didn't know what to make of it. I opened the door with one of the keys on the cord around my neck and swung it open.

'Voilà!' I said.

'There's only one bed here,' Xavier pointed out, after looking around.

'Don't be so bourgeois,' I exclaimed. 'It's all we can afford right now.'

'I'm sorry. I didn't mean to insult you.'

'That's quite all right,' I said with a British accent, and we both laughed.

I turned on the radio on the nightstand the way Harvey did to make things romantic. Xavier sat down on the bed and took his winter coat off. I was happy to see that he still didn't know how to dress. He was wearing corduroy pants and a purple sweatshirt with a Transformer on it. He looked embarrassed when he took his moon boots off because he was wearing gym socks that didn't match.

I sat on the bed next to him. His forehead was sweaty and oily and his bangs were standing straight up. I suddenly liked all the things that were supposed to be unattractive and awkward about kids.

'Look what I have,' he said, digging through his pocket. 'I've been carrying it around everywhere because I knew that I'd eventually run into you.'

He pulled out an IOU for a kiss that I'd written him once on the corner of a piece of paper. He held it up to my face and smiled at me.

'I'd like my reimbursement, s'il vous plait.'

We put our arms around each other and held each other. I almost melted when I felt how small and gentle he was. I was used to men, who could toss me into bed with one hand. I pushed Xavier down onto the bed and pinned him there. He struggled, laughing, but couldn't get me off. We stayed in that strange position, enjoying each other's company.

'You know what would be so cool?' I asked.

'What?'

'If we had a little baby. We could name him Cotton; wouldn't that be the most beautiful name for a baby? I would never ever send our baby to school. I would miss him too much while he was at school. I would kiss him a hundred times a day.'

All street kids wanted babies. It's a terrible kick. You should never start talking about it because once you started, you wanted that baby so bad you could almost faint. I couldn't resist, though.

'I like the name Loulou,' he answered, much to my delight.

'I'd save up our money and buy our baby an electric blanket, I don't care how much money it would cost. He would never be cold.'

'I'd like it if the baby had your hair. You are the prettiest girl in the whole world.'

I let Xavier go and lay next to him. I reached over and touched his cheek. I liked the way his skin was so soft. Touching him felt like picking up a baby animal that you weren't supposed to handle. Because once you touched the animal it was spoiled and its mother wouldn't want to have anything to do with it.

Xavier and I leaned in and kissed each other on the lips. I gave him my most secret unconditional kiss I'd saved up for special occasions. It was like taking the glass off a framed moth and letting it fly.

Then we both closed our eyes. I kept mine closed so tightly. I felt like a negative that had been exposed to light. If I accidentally opened my eyes, then I knew we would both be destroyed somehow. I knew that Xavier was going to keep his eyes closed the whole time too.

He tickled me everywhere that he touched me. I kept laughing and he would laugh too. But then we got quiet. It was like we were hidden in a dark closet playing hide-and-seek. We buried ourselves deep down in the closet, hidden under the sweaters and warm leather shoes and slippers, and we did our business.

When we'd finished making love, Xavier pulled his long johns back on and lay next to me with just one sock on. We hadn't said anything to each other yet because we were both feeling so perfect and quiet. He held his hands up in front of him, seemingly admiring his fingernails. We looked over at each other and smiled.

Then I felt nauseated. I rolled off the bed and ran into the bathroom to throw up. I turned on the water so that Xavier couldn't hear me. Feeling genuine emotion while on junk had made me sick to my stomach. But I felt better once I'd thrown up, and I sat on the toilet lid to make sure it had passed.

As I turned off the water, I heard the sound of the door opening and Xavier saying hello to someone. I had the feeling you have after you've slipped on the ice and your body is stuck in the air a split second before you fall. It is an awful hollow unknown feeling that smashing to the ice afterward hardly compares to. I pulled open the bathroom door and ran out into the living room. Alphonse was standing in the room, staring at Xavier. Xavier was scrambling to get his clothes on.

I thought he had a schedule. I thought that I knew this schedule. I thought that he went over to Leelee's apartment around seven o'clock. They always did that. But I had forgotten that Leelee had gone to visit her parents. All the stars in the sky had decided to change places.

Someone had taken the lights from the Lite-Brite set and had rearranged them in a new pattern. I had forgotten how simple something like that could be.

Alphonse turned to me and looked me right in the eyes. It seemed like the first time that I'd ever seen Alphonse's eyes. The whites had turned yellow. He had eyes that looked like they had been crying, not for an hour but for a hundred years! His eyes were the color of water stains on drapes. They were the color of water in a puddle. They were the color that pennies would make when they left stains at the back of the porcelain sink. I couldn't believe that anybody was allowed to look at me like that. It was wrong. It made me feel as if it had eroded my heart. I felt like I had lung cancer. I felt rotten inside, like a bag of toys that someone leaves outside the Salvation Army in the rain.

Then he turned back to Xavier.

'What the fuck are you doing in my house? You have some nerve coming here. I'm going to call the fucking cops for trespassing.'

'I came up here with Baby,' he whimpered.

Xavier looked horribly worried. He believed he'd done something terrible. He really had no idea what was going on, but I could tell from his face that he knew it was bad.

'This isn't Baby's place,' Alphonse said, disgustedly. 'This is my place. She doesn't pay the rent here. I do. She's a fucking thieving whore. A whore. You're in way over your head. I'd be afraid to touch her.'

'I want to go,' Xavier said, beginning to cry.

'Let him go,' I yelled. 'I just ran into him by accident. I won't invite him here again.'

Xavier went to the corner to gather his moon boots and bent over to put them on. Alphonse kicked him in the ass, and he fell to the ground, completely startled. I ran toward them, but Alphonse shoved me backward and I fell over the chair and was on the ground too.

He grabbed Xavier by the throat and held him against the wall. He whacked him in the face. Everything was going too fast. I just wanted Xavier to get out of there. It was probably the first time that he had ever been hit like that. I wished that Alphonse had hit me instead. It was much, much worse to watch it. He looked terrified, like a baby.

I got to my feet and started jumping up and down futilely. It was like when you tried to get puppets to run just by jerking their strings up and down and they just end up getting all tangled in themselves. There was nowhere to run and nothing that I could do. Alphonse was insurmountable because he was an adult and we were just two kids. All that children can hope for is that the adults who were around them would be kind. All they can do is beg for mercy.

'Please, please, please,' I yelled at Alphonse.

Xavier's nose was bleeding now. Alphonse stood back, giving him enough space to get his things and leave. And he did. The sound of his moon boots going down the stairs sounded loud, like thunder. I didn't feel any pain when Alphonse slapped me on both sides of my face. I could feel both my cheeks getting all warm and tingly.

I couldn't cry, and this was the one time I really wanted to. Crying helps you not see what's going on around you. But I couldn't get the crystal-clear image of Xavier being hit out of my mind. Seeing Xavier in my universe was the most shocking thing I'd ever seen. I put my hands up to my eyes to try and wipe the image from my mind.

'Give me the dope,' Alphonse said, blankly. 'I heard you scored from Stacey.'

I reached into my pocket and pulled out what remained. I took my works out of my pocket and gave them to Alphonse. I had a handful of change that I splattered out on the table too, as if I was trying to prove that I wasn't hiding anything else from him. He would shoot up first and then he would get around to killing me.

'Now we'll have to split before he tells his parents about us,' he said.

'He's not going to tell his parents!' I cried out. 'He's not even allowed to talk to me.'

'We're getting the fuck out of here. We're going to Toronto.'

I whined loudly. Whenever he was annoyed, he threatened to move us to Toronto. I hated the idea of leaving Montreal because I figured that if I did, I would never find Jules again.

He poured the rest of the dope in a spoon, cooked it up, and shot it all at once on the side of the bed. He sat there for a second while the color drained out of his face. He slowly laid his body down on the bed and became perfectly still, not uttering a sound. The storm was over. I remembered how great that heroin was and I wished I had some more of it. Naturally, he hadn't left me any at all. I climbed up on the bed and lay down as far away from Alphonse as I could. I would just have to rely on my natural defenses to erase the events of that evening.

I had lost Xavier. But I had lost all the children that I had been close to, so why had I expected things to be different with Xavier? I was very religious about other children, and I wanted so much to believe that they could save me. I had tried to be rescued by the most powerless group in the world. Children were neither real nor dependable. Alphonse was real. He was the one who would make sure that he was in my life. He was, unfortunately, the one who was strong enough to fight for me.

I didn't ever want to see Xavier again now that he knew all about me. A part of me was destroyed, a part of me that made me feel really good about myself. Before, when I'd been upset, I'd been able to think about the times that I had been with Xavier, like when we had spent the afternoon hugging the cats. But I wouldn't be able to think about those things without remembering what had happened tonight. I didn't know where I was going to find that feeling now. I felt traumatized and dark and ugly.

I needed to have a really pleasant thought so that I could fall asleep like a baby. I thought about this time when Jules and I had brought some paper and pencils down to the riverbank to sketch the landscape. We'd brought along a plastic bag with a picnic in it and had spent the whole afternoon there. I couldn't remember if our drawings had turned out nice, but that was one of my favorite memories.

In the window, the moon had made itself so tiny it was just a hole in the elbow of a black sweater.

I woke around nine o'clock in the morning. Alphonse was in exactly the same position as when he'd passed out. I was cold, which was strange because Alphonse's body temperature always kept me really warm at night. I sat up abruptly, startled by the realization that unnatural things were at hand. As soon as I looked at Alphonse's face, I knew that he was dead, even though I had never seen a dead body before. People still had expressions on their faces when they slept, but his face was empty. His skin was a chalky shade of green that I'd never seen anywhere in the world before.

I had the strange feeling that I was dead myself. It felt as if I were lying at the bottom of a grave and earth was being thrown on me. When death takes someone you know, he holds you and whispers all his secrets in your ear.

I tried to drag Alphonse into the bathroom because people always did that in the movies. It took all my strength just to get him on the floor, and the thud of his body hitting the floor made me dizzy and almost faint. I knew it was pointless to drag him any farther. I threw a glass of water on his face so that I could feel I had done everything I could, and I decided to get as far away from this room as possible.

I put my things into a plastic bag and ran down the stairs of the hotel. I walked quickly down St Hubert and turned onto St Catherine, which was still quiet. The drugs from the night before made me feel completely gutted and hollow. I didn't know what on earth I was supposed to do without Alphonse. Even though I was making all the money, it seemed that since he was the adult, he was the only one who could get us a place to stay and food to eat.

I was thinking that perhaps I could make it on my own. Maybe I could stay at this trick Marcel's house for a bit. He could marvel over how I liked to eat sugared cereal for dinner and how I still liked to watch Walt Disney on Sunday nights. He'd invited me to live with him, but, I knew he wouldn't be nice to me now, even though he swore and swore that he would. It was a lesson

334

I had learned from Alphonse. When you are vulnerable, the worst of society will fail you too.

A cop car rolled up beside me and the cop in the window told me to hold on a minute. 'Shit!' I screamed at myself. I'd always been careful to keep clear of cops and to duck down alleys and take back streets if I spotted them cruising around. I considered running just so they would shoot me, but I didn't even have the energy for that kind of thing.

I stood there freezing, waiting to be punished. They both got out of the car. I noticed they were both very young and similar looking. I was intimidated by how normal they were because I felt they would be disgusted by me. I wasn't exactly sure what they would find wrong with me, but there was a lot they could choose from.

'What do you have in that bag?' one asked me.

'Can we also see what's in your pockets?' the other one added.

I was terrified by them. My hands were shaking horribly as I emptied the bag and my pockets onto the hood of the police car. Together we all examined the contents. I had a big white rock that I had been meaning to paint a picture on. I had a *Peanuts* comic that I had colored in myself with pencil crayons. I had a Smurf with a white coat and a top hat that I was quite convinced was the most wonderful Smurf in existence. I had my 'Kiss me I'm Polish' T-shirt. Thanks to Alphonse taking all my money, I only had about sixty-five cents in my pocket. This was a normal amount for a child to be carrying: enough for a telephone call and some candy.

'What's your name?' he asked.

'Mary,' I lied, trying to come up with the most normal name possible.

'What are you doing here?'

'I slept at my friend's house and we woke up early. I'm going home.'

'Do you want us to drive you home?'

'No, thank you.'

'All right then. Move on. You shouldn't be hanging around here. It's a very bad neighborhood. You'll just get into trouble.'

'Yes. Okay. I will.'

'It's silly to be out on your own around here.'

'I know. I'll go now.'

'Okay.'

One waved to me from the window. The results of their investigation had clearly uncovered the fact that I was still just a child. I had thought every single thing about me was something seedy, but really, there was nothing wrong with me.

When I'd left the hotel, going to see Jules hadn't been an option for me. All I knew now was that I kept walking and walking toward the Mission, the shelter where he was staying. In fact, the only thing that sort of calmed me down was walking in that direction. I felt that if I stopped, even for a second, I would completely collapse and throw up on my shoes. My body seemed to believe this was the only way to escape the mess I was in. The Mission was on St Laurent Street, at the bottom of two hills, between Chinatown and Old Montreal. It seemed to be surrounded by bits of debris, as if the garbage from both parts of the city rolled down there. The Mission was an old building whose stones had been stained black, as if it had been touched by hundreds of people who'd just finished reading newspapers. There were big windows on the ground floor that looked into the soup kitchen, but garbage bags had been taped all over the glass to prevent strayed tourists from looking in at the homeless people. This was where Jules and I had always had our Christmas dinners together until this year.

On the second and third floors were rooms where men slept at night. They didn't allow children to stay at this shelter, so I had never been upstairs. Until I'd run away, neither had Jules.

I cut through the parking lot, which was filled with men smoking cigarette butts. The ones who were worse off had tangled hair and looked like Moses when he came down from Mount Sinai with the Ten Commandments. From the distant looks on their faces, they seemed to be experiencing a level of profundity that could kill an ordinary citizen.

I walked inside the entrance and down the hall to the cafeteria. I was feeling out of place because I was younger than anyone else who was milling around. No matter how old I got, I always seemed to be younger and more immature than everyone else. I accidentally caught my reflection in a mirror on the wall in the hallway. My hair looked dirty, like I had been clogging up a drain pipe. I seemed skinny, and my clothes had become too big for me. My face looked red and bruised from where Alphonse had hit me the night before. I put my hands on both cheeks and tried to somehow fix my face. I don't know why they would put a mirror in that hallway. I couldn't imagine anyone there was in the mood to take a good look at themselves.

When I stepped into the cafeteria, I spotted Jules right away. I hadn't seen him in almost two months, which at my age was an incredibly long time, especially since this time I'd been the one who had decided to stay away. It was almost supernatural to see him in the flesh again, after I'd spent so much time thinking about him. He was sitting on a bench all the way at the other end of the cafeteria beside an upright piano. He had on a large checkered jacket and a sheepskin hat. He was wearing a pair of bright yellow running shoes that he'd bought last year when they'd been on sale for seventy-five percent off because of their unfortunate color. It made me sad to see him in his yellow shoes.

Jules was fiddling with the radio on top of the piano. I could hear the song from where I was standing. It was that old Félix Leclerc song. 'When I don't love you anymore, so as to let you know, I'll be wearing my hat.' The guy next to my dad asked him to change the station, but Jules just ignored him. He had an unlit cigarette in his mouth that he was obviously looking forward to smoking.

I didn't want to call out to get his attention. I decided to stand there and wait until he spotted me. I had an uneasy feeling about standing there. It reminded me of a time when I was little and Jules and I were at a lake. I hadn't had a bathing suit, so Jules had told me to take my shirt off and swim in my underwear. He had said that no one would think there was anything wrong with me. When anyone had looked at me that day, I'd wondered if they were thinking I was a pervert for swimming without a shirt on. It had been terrifying.

I didn't expect anything physical or material from Jules. After all, he was living in a homeless shelter and had nothing. I just needed, more than anything else, for him to love me like he did when I was a baby. That's all I wanted from him. I felt tense as hell waiting for him to turn around and see me. It was as if I were standing on a window ledge of a six-story building. If he was furious with me or hated me, I would just plunge to a certain death right on the spot. It seemed particularly easy to die that day.

Jules turned his head in my direction. Our eyes met and he stared at me for a split second, not recognizing me. I waved slightly. The minute he looked over in my direction, his eyes lit up. They really did. They got bigger and bluer, as if they'd been filled in with a bright blue pencil crayon. His face broke into a grin. And his big smile – in the way that smiles sometimes can – fixed things between us. I felt a rush of relief come over me. It was an unexpected warm feeling like the way your lips feel when you kiss in the rain. He wrenched himself up and hurried across the room to me.

'Where have you been!' he cried and took me in his arms.

He smelled like terrible things. He had that smell that is in the air in the morning sometimes, of animals that had been killed in the night. He smelled like dirty, sweaty clothes and garbage trucks. He was and probably still is, to this day, the worst-smelling person I have ever hugged. But it was wonderful. He just wrapped his arms all the way around me. He hugged me the way that parents hug: with them doing all the work.

'I haven't seen you in so long,' he said, while hugging me. 'I've worried so much that it's taken a year off of my life. Shit, I didn't know where the hell you were.'

He looked at me in the face. I didn't know what to say. I didn't want to say anything because I was so tired and strung out that I felt the sound of my own voice might be too much for me to bear.

'You must be hungry!' he cried.

He sat me down at a cafeteria table and went to get me what appeared to be a gravy sandwich and a glass of milk. He laid the plate down in front of me and handed me a fork and knife that were wrapped up in a napkin.

'Kids get to have a glass of milk instead of pop. Go ahead. It's full of calcium.'

I'd never heard him talk about the nutrients in food before. I found it odd, as if he was a stranger. He seemed like an adult, like a real parent for the first time. I didn't know what he was going to do next. I was starving and was surprised that as soon as I put the food to my mouth, I completely lost my appetite. I chewed on a mouthful of bread for a long time before I could swallow it. Jules watched me eat with a sort of desperate relief in his face. He seemed to know something had been fixed between us, and he didn't want to mess that up. He had to handle this responsibility.

'I've been doing a lot of thinking since you were gone,' he said seriously at last. 'This isn't right. You shouldn't have to run around. You need some stability. This isn't your fault; it's mine.'

'I'm okay. You really don't have to worry about me,' I said, not wanting to spoil the mood. 'I just came to say hello.'

'Don't just say hello. This is fucking stupid. You're a baby. You're a teeny-weeny baby, and I'm going to make sure you're taken care of.'

I started to tremble violently. It was warm in the cafeteria and I still had my winter coat on, but every part of me started shaking. My teeth were even knocking together.

'Look at you, you look like you're suffering from diphtheria, for Christ's sake. You need a change of scenery.'

'Yeah,' I said, shrugging and smiling weakly. I figured that that was some sort of joke.

'I spoke to Janine.'

'Who?' I asked, as I'd never even heard that ridiculous name before.

'Janine.'

'I don't know who that is.'

'You know Janine.'

He said this all natural, not like he was trying to convince me of one of his tall tales. He couldn't fool me, though. I had an almost religious memory for the things that Jules had told me, and I knew he had never mentioned anyone named Janine.

I looked at him as though he was crazy. He pursed his lips for a bit. Usually when he did that, he would say that he wanted a cigarette. Instead he sighed.

'She's my cousin. Janine?'

'I don't know who that is,' I repeated.

'All right!' he yelled, putting his hands in the air. 'I was out of touch with her. You know she wasn't my style. She was the only person that I sort of talked to when I left Val des Loups. I mean she kept calling until I changed my phone number.'

'When was this?'

'I don't know. Ten years ago? Time flies faster when you're an adult.'

'Okay,' I said in agreement, thinking that would end this topic.

I took another sip of milk. I didn't know what he was going on about. I was still in such a state of shock that I had no ability to do anything with new information.

'She came to see me. And we were talking about you.'

'Okay,' I said, for the millionth time.

'I've been talking to a cousin, and she wants you to visit with her for a bit.'

'What?' I asked, sort of startled. I was finally getting the gist of what he was talking about. I was shocked that he was talking about something concrete about my future. I thought he was equally as confused as I was at the moment.

'You knew her when you were a baby,' Jules continued, despite my bewildered look. 'She really wants you to stay with her. She always did. When you were little, she was very aggressive about keeping you.'

'Who is this person again?' I asked.

'My cousin.'

'Okay. You want to visit her. I'll go. That would be nice.' I wanted to be able for us to agree on something. I was being very optimistic. I didn't even care where she was or how we were going to get there. 'For how long?'

'She used to piss me off. I wanted you all to myself, you know. But things are different. I think it might be better for you if you did stay with her.'

'But I want to stay in Montreal. I want to stay near you.'

I surprised myself when I said that. I didn't even know that I knew what I wanted so clearly. I felt my eyes smart. Jules's face got all red and had a goofy forced smile on it, as if he might be holding back tears. Yet, at the same time, I didn't feel so bad about the idea of going. It was making a little bit more sense each second. It was as if I was climbing down a ladder.

'I'll come and see you all the time. It's not a long drive away. It's better for now.'

'Where does she live?'

'In the sticks, outside Val des Loups.'

'What! You said it was like a toilet bowl out there.'

'It's not that bad. Once when I was little, there was a goose that used to follow me around all the time. It thought I was its mother.'

'Really,' I said, pleadingly, as if this goose would be waiting for me as soon as I stepped off the bus.

'I called that goose Peter; I always liked that name.'

I guess if I was a boy, my name would have been Peter. A lot of other things might have been very different too. Jules stared at me, waiting for me to commit. I felt over-whelmed. I wasn't sure what was going on, whether I was losing Jules or not.

'Are you okay? Are you going to be sick? It's all right if you are. People here get sick all the time. Nobody would be surprised by anything.'

'Are you going to come with me to Val des Loups?'

'Sure, I'll stay for a bit,' he said, smiling sadly. 'Look what I have for you. Wait here. Paul, keep an eye on her. I swear to God, if I come down and she isn't here, I'm going to burn this place down. You know I'm capable of it.'

He went into the pastor's office at the back of the cafe-teria. When he came out, he had a wrapped package in his hand.

'Here's a present for you. The pastor put it aside for you. He was like shocked not to see us here this Christmas.'

It was soft and wrapped in purple tissue paper. On it was a little paper tag that said 'GIRL 5 and Up.' I opened it slowly without ripping the paper, but taking it off neatly, as if I was folding a sweater. Inside was a little family of toy mice made out of some sort of real animal fur. There was a mother and a father and two children mice. They were dressed in miniature tuxedos and frilly Victorian dresses. It was, by far, the best gift I'd ever gotten.

'Aren't they beautiful!' he exclaimed. 'Look at the tiny umbrella the girl one has.'

'It's a parasol,' I whispered.

I had to whisper so that I wouldn't start to cry.

'I love you,' he said. He looked a little appalled at how unconvincing that word sounded. He had used the word 'love' to describe everything from flip flops to pickle chips to a soda pop commercial. But what else could he say? 'Will you let me take you out there?'

I shook my head no. I didn't know where out there was. All I knew was Montreal.

'You don't have a choice. We're going, okay. I'm going to call my cousin.'

He jumped up and walked over to a yellow phone that was on a wooden shelf on the wall. I stayed seated, finishing my glass of milk and watching him take action. He went through all his pockets to find the phone number. He took out some candy, a pack of cigarettes, and five or six scraps of paper, which he examined carefully and then threw on the shelf with disgust. Finally, he took out a piece of paper that he seemed satisfied by and dialed a phone number. He looked excited about being in charge. I couldn't hear what he was saying, but I could see that he had a lot of trouble staying still while talking. He took off his hat suddenly and rubbed his hair really hard. It was so dirty that it looked wet. What a bum, I thought, and smiled. He hung up the phone and hurried back to the table triumphantly.

I had been making my own decisions for a few months and God knows I had gotten myself into enough trouble.

I needed someone else to make the decisions, and it suddenly seemed as if Jules was the perfect person to do that. He was completely discombobulated, but he was my parent, after all.

He sat back down next to me. He didn't say anything at first, and I just looked at him closely. He had always been pale, but now his skin was a darker, more reddish color, and there were hard creases in his skin when he smiled. There were two big dark half-moons under his eyes. He would have to sleep for about a year straight to get rid of those bags. He had always looked young for his age, and waitresses had almost always carded him when he ordered beer. I doubted that would happen anymore.

'I'm always going to be a misfit,' Jules said and sighed. 'There's always going to be something wrong with me. But not you. You're really smart. You could go to school or to university. You have a good sense of humor. And look at your tiny little wrists and look at your fingernails. I've never been able to get over how cute you were since the day you were born.'

His compliments were like little cupcakes all lined up in a window. Each one made me a little stronger. I loved listening to him convince me that I deserved better. Now that this was said, things would be good for us. Being apart from him hadn't been the worst thing; the worst thing had been not knowing if he cared or not. I thought I could start over again and he would be proud of me. I was going to get to be whatever I wanted to be. Jules held my hand in his. His fingers were all stained yellow and brown from cigarettes, and mine looked white and small in comparison. It seemed true that one of us could be saved.

'Do you want to see an authentic fossil?' I asked Jules.

I reached into my jean pocket and pulled out a bone that I'd been carrying around. Xavier had gotten it from a museum he'd visited while on a vacation. When he'd shown it to me, I told him that it must be the fossil of some sort of primitive butterfly. Xavier said it was nothing but the fossil of a leaf and was probably only five years old.

Jules pulled himself up when I took it out. He looked at me just like a little kid and he smiled. He held up the fossil for inspection.

'This is some sort of fish with wings,' Jules said confidently. 'It's some sort of prehistoric fish that probably evolved into what we are now! See, these are its little stick legs that eventually became our tibia and our toes and our joints. This little thing could have descended into an astronaut or soul singer. This little great-grandpa is someone who wants to express himself. You can tell.'

'Maybe it was a prehistoric butterfly?' I suggested.

'I think that you're absolutely right,' Jules exclaimed. 'I think that's what it was. And it must have had really beautiful colors. Perhaps colors that do not even exist anymore. Colors that just disappeared right off the spectrum.'

Jules had dropped out of school in the eighth grade. He got all his information off of what people said on park benches. Sometimes he listened to the news on the radio, but mostly he turned the station to hear music. And yet he knew all types of beautiful things. He knew enough to teach me something. His parents hadn't taught him anything about the world. We had conjectured upon the nature of the world and had reinvented it together.

Jules and I were tiny people. We were delicate. We were almost destroyed. We were vulnerable. Like nerds in a school yard of bullies, we could have traded our stamps and cards of extinct animals. That's the kind of people we would be if our situation were different.

'Let me get my bags, Baby.'

He left the cafeteria, and I saw him disappear up the stairs at the end of the hall. He was back down in less than three minutes. His bags consisted of a red school satched overstuffed with clothes.

'Do you have to check out of here?' I asked.

'I guess so!' he said.

He stood up on a chair and called out to no one in particular, 'My stay at this fine establishment is going to have to terminate sooner than I thought, I'm afraid. It's been lovely, however. Business has called me elsewhere. Don't worry. I didn't steal any of the rats.'

I had a strange feeling of freedom as I stepped outside the Mission. For the past couple of months, every time I stepped out of anywhere, I'd always had to check if the coast was clear. Like a rat, I couldn't just go wherever I wanted. I'd been afraid of the cops, but mostly I'd been afraid of Alphonse, who was much more vigilant than any police officer could be. He caught me hanging out at the skating rink once, when I was supposed to be working, and he had yelled at me for hours. Walking down the street, I really felt as if I weighed a hundred pounds lighter now that he was gone. I was afraid that I would eventually feel guilty about the way he died and that I would feel even more guilty about not having felt guilty. I had just the inkling of that emotion and it was deeply unsettling. I tried to avoid that emotion the way that you try to avert the gaze of a creepy person who's staring at you on the bus.

The bus station was a fifteen-minute walk uphill. Once

we were there, we had to wait at the ticket booth for a while because Jules was trying to convince the cashier that I was under eleven in order to get me half fare. I blinked my eyes and tried to look innocent, although that might have only succeeded in making me look older. Finally, the cashier gave in and offered me the reduced fare. Together the tickets came to eighteen dollars, which was perfect because all he had was a twenty. We sat on the bench near the door that the bus would eventually pull up to. Jules lit up a cigarette that he held in a cupped hand so that no one would notice.

'Everything's going to be okay,' he said.

'Yes, sir,' I said and smiled.

He put his hand on my head and messed up my hair. Ever since I was little, he had said that I looked best with my hair messed up.

We didn't even get one good last look at the city as we were leaving it. I wasn't interested. You could put a blindfold on me and I would be able to find my way around. Who needed to take a look? Everything was combat colors. Camouflage. The colors of a dirty aquarium that needed to have its glass cleaned.

The bus wasn't full at all. We sat together, even though both of us had such long legs that they were getting in each other's way.

'Moving away from civilization,' Jules said, and he winked at me. He took out a comb, and as I remember it, he combed his hair for the rest of the hour-long trip.

It always surprised me how after driving for twenty minutes out of Montreal you were already in the sticks. The woods are right there, all around the city, like wolves at the edge of a campfire.

All the trees looked like the tufts you pulled out of hairbrushes. They were like a child's drawing of lightning or the veins on an old man's arm. It was better not to think about those trees or you would get lost over how many of them there were. The forest ended, and the bus passed by some farms and barren fields. I saw a horse standing alone in a field, a little shack painted blue, and a tractor with no one in it. Things were scattered randomly in the landscape like a giant's child hadn't put his toys away. There was something pretty and peaceful about it all.

What could you do for a living out here? And what would you do if your car broke down? My dad and I had never had a car, and all that I really knew about them was that they broke down. Maybe when your car broke down, you just gave up, walked into the woods, dug yourself a grave and jumped in.

I realized as we got farther from the city that I was going to have to go through withdrawal. As soon as I thought of it, I started experiencing some of the symptoms. I started to feel all cooped up in my seat and couldn't get comfortable.

I started thinking about how a neighbor of ours once bought a wolf hybrid on the reservation. I'd see the wolf being walked down the street, and it had this strange lilt, like all the bones in its body had been broken. Even if it wasn't biting throats, eating babies, running across fields, and worrying about his ass getting shot, you could tell the wolf was thinking about those things. It was killing it to think about them all day. That's sort of how I suddenly felt, as if I was moving farther and farther away from my element, from everything that made me feel good.

My skin was itching as if I'd been in a pool all day and the chlorine was drying it out. I didn't like the way that my ribs were fitting into me, as if there wasn't room enough for them in my torso. I wanted the hell out of my body. Then I started feeling my own heartbeat, something which could just about drive me crazy. I was able to hear a woman breathing three seats behind us. I wanted to go back there and put my hand over her face.

I tried not to sigh. I hated how people going through withdrawal always sighed over and over again. They were trying to get people to have sympathy for their condition. But it wasn't a real sickness. There wasn't actually anything wrong with you. Your body would fake any kind of symptom to get another fix. Once you give your body that kind of pleasure, it gets to have a mind of its own.

I started to think about irritating things. I remembered one time when I had got my leg trapped between the rungs in the bedboard and couldn't get it out. I thought about a pair of jeans I had that were too tight. I thought about the tin cans we would get from the food bank that had lost their labels, and so we had no idea what was inside them. I squeezed my eyes shut to try and not think about those cans. These were thoughts that wouldn't normally bother you, but right then, they were making me insane.

I remembered this one time that I had drunk too much at the park and made myself sick. They say that you can't remember pain, but you can when you go through withdrawal. My stomach started reliving the exact pain I'd experienced that day, puking into the bushes.

I tried to look out the window to distract myself from my imagination, but it didn't help. I started thinking about how one night I was sitting on the bed in my underwear reading and Alphonse had come and lain next to me. He had pulled the strap of my underwear and then let it go, snapping it hard against my hip. I had tried to ignore him, but he kept doing it over and over, and each time, as my skin had become more tender, it had hurt a little more. Finally, I had to cry out and beg for him to stop. Now on the bus, I started to feel the burning on my hip again. But I closed my eyes because I knew that this time, if I had patience, the pain would go away eventually. Alphonse was dead and the pain wasn't real anymore. The poison was coming out of me in the form of irritating and unbearable thoughts and memories. I would have to think about these things one by one. When I was done with them, I would be done with junk and with Alphonse.

I started shifting closer to Jules in my chair, like a little kid watching a horror film. I stuck my hand into his pocket and started shaking the change inside it. I took out the lady mouse from my own pocket. I kept running its tail under my nose as if it were a mustache. I opened Jules's hand and made the mouse dance on his palm.

Jules didn't seem to think there was anything wrong with me acting that way. He had told me before that when I was a baby, there were times when he had thought that I was possessed. He said I was always trying to run out into the middle of the street and would lie down on the floor in a subway car. He didn't seem to know that all babies did these things. Anyhow, I guess nothing could surprise him now.

'I was driving the car when your mother died, you know,' Jules said suddenly.

I sat up, startled, forgetting all about dope, and stared at Jules.

'We were driving into town. You were in her arms and I was driving. I was looking at her because I was always staring at her; I couldn't help it. Her head hit the dashboard really hard, but you were okay because you were curled up in her arms. They said it wasn't my fault because the other driver was drinking and driving, which was worse than driving without a license, which was what I was doing.'

This was the first time he had told me the truth about my mother. Before, she'd been a little make-believe thing. I'd pictured her as a pen-and-ink drawing of a little girl in a black dress like in an Edward Gorey cartoon I'd seen once. When I was growing up, Jules and I had been living in a bit of a fantasy world, which had been a lot of fun. But now it felt good to deal with consequences because it meant there was nothing to be afraid of. I suddenly seemed, for the first time since I'd started shooting up, like a real flesh-and-blood person.

'Manon was so sweet,' Jules said. He had a little trouble looking at me. I had a feeling he was just going to tell me everything now and get it all off his chest. He was going to allow me to be angry with him or hate him or forgive him. 'She was really the most beautiful girl I ever met. They say that you can't truly be serious about someone when you're only fifteen. But I haven't ever loved any woman since. I think that your heart can be really old and wise at fifteen. Especially if you've been through some shit together.'

'You loved her,' I said quietly, so that maybe he wouldn't even hear it. It was the first time he had ever started talking about my mother without me begging him to. I knew her name was Manon Tremblay from my birth certificate, but Jules never referred to her by her name.

I'd never heard her called simply Manon. I whispered it under my breath. Your mouth was left in the shape of a kiss when you finished saying that name.

'We liked to go and drink beer together. She was always laughing when she drank. She used to make me swear over and over again that I would never leave her. She really liked music. We sang all the time. We thought that at least one of us was going to be famous.'

'What song did she like to sing?'

'You know that song "La fille Partie"?'

'How does that go?'

'*Quand elle était tellement petite et tellement jolie, on croyait en elle avec beaucoup d'espoir. On la chassait dans les parcs et près de l'école. Mais c'est fini et tout est completement perdu. La fille qui est partie avec mon argent, avec mon auto... When she was so small and pretty, we only could think of her with hope. We chased her around the park and by the school. But when it was over, everything was lost. The girl who has left with my money and my car.*'

I closed my eyes and tried to imagine her singing the song. And for a moment I actually thought I heard her physical voice somewhere.

'She was so pretty,' Jules continued, with his eyes closed. 'Even though she had to wear boys' clothes all the time. She was the only girl in a family of seven. She used to wear shirts with her brothers' names on them. They didn't know what to do with a girl.'

'How did you meet her? God! You must have been in love with her at first sight!'

'Her dad used to sell firewood door-to-door in his truck. He'd bring her along so that people would offer him a little extra.

'She was unlucky, just like me. I'm surprised she

carried you to full term. She was always falling down. She had a habit of falling down stairs. I know what you're going to say. Who has such a habit? But every time we were going down a flight of stairs together, all of a sudden she'd be bang bang bump falling down the stairs.'

'How come you didn't get along with the rest of her family?'

'She was a Tremblay.' Jules sat up all animated and swung his hands around while describing them, as if to imply that they were nuts. 'They were really backwoods people. I mean, we are out in the woods too, but not as far. The Tremblays are always marrying their cousins. They don't know about the rest of the world. They have as much in common with the birds and the raccoons as they do with other people. If they murder each other, nobody will hear about it. There's one birth certificate for every three people. They let nine-year-olds smoke and drive the trucks. Their accents are so lousy and low-class no one can understand them. Your mother, I could barely make out a word she was saying. If anyone from the French embassy came and heard what we're doing to the French language out here, I don't know what they'd say.'

'But you two didn't give a shit, right! You got together and fell madly in love.'

'Yes, and I was so happy when she got pregnant.'

'And was she?'

'She was messed up and paranoid about the whole thing at first. Her family didn't want her around at all once she got pregnant. They stopped talking to her and everything. When she started to show a bit – she was skinny, just like you, and her stomach just started sticking straight out – well, then her dad kicked her out and she came to live with me. She was so unhappy to leave. I had to drag her kicking and screaming out of her house. She was holding on to the door frame and I was pulling and pulling on her like crazy. She was just supposed to go in to get a suitcase, but she wouldn't come back out.'

I stared at Jules, feeling sort of traumatized by this, but he smiled peacefully, as if it was all part of a good memory.

'Why was she so sad to go? I mean, why wasn't she happy to go live with you if you guys were so in love?'

'Your mother was a big shot because there were so many people in her family, and they all lived in the woods together. You couldn't start something with one of them without twelve or thirteen cousins and uncles coming running up. Everyone was afraid. All you have out here is family, and they had just a huge family. She was a good mother, though.'

'Like how do you mean? She kissed me all the time and stuff like that?'

'Sometimes she'd forget where she put you. She left you on the checkout counter one time. She put you in the basket of her bicycle, like you were a loaf of bread. She was a crazy Frenchman through and through,' Jules said, laughing. '*Qu'est-ce que je peux dire?*'

'Did she love me?'

'Yes, my God! She loved you. She treated you like a doll. But if she would have lived, she would have loved you properly. *Elle etait seulement une bébé, comme toi, mon amour*. But of course she loved you. How could anyone not?'

I think it was the first time anyone had told me that my mother had loved me. I felt excited, like when you sneak up onto the roof of a building and you can feel the earth falling through space. There was one thing that I thought

I actually might remember about her. Maybe Jules just told me the story and I stole it as a memory, but I didn't think so. One night Jules made a drawing of a face on a yellow balloon for my mom and me. He kept pushing it up into the air toward the ceiling with his fingertips. I thought that the moon had come into our room from the window. My parents were batting it up in the air with the palms of their hands every time it almost landed on the ground. If we let the moon land on the ground, it would be destroyed. I had always thought that the moon was alive and smiling up in the sky and that any day it might sail in through your window and ask you to keep it from falling.

We were the only two people who got off at the bus stop just north of Val des Loups. There wasn't even a bus station there, just a sign on the side of the road, and behind that a dump of some sort. My bag was knocking against my side as I stepped off the bus. The ground was cold and made the noise of broken glass as I stepped on it. I was feeling vulnerable as hell out here in the open.

The wind on that side of the highway made the sound of a million newspapers flapping around. It made me feel as if I was at the ocean. I picked up stones like I was waiting for the school bus. There were circular marks left on the ground where the stones had been lying untouched for a long time. They were like the marks on your skin after you've picked a scab off, all healed and clean and perfectly smooth.

We walked over to the gate and looked at the pile of debris behind a chain-link fence. There were thousands of crows there that day. We stood there for a while looking at all those crows. Jules took a beer out of his schoolbag and slowly drank it. He finished his beer and threw the can in the air and they barely noticed. He said that if you were able to look at the crows really closely, you would see that their eyes were stolen baubles, like buttons or marbles.

To get real eyes, they had to steal them from children. Older people's eyes were too set in their ways of looking and would be no good for a crow. That's why people don't let their children out after dark. The crow who stole the eyes of a real child was king. With a piece of plastic they could just see what was in front of them, but with a child's eyes, they could see the whole world.

Jules and I stood on the side of the road just waiting and not saying anything. There weren't street names or address numbers to tell you where you were and where you had to go like there were in the city. We were waiting for some sort of sign that we were in the right place. Then a van came rattling down the road. We looked at it not knowing if we should wave yet. It was a big navy blue van that looked like it could fit a dozen people comfortably in the back. It was the opposite of Lester's Trans Am, which you had to bend yourself into all sorts of angles to fit into. As it got closer, I noticed that it had an advertisement for stoves on the side of it.

The van pulled up noisily in front of us, practically parking on our toes. A woman climbed out of the driver seat and slammed the door behind her hard, and the noise of it startled us both. She came running around the front of the van toward us, looking so comfortable in her skin it made us seem all the more awkward. We were like figurines that had been broken, and although they'd been glued together with crazy glue, you still had to be very careful while playing with them.

She brushed a curl of dark brown hair out of her face and stopped a second to smile at us. She leaned in toward Jules to hug him. He shifted his arms around, not knowing exactly how to wrap them around her, as if it was the first time he'd ever hugged anyone. He was grinning with his lips pressed together to hide his missing tooth.

Then Janine stepped over to me and squeezed me hard. I could feel my heart beating when she hugged me against her, but now it felt fine. Then she held me in front of her, taking a good look at me. Her big blue eyes looked just like Jules's, and I guess mine too. Her green winter jacket smelled like rain.

acknowledgements

I would like to thank Charlotte Clerk and the team at Quercus for believing in this book, Courtney Hodell for brillance and support, Paul Tough for being Paul Tough, and Jonathan Goldstein for love and squalor. Also the Canada Council for financial support.

© Michael Crouser

meet Heather O'Neill

Child(hood)

After my parents split up when I was little, my two sisters and I lived in Virginia with my mother. As I remember it, we drove around the South, living in different towns and going to different schools. My mother never had a job because she thought she should somehow just be given money for being eight or nine times more intelligent than the ordinary person she met. She drew hundreds of self-portraits on loose-leaf paper, and she was always in the middle of writing an essay about the trials and difficulties of being a genius.

My mother soon wanted to have nothing to do with us. Since I played with my plastic fake gun and holster and my candy cigarettes, she concluded that I was damaging to her credibility.

For the remainder of my childhood, my mother drifted from town to town wearing a black pea coat and knee-high leather boots, chain-smoking and believing herself to be an incarnation of Oscar Wilde. She carried a rat named Sebastien in her pocket. She scribbled angels on matchbooks that she would sell for a dollar. She had a suitcase filled with figurines that she had spray-painted silver, and books on devil worshipers. We saw her less and less.

After a couple years of living with my mother's relatives, it was decided that we should go live with my father in Montreal. I had no memories of my father, as he hadn't been allowed to visit us. My mother would periodically get startled and say that she thought she saw him hiding in the bushes or standing on the front lawn.

I had a red and navy blue wool jacket that my family put on over my clothes whenever there was some sort of situation in which I was supposed to look good. They would make me wear it over my shorts and T-shirt in the middle of August. So now they put it on me and gave me a plastic pink suitcase with a change of underwear and a toothbrush. I was sent with my sisters on an airplane to Montreal with a ticket on my luggage that said O'Neill, which was to be our new last name, my father's.

It's terrible to be introduced to a parent like that later in life – in the middle of childhood. You wish that they would just hold on to their dignity. But my dad was all weepy and ridiculous at the airport. He scared the hell out of me. He was wearing a big fur hat. His hair was white and sticking up from his head. There has never been any rhyme or reason behind how my dad dressed. One day he would be wearing a suit and fedora, the next day he would be wearing sweat pants and a leather jacket.

There were some nice things about my dad. He would sit across from me on the melamine table in our tiny kitchen with its ripped red tiles, listing crimes he had committed when he was a child. We would go eat oysters out of a can with a toothpick and drink tonic water from the bottle in St Louis Square, a park filled with hobos and drug dealers. And those times were good.

My dad was the youngest of nine kids brought up during the Depression and had been treated like a dog. Back then it was very much the style to be mean to your children if you had been mistreated as a child yourself. He had no patience whatsoever. He yelled at us for hours at a time and would practically murder us for spilling a bowl of soup. He took our dolls and ripped them to pieces in front of us. He'd pick up the mattress and roll me right out of it onto the floor in the middle of the night to ask me a question. He would blow a bugle that he'd bought at a pawnshop to wake us up in the morning. We had a little toy poodle named Butch. He would send me out to walk the dog and tell me not to come back for a long, long time. I would sit in the lobbies of apartment buildings with the dog hidden in my pocket until it seemed okay to go home.

I ran away to California when I was fifteen but only managed to get as far as Vermont, where I was arrested by state troopers and sent back to Montreal. I don't consider my childhood a bad one, though, since the best times of my life always happened when I was hanging out on the street.

I never heard from any of my relatives in the South after I moved to Montreal. An unwanted child is a boogeyman to its relatives, as they have to take responsibility for it. But an unwanted child is a hero on the streets. Being neglected, you have a lot of freedom to develop outlandish, eccentric personalities in order to get love. The neighborhood is the center of the universe to a street kid and you develop a hysterical need to become a superstar there. Being charming, pretty, and clever actually gets you somewhere. Then it didn't matter that you couldn't afford the right shoes or that you lived in a crappy apartment. In fact, I had no envy of kids with money. I thought they were lame. I couldn't stand their houses, their parents, their sensibilities, their stupid new clothes. We wore ridiculous fur hats and leather jackets that were donated to the church. We were pirates who didn't take love for granted. That's when I began to meet criminals and creeps who always had time and more time for me. Children are holy on the street. Whereas they are only looking for a little attention, they are treated like the Second Coming.

A child can have a successful profession on the street, can make real money through panhandling, stealing, and prostitution. But the price for this lifestyle always comes as a shock. It's just like when Pinocchio realizes that he is turning into a donkey in the land of Fun and Games. Suddenly you realize that you aren't a child anymore, you've become a grown-up. When you lose your sense of make believe, your life is no longer wild and romantic, but instead one that nobody wants, including yourself.

In *Lullabies*, I wanted to capture what I remembered of the drunken babbling of unfortunate twelve-year-olds: their illusions; their ludicrously bad choices, their lack of morality and utter disbelief in cause and effect. I wanted to describe the bittersweet relationships between children who hate themselves, but are madly in love with and make heroes of one another. I thought it would be interesting to show how a thirteen-year-old who hasn't eaten in two days and is high on magic mushrooms could be treated as though he were a pivotal figure in the history of mankind, a Truman Capote.

I wanted to capture the fun of that and also that sickening feeling you get when you're little and you climb up on to something and fall. The fall is always longer for kids.

Black-Journal Juvenilia

My uncle gave me a black journal with white pages to write in when I was eight years old. I used to write in it obsessively. From then on I always wrote in notebooks and sketchbooks. It would be great to have them now, but my dad threw them out as soon as I had filled them up, deeming them no longer of any use.

I remember deciding to become a writer in elementary school. I had a teacher who was crazy about my stories, and I used to get published a lot in this magazine for Montreal schools. To my family, who were entirely dysfunctional, being a writer seemed just as bizarre and unobtainable a profession as a job working full-time in a bank. They never cautioned me against being an artist. They assumed it was a step better than deciding to be a drug dealer.

Formative Reading

I started reading when I was three or four, unless my parents are lying. I remember reading fairy tales to myself that made me sick to my stomach, they were so traumatizingly real. I remember burying a copy of *Sleeping Beauty* in the backyard because I was terrified of the book itself. Once I put a particularly frightening book about swamp animals in the bathtub and ran the water. I got into a lot of trouble as it was a library book.

As a kid, I loved Indian myths, books on extinct animals, and *Anne of Green Gables*. I always read a lot, although no one around me did. I think it's the only thing that accounted for me having any brains or reasoning skills. Books helped me formulate the illusion that I was wondrous and the source of great stories.

When I was twelve, I found a volume of plays by Harold Pinter in the high school library. I really liked the way he looked on the jacket cover. I stole the book because I was afraid the librarian wouldn't let me take it out. For some reason, I thought it was like pornography. The plays scared me to death. They were so creepy and I couldn't quite understand what was going on. But they made me feel smarter too. I moved on to Sam Shepard and Samuel Beckett and Eugene Ionesco. These playwrights gave me the life-changing idea that rebels and outsiders could be brilliant.

I was very affected by *The Painted Bird* by Jerzy Kosinski, *Childhood* by Maxim Gorky, and *The Notebook* by Agota Kristof. I loved poetic novels about brutal childhoods. They made me feel so good to be alive. My worship of stuff like that made me happy that I was poor and downtrodden, it made me feel incredibly lucky. I guess that's a little twisted, but it got me by.

I really liked *1984* and wished that I too could live in a fascist regime. And I read *The Clown* by Heinrich Böll a dozen times. It was all about being squalid and artistic and lonely. I found it so beautiful and sweet. I swore I would become a depressed bohemian one day.

Jobs
When I was a kid, I used to sell flowers on the street corner with my sisters. Once I tried outdoor work, building a fence at a construction site, but I fainted three or four times on the first day from just standing in the sun.

I was never any good at holding down a regular job and began trying to write professionally in my early twenties.

Strange Stimulation

I am always cutting out pictures from magazines and thumbtacking them to the wall. There are certain images that I see and right away I feel like writing. I love photographs of shady-looking children. I like the way twelve-year-olds look in T-shirts with decals of deer on them and ripped sweatpants. Something about them holding guns or walking a dog at midnight makes me desperately need to write immediately. They remind me of a state of grace and perfection.

Whenever I hear a really great song, I want to drop everything and write. I feel the same way when I see art. Whenever I'm stricken by something beautiful, I have a craving for writing like someone would have a craving for cigarettes.

Broken-down places make me want to write too. My dad and my sisters and I lived in a tiny, run-down apartment where my mother had painted murals of swans and monkeys all over the walls before she left. My dad used to say that if my mother hadn't left, we would be millionaires. He thought that she could draw cats on rocks and he'd sell them at the Old Port to tourists and make a fortune this way. Her leaving nixed this entire money-making scheme. Whenever I'm in a bleak, famously violent neighborhood, it makes me feel comfortable and happy. It reminds me of the old apartments and sitting up late with my dad as he tried to figure out why and how we weren't rich and famous. The feeling of loss and heartache sometimes makes me feel secure and nostalgic.

Higher Education

People are often surprised that I went to university because I came from a lower-class background and because of what I write about. When I graduated from high school, I won a paltry English scholarship. I knew from reading authors' biographies that the majority went to university, so I went too. Tuition at the time was only about four hundred dollars a semester. Anyone could go. I was accepted to McGill University, the best school in Canada, which turned out to be an institution designed to distract you from reality. The professors gave lectures on their own brilliance and laughed at their own jokes. It was a good program if you wanted to become a mad scientist or a parlor wit. I might not have looked like it, but I was always good at school because I loved it so.

I graduated in two years when I was twenty, which was a mercy because I couldn't have taken much more of being so incredibly poor. I had a friend who worked at a restaurant and I'd get free food there or at the soup kitchen. I lived with six friends in an apartment on St Denis Street. My share of the rent was only forty dollars a month, which I made tutoring French grammar on Sundays and scrounging around. I don't really think university made me a better writer at all. It is my observation, however, that the more knowledge and interesting information you know, the happier you are.

Buzzard-Spotting and Other Diversions

I like to collect things. I love going to junk shops, bad museums, and science fiction shops. I collect screwed-up-looking dolls and figurines. My daughter is a collector too. She collects seashells and rocks. She has scrapbooks that she fills with leaves and bird feathers and puts these pseudo-scientific notes underneath them. She also collects different editions of Sherlock Holmes books. Collecting makes me forget all my problems; it convinces me that I can reorder the universe by its parts. Maybe it's a genetic thing. My dad has this incredible collection of pickle jars and jam jars and baby food jars. Tiny objects are separated into each of them. There's one with doorknobs, and another with safety pins, and another with plastic animals. It's truly beautiful in an ugly way. If you open the right jam jar, you'll probably hear me singing a song as a kid.

I like drawing with pencil crayons. People in my family tend to have a knack for drawing. I draw the same object for a month. Last month my daughter and I drew about five hundred umbrellas.

I like spotting buzzards and crows. When I see a lot of the same number in one day I believe that the universe is conspiring in my favor.

Another thing I'm crazy about is watching stop animation. Jan Svankmajer and the Brothers Quay are my favorite filmmakers. The voices in dubbed films move me in a particular way because they always sound like children pretending to be adults. I tried to pass myself off as an adult when I was a kid, and now, ironically, I am an adult who tries to write in the voice of a child.

'Putting Together a Robot Without an Instruction Manual'

Heather O'Neill on Writing *Lullabies*

I started off writing this book some summers ago. Working on a novel is kind of like putting together a robot without an instruction manual. Each word is a nut or a screw and there are hundreds of thousands of them. You put it together and tinker with it, hoping that it will come alive in the reader's mind. I read an interview with Hotel, a member of the punk band the Kills, where he said that when he was little, he fell in love with a pair of leather boots and his whole personality was inspired by them. Every detail in a novel should have that sort of transformative power.

I don't like to tell people that I'm working on a novel because they ask me literally thousands of times when it's coming out. People around me seemed to get very upset while I was writing this book. They were like: What's with all this paper! This simply isn't right! Nobody really believes you when you say you're writing a novel, and they look at you all suspiciously. I used to get pulled out of a line at customs every time I said I was a writer. They'll dump out everything in your suitcase if you say that you are a poet. The last thing they want is another poet in their country. They apparently have enough trouble dealing with their own domestic population of poets.

It's hard to have faith that you will ever finish a novel. Luckily my boyfriend read everything I wrote and loved it. All any writer needs is one single reader.

Writing keeps me from my more destructive pastimes, like buying clothes. I spent my twenties dressing up in high heels and striped pantsuits. I would have to put my daughter in a baby carriage and wheel her over to my dad's apartment to eat dinner because I'd spent all my money on these outfits that made me feel like a famous rock star.

A lot of the novel takes place around the red-light district of Montreal. I really like that whole area. Kids who hang around there always act like the apocalypse happened yesterday. Even today you can walk there and see a kid with a blanket wrapped around them, pushing a grocery cart containing a dog with a broken leg. But in the novel, I describe Montreal the way that I saw it when I was twelve, not the actual physical place. I had to close my eyes to see Montreal as it is in the book. Lower St Laurent Street is just a string of really crappy dives, but back then, it was the greatest place in the world.

Even though the novel is set in rooming houses and the red-light district, it still exists in the childish realm of make-believe: a world in which plastic swans are real; cracks in the wall are spiders; and an old fan blowing in the corner of the room is the seaside. The inability to properly identify danger exists throughout the book. Whereas children can be terrified by a puppet of a crocodile or a photograph of a shark in a *National Geographic* magazine, they are unable to get it through their heads to look both ways when they cross the street or that there are strangers that you cannot talk to.

The main character is twelve for a good chunk of the book. Twelve is a beautiful and striking age. It's when kids start talking big and thinking about how they could make it on their own: just like angels right before they are cast out of heaven. They have such innocent and dangerous ideas.

When I was eleven, I used to have a friend whose older brother was a junkie. He and his friends were the coolest kids in the neighborhood. Some high points in my childhood were when drug addicts would flip out and come out of their apartments in their underwear with cats on their heads. We kids would dance around them, shouting and laughing with our hands up in the air. I wanted to capture this nonjudgmental attitude a lot of lower-class kids have to drugs. I also wanted to portray the relationships these same kids have with seedy adults. Children believe the lies that adults tell them and are dutifully impressed. Lowlifes are fantastical creatures who animate the world of children, and, in turn, lowlifes love children who are their most captive and adoring audience.

Inspiration

Although much of writing comes from the manufacturing of past impression, you have to feed your imagination on a daily basis in order to keep it productive. Here is a by-no-means comprehensive list of things that moved me while I was writing this novel. It's hard to say in what way they affected my writing exactly, but they made me feel alive:

This clown in a tuxedo who sat in the audience at a little circus, smoking an imaginary cigarette through the whole show. A theatre in the back of a van, out of which an actor climbed with an umbrella. When he stood on top of the van and opened his umbrella, a rain storm of confetti flew out over the audience. Strange dolls we found at the Salvation Army. The library downtown that gets so full you have to wait a half hour in line to check out a book. Watching Jean-Luc Godard's film *Bande à part* for the hundredth time. The music video 'What's Up Fatlip'. Revamped cars. My daughter when she rides her low-rider bike down the street in bare feet and track pants. Anyone who tried to talk me into buying batteries on the street. Les Cigales wine,which hits me just right and doesn't make me philosophize. Anyone who can dance as well as I used to. Fashion magazines with girls in fancy clothes,weeping. All the parks and cheap zoos and public swimming pools I went to with my daughter. Jan Svankmajer's film *Alice*. The Brothers Quay film *Street of Crocodiles*. Jean Rhys's lesser known novels. The Moldy Peaches. Any time a swan appears in a description in a novel.